The Seeker of Lost Paintings

Sarah Freethy

**SIMON &
SCHUSTER**

London · New York · Amsterdam/Antwerp · Sydney/Melbourne · Toronto · New Delhi

First published in Great Britain by Simon & Schuster UK Ltd, 2025

THE WRITERS' ROOM

1 3 5 7 9 10 8 6 4 2

Simon & Schuster UK Ltd, 1st Floor
222 Gray's Inn Road, London WC1X 8HB

Simon & Schuster Australia, Sydney
Simon & Schuster India, New Delhi

www.simonandschuster.co.uk
www.simonandschuster.com.au
www.simonandschuster.co.in

The authorised representative in the EEA is Simon & Schuster Netherlands BV,
Herculesplein 96, 3584 AA Utrecht, Netherlands. info@simonandschuster.nl

A CIP catalogue record for this book is available from the British Library

Paperback ISBN: 978-1-3985-3071-3
eBook ISBN: 978-1-3985-3069-0
Audio ISBN: 978-1-3985-3070-6

Typeset in Bembo by M Rules
Printed and Bound in the UK using 100% Renewable Electricity at CPI Group (UK) Ltd

MIX
Paper | Supporting
responsible forestry
FSC® C013604

Sarah Freethy worked as a writer, script consultant, producer and development editor in television before turning her hand to writing novels. She is the author of *The Porcelain Maker* and lives in England with her family.

Also by Sarah Freethy

The Porcelain Maker

Dedicated to all those fighting fascism and
the loving fathers in my life. To Philip,
and to Nicholas, my own dear daddy,
gone so long and sorely missed.

PROLOGUE

Naples, 1610

The threads of the canvas are thick and sparse, a single piece of woven Roman linen, plain and unadorned. Before the painting can begin, it must be readied with a ground – dark as night and deep as a wound, obscured by shadow. What lurks there, hiding in between the strands, waiting for a single source of light?

The ground is a primer, like honey with a grainy bite which satisfies the blade. This *mestica* provides the foundation. A wet soil, brown and loamy; a thick and fertile paste of pigment, gypsum, linseed oil. No tentative strokes or rough approximations – what's planted there is fully formed already. Each line laid down in certain knowledge that what grows there was always present, just obscured.

The artist picks up his knife and scores the base, as one might carve into flesh. He's had cause to do that on one or two occasions: to spill a man's colour onto the canvas of the street. His own scars are a testimony to that, itching where the flesh knits back together. They sometimes blind him with an awful light, but he must push on. He can't return until it's done.

Who will he paint and in what guise? There is one . . . spirited and quick to take offence. He sought him out for strength of will. A man must be memorable to be immortalized. He's seen his muse in many moods; transformed by agony, drowned in wine and burning hot in anger, but this time must be different. Well then, let it be ecstasy.

Colour comes last, built by blending pastes together. This earth will soon be scorched by umber. Butter yellow, cinnabar and ochre; charcoal grey and copper green. The faintest touch of luminescence; a sheen of tempera where the light hits, swimming on the still-wet slick of oil. The drape of his cape, scarlet as a cardinal's shoe; his mouth, darker than rose madder. What colour is regret? Lead-white, dragged across a blood-black ground.

Time is a fugitive, and he must get to work. Every picture has a memory. Where there are layers, some imprint will be left behind. A trace, a trail, an inadvertent map. You might escape, but those who seek shall surely find.

All that is yet to come. For now, the ground is laid, the canvas ready and so the painting must begin.

CHAPTER ONE

LONDON, JULY 1997

London was wilting on the first truly hot day of summer. On Piccadilly the tide of tourists jostled, hot thighs rubbing, slick with sweat. A pall of grey fumes filled their nostrils and light bounced off the buildings, slicing through the shadows.

Behind these populated streets, the rest of the city lay dormant. The tail of the Thames slithered from the suburbs to the centre, past the mansion blocks and villas, the upmarket galleries with their blinds at half-mast. There were few indicators of the life which would soon return to these streets: a flyer advertising an auction in September, posters for an autumn exhibition, the promise of Gentileschi, Mondrian or Mueck. The windows of the antiquarian booksellers were wrapped in yellow cellophane, like bottles of medicinal tonic, yet somehow sunlight persevered and browned their paper petals with its scorching rays.

On a busy western artery, choked with traffic, there stood a row of silent houses. The roofline was cluttered with iron finials and flourishes and vast skylights, which bathed the rooms beneath. Nothing stirred the air. The rumble of the road was ever-present, but could not penetrate the soup of summer. A floorboard creaked from deep within, stretching its spine in the heat.

Beatrice Fremont leant her head against the window. She gazed out listlessly, waves of dark hair pressed against glass. The room was always sunk in shadow, the faded nets and curtains rarely open, but she was keeping watch today. As always, the road was gridlocked, night and day; visitors entering the city, while the locals sought escape. Exhaust fumes filled her nostrils and for a moment she felt a yearning to take flight – to Italy, perhaps. The home of childhood holidays, of terracotta hill towns and olive groves, shaded fountains and piazzas. If only she could take her mother back there, one last time . . . But that was now impossible, she knew. The expense for one thing, and besides, Maddalena was so frail, she'd never manage.

Beatrice envisaged her mother next door in the dim twilight of the study, converted to a bedroom since she could no longer manage stairs. She lay there even now, half in, half out of sleep, a threadbare linen sheet pulled up around her shoulders. She was invariably cold, even in this suffocating heat.

Beatrice knew her mother would not live to see Rome or Sicily again, much as that saddened her. All she could do was make her comfortable in the time she had remaining. Money was the salve required, but the one thing which they lacked.

She stared down the street, waiting and watching for the man she hoped would help.

Buffeted by the hot wind of a passing train, Jude Adler stepped onto the platform at Baron's Court. The station teemed with life: excited teenagers on their way to town, a gaggle of young mothers and their fractious babies, protesting at the crush of bodies and the closeness of the day.

Jude squeezed through them all and ran up the stairs, out of the gate and onto the street. Realizing he was late, he pulled the *A–Z* out of his pocket to check its dog-eared pages. Talgarth Road was close. No more than a few minutes, if he took it at a clip.

He was anxious to find out what this collection had to offer. From the little information Beatrice Fremont had given him on the phone, her father's art and photography collection could be a step on the road towards redemption. It had been three months since Jude made the worst decision of his career, which had all but destroyed his reputation. A decent valuation wouldn't fix that, but it would help.

His mistake still haunted him, both waking and asleep. He'd come across the little painting on the website of an auction house in France. A small, pixellated image which captured his attention. It showed the roof of a red barn floating above a sea of muddy green, a clotted cream sky – thickly textured – over fields of undulating grass roiled by an unseen wind.

The listing had cited the painting as unsigned, the author unnamed, but Jude had known. He'd understood instinctively. That was his skill: to recognize the wheat among the chaff, to separate the artifice from art. To trust his instincts, which had never let him down.

He'd known in his gut that the painting was by Paula Modersohn-Becker, the German expressionist, who'd died in 1907. He was as certain as if it was a portrait of the artist's face; those oval eyes which saw her small, domestic world in a specific way. He knew that it had been missing for more than half a century, swept up in a purge by the Third Reich. It was exactly what he needed it to be.

He'd felt the rush of blood, a pricking on his skin which told him this was . . . something. Like all gamblers, he knew his own tells intimately. In the days before the World Wide Web, he'd often feared those signs would prove his undoing. Now he could hide behind a screen, anonymous and unobserved. Following his gut, he'd borrowed money and bought the painting at auction. When it arrived in London one week later, he'd been thrilled to hold it in his hands, to see that red barn roof up close. He'd taken it to Oxford right away, so his friend, Kit Worseley – art historian, teacher and curator – could authenticate the find. Then Jude called up a handful of trusted confidantes to tell them news was coming; watch this space. It felt exciting, to know his peers were out there waiting, willing him on, and then all the more traumatic when Kit called to tell him the striking russet pigment of the roof was not produced until 1968. Jude had listened to him carefully, each word landing like a blow. Kit tried to make it better – reassured him it was a masterful forgery, made all the more elegant by the fact the seller never laid claim to it being a Modersohn–Becker in the first place, but for Jude, the finesse of the fraud did nothing to lessen its sting.

Months had passed, but the shame of it weighed heavily and he still owed a debt he couldn't hope to pay. He would often wake from dreams where he was watching the price rise on the screen, creeping up like floodwater. He'd see the whole thing for the folly it was, and yet be unable to stop until he woke up sweating and ashamed. He turned his back on investigations and started doing minor valuations, just to pay the bills. They gave him no pleasure and little profit, but he knew he wasn't ready to trust his instincts again, wasn't sure he ever could.

When he turned the corner into Talgarth Road, Jude only prayed the Fremont job would be straightforward – a simple valuation of a small, mid-century collection. It was a million miles from the Modersohn-Becker, and that was just how he wanted it to be.

He saw ahead a row of red-brick houses; he'd driven past them on innumerable occasions, always wondering who lived there. They looked even more imposing as he approached on foot. He had to crane his neck to take them in; the elegant facades were notable enough, but the skylights were what caught the eye. Each one, a feat of Victorian engineering: metal-framed glass, topped with an ornate arch.

Jude checked he had the right number and climbed a flight of steps to the front door. He pressed the bell and heard foot-steps approaching. The door opened to reveal a woman in her early thirties, wearing jeans and a loose white shirt. She had pale olive skin and was delicately beautiful with large, brown eyes. Her thick dark hair was almost black and curled down to her shoulders.

'Miss Fremont?'

He extended his hand with formality. She smiled.

'Beatrice will do. Please come in, out of the heat.'

Jude stepped into a bright and airy hallway with several closed doors on the right-hand side. On the left, a flight of steps descended to a basement floor below. Beatrice led the way along the passage, opening the first door they came to.

'Come through.' She walked to the front window and pulled back the curtains. The light revealed a cosy, cluttered room: two armchairs and a drab green sofa, a wall of bookshelves, piled with paperbacks. It looked like it was decorated twenty years before but hadn't been touched since.

'Mum always insists we keep the curtains closed to "save the furniture", but honestly, that ship sailed years ago.'

'You live here, too?' asked Jude.

'I moved back a few months ago when Mum got ill. I've been kind of camping out here ever since.'

Outside, the ever-present road noise grumbled: lanes of traffic, only metres from the door. Jude looked around and noticed a dozen or so large, framed paintings stacked against the empty fireplace.

'Are these part of your father's collection?'

Beatrice nodded. 'I brought them down here after we spoke. Turns out Dad didn't have that many paintings – his real passion was photography. I laid all those out over there . . .'

She pointed to a mahogany sideboard, its surface entirely covered in stacks of framed photographs and several large leather-bound portfolios, with more prints neatly filed away. Nearby, a smoked glass coffee table held a pile of albums.

'There are some old engravings in there, and a few sketches and watercolours I've no idea what any of it is worth, but my dad always told us they were valuable.'

'Fingers crossed,' he said, eager to get on.

From the mantelpiece came the glass chime of a clock. Beatrice checked her watch.

'I need to prep Mum's medication. Would you mind if I just go and sort her out? It shouldn't take too long.'

Jude nodded.

'Take as much time as you need.'

He preferred to work unobserved. Beatrice seemed relieved.

'I didn't tell her you were coming – no point in needlessly upsetting her and I haven't had the heart to break it to her yet. My dad died twenty years ago, but she doesn't like the thought of selling any of his possessions.'

'It can be hard to say goodbye to things we love.'

'Yeah, well – needs must, but I'll cross that bridge when we come to it.'

She gave him a tight smile.

'Can I bring you back a tea or coffee?'

'A glass of water would be lovely.'

After she left, Jude went over to the coffee table and flicked through the first book of engravings. They were Biblical studies: intensely dramatic, full of fire and brimstone, of looming towers and turgid skies. He guessed they were late nineteenth century, decent quality, though not especially valuable.

It was the same story with the oil paintings stacked against the fireplace. Some were so dark, he had trouble making out much detail. Even so, most were reproductions and those that weren't seemed fairly standard.

He crossed over to the sideboard, to the stack of photographs in frames and he knew right away these were of a different order. The subjects were varied but shared a commonality – light as a source of both beauty and illumination. Many of them featured architecture: empty streets and courtyards, statuary, details carved in stone. He was no specialist, but he recognized a few of the greats: Brassaï, Mario De Biasi and Man Ray, among others. He removed a few from their frames to check the age and patina, and felt a tingle of possibility – these might make decent money for her. They were beautiful, in limited runs and excellent condition. Excitingly, there were one or two by a photographer he didn't recognize, but who displayed the same sensitivity: meditations on the interplay of light and dark, the contrast so much greater than the sum of its parts. Could there be something hitherto unknown among the classics? The possibility of an undiscovered talent buoyed him up.

A few prints showed signs of ageing – their edges speckled with tiny, sooty spores – but overall, the collection had potential. Most were good, a few were quite exceptional.

The mantel clock began to chime again. Jude wondered where Beatrice had got to. She was clearly worried about their finances, and he was keen to share good news, so he stepped out into the hallway. There was no sign of her. Apart from the endless rumble of the traffic, the house was ominously still. The door to the next room was slightly open and a warm glow of light spilled out. Jude walked toward it, peering in. The air inside was stuffy: a heavy curtain hung across a window at the rear, blocking out the sun and deadening the noise. The only light source was a picture lamp, which hung above a small, square canvas on the wall opposite the door. Beneath it was a chest of drawers. The painting had no surrounding frame. It showed the head and shoulders of a young man whose pallid skin shone like ivory. He had curly, ruffled hair and an impish, playful grin. The background lacked discerning features, only colour – bitter chocolate, dense and rich.

To Jude, the image was striking and familiar, although he could not place it straight away. He crossed the room to take a closer look. Was it another reproduction? If so, exceptionally good. The subject's bright complexion stood in contrast to his tenebrous surroundings. There were fine brushstrokes, barely visible in the warm light which pooled beneath the lamp.

A strange sensation came over Jude as he looked at it, not unlike déjà vu. He felt – no, *knew* – that he had stood in front of this very image, or something close to it, before. He nearly had it, then it slipped away. Instead of trying to chase it down, he turned his mind and then it came to him, with force:

Caravaggio's St John.

This youth, his glowing skin and dark surrounding, was the embodiment of *chiaroscuro*, the interplay of light and shadow. A word whose magic made little sense in the abstract but which, once witnessed, couldn't be ignored.

He put out a hand to lift the canvas down, unable to deny his curiosity. The fibres were rough beneath his fingers, a ragged fringe, pinned into place. He turned it over in his hands: dense linen with a coat of cracking paint. He turned it back and gazed down at the young man's features: the sharp blades of his cheekbones, lips curved as tightly as the framing curls. It was St John the Baptist in *Youth with a Ram*. He was certain, and yet it somehow seemed transformed. He recognized the model. What was his name ... Cecco? Yes! Francesco Boneri. An artist in his own right, but best remembered as a muse.

Jude stared down at the young man's features, straining to make out details in the gloom. Keen to see him in the light, he reached out to pull the curtain open, wincing at the sudden beam of light. From across the room came a low moan, which informed him, far too late, that he was not alone.

He turned towards the sound and saw the weathered face of an elderly woman, looming at him from the shadows. She heaved herself up from the confines of a narrow bed. White sheets wrapped around her.

'*Cosa fai; chi sei? Mettilo giù subito!*'

She called out, 'Be-ah-tri-chay', the name broken into four clear syllables.

Jude put out a hand to quieten her, to reassure her in some way, forgetting he was still holding the canvas square. It knocked against the chest of drawers and clattered to the floor.

'I'm so sorry,' he stuttered. 'Please, there's no need to get up ...'

He dropped to one knee and cast around him blindly, trying to locate the canvas on the floor. Footsteps sounded, running along the corridor. The old woman was already up and speaking in some unknown dialect, although her alarm was clear enough. One hand gripped hard on the iron bed frame, the other clutching at the collar of her nightgown. She wavered there on stick-thin ankles, her bare legs roped with veins.

Beatrice rushed in, dashing to her mother's side, shushing her and gently guiding her back to bed.

Jude finally caught hold of a corner of the picture. He stood and fumbled it back into place, then stumbled from the airless room and slumped against the wall. He tried to catch his breath and listened guiltily to the old woman's quiet crying, her daughter's whispered reassurances, until at last there was quiet.

Beatrice stepped out of the room and closed the door behind her.

'Are you okay?' she asked.

Jude nodded, though his heart was still racing in his chest.

'I'm so sorry,' he apologized. 'I had no idea.'

'It's my fault – I should have warned her you were coming.' Beatrice glanced towards the door.

'I ought to go back in. Would you mind seeing yourself out?'

Jude shook his head. 'Of course not.' He added, 'Call me, when you get a moment? Once things have settled down?'

She gave a nod and then went back into the room.

He was left standing in the corridor, heart rate slowing, wondering if he might have dreamt it all.

It was dark when the phone began to ring. Jude lived in a narrow mews in Pimlico. On the ground floor was his gallery: open-plan with white walls and wooden floors. Above,

his private space. Bedroom, bathroom, kitchen, sitting room.
Work and life, all overlapping.

Jude had fallen asleep on the sofa. The orange tungsten of
the streetlights cast the room in their synthetic glow. At the
first ring, he sprang up and started for the stairs, before he
even realized he had momentum. He ran down to his desk
and lifted the receiver.

'Hello?'

'Mr Adler? It's Beatrice Fremont. I'm sorry for calling you
so late.'

Jude looked down at his watch. It was almost 11 o'clock.
He rubbed his eyes as she continued.

'I was just waiting for my mum to fall asleep.'

'I'm really sorry if I upset her. I'd no idea anyone was in
there. I shouldn't have gone wandering off on my own.'

'My fault. I should have warned her in advance.' Beatrice
paused. 'But some good came from it. It spurred a conversation
I've been avoiding for too long. She's agreed to let me sell my
dad's collection. If you think anyone would be interested in
buying it, of course.'

'Certainly – your father had good taste.'

'You really think so?'

'The photographic prints have real potential.'

'Oh, that is a huge relief. Mum got herself in a financial
pickle a few years back. This is my last hope to repair it.'

Jude felt the need to strike a note of caution.

'We must do due diligence, of course. Make sure they are
what I think they are. I know someone, a photography curator – I can ask him to take a look.'

He hated that he'd allowed so much doubt to creep in. Still, he couldn't afford to make the same mistake again. Beatrice seemed unconcerned.

'Better safe than sorry. I could put a few of them together in a portfolio and drop them round?'

'Good idea. How about we meet in the restaurant at the top of the National Gallery one day next week? I'll stand you a coffee.'

'Would Monday morning be okay – say 10 o'clock? That's when the district nurse comes round. Otherwise, it's hard to get away.'

'Monday morning sounds great.'

Jude was about to say goodbye, when he remembered the portrait.

'That picture in your mother's room . . . was there a reason why it wasn't among the rest of the work you wanted valued?'

'The smiling boy? I forgot he was even there, to be honest.'

'Do you know anything about it?'

'Not really. It's been hanging in Mum's room for as long as I remember. I don't think it was my dad's. It's so old and shabby – probably just some print my mum picked up from Woolworths years ago.'

Jude's fingertips recalled the texture of thick paint and rough threads . . . it was certainly no print. He was about to say as much when Beatrice interrupted.

'I'd better get on. Mum tends to wake up early.'

'Of course.'

'I'll see you Monday, ten o'clock?'

'See you then.'

After he hung up, Jude stood in the quiet darkness thinking

about the painting. The delicacy of the brushstrokes, the sucking darkness of the ground against the brilliance of the skin. It whispered to him, like a red barn roof. He shivered and pushed the thought away.

CHAPTER TWO

Jude crossed to Trafalgar Square by St Martin-in-the-Fields where a steady stream of vehicles churned round the periphery and the incessant noise of roadworks rattled at his jaw. He wove a path through the tourists and up the steps to the portico of the National Gallery. As he pushed his way through the great doors a sense of calm enveloped him. Although the marble entrance hall was bustling with life, Jude felt as if he'd entered a more rational and ordered space.

Throughout his childhood, the gallery had been his sanctuary. Eager to fill their days and minds without emptying her purse, his mother had made it their frequent pilgrimage. He'd fought against it at the time, kicking back against the imposition, but in the end, he always got pulled in. Some small painting he'd never seen before would catch his eye and he'd forget to feel morose.

When he was very young, his mother had made a game of going round the rooms to count the dogs, an endless fund of puppies cowering under damask tablecloths and faithful hounds sat at their master's heel. As Jude grew a little older, Rousseau's slinking tiger became his favourite, followed by the Impressionists, then Gainsborough and his daughters, all three maturing before his eyes. In time each room had its moment, except for the Renaissance, which he took pains to avoid. Even as he entered adolescence, something about the outsized, vivid canvasses disturbed him. He was secretly terrified of all the blood and gore in Judith and Holofernes and the grey face of the beheaded Baptist. Other people seemed to wallow in their gore, but Jude worried they'd somehow find him in his dreams.

After his mother died, he stopped going to the gallery altogether. Several years passed before he returned and it was only teenage boredom which forced him up the steps one winter afternoon in the mid-1980s. Seeking shelter from the rain, he'd trudged around reluctantly, the familiar sight of myriad hounds only darkening his mood. When he realized he'd drifted into the Renaissance, he almost turned straight back round, but then he found the novelty pulled him in and served as a distraction. Finally summoning up the courage to face their vibrant horrors, he discovered their humanity instead. Blood, yes, bright red and in abundance, but also real expressions of guilt, grief, terror and remorse, all of which he now recognized.

Fifteen years on, the building was comfortably familiar. He knew all the shortcuts through its crowded halls. He'd arranged to meet Beatrice in the restaurant which overlooked the square and made his way up in the lift. Jude loved the view from here: picture windows ran the full length of the room, displaying the great sweep towards the river, the Admiralty and The Mall. Nelson stood almost parallel and Jude delighted in the little roll of vertigo he felt, imagining himself in that position.

The restaurant was all but empty, the waiting staff gliding between tables, laying out linen and polished flatware. Jude took a seat and ordered an espresso, then stared out at the flat steel sky.

'Not too shabby.'

He turned to find Beatrice looking more polished than when they first met. She held out a black portfolio.

'A sampling of prints, as you requested. I hope I didn't put too many in – I didn't really know what you might need.'

Jude thanked her and set it down next to his chair.

'I hope I didn't sound alarmist, but a second opinion is good for both of us. I contacted a curator at the Photographers' Gallery who has agreed to take a look.'

Beatrice sighed.

'Well, fingers crossed. We could really use the money.'

'Do you mind if I ask why?' She blushed and he hastily apologized, 'Sorry. None of my business. You don't need to tell me.'

She waved his guilt away. 'It's fine – no deep dark secrets, just normal human frailty. My parents both moved here from Italy. After my dad died, Mum did an amazing job of looking after me but managing the finances has never really been her strong suit. I thought she was doing okay, until last year when she got ill. I was living up in Manchester, working as a translator. I moved back here to take care of her, then discovered she'd remortgaged and hadn't been able to keep up with the payments. By the time I found out, she'd racked up a lot of debt, tens of thousands. On top of that, she now needs full-time care, which means that I can't work. All in all, it's been a lot.'

Jude felt bad for asking, though she didn't seem to mind.

'If the pictures are as good as I hope, they should sell really well at auction, but I don't know how much you were hoping for . . .'

'It would need to be at least six figures to secure the house. I'm guessing they won't get anywhere near that.'

'Sadly not.'

She sighed. 'That's okay. Given the way things are, I know I'll have to sell eventually, though it will break my heart. I just want to hold the bank off long enough so Mum doesn't have to know.'

A waiter came to take their order.

After he left, Beatrice turned back to Jude. 'You came highly recommended by someone at our family solicitor's office. They said you don't normally do straight valuations – is that right? If so, I feel very fortunate to have your expertise.'

'No problem.' She seemed unaware of his recent humiliation much to Jude's relief.

'So how did you get into this line of work?'

He shrugged. 'By luck. History of art was always my favourite subject. I got offered a place to study it at Oxford, much to everyone's surprise – not many kids applying from an inner-city state school, but I did okay. After that, I spent a few years working in Europe, tracking down works of art which had been lost or stolen. I was interested in the potential of the World Wide Web as a new frontier, but that's on hold for now. I'm just going back to basics. I have a little gallery in Pimlico and I'm trying to fill it with interesting work. Like your dad's collection, with any luck.'

The waiter brought their drinks and set them down.

'Can I ask how he came by them? He clearly knew his stuff.'

'My parents moved to London at the tail end of the war. They both left everything behind, and I think he was keen to replace what he'd lost. He always loved photography; in fact, he took a few of them himself.'

Mystery solved.

'To my eye he had real talent. It'll be interesting to hear what my friend at the Photographer's Gallery makes of his work. What was his name?'

'Luca Fremont.' Beatrice looked bemused. 'Do you really think anyone would want to buy his pictures?'

'Absolutely. Photography is growing in popularity as a medium. Those early Europeans – Sudek, Brassaï – some collectors pay a lot. Your father may not have their reputation, but if we put together a small exhibition, we might generate some interest.'

She looked surprised. 'He would have been delighted. I wish he could have known. Makes me sad but proud, if that makes sense?'

'It does. I lost my mum when I was thirteen. Not much left now to remember her by.'

'Oh God, I'm sorry. But what about your father?'

Jude shrugged. 'Never really knew him. He found out she was pregnant and didn't stick around.'

Feeling her discomfort, he drained his coffee.

'Listen, I know you need to get back to your mum, but can you spare ten minutes? I want to show you something downstairs, in Room 32.'

When Beatrice stepped out of the lift, the quiet tranquillity of the restaurant was replaced by a riot of people and paintings. Jude sped them through rooms of art from a dozen eras, pointing out developments in style. It was all so overwhelming; she found herself observing him instead. Striding through the gallery, he seemed to be in his element. He turned to her, pushing back his sandy hair.

'What do you know about Caravaggio?'

'The painter? Not much. Didn't he do that mad painting on a shield: the woman with all the snakes in her hair?'

He grinned and nodded. 'The Medusa – that's in Florence, in the Uffizi.'

'That's where I saw it! My dad took me there when I was little. Scarred me for life.'

'Yeah, well, he can have that effect. Ah, here we go . . .'

They'd reached Room 32, their destination. Pale green damask walls were covered with a feast of the Baroque. Huge, densely populated canvasses, hanging from the ceiling on long chains. There was no restraint – they demanded your attention.

'This was what I wanted to show you.'

A crowd of people stood in front of three paintings; so many that they blocked the view. Jude steered Beatrice by the elbow, and they squeezed through. The first painting they came to was quite small and showed a startled boy bitten by a lizard, the offending creature still hanging from his hand.

'Caravaggio, if you hadn't already guessed it. One of his early works,' said Jude. He pointed to the bottom right-hand corner. 'See that rose and its reflection? He was a master of still life from early on – the whole painting is thought to be an allegory for the pain of love. There's something very feminine about his depiction of the boy, the flower in his hair, the physicality, but then Caravaggio was always pushing boundaries. Choosing to depict a moment like this was a radical choice for an artist at this time. All the energy, the life.'

Jude pointed her towards the next painting.

'This is *The Supper at Emmaus*.'

The second painting was much larger, four figures grouped around a table laden down with food. Every element was rendered in exquisite detail, but it was the theatricality that Beatrice was drawn to – a seated figure on the right-hand side, his arm flung out, seeming to project beyond the canvas, inviting the observer in. A fruit basket teetered on the table, looking like it might tip and spill its contents out onto the floor. Jude leaned in close so he could be heard above the chatter which echoed round the room.

'The central figure is Christ after his resurrection. This is the moment his disciples realize who he is, so Caravaggio painted in little clues for the viewer ... See, there?' He pointed out a twist of broken wicker, shaped like a fish. 'Early Christians were called the "fishers of men" and used that symbol to identify each other. There's another fish shape there, in the shadow of the fruit bowl on the table.'

Now he mentioned it, she saw it clearly.

'This painting is a great example of *chiaroscuro* – the interplay of light and shade. The dark background makes such a contrast to the illumination, which favours Christ and throws his shadow on the wall. You see there – what looks like a halo? His painting was unparalleled. Incredibly detailed and as polished as they come.'

Jude moved her towards the last picture of the three, a darker and altogether more disturbing image. 'This is Salome, receiving the head of St John the Baptist. It's said that she danced so skilfully, Herod promised her anything she wanted. She chose the Baptist's head.'

The executioner presented the decapitated saint to her on a platter, grasping at a handful of his hair.

'It's fairly gory.' Beatrice recoiled.

Jude nodded. 'It's a gut punch, both the story and Caravaggio's depiction. I've always thought there was something brilliantly ambiguous about Salome's expression, the way she has her eyes averted. Is it disgust, revulsion, perhaps regret? We can be sure Caravaggio saw his fair share of real beheadings. This was painted in Naples, towards the end of his life. He died under fairly murky circumstances at the age of thirty-eight. Compared to *The Supper at Emmaus*, the brushstrokes here are freer, more expressive, the background only hinted at, the colour palette dark.'

Beatrice was staring at the Baptist's deathly pallor; she found it hard to look away.

'Come on, there's a bench free – let's grab it.' Jude led her to the centre of the room where they sat down. Reaching into his pocket, he pulled out a small glossy hardback book with 'Caravaggio' embossed in gold across the cover. He rifled through the pages and stopped at a small plate reproduction, which showed a dark-haired youth. Wrapped in blood-red robes, his skin was luminous, his figure muscular but slender.

'This one is called *Youth with a Ram*, painted in 1602, around the same time as *The Supper at Emmaus*. The youth is St John the Baptist.'

Beatrice studied it for a moment, then gasped in recognition. 'It's him! It's just like the portrait in Mum's room.'

Jude nodded, seemingly delighted. 'I think so too. Caravaggio made at least eight depictions of St John. He painted this one twice; both the original and a second version are on display in different museums in Rome.' He looked at her intently. 'Some artists are incredibly prolific – Picasso painted maybe 10 to 15,000 works. Rubens well over a thousand, but Caravaggio managed less than a hundred in his short life, that we know of. That meant an awful lot of people wanted copies. To me, the similarities between this picture and the portrait in your mother's bedroom are undeniable.'

Beatrice stared at him; Jude put up his hands.

'I'm not saying Caravaggio painted it himself – that would be utterly incredible – but the painting in your mother's room looked very old and very good. It's impossible to say without getting it examined, but if it is a copy by one of his followers, the *Caravaggisti* as they were known, you could be looking at something worth tens of thousands.'

She stared at him.

'You're kidding.'

He shook his head. 'I promise you, I'm not. You might have something special there, Beatrice. Something worth exploring.'

When she got home, Beatrice went to check in on her sleeping mother straight away. She sat down on the edge of the bed and stroked her hair. The light from the open curtains cut across her face, casting deep shadows in the hollows of her cheeks. Old age had brought with it a kind of second infancy; Maddalena Fremont's days now comprised of several short cycles of sleep, followed by a few restless hours when she might be helped to eat a little, then rest again. She'd often toss and turn for hours through the night, unable to get comfortable, so little flesh left on her bones to cushion her.

Beatrice pulled the linen bedsheet up around her mother's shoulders. Trimmed with ancient lace, the knotwork had been a source of Maddalena's pride. She'd been a dextrous lacemaker until arthritis came and robbed her of her tools. Beatrice had always admired her mother's practicality. Whether her hands were plaiting hair, shelling peas or rolling gnocchi, her love was always tangible, woven into the fabric of their daily lives.

Beatrice went over to look at the painting on the wall.

Hidden in the corner of an often-darkened room, she'd barely noticed it in years. She took it down and turned it over in her hands. It always looked like such a shabby thing to her, no more than a remnant. Could Jude be right? Could it really hold so much value? She stretched to hang it back up on the wall, then switched off the lamp and tiptoed from the room.

She went downstairs to the basement kitchen where the strip light cast its wan blue glow across the room. Taking down the pasta flour, she set to work, hoping some fresh tagliatelle might tempt her mother to eat a little more than usual.

When Maddalena woke a few hours later, Beatrice was pleased to find it did the trick. She sat beside her and swirled a fork in the thick ribbons, spearing a cube of roasted squash and feeding it to her patiently. By necessity, it made their communication one-sided, so Beatrice kept up a running commentary on her day instead.

'I went to the National Gallery, to meet Jude Adler. You remember, the one who came to look at Daddy's photographs and paintings.'

Her mother regarded her steadily and slowly chewed her food. She clearly did remember him, and none too fondly.

'He thinks some people might be interested in buying Daddy's pictures too, can you believe it? He would have loved that! They're looking at the other prints, see what might be worth selling, how much money they could raise, fingers crossed.'

Her mother swallowed, but didn't say a word.

'There was something I wanted to ask you. The portrait of the smiling boy. Can you remember where you bought it?'

Maddalena turned away.

'Mum, are you listening?'

Her brown eyes were cloudy and her expression vague. Beatrice wondered how much of what she said was going in.

'The picture of the man, up there on the wall?'

Beatrice turned and pointed. Her mother's eyes drifted up to the painting.

'*La luce* . . .'

Although she understood English perfectly, Maddalena refused to speak it anymore.

'That's right.' Beatrice nodded encouragingly. 'The painting in the light.' Getting no more response, she tried again. 'Jude thinks it's a painting of St John. Did Daddy buy it for you, do you remember?'

At the mention of him, Maddalena's eyes dropped back down to the lace-edged counterpane, her agitated fingers plucking at a row of little knots. Beatrice reached out and wrapped a hand around her mother's fingers.

'It's okay. I didn't mean to upset you. It doesn't matter.'

Maddalena's chin trembled. She shook her head.

'*Mi ricordo* . . .'

I remember. 'Remember what, Mum?'

A tear rolled down Maddalena's cheek. Her voice was quavering, '. . . *Sono maledetta.*'

Beatrice squeezed her mother's hand. 'You're *not* cursed, Mum. Don't be silly!'

Maddalena pushed her plate away. Beatrice picked it up and put it on the tray. As she left the room she glanced over at the painting, puzzling the meaning of her mother's words.

CHAPTER THREE

ROME, JUNE 1939

The morning of Maddalena's seventeenth birthday was like every other since she'd first arrived at Villa Velare, three months before: she'd risen in the half-dark, set a fire in the kitchen grate and gone straight out to the fountain in the courtyard to fill the copper water jug. These were her primary tasks, come rain or shine. She fetched and carried, cleaned and tidied, chopped and peeled. The one thing she was not yet allowed to do was cook. That task fell to Dolorosa Senese, a short, indomitable woman, firm but relatively fair. She expected a great deal from Maddalena but worked as hard as anyone herself. Dolorosa had a vast bosom and hair like wire wool. She wore her sleeves rolled up, and her red face shone from the kitchen's heat and her own exertions. She described herself proudly as a *gattara* and Maddalena sometimes wondered if she felt more affection for the stray felines of the

Aventine than she did for her new charge. Every morning, cats and kittens came to scavenge at the kitchen door. Sometimes Dolorosa would sit with a barrel of sardines and a pair of scissors, snipping off the little heads and tossing them out to the wiry creatures who lay in wait.

All day long the cook kept up a steady flow of instructions for Maddalena: wrap the stale bread in a damp cloth, whip the cream and beat the eggs. No, not like that – like this! Despite every provocation, the young woman held her tongue and tried her best. She yearned to cook, but knew the first step was to earn Dolorosa's trust.

As the cold water of the fountain slowly filled the copper jug, Maddalena savoured a moment of solitude and peace; the birds were singing and steam rose from the garden as the first sunlight warmed the dew. It wouldn't last – Dolorosa would soon be giving her instructions, and the house would wake up, one by one. The master and the mistress, Conte and Contessa Montefalco, their two daughters, Costanza and Sophia, and all the staff, who tended to their every need. This day, the anniversary of her birth, would pass unnoticed, like any other.

Maddalena reached down into the pocket of her skirt to find the letter from her mother. It had arrived the day before, but the kitchen had been too frenetic. She hadn't had a chance to open it till after dark and by then she'd been too tired. Now she removed the single sheet of writing and gazed at the sprawling letters; her mother had probably dictated it to Father Brancuso after Mass. Maddalena was grateful to the priest, but wished he'd written it more slowly. She tried to decipher his words while the water filled the jug, but then gave up. Her presumed birthday greetings would have to wait till Sunday, when she'd have a few hours to herself.

Maddalena had only been sent to work in Rome in the first place thanks to Mussolini's eternal quest for empire. After her elder brother Dario died on a battlefield in Ethiopia, their widowed mother had tried to scratch out a subsistence for her six remaining children. As the eldest, Maddalena had left school to take the reins at home – she'd known how to cook already, but with her younger siblings relying on her, she learned to do it frugally and well. She gained a good reputation, and her mother determined they could all benefit from her culinary skills. The parish priest had been persuaded to recommend her to a friend of his in Rome: might he know of anywhere in need of service? A reply came back by return, telling of an opening for a *sguattera* in the kitchens of Villa Velare, home to Roman aristocracy – the scion of the House of Montefalco, no less. She had been dispatched with haste and found herself in the well-appointed kitchen of a palatial villa, high up on the Aventine, one of the seven hills of Rome. It was a world away from Sicily.

On the terrace Maddalena stood up. She balanced the conca jug, now heavy with water, on top of her head, keeping her focus straight ahead. When it was solidly in place, she stepped forward quickly and assuredly. She didn't see the tiny cat as it streaked in front of her, only felt its presence when her foot connected with its skinny flank. The cat flew forward, yowling and spitting out a protest, which caused Maddalena to hesitate mid-step: Icy water splashed across the rim and down her back, causing her to gasp and stumble. The wave slopped back the other way and took the conca over with it, drenching her from head to toe. The jug landed and bounced across the cobbled courtyard, sounding like a clamouring of bells. It sent the frightened kitten streaking off as the jug spun and came to rest by the open kitchen door.

There was a moment of absolute quiet and then the wailing started up. It came from the nursery, whose shuttered windows looked out across the courtyard, two floors up. The cry was piercing and sliced the stillness like a knife.

Dolorosa dashed out through the kitchen door, a shocked expression on the old cook's ruddy face. She kicked the copper jug where it had fallen, so it slammed against the metal cover of the coal chute. The shutters of the nursery flew open and the Swedish nanny, Balia Carolina, poured furious invective onto both their heads. In return, Dolorosa made a rough gesture with her arm, then growled at Maddalena.

'Go inside.'

From the nursery, the piteous cry of young Sophia was joined by howls of protest from her older sister. The nanny slammed the window shut. Drenched to the skin, Maddalena slunk back into the kitchen and tried to wring her skirt out in the sink.

'You woke up half the house, you little fool,' Dolorosa tutted. 'Better pray you didn't wake Signora Bianchi, too.'

But of course nothing escaped the housekeeper's notice, and so Maddalena found herself summoned to her office on the second floor, a narrow box room filled with shelves of dusty ledgers. The Signora looked up as she entered: a gaunt woman with drooping jowls and a hard-set mouth, thick kinks of salt and pepper hair scraped tightly in a bun. In pride of place on her desktop was a framed photograph of her deceased husband, a fascist captain, and beside it an even larger portrait of the leader, Benito Mussolini.

'Your antics this morning upset the girls and disturbed the master and the mistress. No doubt you do things differently in Sicily, but in Rome we expect certain manners and decorum.' The woman puffed her flat chest out. 'I'm inclined to be lenient as you are relatively new, so I shall merely dock your pay and send a letter to your mother, but consider this a warning: if I see no improvement, you will be sent back home.'

Shamefaced, Maddalena nodded. As she moved toward the door she caught a single muttered word, *terrona,* loud enough for her to hear. Filthy southerner, less than dirt to be swept out into the gutter. Maddalena said nothing in reply but was shaking as she went back down the stairs, an angry knot lodged inside her chest. From the neck of her black uniform, she pulled out a medallion on a scarlet ribbon. Her mother had given it to her on the day she passed into the Signora's care.

'This is for your protection – it's the Holy Face of Jesus, who will shield you from the age of lust.'

It gleamed dully. To Maddalena it looked like a tiny death mask, pressed from tin.

'His light will imprint itself on you. If you are always good and try hard, I'm sure they'll treat you well and fairly. Do not put me to shame.'

Maddalena had sworn to be obedient and do her duty then, but still, an ember of injustice burned. It wasn't her fault the cook encouraged the starving creatures in the first place; only sheer bad luck sent the kitten through her feet. Now her family would go hungry and her mother would think she was to blame.

She rubbed hard at her tears before they had a chance to fall. If she was dirt then, so be it – she'd be grit in their eyes and hard as flint. She would not be her mother, defeated by life's bitter disappointments. She'd be like the little feral cat and spit and scratch and streak between their heels, and do what she must, to flourish and survive.

Maddalena spent the rest of the day doing drudge work, from scrubbing pans with wood ash paste, to sluicing out the drains with scalding water. By the time she finished it was long past midnight, the house was sunk in darkness and her fingers were as raw and pink as baby mice.

She wandered out into the garden, the letter from her mother still tucked inside her pocket. She'd deciphered barely half of it, a fact which saddened her as much as anything that day. She walked up the path and breathed in the perfume of the damask roses, their scent strongest in the hours before the dawn. The sky spread out above her, a moth-bitten cloth which let in tiny specks of light. At the garden's highest point, a stone bench had been placed to take the view of the Altare della Patria, a yellow moon reflecting off its columns. Maddalena sat down and having held it in all day, allowed herself to cry. The tears fell fast and passed quickly, like a summer storm. She sighed and sniffed and wiped her nose along her sleeve. She was about to get up and go back down when she heard a gentle cough. Maddalena spun round in her seat, startled, and saw the figure of a man silhouetted on the hill.

'I'm sorry,' he said. 'I didn't mean to scare you. I only wanted to make sure you were all right.'

For a moment she considered dashing down the path, but then the figure took a step towards her, out of the shadows.

'I hope you will forgive me the intrusion.'

She saw at once it was Conte Luciano Montefalco.

'It's Maddalena, isn't it? We haven't been properly introduced.' He put out his hand and she thought for a moment he wanted her to shake it, until she saw the pressed white cotton handkerchief. 'Perhaps you might have need of this . . .'

So, he knew she had been crying. She began to stammer an apology, until he interrupted.

'I'm the one who ought to ask forgiveness – I disturbed your peace. I just didn't want you to turn around and find me without warning.'

Now she saw that he had been standing next to a large camera on a tripod, the lens trained on the very bench where she was sitting. She jumped up, but the conte gestured to her.

'Please stay.'

She cautiously sat back down.

'That's better. Besides, I need you in my composition.'

'You were taking a picture of me?' She sat up straighter.

'After a fashion – if you remember, you sat down in my frame.'

Maddalena looked across the vista of the city. 'But how, when it's the middle of the night?'

'Well, there's the moon, the stars, the streetlights . . . Rome is never truly dark.' The conte moved back to the camera and made adjustments to the lens. 'I've been conducting some nocturnal experiments using only available light. There's a photographer who lives in Paris: Brassai, perhaps you've heard of him?' She shook her head; the conte continued. 'The photographs he takes at night are just incredible; puts all my little efforts here to shame, but I do love this view. I thought I'd try to capture it with a very long exposure.' He took a cloth out of his jacket pocket and wiped the lens. 'I quite like the notion of a figure in the foreground – makes you a proxy for the viewer, if you will. Do you mind?'

She shook her head again, and he smiled at her.

'Well then, stay very still . . .'

Maddalena looked out, conscious of the glittering eye of the camera lens which focused on her. As the minutes passed, she hardly dared to breathe.

'There now. You can relax.'

She watched as he began dismantling the camera. From a distance she'd assumed he was serious and terribly mature, but now seeing him up close, he seemed much younger. He was tall and elegantly dressed but not in the least bit stiff or formal. He had a deeply dimpled smile and thick, dark waves of hair.

'Shall I walk you back down?' he asked, once the camera was packed away. 'The path can be fairly treacherous at night if you're unfamiliar.'

'Thank you.' She handed back the unused handkerchief; hadn't wanted to tarnish the pristine cotton.

'I do hope it was nothing serious, whatever made you sad?'

Maddalena flushed.

The conte added, 'Not that it's any of my business. I didn't mean to pry.'

'I was just a little homesick.'

'And where is home?' he asked.

'Sicily,' she replied, the word *terrona* an echo in her mind.

The conte regarded her with sympathy. 'Well then, no wonder. I've only been there once, but I liked it very much; untamed and absolutely beautiful.'

As they drew near the house, the path diverged. The moon cast shadows of the cypress. The conte slowed.

'I'll say goodnight. You should be safe enough from here.'

'Aren't you coming in?' she asked.

'I think I'll head down into Testaccio with the camera. See what kind of lunacy the full moon brings.'

'But it's so late.'

He shrugged. 'Some subjects only come out after dark. Brassaï's pictures take you places, show you people you might not realize exist.'

'You aren't afraid?'

He shook his head. 'The camera keeps it at a distance.'

Not knowing what more to say, she started down towards the fountain.

'Maddalena?'

She looked back; he was a silhouette once more, a sheen of light in the dark sweep of his hair.

'I hope tomorrow is a better day.'

'Thank you, sir.'

'Please, call me Luca.'

She watched him leave and stood a moment in the kitchen courtyard, now a place of shadows, entirely altered by the dark. For better or worse, this was her home now, where adult life began.

CHAPTER FOUR

LONDON, AUGUST 1997

The sky was flat and bright on the morning of her mother's funeral. Beatrice stood outside the church with Father Morgan, waiting to greet the congregants as they arrived. He'd made few attempts to speak to her beyond giving a perfunctory schedule of events when she'd arrived. Now he hummed quietly to himself, a hymn she recognized but could not name.

At least the building was familiar. Modern Catholic, brutalist – an airy, open space. Above the entrance, a clock was built onto the brick. No numerals, just plain white dashes which told her the service was due to start in a few minutes. Father Morgan had been firm – they must begin promptly on the dot of two o'clock. Funerals, like trains, should run on time.

From the moment she learned about her mother's death, Beatrice felt her autonomy diminish. Everyone demanding something of her but no one giving her what she needed, which was simply time and space to grieve. In late July, Maddalena's body had finally betrayed her. Beatrice spent long days at her bedside in the hospital, willing her to persist. She'd only gone back home to shower and change her clothes, when the call came from the nurse. Even though she was expecting it, the end was still a shock.

'You think they'll want you with them,' the nurse had reassured her. 'But they often wait until their loved one steps away.'

Standing outside the church in the summer heat, Beatrice watched the pallbearers lift the coffin, the new centre of her gravity – she knew where she was in relation to it, at every moment. Conscious of her posture, she forced her shoulders back and made sure her stoic smile was set, anxious to signal to everyone she was coping.

'Ready?' Father Morgan asked.

'As I can be,' her taut reply.

She began the long walk to the front pew, awkward and self-aware. She took up her position and watched the procession of the coffin being carried down the aisle: one narrow wooden box borne on the shoulders of six tall men, though the effort was drawn clearly on their faces.

But Mum's so small, she thought. *How can she be so heavy?*

They set the coffin down and Beatrice fixed her gaze on the flowers, her mother's favourite roses, so wine-dark they were almost black. A brass thurible smoked and filled the air with a scent like the incense which lingered in her mother's room. Maddalena's body had lain there overnight; Beatrice had taken down a little cut-glass bowl of keepsakes from her dresser – a silver medal, which bore the face of Christ, on a faded ribbon, and a little donkey carved from wood, small and smooth as a pebble. Both had been items of intense interest to Beatrice as a child, as if they might possess some magic. She'd tucked the medal into the palm of her mother's hand before they closed the coffin; a totem to take with her. She'd kept the donkey for herself. Even now, she had it in her pocket; the worn blonde wood soft to the touch.

The organ came to a wheezing halt, leaving silence in its wake. There was a whisper as the pages of the service sheets were turned, a ripple of sniffs and coughs and then the priest began intoning words, half spoken and half sung.

'God of faithfulness, in your wisdom you have called your servant Maddalena Fremont out of this world. Release her from the bonds of sin, and welcome her into your presence, so that she may enjoy eternal light and peace.'

From the rear of the church there came a rattling sound as someone wrestled with the doors. A few people turned their heads, including Beatrice. Jude Adler stepped into the vestibule, dressed in a dark grey suit and tie. Flushed and breathless, he made his way towards an empty seat, almost clumsy with embarrassment. Beatrice flashed him a swift, reassuring smile, which he gratefully returned.

Father Morgan signalled to her it was time to speak and she felt the world tilt a little at the prospect. When she'd enquired about a eulogy, the Irish priest had been reluctant. 'Are you sure you won't get upset, now? I wonder if it isn't more dignified to go without ...' But she'd insisted, so he finally assented – perhaps a few short words might be appropriate. The basics, mind, no need for *War and Peace*.

Beatrice kept her eyeline fixed above the congregation's heads, determined not to cry.

'My mother was, first and foremost, an amazing cook. When they fled Italy in 1944, my parents came to England with nothing but her recipes. She used to call me her *piccola pallina di pasta* – her little dough ball – and could never understand why I didn't find that very flattering!'

A wave of gentle laughter buoyed her up and willed her on. She relaxed a little and spoke about her mother's life, her own late arrival in her parents' world, the terrible, sudden loss of her father and the resulting bond they formed.

'Mum and I became a unit, the power of two. She did her best to fill his shoes. She tried so hard, and she succeeded.'

The words Beatrice had scribbled swam before her eyes. She'd written more, but realized she had nothing left to say. She picked up the sheet and walked back to the pew, fearing her legs might give way. Looking slightly vindicated, the priest hurried to take her place.

Beatrice kept her eyes on the order of service. She'd chosen a picture of her mother, taken in this church a few years earlier. She looked fiercely handsome, even then – a proud woman, tiny but determined, her auburn hair turned grey.

'Lamb of God, you take away the sins of the world, have mercy on us.

'Lamb of God, you take away the sins of the world, have mercy on us.

'Lamb of God, you take away the sins of the world, grant us peace.'

*

Afterwards, the guests filed out from the front, each stopping to press her hand as they passed by, to murmur their condolences. Jude Adler was among the last. He went to shake her hand as she stepped in to hug him. They came together awkwardly, each patting the other on the shoulder.

'I'm so sorry I was late.' He seemed flustered.

'Don't be – I'm very glad you came. I think you tipped us into double figures.'

She'd told him about the service a week before, when she'd called to say she needed to delay the auction. 'I just can't think about anything until after the funeral.'

'I get it, absolutely,' asking when and where the service was. She'd told him, though she hadn't really expected him to come.

'So, how are you doing?' Jude frowned. 'No, scratch that, don't answer; such a stupid question.'

'Let's just say I'm coping, shall we?' She stuck her chin out, proving her resilience.

'Fair enough. Can I give you a lift somewhere?'

'That's kind, but this is just the start. Mum insisted on cremation, though I'm not sure Father Morgan quite approves.'

'What's wrong with cremation?'

Jude was clearly as unfamiliar as she with the Catholic rites of passage. She parroted the priest's broad brogue.

'Apparently, "A burial asserts the bond between the living and the dead, Beatrice". Nevertheless, he's allowed it.'

'Well, let me know if I can do anything to help. I remember how it feels, when there's no one left. The concept of being an orphan sounds awfully Dickensian, but still . . .'

She'd forgotten he'd been through something similar. 'I'm so sorry. I ought to have remembered.'

'No reason why you should. Besides, it's ancient history for me.'

Beatrice sought a change of subject. 'If it's okay, I would like to pick up where we left off with the auction.'

'Are you sure? I figured you might need a break – you've had a lot to deal with.'

'Honestly, I could do with the distraction. Arranging all this kept me busy, till now . . .'

She heard a cough behind her.

'Sorry to interrupt.'

The voice belonged to an overbearing man with a barrel chest.

'Charles! I didn't see you there. Thank you for coming.'

'Need to get back to the office but wanted to pass on my condolences.'

'Charles, this is Jude Adler. He's helping me to sell Dad's photography collection. Start paying off the bank.' She explained to Jude, 'Charles Ingram is our family solicitor.'

He gave Jude a curt nod. 'Good idea. Art dealer, eh?'

'Not a dealer, as such,' Jude replied. 'I do valuations.'

Beatrice interjected, 'Your secretary recommended him.'

'Did she?' Charles Ingram sniffed. 'Well then, let's hope you do a good job.'

He gave Jude a thin, rather predatory smile, then turned back to Beatrice.

'Will you be home on Thursday, late morning? I'd like to drop by with the deeds and a few other things for you to sign. Oh, and a note about disposal of the ashes, from what I understand.'

She nodded and they watched him as he walked away, Beatrice waiting to speak until he was out of earshot.

'Sorry about him – he's rather old-fashioned but he's been pretty good, advising me on the best way to proceed, in legal terms. The bank is relentless. If I can give them a better picture of my financial situation, I'm hoping they'll back off.' An idea suddenly came to her. 'Could you come over Thursday, too? Get the ball rolling, give the bank something to chew on for a while?'

'Of course,' said Jude.

'And that painting – the laughing boy? Mum didn't want to get it valued, but maybe you could look into it, do some sort of investigation?'

'I'm afraid I'm not taking on that kind of work just now, but I could put you in touch with some friends of mine in Oxford, if you like. No pressure. Have a think about it. It's entirely up to you.'

'Okay, I will.'

He's chivalrous, she thought. Such an old-fashioned concept, and yet it seemed to fit him perfectly.

'Well then, I guess I'll see you Thursday morning? Hope it goes okay this afternoon.'

As he began to walk away, she felt a powerful desire to reach out and touch him; to feel the warmth between his shoulder blades. A sudden yearning for simple human contact. The moment passed. The pallbearers were readying the coffin for the journey to the crematorium. Beatrice braced herself, knowing she was facing it alone.

CHAPTER FIVE

ROME, DECEMBER 1939

'Come in.'

Luca opened the door and saw his wife of seven years was at her dressing table, patting the dark waves of her hair into place. Contessa Violante Montefalco looked sternly at his reflection in the mirror.

'Can you please have words with Cook? Tito and the other boys have been throwing fireworks again. They scared Costanza and the guests will be arriving soon.'

Luca frowned. 'It's New Year's Eve. Perhaps we ought to let them have their fun.'

'You think I'm being unfair.'

By making it a statement, Violante placed the responsibility on him. He thought it better to conciliate.

'I'll speak to Dolorosa when I get a chance, but the kitchen has been busy and you know how hard it is to keep the boys in line. I'll see if I can persuade them to take it to the streets instead.'

He hoped to go into the new decade with more felicity than the last.

Violante picked up a small diamond drop earring: expensive, but discreet. She did not go in for great displays of wealth or fashion but was never less than well maintained. Her hair was her greatest affectation: a coronet of curls set fast, which she'd worn the same way since the day they'd met, when he was twenty-one and she was thirty. He'd admired her sense of purpose then; she didn't simper. She was sometimes haughty, but not unkind. They'd married within months of meeting. Both sets of parents had been keen – Violante was not getting any younger and Luca was deemed to be in dire need of a wife. His older brother Roberto had shocked the entire family when he decided to renounce his title and take up Holy Orders instead. Luca found himself suddenly thrust into the role of the successor and everything which went along with it, the need to produce an heir the chief among them.

Along with the title, he took possession of three houses: Villa Velare in Rome, Castel Gedächt, a fortress in the Dolomites, and a seaside property, up the coast. His desire to be a photographer could no longer be supported, so a suitable role at the Vatican's Photographic Cabinet was procured instead – close enough and more appropriate for his situation.

Violante soon fell pregnant and then Costanza was born, the vast rooms of Villa Velare echoing with her cries. A second daughter, Sophia, followed on a few years later, then finally a third much-wanted pregnancy, which both had hoped might be a son. It proved to be so, although his body, born too small and far too soon, could not long sustain his life.

Both Luca and Violante mourned his passing in their different ways: he threw himself into work while she lost herself entirely for a time, then found some sort of equilibrium by focussing on God and her surviving children. The doctors informed them there would be no more, and so a certain coolness came over their relationship. They did not fight and Violante rarely disagreed with him outright. She just retreated from the world, relinquishing many of her responsibilities to Signora Bianchi, the housekeeper, who gladly took them on. To the outside world, the couple looked the picture of domestic harmony; only they knew the truth, as chilly and as complex as that could often be.

'Do you need something else?'

Luca realized his wife was scrutinizing him in the mirror; he pulled a slim box from his inside pocket and handed it to her.

'It's nothing, really. Just a gift to mark the new year.'

She frowned, a little pinch between the eyebrows, then peeled back crisp layers of white tissue and lifted out a scarlet camisole and knickers. Her cheeks flushed and she dropped them back into the box, placing it on the table and pushing it away.

'I'm not sure Father Colonni would approve.'

'I can't imagine how he'd ever know,' Luca replied. 'Do you intend to show them to him?'

'Don't be ridiculous.' She shot him a reproachful glance.

Seeing his gift had fallen flat, Luca bristled. 'You never

know, Colonni might like to wear a little silk himself, beneath his vestments.'

Violante's lips were set thin. 'I know you think you're being funny, but given your own brother's position, I sometimes wonder at your sense of humour.'

'Roberto is not as pompous or dictatorial as Colonni.'

He could tell he had offended her and tried to make amends. 'It's just a fun tradition. It was meant to make you laugh.'

'Oh, I know what it was meant for.'

In the silence which followed, they both heard shouts coming from outside: a squeal of tyres skidding on the driveway. Luca glanced out of the window. It had been snowing heavily for days and all Rome was submerged under its deadening white weight.

'This weather's quite atrocious. Perhaps we should have cancelled after all.'

Violante resumed patting her hair into place and refused to meet his gaze; silence was always the most effective weapon in her armoury. Luca considered reaching out, but found he had neither the will nor inclination, so simply turned around and left the room instead.

The party ended up being a rather tame affair, at least by Villa Velare's usual standards. The heavy snowfall meant that fewer than a hundred guests assailed the Aventine's steep inclines. Some telephoned with their apologies, having decided against any unnecessary journeys in such adverse conditions. Many of those who did brave them voiced their intention to leave shortly after midnight, though Luca was appalled.

'Where's your spirit of adventure?'

'You can't blame us,' said one American diplomat. 'It took three of your boys to push my car up the drive. I was terrified we were going to plough them down!'

Despite it all, the rooms were overflowing. Dozens still descended, to drink their share of his spumante, the golden bubbles running up the edges of their coupes. In times of restriction, nothing tasted half so good as someone else's food. Noblemen drifted through the grand, high-ceilinged rooms, while the women in their thin silk gowns gravitated to the fireplace for warmth.

'I don't think I can remember it ever snowing quite as much as this, can you? The thermometer on the transept wall read minus five this morning.'

Luca liked his parties to include people from different walks of life. Along with the patrician class, there were diplomats, actors, film-makers and photographers, as well as many stalwarts from the Vatican, Luca's older brother chief among them. Father Roberto Montefalco arrived late, his hat covered in a fresh dusting of snow, the hem of his robes soaked through. The housekeeper, Signora Bianchi, cleared a path for him and led him to the fireplace. Luca kissed his older brother on both pink cheeks.

'Well done for braving it. I wasn't sure you'd come.'

'I couldn't disappoint my stomach. It's been rumbling at the prospect all day long. Your kitchen is vastly better than that of the refectory.'

As he warmed his hands, Roberto asked his brother, 'How is your work? Going well?'

The Vatican Photographic Cabinet was in the process of logging and recording every precious item in the Holy See's extensive archives, from priceless paintings to illuminated manuscripts.

'It's a slow process and there are challenges, but I believe we're beginning to chip away.'

'All thanks to the forethought of il Papa, may he rest in peace.'

Roberto gesticulated to the heavens. It was less than a year since the death of Pius XI, who'd been responsible for the Cabinet's formation.

'Very prudent of him,' agreed Luca. 'I fear that if we go to war, as seems inevitable, then nothing will be sacred. What's the latest from the Vatican spies? You hear more gossip than the papers do, at least the ones who only publish what they're told to.'

Roberto sighed. 'I don't think there's any chance Italy won't get drawn in. Herr Hitler seems determined to force Mussolini's hand.'

Luca gave a hollow laugh. 'But haven't you heard? We aren't allowed to question our great leader. What is it they say, don't ask the pilot where he's going while he tries to fly the plane? Seems like a fine way to conceal the destination, if you ask me.'

'I'm ever thankful the Vatican is a nation state,' replied Roberto.

'Good luck with that. You may be neutral, but you're surrounded by a country which seems hell-bent on self-destruction.'

Roberto put up his hands. 'Then let us pray that doesn't happen.'

'I'm not sure how much our peerless leader listens to prayers, or to his people, come to that,' Luca snorted.

'The new Pope does, and for that I'm truly grateful.'

'Damn it, Roberto! How can you be so complacent? You must realize the fascists have no love of God?'

Luca generally concealed his distaste for the government, but his brother knew him better.

'Come, Luca, though we may enjoy sparring, your other guests may not.' Roberto looked about him, lowering his voice. 'Mussolini has been a friend to the Vatican, so far. Many in the Church see an advantage in having a strong leader who is broadly sympathetic to our needs.'

'Until they no longer suit him.'

Luca sometimes wondered if his brother's loyalty to the Church meant he would choose it over him.

'Perhaps we ought to change the subject,' Roberto said mildly, putting a hand on his shoulder. 'You never know who might be listening.' Luca felt the flame in him diminish.

'You're right, I'm sorry. It's my duty to be a thorn in your side, as your younger brother.'

'So I understand.'

'Let's hunt out something for you to eat instead.'

Luca led Roberto to the dining room. A long table was laid out with tureens and chafing dishes, filled with food at the start of the evening, but now picked almost clean. Luca began to apologize for the lack, when Maddalena entered with a steaming dish of sausages and lentils, fat as golden pennies. Seeing the two men, the young woman dipped into a curtsy.

'Good evening.'

'These look good,' said Luca. 'May I take a bowl for my brother?'

Maddalena looked concerned. 'But Cook said they're supposed to be served after midnight?'

He winked. 'I promise we won't tell.'

She grinned as she ladled a generous serving out for Father Roberto. He dug his fork in straight away.

'Did you make these, young lady? They're utterly delicious!'

'Thank you, Father. Cook let me make them for the first time, so I'm glad to hear you like them.'

He speared a sausage, still speaking while devouring it. 'Perhaps I ought to try to poach you for the Vatican refectory. Our cooks are good and pious women, but they rarely make anything as flavoursome as this.'

'Don't you dare!' Laughed Luca. 'Maddalena is indispensable.'

She blushed. 'A little more piety might do me good. We had a game of tombola last night in the kitchen – it went on so long, I almost forgot to soak the lentils. The Signora would have my guts for garters if she'd known.'

'Maddalena!'

The exclamation caused all three of them to turn. Signora Bianchi stood glaring in the doorway, her white face stiff with fury.

'How dare you speak like that! Get back downstairs at once.'

The young woman shrank at the sight of her. Cheeks aflame, she bowed her head and ran out of the room.

The housekeeper approached Roberto. 'I'm sorry, Father; please forgive us. She knows no better, I'm afraid.'

'But we interrupted her,' said Luca. 'She was only trying to be polite.'

'She ought to know her place. I will endeavour to instruct her.'

'I assure you, there's no need, Signora. She did nothing wrong.'

Signora Bianchi gave him a tight smile. 'Very good, sir. As you please. Do excuse me.'

Luca watched her go, hoping Maddalena would be able to keep out of her way. Roberto regarded him with some sympathy. 'Must be quite a responsibility, being master of this house. You make it seem so easy.'

Luca raised an eyebrow. 'You don't regret giving it all up, then?'

Roberto shook his head. 'I feel certain I wouldn't have done as good a job as you.'

'I don't know about that. Violante trusts that woman implicitly, but I fear she's been given far too much leeway.'

'I'm sure she means well,' replied Roberto, ever diplomatic.

'You're more charitable than me.'

'You know I'm here as your brother, if you should ever need to talk?'

For a time, the noises from the party flowed around them: sounds of laughter and indulgence. As tempting as it might be to share his worries, Luca thought better of it. They were his to deal with, on his own.

'Don't worry. I know I have much to be thankful for. It's nearly the start of a new decade, after all.'

Roberto clapped him on the back. 'Come then, let's go out and see it in.' The priest's eyes twinkled and he rubbed the rotund belly concealed beneath his robes. 'But first, perhaps I might trouble you for another portion of those excellent *lenticchie . . .*'

At the stroke of midnight, the assembled throng raised their glasses to prosperity and said a toast to new beginnings. Their glasses chimed together with the mantel clock, echoing bells which rang throughout the city. The song remained the same, in peace and war, sounding out for celebration and alarm.

The assembly tucked into their bowls of *cotechino,* then started gathering up their coats of silk and fur and fine-cut wool before setting off into the night. They were protected by these insulating layers; though none knew what lay ahead, they'd less to fear than most.

In the backstreets children played at soldiers, hurling snow grenades. Young boys ran in packs, letting off fireworks which turned the white to red and filled the air with soot and cinders. Infants in their cots cried out, their sleep disturbed by such uncommon sounds.

The state rooms of Velare were cleared and all the lights extinguished. Signora Bianchi moved through the empty spaces, making sure the fires were dampened, the candles all snuffed out. She took her husband's watch out of her pocket; it was shortly after one o'clock. She ran a fingertip across the cracked glass face. He'd been wearing it when a bullet struck him in the eye, dead before he hit the ground, the casing cracking as he landed. Despite all that, it kept good time. She hastened to her bed.

Luca was last to retire. When the guests had gone, he retreated to his study and scanned the airways for news on his radio: from Paris, Prague and London. When the house was still, he stood and stretched, then went back downstairs. He knocked lightly on the door to the dressing room. Getting no reply, he eased it open: the bedroom beyond was dark, the only source of light a small lamp by the mirror. He wondered if the silence was an implicit invitation: was she sleeping or awake? Then he saw the slim black box, which lay discarded in the waste basket. He reached down to pick it up and found the silk still wrapped inside, unwanted and rejected. Now the silence of the bedroom took on a different tenor, as if the occupant might be lying there holding her breath, hoping to repel his intrusion. He waited for some indication and when none came, dropped the box into the basket and climbed back up the stairs.

He pulled out blankets from an old campaign trunk in the corner and made up the daybed. He put more fuel on the fire and got undressed, his skin pale in the amber glow. By the time he put his head down on the musty pillow it was almost three o'clock. He fell into a restless sleep.

Three floors below, in the small box room next door to the kitchen, Maddalena lay on her narrow iron bed. She watched her breath rising, a plume of steam. Outside the window, feral cats prowled, calling to each other: to hunt, to play, to procreate. They roamed rooftops covered with a blanketing of snow. She touched her fingers to her cheek and felt it sting where the Signora's hand had slapped her. Shame stained her wax-white skin, while ice as fine as filigree spread feathered wings across the window. Full of cold fury, Maddalena willed herself to sleep.

CHAPTER SIX

LONDON, AUGUST 1997

As Jude turned onto Talgarth Road late on Thursday morning, he felt lighter in his spirit. When he'd got back from the funeral there was a message on his answering machine to call his friend at the Photographer's Gallery. Ben had sounded uncharacteristically excited, declaring the Fremont prints to be 'a delight' – excellent quality, in good condition and likely to interest collectors from around the world. He'd earmarked a dozen of them which could go as high as two to five thousand pounds each. Certainly nothing close to the six-figure sum Beatrice needed to save her home, but perhaps enough to buy some time. Jude knew how empty the future could look to someone newly grieving, and it came as a relief to him as well; even this small commission would mean he could pay the mortgage on the gallery and start to chip away at the debt he owed for the forged painting. It would take him years to get back to where he'd been, but safer to make steady gains than risk chasing phantoms.

He'd woken that morning with an energy he hadn't felt in months, although he couldn't reason why. Relief and perhaps some measure of excitement at the prospect of seeing Beatrice again. When he arrived at the house, she was standing on the front steps with the family solicitor he'd met at the funeral. Beatrice noticed him and smiled.

'Jude! You remember Charles Ingram?'

'I do indeed.' He put out a hand, which the older man gripped hard.

'I was just telling Beatrice, selling art's a risky business.'

'It can be,' Jude agreed.

Beatrice patted the solicitor on the forearm. 'Don't worry, Jude hasn't tried the hard sell. Quite the opposite, in fact.'

'Glad to hear it,' Charles Ingram replied gruffly. 'I promised her mother I'd watch out for her best interests, you understand.' He turned his attention back to Beatrice. 'Sorry to dash, but I've got a table booked at Daphne's.' He patted his mustard-coloured waistcoat. 'Don't forget to sign that probate document now, will you?'

Beatrice held up a thick stash of letters, wrapped with an elastic band. 'I'll do it straight away, I promise.' She watched him as he strode off down the road, then smiled at Jude. 'Come on in. I'm afraid it's in a bit of a state. I started a clear-out late last night, which I'm beginning to regret.'

They picked their way through towering stacks of *Reader's Digest* magazines and Beatrice led him downstairs to the base-ment kitchen. The room was cluttered and chaotic; it smelled of rich spices, yeast and the fresh herbs growing in a tangle on the window ledge.

Beatrice sighed. 'I'm trying to get on top of it, but there's a lifetime of hoarding here; not sure she threw anything away. I keep finding tins that are years out of date.'

'No need to apologize.'

'Cup of tea?'

He nodded.

'Only builder's, I'm afraid.'

She crossed to the sink to fill the kettle. He observed her as she moved around the kitchen. At the funeral she'd seemed so pale, but now she had some colour back. She caught him watching. Feeling suddenly self-conscious, he reached for a new thread of conversation.

'What does Mr Ingram think about the auction?'

Beatrice spooned loose-leaf tea into the pot. 'Cautious, I think it's fair to say. I just wish he'd been equally circumspect when Mum decided to remortgage. Without that, none of this would be necessary.'

'I have some news on that front. I spoke to my friend last night and he agrees that your dad's collection is very saleable. If you're happy, we can start to move forward.'

'Oh, that's fantastic, thank you!'

He thought briefly she might hug him, but the moment passed.

'Milk?'

'Just a splash.'

She pulled out a bottle from the door of the fridge. 'Do you have any idea how much they might make?'

'I try to be conservative as auctions can go either way, but I'd be looking for something in the region of ten to twenty thousand.' Jude knew she'd hoped for more.

'Oh. Okay.' She handed him his tea and tried to hide her disappointment.

'It could go higher; I just think it's better to be cautious.'

'Honestly, that seems like a fortune for some old photographs. I suppose I keep hoping some miracle will let me stay. Do sit down . . .'

She pulled a chair out from the kitchen table and picked up the bulging pile of envelopes which Charles Ingram had given her.

'These are the last bits my mum sent to the solicitors, apparently.' She levered off the elastic band and began to rifle though. 'All this death admin is exhausting. What did you do about probate when your mum died?'

'I was only thirteen, so my uncle handled most of it. Not that she had anything to settle, except debt.'

'Same. Charles says there's little more in the way of assets, except for a safe deposit box in Rome that's just been sitting there for years. If that held anything of value, then Mum wouldn't have had to remortgage in the first place.'

She opened the first envelope and retrieved several sheets of Green Shield stamps and a sheaf of Premium Bonds. Beatrice laughed and fanned herself with them.

'Call off the hunt – I think I've found my fortune.' She handed the sheets of stamps to Jude. 'What do you reckon they're worth?'

He peered at the fine print.

'Two shillings each. So, maybe ten, twelve pounds?'

'Ah well, maybe not.'

Next came a padded envelope. She shook the contents out on to the table – a set of keys and a sealed envelope. 'These must be for the safe deposit box in Rome.' She tore the letter open and scanned the first few lines, then stopped abruptly and reached for a box of tissues, exhaling deeply.

'Are you okay?' asked Jude.

She nodded stiffly. 'It's a letter from my mum about disposing of their ashes. Hers and my dad's, by the looks of it – I only read the first few lines.' She stared at the paper as if it was an incendiary device. 'I'm so sorry, I wouldn't have opened it in front of you if I'd known. I thought it was just another bit of admin. Didn't get myself prepared.' She gave a brave smile, which quickly faltered.

'I can come back later, if you like?' suggested Jude. 'Give you some space . . .'

Beatrice shook her head determinedly.

'Not at all. Stay here and drink your tea, though I might just pop upstairs to read it on my own, if you don't mind?'

He nodded. 'Of course.'

Picking up the letter and the box of tissues, she slowly climbed the basement stairs. Jude gazed round the room as he sipped at his hot tea. It was a proper working kitchen: shelves filled with bottles of oils and vinegars, a little salt pig and a great many cookery books. For Jude, who existed primarily on a diet of takeaways, it seemed like a foreign land. He sat in silence for a minute, wishing he'd brought a book. He didn't want to disturb Beatrice by venturing upstairs, so went over to the shelf and read the titles on the spines: most appeared to be Italian. At the end of the row was a thick ledger, a battered, linen-covered book of recipes, which he began to rifle through. There were loose pages and cuttings from old magazines, a pamphlet from Be-Ro and shopping lists of exotic ingredients written in Italian, all in the same small script. There were annotated passages written tightly in the margins. Jude tried to parse out the dishes from the few words which he recognized and flicked through recipes for arancini, cannoli, gnocchi.

At the sound of Beatrice's approaching footsteps, he tucked it hastily away, worried she might think he was prying. She held the letter in both hands, her face was wet with tears.

'I think Mum must have written this after you came here. That painting stirred something up, some dreadful memory. It doesn't make much sense.' Trembling, she sat back down. 'Can I read it to you? It's in Italian, only I need to know I'm not going mad.'

'Of course.'

She began to read, her voice hesitant.

My darling Beatrice, this is hard to write. It is my wish to have my ashes buried with your father's in the rose garden of the Villa Velare in Rome. Take us back to the Aventine, where we met and fell in love.

I leave you everything, to do with as you please, but there is something I must ask. The portrait of St John – the one you always call the laughing boy – it is not ours. We brought it here from Italy. We had no choice, but still, such sins will not stay buried. Keeping it so long has been a curse.

I planned to take this secret to the grave, but now I'm
close to death I cannot bear the thought of my damnation,
condemned forever by the memory. For the sake of my eternal
soul, find the rest and return the painting to its rightful owner.
Please forgive me. Make right what we did wrong.

Beatrice slumped back, her face as drained of colour as the
paper. She shook her head.

'It's like some awful riddle. What does any of it mean?'

'Was there anything else in the envelope?'

'Just the keys I showed you, to the safe deposit box in Rome.'

'Maybe you start there?'

Beatrice looked perplexed.

'You don't think it all sounds crazy? Because I do.' Her dark
eyes glittered on the edge of panic. 'And I can't just run off
to Rome. I wouldn't even know where to start and besides,
I can't afford it!'

He considered for a moment. 'Maybe it's worth trying to
find out more about the painting first.'

Beatrice jumped at the idea. 'Could you help me?'

He instantly regretted saying anything. 'I don't think that
would be a good idea.'

'Isn't that what you used to do?'

'But I don't do it anymore.'

'Please, Jude. I really need your help. I know next to nothing about art.'

He wanted to say yes, to appease her and to scratch his own
itch of curiosity, but no. He recognized temptation; it would
be all too easy to fall back down that rabbit hole.

'I can't. I'm sorry, Beatrice.' He felt the flush creeping up his throat.

She nodded but couldn't meet his eye. 'I understand. I've imposed too much on you already.'

'It isn't that.' He thought about the red barn roof. He couldn't bring himself to voice that shame to Beatrice. 'I'm just not the right man for the job, but I know someone who might be. Those friends I mentioned, Kit and Anita Worseley? They live in Oxford. He works at the Ashmolean and she's a conservator. I can ask them if they'll take a look.'

'I don't want to be a nuisance.'

'You're not. I wish I could do more.'

She stared down at the letter in disbelief.

'Poor Mum. No wonder she was so weird when I tried to discuss it.'

Jude hesitated. 'Was she lucid, at the end?' He didn't want to seem insensitive, and yet the whole tone of the letter begged the question.

'I thought so, but all that talk of sin . . . My dad might not have believed in it, but Mum did in a very real way.' Beatrice could not forget their conversation. 'She told me she was cursed. I thought she was just being overly dramatic, but what if she believed it? What if she couldn't live with the recollections it brought up?'

Jude shrugged, aware he'd spent a lifetime avoiding so much of his own history.

'Memory can be a very unreliable narrator. It's sometimes better left alone.'

CHAPTER SEVEN

ROME, JUNE 1940

The kitchen was sweltering. No breeze to stir the air or break the noisy syncopation of the insects, which rose and fell the whole day long. A battery of tiny ants crawled into everything which wasn't covered, so bread and other sundries had to be stored in string bags and hung among the copper pots and pans.

Maddalena had risen at 4 a.m. to get ahead, doing much of the day's preparation before the heat became too overwhelming. Neither the temperature nor the restrictions imposed by rationing meant Signora Bianchi had lower expectations. She simply required the two cooks to make up any shortfall with their effort and imagination, getting up early to spend hours waiting in a line for very little. Her priorities were clear: Italy might not yet be at war, but Velare's staff were part of Mussolini's standing army, and the cooks were foot soldiers in the fight.

In the fifteen months since she first arrived at Villa Velare, Maddalena had gone from a mere *sguattera* to a proper cook, in part because of her extraordinary bread-making skills. Flour was at a premium, but Maddalena's Sicilian loaves lasted for days and could be stretched out in a variety of ways. Dolorosa had been happy to encourage her; kneading large quantities of dough was heavy work, so she often supervised while the younger woman worked up a sweat, her shoulders rolling, fists punched deep into a trough of dough.

On this morning in early June, Dolorosa sighed at the sight of such exertions while fanning herself and stirring a pot of starchy rice. She poked it with a ladle and muttered her disapproval.

'So bland. The men complain.'

Still pummelling, Maddalena laughed. 'It doesn't stop them eating it. Besides, Bianchi would go after them if she heard any word of protest.'

Dolorosa snorted. 'There's little she can do to them. It's our lives she makes hell.'

Maddalena stopped kneading and wiped her brow. Complaining was the language of the kitchen – it fuelled the labour, but it meant their tempers often frayed.

'We're already working in an inferno. I don't see how Hell itself could be much worse.' The sweat was pouring off her. She plucked at the neck of her uniform. 'I'll make some arancini with the leftovers, they won't miss their pasta then.'

The Ministry of Food had declared that eating pasta was a sign of weakness, so Signora Bianchi insisted they only cook with rice, one more salvo in the ongoing battle between the housekeeper and the kitchen.

'What's wrong with pasta, for pity's sake?' Dolorosa snorted.

'You don't have to convince me.'

'I'm hardly likely to convince that dried-up witch now, am I?'

They stifled their laughter, fearing they might be overheard. Signora Bianchi often seemed to possess a sixth sense for their mutiny. Dolorosa picked up a bowl of green beans and a paring knife.

'When you finish with that dough, come and sit with me outside.' She wandered out into the cool of the courtyard, a rolling wallow from one stiff hip to the other.

Maddalena went back to the dough, working it between her fingers and feeling the coarse grit of semolina, like grains of sand in silk. She dipped her fingertips in water and scraped the strands together, before flattening it out to begin again. Later she would make some little mouse-ear pasta for the girls. It was their favourite and the Signora's edicts about rice applied only to the staff. The family still ate as they pleased – they could afford to supplement the rations, as long as the ingredients could still be bought on the black market. The cook's son, Tito, was often sent to buy illicit items from the *borsa nera*, riding his bicycle at speed down narrow alleys. He was a true son of the kitchen, motivated by greed and fast enough to evade pursuit.

Maddalena shook the wet dough from her fingers and began to put the bread to bed, wishing she could do the same for herself; her back and shoulders ached from all her effort in the heat. These days life seemed incrementally harder: most people were hungry, making them a little more selfish, a little less patient. Some changes showed themselves in unexpected ways; she'd seen several fights break out on the street in daylight and there were more stray cats than ever. With scraps at a premium, even Dolorosa declined to share as much. A trickle of sweat rolled down between her breasts as Maddalena began to cut hunks of dough from the trough, rolling them on the floured tabletop. She laid them on a damp sheet and blessed each fleshy dome in turn. A snort of laughter made her jump and gasp out loud. She turned to find Signora Bianchi smirking in the doorway.

'What do you think you're doing?' She waved her hands, mocking Maddalena's little ritual.

'You have to bless the bread, or it won't rise.'

'Superstitious nonsense; I despair.' She sniffed. 'Where is Dolorosa?'

'In the courtyard, paring beans.'

'Tell her the contessa has been calling for refreshments. It's very close and the children are becoming fractious. Make them a granita.'

'Yes, Signora.'

The gaunt woman grunted. 'And tell Dolorosa we've been informed Mussolini will address the nation later. The household must be present to listen to the broadcast, including both of you, so meal preparations should be finished in a timely fashion.'

Maddalena moaned. 'Again?'

The same thing happened the day before, to no avail. No

word from Mussolini, just a great deal of waiting around, followed by a long report about a bike race.

'You think the affairs of state are yours to question?'

'No, Signora.'

'Quite right. Now hurry up with that granita.'

Maddalena brushed the dry dough from her fingers and went outside. Dolorosa was dozing in the shade, the bowl of trimmed beans at her feet. She sat up at the sound of Maddalena's approach.

'The contessa is asking for refreshments.'

The cook yawned and rubbed her hands across her face. 'She hates being in the city in the summer, that one. Always has.'

Maddalena wondered what it must be like to have worked in one place for so long.

'Why don't they just go away then, for the summer? They did last year.'

'The conte won't let them, not until he knows what's happening with the Germans. If we join the war he might decide to keep them here.'

Maddalena frowned. The prospect of war seemed impossible to her, despite all the rumours to the contrary.

'Do you think it might really happen?'

'War? Who knows. The government said it wouldn't come to that.'

Maddalena chuckled. 'Luca says only a child would believe anything the government says.'

'Don't be so familiar!' Dolorosa sucked her breath across her teeth. 'Luca indeed. He's sir or the conte to you.'

Maddalena pouted. 'He *told* me to call him Luca.'

'He's the conte and don't forget it.' Dolorosa pulled herself up, out of the chair. 'Still, he's not wrong. They've been installing loudspeakers throughout the city, and they wouldn't do that if there wasn't something to warn us about, now would they?'

Outside the Vatican the roads were packed: buses, cars, pedestrians and motorbikes, all jostling for space, each one unwilling to surrender to the other. Men in smart white uniforms stood on stripy podiums at busy intersections, conducting traffic with their white gloved hands, like doves in flight.

Driving through it all, Luca often wondered how it did not descend into anarchy, and yet overall, the city functioned. These last few days had been worse than usual; the heat of summer had arrived in earnest, but more than that, after months of angry rhetoric, the newspapers had all gone strangely quiet. A summons came and thousands gathered to listen to the radio in homes and factories, cafés and piazzas, all waiting for Il Duce's bullish tones. Still, no pronouncement came, only a detailed description of the last leg of the *Giro d'Italia* bike race. A nation simultaneously released its breath and went about its day.

The call had come again this morning: every household must stand by at five o'clock. Luca telephoned his wife reluctantly.

'Can you ask the Signora to gather all the staff at five o'clock?'

'What for – the results of a tennis match? She says we lost an hour of work yesterday.'

'What can I say? I asked Roberto and he's certain news

will come today. He's seen the intelligence: Mussolini will join Hitler and declare war against Great Britain and France.'

After the call, Luca left the Vatican and drove across the Tiber. The avenues thronged with people, including tourists, although fewer than before and mostly German. Almost all the British, even residents who'd been living here for years, had abandoned Rome completely and gone home. Luca had been sad to say goodbye to friends from the consulate, intelligent men who'd warned him what was coming.

The prospect of war made him fear most for his daughters. Sophia wouldn't understand – her world was hardly any bigger than the nursery – but Costanza was her mother's child. She took her cues from Violante, who tended to pessimism at the best of times. How would they manage in the face of real danger? Even wealth and the high walls of Velare could not shield them from a war.

Luca slowed the Alfa as he passed a cluster of market stalls on the Campo de' Fiori, turning the steering wheel to park up alongside. He wound the window down: a dozen older women sat in headscarves, with baskets of gladioli and ornate cruciforms woven out of palms. Nearby, a sad-looking donkey stood, harnessed to a gelato cart and laden down with bridles and rosettes. The poor creature was being tormented by a swarm of flies; it slowly blinked its gentle eyes and kept its head bowed low. Luca picked up the little Leica camera which he carried with him everywhere. The dispirited donkey seemed so emblematic of the day, he framed the creature in the foreground, the empty piazza behind it. Suddenly a group of men walked through the shot. They wore the black shirts of the *squadristi* and slapped each other on the back, jostling and joking. More of them kept coming, wave after wave, until hundreds filled the square, heading east towards Palazzo Venezia. Towards Mussolini.

Even in the heat of the June day, Luca shivered with foreboding. He wound the window shut, started up the engine and turned the car south, towards home.

When he pulled up the driveway, there was no one to be seen. As he came to a stop in front of the garage, his mechanic, Santino Marchetti, emerged from the shadows, wiping his hands on a greasy rag. He nodded a greeting, and Luca handed him the keys.

'You heard they're making an announcement?'

Santino grunted. Luca checked his watch.

'We were told five o'clock. Best come up to the house soon.'

'I'll put the car away first. Give it a quick polish.'

The garage was uncommonly quiet; no sign of the young men who often hung around there, eager to get their hands on any engine they could find.

'You on your own?' asked Luca.

'They've all gone down to watch the speech.'

'I saw hundreds heading that way as I left. It'll be pretty crowded by the time they get there.'

'They're young.' Santino shrugged. 'They just want to be in among it.'

'I have a feeling they might get their wish,' sighed Luca. 'Much good may it do them.'

The mechanic made the sign of the cross. *'Ci siamo.'*

Here we go.

Luca walked towards the house. After the glare of the road, the villa's interior was cool and quiet, the height of the ceilings lost to shadow. He crossed the empty rooms, accompanied only by the sound of his footsteps on the marble floor.

He went upstairs and found that even the nursery and his wife's sitting room were empty, the doors left open, toys abandoned. He climbed the final flight up to his study and looked down onto the terrace. Almost the entire household was in attendance there already. Violante and the girls sat near the shade of the loggia, while the groundskeeper and household staff stood out in the sun. Snatches of their conversations drifted up.

Luca took his camera from his pocket, focussing on the elongated shape of their shadows, which cut across the ground. Up here he had a bird's eye view of the distinction between employer and employee; together and yet separate. War would touch them all in ways which none of them could guess. He checked his watch: it was almost time.

When Luca finally stepped out onto the terrace, Signora Bianchi was instructing the maids to hand round water from the fountain. The Geloso radiogram had been moved outside from its position in the salon. Balia Carolina was trying to prevent the children from pestering their mother, while Violante sat apart, fanning herself in the heat. One of the privileges of such a large and graceful home was that they rarely saw how much human endeavour it took to maintain; occasions which brought them all together were few and far between.

The tensions of the day simmered just beneath the surface. All the adults understood the threat of war was hanging right above them and their expressions reflected their concern. Signora Bianchi barked out terse instructions, and the young women jumped to do her bidding, keeping their heads down and their eyes averted. The housekeeper spied Luca and bustled over straight away.

'I took the liberty of asking the men to carry out the radiogram, sir, but told them to wait for you to tune it in.'

Luca crossed to the walnut cabinet and turned the dial, rocking on his heels until the sound of patriotic airs erupted from the speaker. He lowered the volume quickly – he'd had more than his fill of such pomposity the day before.

Ordinarily this space was his sanctuary. He could escape out here to take the evening air. The ceiling of the loggia itself was painted with frescoes of a cerulean sky filled with the underbellies of songbirds and frothing clouds. Beyond that came the open terrace and the rising levels of the garden, a row of trees like exclamations, stepped against the sky: Lebanese cedar, cypress, laurel, bergamot – the threshold, where domesticity gave way to nature. Today a large group of garden labourers sat on the terrace steps, and he could smell the diesel fumes, the soil, sweat and tobacco which radiated from them. The women of the household stood together, quite close by. Only Violante sat alone, her face a mask of calm restraint. The sleek black pin-tucked waves of her hair barely stirred in the air from her fan. An ebony rosary lay in her lap, and she idly thumbed its beads. Luca drew a chair up next to her.

'How was your day?'

She barely glanced in his direction. 'Tiresome. The children will not settle in this heat.'

He knew she was desperate to escape the city, but she possessed a passive fatalism and would never challenge his decision to stay, at least not directly.

'I wish the men wouldn't loll around so.' She nodded at the gardeners.

'They're not doing any harm.'

Signora Bianchi, who'd seen and understood the signal, strode towards the men and ushered them to stand. As they reluctantly did so, Santino joined them. He stood next to his young wife Maria, who ran the laundry, bridging the gap between the men and women. Luca nodded to the mechanic and retrieved a cigarette case from his inside pocket. He took out a cigarillo, tapping it at either end. He rarely smoked, but found he needed occupation. As he drew the smoke in, his eye was caught by the swifts darting overhead. Only days before, a squadron of bombers from the *Regia Aeronautica* had flown directly overhead, startling them away. He was glad to see they had returned.

A sharp voice came over the radio. *'Attenzione, attenzione!'* Luca turned up the volume as the Signora bustled across to Violante.

'Should the Swede be here, I wonder?'

Violante called out, 'Balia Carolina, could you take the girls upstairs?'

As the young woman ushered the children back inside, the patriotic music was replaced by the roar of the crowd outside Palazzo Venezia. The amplified voices echoed round the loggia and a sudden shout broke through.

'Salute iI Duce!'

A hush fell over the multitude, bar a few shouts of

encouragement. The terrace was completely silent, the only sound the chirring insects in the trees until Mussolini's voice began to pepper the crowd like a machine gun.

'Fighters of the land and sea and air . . .'

They listened as he told them this was an hour marked out by destiny, which struck the heavens of the fatherland. A time of irrevocable decisions.

On the terrace, every face was gaunt. Luca exchanged a glance with Santino. They'd known of course; this was only confirmation.

'The declaration of war has already been handed over to the ambassadors of Great Britain and France.' Then came the roar; thousands shouting with one voice.

'War, war, war!'

Despondent, Luca listened. How could people celebrate; how did a country turn against its own best interests? What could make so many cheer on their own demise?

The bulldog barked at them from his balcony. 'People of Italy, run to take arms. Show your tenacity, your courage and your valour!'

Signora Bianchi thrust out her chin and began to clap her hands together, until the rest joined in. A desultory applause broke out, no one wishing to look less than patriotic, though their support for Mussolini had long been based on the belief that he would keep the country out of the war.

Luca noted those who stopped applauding first: Santino, Maddalena and Dolorosa, the head cook folding her arms across her ample chest in protest. With one son in the army and another not yet of age, she had more to fear than most.

He looked for the Signora and saw from her expression she'd been watching too.

Violante spoke quietly. 'Can you turn it off now? All that shouting is giving me a headache.'

Luca stood up and flicked off the radio, then realized every face was turned towards him, waiting to hear what he would say. They wanted words of reassurance, though in that moment, he had none.

'No doubt we all have a great deal to digest. I'm sure nothing much will change immediately. Let's wait and see what the weeks ahead will bring. We thank you all for your service, today and every day.'

After that, the staff began to leave the terrace. Luca watched Maddalena put an arm round Dolorosa, then lead her away. Eventually, he was left alone with Violante.

'What now?' she asked.

'We must hope for quick appeasement. No one wants this, least of all the French. The Germans are advancing there already – they'll have to come to some accord.'

'And if they don't?'

He was torn between wanting to keep the girls with him and removing them from harm. Finally, he sighed in resignation. 'You should take the girls away for the summer, although I shall miss all of you dreadfully.'

'Where to, the castle or the coast?'

'Perhaps the beach might be safer, given Castel Gedächt's proximity to Austria and France, though I don't think we're at imminent risk of an invasion.' He didn't want to imagine what might happen if peace did not come soon. 'I shall join you when I can, though no doubt the threat of bombing will accelerate our work. I'll speak to my brother in the morning, find out what intelligence he's heard.'

Violante stood and put her hand on his shoulder. He couldn't remember the last time they'd touched.

'I'll inform the Signora; she'll want to make a start on packing. You'll be all right here, fending for yourself?'

'Of course, take everyone you need. A skeleton staff can keep this place ticking over till you return.'

She bent down and brushed her dry mouth against his cheek. 'Thank you, Luca.'

He sat out on the terrace for an hour or more, watching as the light dimmed and the swifts wheeled overhead, swooping after fireflies. Eventually, the Signora brought out a lamp, which he thanked her for. He lit another cigarillo, which glowed in the growing dark. He saw himself as the swifts must, alone in a pool of light and realized the loudspeakers in the public squares were there to serve a dual purpose – to call the men of Italy to arms and to warn them when predators were on the wing. War had come at last, as he'd both dreaded and predicted.

Ci siamo. Here we go.

CHAPTER EIGHT

OXFORD, AUGUST 1997

A week after the funeral, Jude drove to Talgarth Road in his ageing Karmann Ghia to pick up Beatrice and drive them both to Oxford. He'd sent the small square portrait of St John ahead and then got a call from Kit to say he and Anita had preliminary thoughts to share.

Jude set a course towards the straight path of the Great West Road, past arcing smoked-glass structures and rows of grey-faced houses hugging tightly to the road. Beatrice seemed subdued; his offer to drive them both assuaged the guilt he felt at turning down her plea for help. She stared out of the window, barely speaking till they broke through the surface tension of the city. The urban palette gave way, first to green, then gold and finally, the spires of Oxford began to gather on the horizon.

Jude drove them through the city and past the Ashmolean,

pointing out the places he'd spent time as a student. Finally, he turned the wheel and pulled into the car park of a pub on the eastern edge of Port Meadow. The Hound was a jumble of red-brick Elizabethan buildings, with a sweeping, low-tiled roof.

'I thought we'd get some lunch and then walk down to the studio,' Jude explained. 'I told Kit we'd be with them for roughly one o'clock.'

Inside, the wooden beams were so low he had to duck his head. 'What can I get you?'

'I don't mind.'

He recognized Beatrice's sense of disconnection: the unseen wall between grief and the relentless world.

'They do a legendary ploughman's. Why don't you go and find a table, and I'll order for us?'

Beatrice sat down next to a mullioned window in a patch of sunlight. She looked out across the flat landscape of the meadow, buff-toned and wild at the height of summer. It had often worked its magic on him; he hoped it would do the same for her. He brought their drinks over to the table and set them down. The rhythm of a roosting pigeon drifted through the window. Beatrice yawned and stretched, and rubbed her eyes.

'I like it here.'

'I like it too,' said Jude. 'It feels outside of time somehow.'

'Tell me again who we're meeting?'

'Kit and Anita Worseley.' He smiled fondly. 'Kit was my tutor and later we became good friends. He's lovely, fiercely bright and kind and funny. An expert in the Italian

Renaissance and Baroque. He knows far more than I do about Caravaggio and his followers. Unlike some great masters, Caravaggio had no studio. People only learned to replicate his techniques by copying his paintings. Kit knows all about that world.'

'And what about Anita?'

'She's a conservator, one of the best; she can read a canvas like a map. There's always so much more than meets the eye. She'll look at your laughing boy in forensic detail: take samples of the paint, the base frame and the canvas, get them under a microscope if necessary. Conservators are scientists and artists in equal measure and Anita is also generous and tolerant, especially of Kit and all his eccentricities. I think you'll like them both.'

Jude considered how integral the couple had been to his own survival. 'I didn't take to Oxford easily. I felt out of place, like everyone had been given instructions which never came to me. I think I might have left in my first year if they hadn't taken me under their wing.'

The waitress brought their meals over: huge oval plates with slabs of cheddar and a wedge of crusty bread; golden pickles and tiny fire-red tomatoes. Jude tucked in with gusto, while Beatrice grazed around the edges.

'Can I ask you something?' Her voice was hesitant. 'After your mum died, how did you cope with it? You were so young.'

He considered saying something glib and reassuring, then surprised himself by telling her the truth.

'I'm not sure if I dealt with it at all. I only cried once, at the funeral. That was it.'

She tried to hide her disbelief. 'Really? I feel like I could cry all day. It takes nothing to set me off; I found a half-used tube of toothpaste this morning and that was it, I was toast!'

Jude laughed. 'Your way sounds better. If you ask my friends, I flunked it. Must try harder.'

'I don't know, do any of us have a choice how we respond?'

He looked at her plate of half-eaten food.

'Are you going to finish that?'

She shook her head. He picked up the bread and cheese and gulped it down, along with the last dregs of his pint.

'Ready? Then let's go.'

The hedges of Port Meadow were filled with the smoke of old man's beard and russet berries shone against an ice-blue sky. Jude tramped ahead across the long dry grass.

'This way.'

He watched Beatrice from the corner of his eye as she stretched her legs to match his pace. There was a violet undertone to her skin, like someone who'd been indoors far too long.

'How's it going with the bank?' he asked.

'Not great.' She frowned. 'It's a rat's nest of bureaucracy, to be honest. Some people there are normal human beings, who try to help, but the rest seem pretty callous. I'm applying for a bridging loan, but I have no measurable income – I gave up my job to look after Mum. The auction helps, but that's going to take some time.'

Jude had warned her it could be a slow process. 'I keep thinking about Mum's letter and bouncing between extremes . . . From hoping the painting is the answer to all my problems to being terrified in case your friends have found out it was stolen, or even worse.'

Jude felt a pang. 'Digging into art can be a complicated business.'

'If it wasn't for you, it would still be hanging on the bed-room wall.'

As they loped through the field together, their strides began to synchronize. He imagined his hand brushing hers, how it might feel to take hold of it . . . Would she have wanted that? Perhaps, if Maddalena hadn't died and Beatrice hadn't crossed the gulf of grief. It couldn't happen now. Most likely, she'd never looked at him that way. He saw himself as she must: younger, awkward, gauche. The flat Estuary accent, which gave so much away. He consigned hope and his growing feelings for her to the place where all such issues went: to be dealt with on another day. This year, next year, sometime, never.

Wisps of cloud obscured the sun, a high and faint corona. Beatrice squinted in the light as Jude pointed out a tarmac path ahead, its tongue cracked and overgrown: Jericho lay before them. The mottled ground of the meadow gave way to hard paved streets and she followed as he led the way, weaving a path through rows of Georgian buildings. They came to a stop on a residential street, in front of an anonymous house. Beatrice looked around.

'You sure this is the place?'

He pressed his finger to the doorbell. 'Doesn't pay to

advertise when you might have paintings worth millions lying around inside.'

After a moment, the door opened and a small woman with bronze skin and dark plaited hair enveloped Jude in an enthusiastic hug.

'Anita, this is Beatrice.'

Half expecting to be embraced as well, Beatrice felt relieved when Anita simply clasped her hand.

'We've heard so much about you.' She smiled conspiratorially. 'Don't worry, nothing bad. Come on inside.'

'Where's Kit?' asked Jude.

'Out back, in the studio. Follow me.'

Anita led them along a hallway, through a cheery kitchen, then outside to a gravelled courtyard behind the house. Beyond it stood a stable block, with a sliding blue barn door. Anita put her weight against it and pushed, revealing an open workshop with stacks of empty picture frames, lined up against the wall. It reminded Beatrice a little of a school art department: several large oils were set about on easels, their dark patina visibly lighter in some patches. The air was thick with the warmth of a summer's day and the heady tang of turpentine and varnish. The workshop seemed at once cluttered and yet fastidiously clean. A fixed workbench ran along the right-hand wall with a microscope and sundry other scientific items. Above them, rows of shelves with jars of pigments and bottles of all sizes; pots of inverted brushes and sharp implements, palette knives and files.

In the centre of the room stood a broad-backed wooden table with a north-facing skylight overhead. Beside it stood a portly man: fair-skinned with a ruddy pink complexion. Despite the heat, he wore a brown tweed suit and heavy polished leather brogues. Hands laced behind his back, he bounced on the balls of his feet, his face alight.

'Jude!'

'Hello, Kit.'

The two men embraced and clapped each other on the shoulder. Kit Worseley turned and beamed at her.

'And this must be *Beata Beatrix*, just as you described.'

'Beatrice Fremont,' she clarified, putting out her hand. 'Nice to meet you.'

'Ignore Kit,' said Jude. 'He can't help associating people with famous works of art.'

Kit clasped her hand and shook it up and down.

'*Beata Beatrix*, by Rossetti – a pre-Raphaelite tour de force. My dear, I'm so excited.'

'Me too.'

She glanced at Jude who smiled wryly at Kit's enthusiastic greeting. Seemingly oblivious, the flush faced man carried on.

'Miss Fremont, may I introduce you to your painting in all its unbound glory? Liberated at long last . . .' He stepped sideways with a flourish of his hand, allowing Beatrice clear sight of the table. It was covered by a large expanse of canvas, the edges of which showed peaks and troughs, not unlike a folded paper map.

Only one section was familiar to her: the face of the smiling boy, who she now knew to be St John. His head and shoulders were there, but she was amazed to see so much more besides: a muscular arm and torso and a strong, flat stomach. Unbound, the canvas was at least three times the size of the original – where that had appeared to be small and neat and square, this was a rough rectangle, the edges slightly frayed.

Fascinated, Beatrice bent over to examine it more closely. From the light above, she saw the patina of the original square was slightly darker than the rest. Those parts which had been folded bore scars along the creases, where the pigment rubbed away. Tiny chips of paint were missing, exposing coarse threads of canvas underneath.

St John was surrounded by vegetation – hadn't Jude mentioned they were oak leaves? She turned round to ask him and saw that he was utterly transfixed.

'It's unbelievable,' he muttered.

Kit and Anita watched them both intently.

'But why was so much of it hidden away?' asked Beatrice.

'It's not uncommon,' Kit replied. 'Paintings get damaged, people cut them back or fold them to make the most of what remains.' He pointed to the frayed edges on the right side and the bottom. 'At some point, many years ago, someone cut this fragment from a much larger piece. Then they decided to focus on the portrait of the face and fold the rest away, tacking it onto a pinewood base.'

He picked up a square frame and handed it to Beatrice.

'Anita very carefully removed the nails, and, well . . . you can see for yourself how it all unfolded: St John revealed himself to us!' Kit was warming to his subject and back to bouncing on his feet. 'It is faintly miraculous that something so delicate should survive this long intact. He hasn't received the same kind of attention most others are afforded.'

'How so?' asked Jude.

Beatrice realized this was just as much of a revelation to him.

'No lining, for one thing,' Kit replied. 'Usually, a piece like this will have a secondary canvas behind it – common practice in the nineteenth century, a way to strengthen and preserve. Something so old and yet unlined is rare to the point of being noteworthy itself. I've only ever seen a few.'

Anita nodded. 'It's certainly peculiar. From the corrosion on the nails, I'd say it was put on this frame some forty, fifty years ago. Why it wasn't lined at that point is a puzzle.'

'So how old do you think it is?' asked Beatrice, trying to come to terms with the painting which lay before her, utterly transformed.

'I think early seventeenth-century Italian. Not definitive, of course, but that's what everything points to. I've collected a few samples: chips which had separated from the canvas where it was folded. I suspect there may be a specific type of gypsum in the primer, made from limestone which is only found in Malta. That might give a stronger indication of when and where it was painted. Help us pin him down.' She picked up a small cube and handed it to Beatrice. 'We suspend these chips from the painting in resin and shave them down until the stratigraphy of the priming, paint and varnish is exposed. Then I pop it under a microscope and see if my hypothesis is confirmed.'

Kit interjected, speaking directly to Anita. 'Ought to get an X-ray, too, while you're at it.'

'Why do you need an X-ray?' Beatrice asked, bemused.

Kit chuckled. 'All paintings have a memory, eh Jude?'

'So I've been told.' Jude grinned, then explained to Beatrice, 'That's the opening line from Kit's lecture on "An Introduction to a History of Painting". Very famous among his students. Basically, an X-ray will reveal if any parts of the composition have been changed or covered up.'

He turned back to Kit. 'The pentimenti show the way! Except . . . there won't be pentimento on a copy.'

He said it flatly, but Beatrice heard the question in his tone. She asked Kit, 'What does pentimento mean?'

'A kind of residue, a mark left where the artist might have made a mistake or changed their mind. The word literally means repentance or regret. On first attempt, a painting may not be planned in much detail – the artist develops their ideas; boundaries might move. In the hands of a skilled artist, a finished piece appears as if it was ever thus but look closely and you will always find evidence, a trace of their original intent. Like an imprint left behind, lying underneath the surface.'

Anita interrupted, 'And don't forget, ageing plays a part. Over time, oil paint can become transparent and make the pentimenti more acute.'

Beatrice looked between the three of them. 'I'm totally confused – is this a copy of the painting Jude showed me in the book, or not?'

Kit beamed at her. 'That, Miss Fremont, is the question!'

She noticed Jude was hanging on to every word Kit said.

'When an artist makes a copy, they know where they are going – a map of the journey already exists already, if you will. They simply retrace those steps.' He gestured to the canvas on the table. 'We think this is no mere copy, but more like a reinterpretation. The artist started with a familiar roadmap, but the final destination was unknown. They fumbled here and there before they found a foothold. Let me show you . . . Darling, would you mind?'

Anita wheeled over a tall lamp on a stand, and positioned the bulb at an angle to the canvas.

'Let us use a second light source,' said Kit.

Anita flicked the switch on and beckoned Beatrice over.

'See these marks scratched into the preparatory layer over the canvas? They are known as placement lines, which some artists use as a guide. In my view, the presence of them here indicates the artist always intended this painting should include two figures.'

Anita looked at Beatrice expectantly, as if she'd delivered some great insight.

'I'm so sorry – I don't understand. What am I missing?'

'Here . . .' She pointed to a shadowy indentation on St John's thigh where the fingers of another hand gripped the flesh below his hip. 'And here . . .' At the ragged edge, close to St John's right ear, Beatrice thought she saw the profile of another face. She moved closer to the painting and saw the suggestion of a nose and mouth, as if someone was whispering to him.

Beatrice looked to Jude, confused. 'But in the painting you showed me, St John was alone. There was no hand, no other person. There was only the ram, but there's no sign of it here.'

Jude looked as baffled as she felt. Anita answered for him by posing a question to Kit.

'How many different iterations of St John did Caravaggio paint in his lifetime?'

'By my reckoning, eight of the youthful St John as a solo figure, three more of him at his death, all of which included other people.'

Anita continued, 'So, it's not beyond the bounds of reason to suppose he might decide to reapproach the subject in later life. Why not the St John he painted as *Youth with a Ram*, but this time with someone else entirely? This has so many of the hallmarks of his later work: the Maltese lime, the colour palette, the looser, more expressive forms ...'

'We believe it's not a copy, Miss Fremont; not a copy at all,' Kit broke in, his face shining with unrepentant joy. 'We feel fairly certain, this painting is an original, by Caravaggio himself.'

Twenty minutes later, Beatrice sat with Kit and Jude at the kitchen table, while Anita bustled round making a pot of tea. The conversation between the two men had developed into a discussion about their best next move: whether Beatrice should go public or get more corroboration. Jude argued for caution, saying that they needed evidential voices on their side, while Kit wanted the academic community to weigh in. The two debated the merits of both approaches, leaving Beatrice feeling mystified and exhausted. She stared down at the waxed tablecloth, clean but sticky, covered in a pattern of birds and brambles. Finally, she realized someone was repeating her name.

'Beatrice dear ...' Anita was smiling at her. 'Would you mind diving into the pantry over there, see if you can lay your hands on some digestives?'

'Of course.'

Relieved to escape the discussion, Beatrice walked over to the little room: three walls lined with floor-to-ceiling shelves. It smelled of cumin and turmeric and earthy vegetables, a scent which reminded her of her mother's basement kitchen. Beatrice felt her eyes fill up with tears.

'Knock, knock.'

Anita squeezed in to join her in the small space. Somehow sensing how she felt, the small woman briefly, wordlessly, wrapped her arms around her, then stepped back and squeezed her hands.

'I should have warned you, I'm a hugger. I hope you don't mind.'

Beatrice shook her head, overwhelmed by the simple comfort of another human's touch.

'Now, don't forget to breathe.'

Beatrice took a deep, shuddering breath. Anita fixed her with a frown.

'Do you want me to go back out there and tell them both to quiet down?'

'It is . . . a lot.'

'They're excited. It's not every day someone finds an undiscovered masterpiece hanging on their wall!'

'I feel so stupid that I never saw it,' Beatrice replied morosely.

The older woman gently wagged her finger. 'Don't do that to yourself. Context is everything. If we see something in a gallery, we have no doubt it has value. But seeing something in your own home, day after day? That will alter your perception.' She picked up a square tin of chocolate biscuits from the top shelf. 'Bugger the digestives. Let's break out the big guns.'

They returned to the table together and Anita began chastising both the men. 'You're a pair of idiots with no consideration. Can't you see you're overwhelming Beatrice with all your prattle? The poor woman doesn't need to hear you arguing a thesis.'

Beatrice flashed her a grateful grin. 'It is a lot to take in all at once,' she agreed.

'I'm so sorry,' Jude said contritely. 'It's just . . . it's blown my mind. It's the find of the century and, as far as we can tell, this might be just a quarter of the painting.'

Kit explained to Beatrice, 'The canvas is torn along the right side and the bottom, so this looks as if it might be the top left quadrant of a much, much larger painting.'

Jude's eyes gleamed with excitement. 'If it is, the full scale of the canvas is larger than the original St John by quite some margin.' Beatrice hadn't seen him so impassioned. 'We need to find those other three quarters, but I've never heard of a famously lost or missing Caravaggio, have you?'

Kit shook his head. 'Not as far as any scholars I'm aware of are concerned. It's not in any of the textbooks. Officially at least, this painting should not exist.'

'That's a relief – I thought from what my mother wrote, it might be stolen.' Beatrice delved into her handbag for the letter. 'She says, "The painting of St John does not belong to us" and later, "We brought it here from Italy". But that doesn't give us any clue where it came from or where the rest of it might be.'

'The safe deposit box!' exclaimed Jude. He explained to Kit and Anita, 'Beatrice was left a set of keys to a safe deposit box in Rome – it belonged to her parents. Maybe the rest of the painting is there. That's where we ought to start, don't you agree?'

Beatrice raised an eyebrow at him. 'I didn't know *we* were starting anywhere. You said you didn't do that kind of investigation anymore. And I quote: "I'm just not the right man for the job."'

She watched Jude blush, the pink hue spreading upwards from his chest. 'In my defence, an unheard-of Caravaggio would be enough to bring anyone out of retirement.'

Kit watched the whole exchange with obvious amusement. 'As well it should. You were the best and the brightest of my students and you mustn't waste your skills for no good reason. I know you had your fingers burned, but it's long past time you faced your demons.'

He spoke more gently to Beatrice. 'Anita and I can tell you all about the mechanics of the painting, but that won't help you trace its origins or find the missing pieces. That requires an entirely different set of skills.'

Beatrice looked to Anita. 'What would you do, if it was up to you?'

Anita grinned. 'I'd be on the next flight to Rome, no question. This is the opportunity of a lifetime for the pair of you.'

CHAPTER NINE

ROME, APRIL 1941

On the first good spring day, Luca left the villa and walked down the hill towards Testaccio, crossing an invisible divide which separated lofty Aventine from its more earthy neighbour.

He never felt more conscious of his own wealth and good fortune than when he travelled the short distance to the meatpacking district. He came here often and had done so for years, to photograph its occupants both day and night. The butchers carrying livid carcasses across their shoulders, the market traders touting wares and the housewives, who patronized their stalls.

When Luca had first taken his camera out onto the streets, he'd felt conspicuous; he'd taken pictures surreptitiously, from a distance. If there was any sign of friction, he'd walked away. Over time, some of the locals came to recognize him and would demand he take their picture or suggest a subject he might not be aware of. 'You need old Berenini on the line – he's as strong as an ox at sixty-two!' Luca was obviously an outsider, yet his purpose seemed benign. The men he talked to in the small hours of the morning would have been shocked to learn he had a title. To them, he was simply Luca, the crazy man who stood out in the rain at 2 a.m., who snapped pictures of the pimp in the doorway, or the pig's blood washing down the drain. The camera was a shield, which gave him licence to pass among the prostitutes, the workers and the nighthawks. Even so, he knew his luck, knew he could escape and climb back up the hill to the comfort of his bed.

Today he'd left his camera in his study and arranged to meet his older brother at his favourite trattoria. He wanted to get some red meat into Roberto's system. A hard winter had left him with anaemia and a chesty cough. The priest often prioritized the spiritual over the physical and forgot to eat well. He needed iron now, not prayer, and with so little meat available in the shops, Luca's only solution was to take him to Felice and pay a premium for the pleasure.

When he arrived, Roberto was there already, waiting for him at a corner table. Luca asked the waiter for the best cut of meat they had, cooked rare.

'Am I so terribly naive?' Roberto asked. 'I'd rather thought the war and rationing would shut all the trattorias down. I'd no idea somewhere like this could stay open.' In the ten months since war had been declared, Roberto had rarely left the confines of the Vatican and had little understanding of what passed for normal life in Rome.

'A lot of restaurants have been forced to close and I'm sure there are days they can't open, but the answer as to how, comes when we get the bill.' Roberto looked alarmed, but Luca brushed his concerns away. 'Don't worry, I'm happy to pay. Your health is the important thing.'

'Well, I'm grateful.'

'It's our family's money, not mine alone. Besides, I'd go hungry if we weren't eating here today. The staff at the villa have a few hours off so they can attend the parades.'

It was *Natale di Roma,* the annual celebration of Rome's birth and one of the few days of the year when Luca was left to fend entirely for himself. Once the food arrived, the two brothers settled comfortably into their usual positions: Roberto avidly consuming his meal, while Luca fretted over the state of the country.

'It seems like this Greek debacle is nearly over, now that Herr Hitler has decided to come in and save face. Mussolini is claiming they'll force the Greeks to pay for their own occupation, if you can believe it.' He kept his voice low – rumour had it half of Rome was spying on the rest. 'Il Duce's hubris has us in running battles across half the Mediterranean, over-extended on every front, and that doesn't even begin to take Africa into consideration.'

'But to what end?' Roberto asked.

'Food sovereignty. We can't grow enough ourselves, so we force the occupied states to be our granary. Resources are always at the heart of any conflict.'

'Ah yes. Indeed.'

Luca was relieved to see the colour returning to his brother's cheeks. Roberto didn't share his ire at Mussolini, but never minded Luca's need to express it.

'That's autocracy for you. Governance by bombast; the empty rhetoric of threats and bullying. Mussolini cannot tolerate his authority being questioned. He calls himself a strong man, but Hitler sees him as no more than a pet.' Luca shook his head despondently. 'I will never understand how one man has the capacity to make an entire country act against their own best interests.' He chewed his meat, lost in thought until Roberto's gentle tone interrupted.

'You seem more than usually irascible today, dear brother. Is everything all right?'

Luca considered what answer was appropriate. He decided on the truth, or at least a palatable version of it.

'I find myself wishing I could do more. I've no desire to fight in this futile war, but some moments require action. I'm thirty this year, Roberto, and ... I wonder if this is all there is.'

Roberto smiled. 'I think you know my answer to that already, but this is not about the next life, is it? You are unhappy in your current situation. Perhaps if I hadn't rejected the title of Conte Montefalco in favour of my calling ...'

Luca shook his head forcefully. 'Neither of us had any choice in the circumstances of our birth. I don't complain; I have so much to be grateful for.' He trailed off, his voice now much diminished. 'Only, I sometimes worry if I've allowed those circumstances to dictate who I am.'

Roberto had taken decisive steps to live authentically,

understanding who he truly was. Luca couldn't help but feel jealous that he hadn't done the same.

Before the occupants of Villa Velare could go and join the celebrations, the Signora lined everybody up. It was one of the few occasions when they might be seen together as a household, so she wanted to ensure they all passed muster.

Sophia and Costanza were dressed prettily in matching outfits, little pleated skirts and tailored jackets, with velvet bows in their hair. Next in line was the cook's son, Tito, uncharacteristically neat in a clean black shirt. His entire school was due to march in formation, though he'd already confided in Maddalena he intended to escape.

The young women of the household were wearing their best outfits and smart, brushed overcoats. Maddalena had dressed as well as she could manage in her tired housedress and a little jacket, now too short on the sleeves and rather tight around the bust.

'You have nothing better, I suppose?' the Signora sighed, despite knowing full well that almost all the girl's wages were sent home to Sicily each month. Maddalena shook her head. 'Well then, I suppose you'll have to do.'

As she moved on, Balia Carolina, who was standing in line beside her, whispered, 'I think I might have something for you. Come with me.'

The nanny took Maddalena by the hand and pulled her up the stairs, taking her by surprise. Despite living under the same roof for nearly two years, she felt as if she barely knew the young Swedish woman. Almost every moment of Carolina's day was devoted to Costanza and Sophia. Her small bedroom was on the first floor, next door to the children's suite. Maddalena felt intense curiosity, having never been inside. The room was plain and tidy: a neat single bed, a small wardrobe and a table by the window. As Carolina opened the wardrobe door, Maddalena saw the inside had been entirely covered with pictures cut out from magazines. The images were all of film stars – she recognized Hedy Lamarr, Greta Garbo and Clark Gable, among others, including all the stars of Cinecittà Studios. The pretty blonde flashed her a glare.

'Don't you dare breathe a word. The Signora would be furious if she knew.'

She pulled out a light brown trench coat, which was hanging at the back, and handed it to Maddalena. 'Here, try this on. I think it ought to fit you – we're almost the same size.'

'Are you sure?' Maddalena took hold of it gingerly, astonished by her generosity.

Carolina shrugged and said simply, 'I don't like it. I haven't worn it in years.'

Maddalena slipped her arms in, brushing down the sleeves and marvelling at the fit after the tightness of her jacket. It was in good condition and must have cost more than all the rest of her clothing put together.

'Thank you, Carolina. Truly.'

The young woman nodded her approval. 'I just thought we ought to look out for one another, you and I.'

Maddalena felt a twinge of guilt. She'd always viewed the blonde girl as exotic, a foreigner with an accent and tastes so vastly different from her own. It made her sad to realize she saw Maddalena as an outsider, too.

'It's so kind of you.'

Carolina shrugged it off as if the gift were unimportant. 'Come on. We'll get the worst of the Signora if we make everybody late to the parade.'

The streets of the capital were busier that day than they had been in months, as if the war could almost be forgotten. And yet the atmosphere was still subdued, at least in comparison to the year before. Maddalena overheard Signora Bianchi saying Churchill had threatened to bomb Rome if Athens sustained any damage during the Greek offensive. The housekeeper applauded the Germans for joining in the fight, though she maintained Mussolini could have managed it without their help.

The bells of Rome had been ringing out since morning. When they reached the main piazza, crowds were standing ten feet deep, and every wall was hung with banners and festoons. Carts were set along the road, selling buckets of spring blooms, little carved horses and toy tambourines. The Montefalco girls held tightly to the expensive dolls they'd been given that morning, though Costanza complained hers ought to have a pram because her little legs were tired already.

Walking a few feet behind them, Maddalena was fascinated to watch how the family interacted with the world. She so rarely saw them all together, outside the villa. The contessa had on a light rabbit fur jacket and a neat brown hat pinned to one side of her shining waves. She seemed bored and spoke only to Signora Bianchi, or to give the nanny sharp instructions: 'Carolina, don't let the girls get their hands dirty' or 'Carolina, tell Sophia to pull up her socks'.

Maddalena overheard the contessa making critical observations about the manners of the masses, which the housekeeper echoed enthusiastically.

'I do wish we could just go out to the lido and escape the crowds, as we used to.'

'I so agree, ma'am. Better days.'

Maddalena spotted the children's physician in the crowd: a kindly middle-aged man with a substantial paunch. She was surprised to see him in full fascist regalia, a blue cummerbund stretched tight around his waist so he looked like he might burst. She exchanged a conspiratorial glance with Sophia, who'd seen him too. They grinned at one another. Maddalena was bemused by the vast array of uniforms on display. There were tall, feathered helmets, alpine headgear and felt fez hats. How, she wondered, could they go into battle when none of it seemed practical at all? The family passed a group of young women in white togas, with wreaths of bay around their heads, so beautiful and ethereal that Costanza and Sophia drifted after them.

'Don't go too far,' cautioned Balia Carolina.

Costanza pouted, then sighed extravagantly. 'When I'm older I'm going to dress like a priestess and jump over the bonfire, too.'

Maddalena giggled. 'I don't think jumping over a bonfire sounds like a good idea. You might burn your lovely gown.'

The little girl appeared affronted. 'That's the tradition on

Natale di Roma. Even Sophia knows that!' she sneered. 'You're so stupid, Maddalena.'

'Costanza!' Carolina gasped, pulling sharply on her charge's arm.

Signora Bianchi intervened on the little girl's behalf.

'You're quite right, Costanza, she *is* stupid – fancy showing off your ignorance that way. Is it too much to ask you to respect our traditions?'

Maddalena realized all eyes were upon her. 'I'm so sorry, I didn't know. I didn't mean to be rude.'

She felt her chest tightening. Everyone around could hear the scolding.

'You don't hear us mocking you Sicilians now, do you?'

Maddalena wished the crowd would swallow her up.

Signora Bianchi raised her voice. 'What is it they say about you southerners? That you eat cat food, or the cats themselves? I never can remember.'

'That's not true!' Maddalena felt like she might cry.

The Signora glanced at her with mild distaste. 'Oh, for pity's sake, I was only joking. There's really no need to take offence.'

She stalked away from Maddalena. 'Come on, girls, keep up.'

Balia Carolina took hold of both girls' hands and trailed after the Signora. She looked back with the briefest flash of sympathy, then turned and they were gone.

That evening, after a long and solemn Mass in honour of the day, the family sat down to a hearty dinner of *carciofi alla romana*, fresh artichokes grown in the garden served alongside nettle risotto. Maddalena was in the kitchen, writing up some notes on the recipe in her ledger, when Signora Bianchi entered.

'The contessa asked me to pass on her thanks for the meal. It was very good, I'm told.'

Maddalena couldn't meet her eye, but replied stiffly, 'There are some leftovers in the chafing dish. I was going to heat them up for staff lunch tomorrow, but you're very welcome to some now.'

'No thank you, I don't like to eat too late.' The Signora's rail-thin physique was sustained by keeping tight control over what she consumed and when.

'Suit yourself.' The exchange at the parade had left Maddalena feeling bruised, her tone more tart than normal. As soon as the words slipped out, she braced herself for a response. There was a terrifying moment of silence, but the Signora seemed content to let it slide.

'The conte is in the loggia. Would you take him a digestif? I feel a migraine coming on and I've sent the maid home already.'

'Of course, Signora,' Maddalena said with some relief.

She went straight down to the cellar with a candle, fetched the bottle of Amaro Averna and hacked some ice from the box. She poured the bitter liqueur into a fat-bellied glass and added a twist of orange, then placed the glass onto a tray with a couple of *cantuccini* biscuits and carried everything upstairs. When Maddalena stepped out onto the darkened loggia, it took a moment for her eyes to adjust. The moonlight shone to light the way and the radio was playing a sonata, a mournful cello, accompanied by piano. Luca turned at the sound of her footsteps on the stone floor.

'Oh, thank you, Maddalena. I was about to come back in; it's a little cold just yet to sit outside for long.' He lifted the glass and took a sip. 'Delicious, though I must admit the thing I miss most is a coffee after dinner. Not flour, not sugar, not good cuts of meat, but what I wouldn't give for an espresso to go with this.'

'I could make you a cup of chicory, or roasted grape seeds if you like?'

Luca shook his head decidedly. 'That's very kind of you to offer, but it isn't quite the same.'

'You're right, I know. I've tried every alternative I can think of, but they never turn out well.'

'If you can't make something taste good, I doubt anyone could do better. That *carciofi alla romana* at dinner – was it one of yours?' She nodded shyly. 'It was delectable. Truly. We have no right to eat so well when there's a war on.'

She blushed. 'That's just the joy of the right meal for the season – almost none of the ingredients were rationed, so I had no need to compromise.'

'I think the key ingredient is your skill as a cook.'

She brushed his kind words aside. 'I'm just lucky it's spring. We have so much growing in the garden this time of year.'

'Did you enjoy today? I don't suppose you celebrate *Natale di Roma* in Sicily.'

'No, we don't.' She'd forgotten she'd once told him where she came from. Was amazed he would remember.

'You must go to the Pantheon next year. The sun comes through at midday, and shines directly on the door. It really is quite something.'

Maddalena said quietly, 'I'm afraid I'm terribly ignorant of all these Roman traditions. Ignorant full stop.' A hard mass of shame lodged in her chest.

'Don't say that.' Luca frowned. 'I wonder if you realize how far you've come, both literally and metaphorically? You've done more in your young life than most.'

Maddalena looked down and shook her head. 'I didn't have much education. I had to leave school early, so I have no understanding of art, or music or culture.'

Luca said earnestly, 'But none of those things need be taught. You keep your eyes and ears and mind open and you learn. That part is easy.'

On the radio, the cello and piano soared together, so different yet harmonious.

'Do you like this music?' Luca asked.

She nodded, 'Very much.'

'So, there you have it! Easy as that. It's by Guido Alberto Fano, *Cello Sonata in D Minor*. Remember that or write it down and if anybody ever asks, you have an answer. I like it too.' He smiled warmly. 'You get the afternoon off on Sunday, is that right?'

Again she nodded; a few short hours she spent lying on her bed, writing recipes and letters, missing home.

'I might be biased about my city,' Luca continued, 'but you can walk into almost any church and see art made by the greatest talents in the world. If you want to enrich your spirit, you could do worse than start there.' He looked intently at her and she felt seen, not as a *sguattera*, or a Sicilian, but a person in her own right.

'You must never feel that you are worth less than someone else, Maddalena. I assure you – you are not.'

She felt all words escape her and could not think of a response. Luca seemed to sense her consternation.

'Do ignore me banging on. I didn't mean to keep you out here in the cold.' He gave her his empty glass and she placed it on the tray, turning back to go inside. He called after her.

'Rome doesn't have the monopoly, you know. Sicily is responsible for great art and culture – it gave us Amaro Averna and your cooking, after all.'

Maddalena walked downstairs to the kitchen and finished clearing up. Grease had congealed on the plates and the heavy-bottomed pans were thick with hard cooked rice but she was lighter in her spirit. She could not say why it felt so much easier to talk to him than almost anybody else. It just felt like a conversation; not master to servant, or man to woman, but human to human. Almost friend to friend.

A few days later she found a folded piece of paper left on the kitchen table, with her name on it. It was a simple map of Rome, with little comic sketches of the famous sights – the Mouth of Truth, the Spanish Steps and Trevi Fountain. Marked on it were a dozen churches with notes about the art she would find there – Michelangelo's Moses in *San Pietro in Vincoli*, Bernini's *Ecstasy of Saint Teresa* in Santa Maria della Vittoria and Caravaggio's *Madonna of Loreto* in the Basilica of

Sant' Agostino in Campo Marzio. There were places marked nearby like the Pyramid of Cestius in Testaccio, and others at a greater distance – a rural park on the Appian Way. Some places she'd never heard of, like Quartiere Coppedè and Palazzo Doria Pamphilj. The artist had even noted an ice cream parlour, Giolitti. At the bottom, in a precise but flowing hand:

In Rome some things cost nothing, but they are priceless. I hope you grow to love this city, as I do. Luca

CHAPTER TEN

ROME, AUGUST 1997

Jude felt the heat as soon as they stepped off the plane at Fiumicino Airport, a veil of humidity which left him sticky and wrung out within minutes. He and Beatrice navigated low corridors lit with fluorescent strip lights, located the arrival hall and wrestled their cases from the carousel. Beatrice knelt down to open hers immediately; she was anxious about the painting and her parents' ashes, both too heavy and unwieldy to carry in her handbag.

'I mixed Mum and Dad together,' she confessed. 'I didn't think they'd mind.'

The canvas was rolled up in a long cardboard tube she'd laid on the diagonal of the case. Thankfully, it had survived the journey well enough.

'Do you think I ought to mention it, when we go through customs?' asked Beatrice.

'No,' said Jude. 'I really don't.'

She'd booked them both tickets on the Leonardo Express, keen to show she could keep a tight rein on their spending. Jude had agreed to cover the expenses, against funds raised from the print auction, but Beatrice still insisted on keeping a note in her Filofax of every penny spent.

'I mean to pay you back.'

After her fifth time of asserting it, Jude responded gently, 'Please, try not to worry about the money.'

'But I do! What if all this leads nowhere and I just end up costing you a bloody fortune?'

'That's my choice and for what it's worth, I think what we're doing is important.'

'Really?'

'Truly. If we don't find anything, we might decide to cut our losses, but for now I see this as a risk worth taking.'

When the express train pulled into the station, he hoisted both their cases on board.

'Thank you.'

'And no more saying thank you, either!'

'Okay, okay!' She put her hands up. 'I promise, that's the last time today. But I am truly grateful, for everything you're doing.'

Jude had consciously avoided any mention of Maddalena till now, but in the quiet of the train carriage it seemed impossible to ignore.

'How are you doing?'

She shrugged. 'I'm okay. At least, I think I am and then it's like it's kicked me in the guts again and I just want to curl up on the floor. Other than that, perfectly fine.'

'I remember that feeling. You make space for it somehow and then, one day, you realize it's diminished. You're remembering a memory and like a copy of a copy, it just keeps on degrading, getting blurry. It's easier somehow, but sad in its own way.'

When the train pulled in at Roma Termini, Jude steered them through the concourse to the first internet café he could find. He paid for thirty minutes and sat down at a monitor, searching online for a hotel nearby with late availability. Beatrice went and bought them both a coffee while he searched. By the time she returned, he'd had a response from a pensione not far from Santa Maria Maggiore.

'Let's just walk, we could be there by the time it takes to find a cab.'

They exited the building and plunged straight into the city. Wrestling with their cases, they made their way through narrow passageways and across a broad piazza, past citadels and fountains. Scooters buzzed around them like mosquitoes, whining engines warning their approach. Jude felt re-energized: this was the Rome he loved. The city of Fellini, Wyler and Rossellini, always shown in black and white, now so full of life and colour it was almost psychedelic.

They found the pensione tucked down a quiet side street – ochre walls and terre verte shutters. Inside was an endearing mix of romance and functionality. The young woman working on reception showed them a little breakfast room with plastic chairs and tables, and a shady loggia – a columned terrace which ran around the second floor and overlooked a busy square. They had separate rooms connected by a shared bathroom, with white walls, high ceilings and tiled terrazzo floors. Jude put his case down and threw the shutters open to reveal a view across the city: a thousand tones of terracotta stretched to the horizon. It was impossibly charming, though the humidity was brutal. No air conditioning, only small electric fans which pointed at their pillows and barely stirred the air.

'What do you say we just dump our stuff, get something to eat then go and find the bank?'

'Give me ten minutes?'

Beatrice dragged her case into the other room and Jude closed the door behind her, leaning out of the open window to look across the city. He could feel its vitality. Despite his words of reassurance to Beatrice, he still harboured doubts, but they were here now. Rome was waiting for them, come what may.

Beatrice locked the door between the shared bathroom and her room, dropped her suitcase on the floor and sat down on the corner of the bed. She took out a powder compact from her handbag and assessed her reflection: tired, pale and crumpled from the flight. She'd barely slept the night before, her head filled with ruminations looping endlessly around. They had four days ahead of them, more than enough time to visit the bank and dispose of her parents' ashes. She still had no idea what she might discover in the safe deposit box, but was eager to find out.

Beatrice looked at her suitcase, bulging with all the hasty second thoughts she'd shoved inside. She certainly didn't have the energy to unpack or face the metal canister of her parents' ashes. For months she'd been yearning for escape, yet now sitting in this pensione, like something from a Merchant Ivory film, she almost laughed aloud. Be careful what you wish for.

From the bathroom next door came the sound of running water. She pictured Jude standing at the sink, splashing water on his face and looking at his own reflection, just as she looked at hers. She shut the compact and pushed away the thought. Ever since the funeral, she'd caught herself in idle fantasies of Jude at moments such as this. Was it weird, she wondered, or just depressingly normal to experience a flicker of desire amid the grief? Perhaps it was rationally irrational, simply her body's defence against too much sadness. She had no intention of acting on these thoughts, but it didn't seem like she could prevent them. She tried to see herself as he must: distracted, scattered, at the mercy of emotion. Not desirable in any way at all.

As if he might have access to her thoughts, Jude knocked on the adjoining door and made her start. His voice echoed off the tiled walls.

'How are you getting on? Maybe we ought to get going, find somewhere to eat and then make our way to the bank. I'm not sure what time they close here.'

'Be right with you.' She bit some colour into her lips and thought about reapplying her make-up, then dismissed it. Time to put such silliness away.

'How hungry are you?' Jude asked, when they finally stepped out into the sunlight.

'Starving,' she replied.

The pensione backed onto a busy square. They scanned it for possibilities and settled on a café at the corner with a simple menu, the chairs and tables screwed firmly to the floor.

'I chose our lunch at The Hound. This time, I'm deferring to the Italian.'

Beatrice ordered them both a toasted focaccia and two bottles of bitter *chinotto* soda, which she remembered from her childhood. She paid at the till, and they sat together at a small Formica table, each of them relishing the warm bread and dripping oil in all its rich simplicity. From her bag, Beatrice pulled a copy of Lonely Planet *Rome*, which she'd picked up at the airport. Searching for a map of the *centro storico*, she located Banca Casa Romana on Via Borghese and estimated it was a ten-minute walk away.

Jude wiped his fingers on a tiny paper napkin. 'I keep having visions of us being escorted down to a vault deep underground, like something from James Bond.'

Beatrice raised an eyebrow. 'It's probably incredibly mundane. Charles Ingram sent me loads of paperwork to prove who I am. I only hope it's not too bureaucratic.'

'So, what's today's best guess as to the contents of the box?'

'Ooh, I'm going gold bullion and a crystal skull. What do you reckon?'

'Sounds plausible enough.' He grinned. 'I've been waiting for the right moment to tell you, we have cause for celebration.' He held up the plastic cup of *chinotto*. 'Not vintage champagne, but it will have to do. Anita called last night to say she has the results on those paint chips she sampled. They contain traces of Maltese lime white, the one Caravaggio used after he lived there. She says it's almost tantamount to a signature. The pieces all stack up.'

'Wow. That's good, right?'

He grinned again and nodded. 'It's very good.'

Beatrice felt a brief thrill of excitement, but it dropped away when she turned the page to see a map of the Aventine, a sombre reminder of the reason she was here.

'The Aventine looks pretty far away.'

Jude turned the book around. 'Yeah, bit of a schlepp all right. Maybe we just get a cab. Do you know where we're going when we get there?'

'I know the name of the house, but not the street: Villa Velare. Mum said she met my dad there, when she was working as a cook.'

'With luck it won't be hard to find.'

Beatrice balled up the greasy napkin and dropped it on her plate.

'But then what? Am I supposed to just rock up at someone's door and say, "You don't know me, but is it okay if I bury my parents' ashes in your back garden? Only, it was my mum's dying wish, so ..."' Beatrice sighed and piled up their empty plates. 'It feels unreal. I can't quite believe I'm here; do you know what I mean?'

'I do,' he replied. 'But that's tomorrow's worry. Until then, let's get on with today's.'

After several wrong turns, they finally located the bank on the Via Borghese and stepped into an air-conditioned lobby. The bank was in a former grand palazzo: marble panels lined the walls and two vast chandeliers hung from the ceiling, their light reflecting on the highly polished floor. A row of tall glass cubicles ran along one wall, and the tellers sat inside, like priests in the confessional. A queue of bored Romans stood in line, so Beatrice took her place while Jude sat down to wait. She checked through the paperwork and rehearsed what she had to say in Italian. Maddalena had sometimes teased her for speaking her mother tongue with an English accent.

When she finally spoke to the teller, Beatrice stumbled her first words and had to start again. She haltingly explained she needed to gain access to a safe deposit box, which she'd inherited from her mother, though it was rented in her father's name.

'*Che anno?*' asked the teller.

'1973.'

The man let out a long whistle of appreciation. He took her paperwork away and left her waiting. When he returned, he explained she would have to wait to see his manager. Beatrice returned to Jude and took a seat next to him on the sofa.

'I don't feel quite so optimistic. Will you come in with me?'

Half an hour passed, and Beatrice was becoming frustrated when they were finally ushered into the manager's office. He wore a crisp black suit and an expression of exaggerated boredom, staring off into the distance as Beatrice repeated her request and presented the paperwork Charles Ingram had supplied.

'*Mi dispiace*, it is not possible,' the manager stated flatly. 'This box is not in your name.'

She pleaded in Italian. 'But after my father died, my mother continued to make the payments for over twenty years. She died a few weeks ago, so the contents now belong to me. Please, Signor, I've come all this way . . .'

She was on the verge of tears when the manager threw his hands up in despair and left the room, expressing his feelings *sotto voce*. Minutes later he returned and spoke in English, rather stiffly.

'You will come back in the morning. Nine o'clock.'

'*Grazie mille,*' Beatrice gratefully replied.

She and Jude left the building together, the afternoon sun warming them instantaneously.

'Listen,' he said in a consoling tone, 'I know you're disappointed, but we're in Rome. There are worse places to kill time. We could go and find the villa now, or something else – your choice.'

She shook her head. 'I left the urn back at the hotel, and besides, I'm not sure I could muster the energy for another confrontation. Would you mind if we just pretend we're tourists for a bit? I haven't been here since I was a kid.'

'Then you get to choose our itinerary.'

They lost the rest of the afternoon to idle wandering, until their legs began to tire. They strolled west, through Palazzo Venezia, heading towards the River Tiber. A thin haze of smog cast a veil across its wide expanse and cormorants perched on the bridges, dark sentinels observing as they slowly travelled north. The walls were hung with vines of vivid green, a living curtain over the graffiti.

'Where now?' asked Jude.

'Spanish Steps, please. Since we're still being tourists.'

They stopped to buy gelato in front of the Villa Medici, pistachio for him, while she chose sour cherry. The steps were thronged with tourists as they leant against the metal balustrade and looked across the city.

Beatrice sighed. 'Eat your heart out, Audrey Hepburn.' For weeks, a fist of anguish had lodged deep in her sternum; now she felt it loosen, just a little. She closed her eyes and turned her face up to the sun.

'When were you last here?' asked Jude.

'I think I must have been eight or nine years old, so maybe '72, '73? Something like that.' She held up her hand to shield her eyes. 'I don't remember much, to be honest. A lot of ice cream, a lot of pasta, a lot of people. Only one day in particular stands out. My dad took me to a theme park. He was not at all the theme park sort, more into galleries and museums. Anyway, this place was absolutely terrifying: haunted houses and some weird dinosaur thing which leapt out of a pond.' She laughed and shuddered at the memory. 'I refused to go on any of the rides, apart from the carousel. I just remember going round and round on it for what seemed like hours, until I threw up in a rubbish bin and he had to take me back to our hotel.'

Jude laughed. 'Sounds like a formative experience.'

'Yeah. I think he got it in the neck from Mum when we came back to London. I don't know why she wasn't with us. I wish she had been. He died not too long after that. A massive heart attack at sixty-three.' Beatrice looked down at the families and couples sprawled across the steps. 'I loved Rome, though. I do remember that. Loved being on that carousel; I didn't ever want to leave.'

The sun had begun to dip, casting a glow over the walls and domes and rooftops of the city, suffusing it with shades of rose and melon, peach and apricot. Beatrice felt a wave of exhaustion.

'What's next on the itinerary?' asked Jude. 'We could throw some coins into the Trevi Fountain or find somewhere to eat.'

'I think I'd rather head back and get an early night, if you don't mind. I feel done in.'

'Of course.' He nodded. 'Early start tomorrow.'

Beatrice felt dismayed by the prospect. She couldn't wait to be on the other side.

They returned to the bank the following morning and were met by the manager's secretary, a trim woman in a tight skirt and impossibly high heels. She led them to a room with a large walnut table in the centre and directed them to take a seat.

'Wait here, please. They will bring the box up shortly.'

Trying his best to ease Beatrice's obvious anxiety, Jude looked around them.

'Not much of a Bond villain's lair, is it? More like a municipal boardroom. Very disappointing.'

Beatrice smiled and seemed to relax a little. A short while later, a young man entered the room, pushing a trolley with a long, rectangular metal box. He picked up a length of green baize cloth and rolled it out across the table, then lifted the box with the full span of his arms and placed it carefully on top.

He turned to Beatrice. '*La chiave, per favore?*' She handed him the key, which she'd brought with her from London. He placed it in the lock and turned it, ensuring it was open before clasping his hands behind his back, giving her a curt nod and then exiting the room.

Jude looked at Beatrice. 'You going to do the honours?'

'I suppose so.'

He stood beside her as she lifted back the lid and felt his heart sink straight away – no sign of the missing painting, no rolled or folded canvas whatsoever, just a leather-bound folder and a few sheets of yellowed newsprint. They exchanged a brief look of disappointment. Beatrice picked up the folder and turned it over in her hands: the cover was embossed with a double-headed eagle and a heraldic shield. She opened it to reveal dozens of loose papers. She slid the contents out onto the baize and started sifting through. There were receipts and cinema tickets, news clippings and coupons. She plucked out a black-and-white photograph, eight by ten, and stared at it for a moment, then handed it to Jude. It was an image of the painting of St John: two portions of the canvas lying on a tiled floor. The top part was even now rolled up in a cardboard tube in Beatrice's handbag on the floor and showed the face and torso of the 'laughing boy'. Underneath it lay a second piece, almost the same size: the lower left-hand quadrant of the painting. Jude examined the photograph closely. As in Caravaggio's original, it was a continuation of the youthful St John's side profile and showed the rest of his leg – the calf and foot. Where it departed from the original was the presence of a strong, male hand, which gripped the flesh of St John's thigh. This second figure seemed to be kneeling in between his legs – a full-grown adult male.

'Kit and Anita were right, this is certainly no copy.' Jude took the photograph over to the window to see the details in a better light. 'These two sections make up the painting's entire left side – you can see where it was cut. I think the painting was divided into quarters. Surely it's a fair assumption your father had both these pieces in his possession at some point, if not the rest. The cuts are very clean; I daresay a good conservator could knit them back together. The question is, where is it? Where's this missing left-hand quarter and all the right?'

'Well, one thing's certain. None of it's in here,' Beatrice replied sardonically. She lifted out the sheet of newsprint which lined the box. '*L'Osservatore Romano* – *Gennaio 21, 1973* ... My dad must have set this all up on that holiday, though I have no memory of coming here.'

She put the paper down and picked up the leather folder; inside the back cover was a document pocket. Ferreting with her fingertips, she retrieved a faded, royal blue passport.

'Now, what have we got here?'

The cover was stamped with the words: *Passaporto Diplomatico*. A glance inside revealed a signature, written in a swooping, cursive script.

'Conte Luciano Montefalco.' Beatrice read the name out loud, seeming to enjoy the way the syllables rolled off her tongue. Jude smiled, turning his attention back to the photograph of the pieces of the painting and asking, 'Do you recognize this tiled floor?'

Getting no reply, he glanced up. Beatrice was staring at the passport, a frown pinched between her brows.

'What is it?' he asked.

Wordlessly, she held the open passport out. On the page was a small black and white photograph, a portrait of a handsome, dark-haired man.

'Who is that? Do you know him?'

She stared at him in disbelief. 'That's my daddy.' Registering her unconscious choice of phrase, she flushed. 'I mean, it says Conte Luciano Montefalco, but that's not his name. He's Luca Fremont. He's my dad.'

CHAPTER ELEVEN

ROME, SEPTEMBER 1941

'Tito!'

Maddalena called out through the open kitchen door. The boy put his head in and she handed him a plum from the bowl on the table, eager to get on his good side.

'Can I borrow your bike this afternoon? I need to go into the city.'

'What do I get in return?' He was fifteen and entirely self-centred.

'I'll bring you something back,' she promised.

'Food?'

'Of course.'

Tito considered her request while chewing. Mercenary and eternally hungry, he'd bolted like a weed over the summer. Dolorosa was away, cooking for Violante and the girls on their summer sojourn from the city. They'd chosen the

Dolomites this year, leaving Tito behind to help in the garage and the gardens. Though he was cocksure and full of cheek, Maddalena had grown quite fond of him. He saw himself as something other than a child, if not yet quite a man.

'You can borrow it, but I'll destroy you if you damage it. I can't find parts anywhere.'

He spat the plum stone into his hand and threw it out of the back door.

'I can look after it,' she reassured him.

He scoffed. 'Everyone knows that girls can't ride.'

Maddalena moved to clip him round the ear, but he was too fast and dodged past, stealing a second plum and stuffing it into his mouth. He wiped the juice from his chin, which bore its first shadow.

'*Buffanato.*' She chided him mildly, worried he was lonely. He'd been alone for months, his mother in the mountains and his older brother far away, fighting in North Africa.

'The post came earlier; any word from Matteo?'

The boy shook his head. 'He only writes to Mamma and all he does is complain about his rations.'

'Don't we all.' She handed him the bowl with the remainder of the plums.

'Take these out to Santino. He needs your help.'

After he'd gone, she made a note in her ledger to remind herself to find Tito some special treat while she was in the city. She had a lot to do today. Despite the ongoing war, school would start again soon. The Contessa, her daughters and all their attendants were due to return within the week. They'd decamped to the Dolomites as soon as school finished for the summer. The north seemed safer than the coast's exposed west flank, but Castel Gedächt was nowhere near as comfortable as the beach house, so it took a sizeable contingent to help them feel content: Signora Bianchi had gone with them, along with Dolorosa and the children's nanny, Balia Carolina. They'd taken two young housemaids to augment the locals who helped with laundry and with driving. The small number of staff who stayed at Velare settled to a dull but pleasant state. Now, as summer's end drew near, that rhythm was disrupted. Resuming life at such close quarters would be difficult; it had taken them weeks to adjust last summer and they'd been apart even longer this year.

If she could get her work done early, Maddalena thought she might have time to go exploring on her own. Knowing this might be her last chance of freedom, she made up her mind to do something she'd been contemplating all summer long.

An hour later, Maddalena freewheeled Tito's bike down the cobbled Clivo, a warm wind buffeting her hair. The scent of wild oregano and pine needles rose from the ground, as if the world was gently cooking. This was one more thing to savour while she could – Signora Bianchi would no sooner see one of the Velare women riding a bike around the streets of the Aventine than she would climb on board herself.

At the bottom of the Clivo, Maddalena turned the handlebars towards the city, following the tramlines which threaded through the cobbles. She found herself in the slipstream of a carriage packed with people. On the back hung twin boys in shorts, with filthy plimsolls on their feet. Maddalena felt a lurch of terror as she watched them shoving one another, dissolving into fits of laughter when they came close to falling off. As the tram reached the turn, the first boy jumped easily enough, but the second couldn't muster up the courage. Eventually the jeers of his brother seemed to goad him into action. Heart in her mouth, Maddalena watched as he leapt and landed on his knees, then got back up and started sprinting straight away. He ran full pelt across the road, an obdurate expression on his face. Glancing back, she saw them wade out into the river and envied them their freedom.

Though Rome had not suffered bombings like the industrial cities of the north, the war made every day more challenging. The grind of blackouts and restrictions, of sirens and heavy-handed fascist interventions took their toll, but despite all that, she would be sad to see the summer go. Though she missed Dolorosa and Carolina, she'd discovered greater independence than before. Only the prospect of Signora Bianchi's return gave her pause. The woman always viewed her with suspicion and time apart would likely only make it worse.

When she reached flat ground, Maddalena realized how tired she was. She slowed as she passed through Campo di Fiori, but didn't stop. Since her nineteenth birthday, her wages had increased a little. She still sent most of it home, but she had enough to buy some small luxuries: a comb, a lipstick and some powder. Santino's wife, Maria, had shown her how to sew a simple dress and even helped her style her hair. Almost overnight, Maddalena found herself an object of fascination. The local boys would loiter at the kitchen door and ask her for a glass of water. She found it all unsettling. She'd been alone in the world so long, she felt older than her years.

She cycled past the fascist headquarters at Palazzo Braschi, where the walls were plastered with images of Il Duce's brutish face. He would not approve of where she was heading – to the *borsa nera*: the clandestine market stalls of the Via di Tor di Nona. For a time, she'd thought the black market was so named because the street itself was dark – the buildings so tall, the way so narrow, permanently in shadow. Everything about the *borsa nera* frightened her: the mess, the chaos and the illegality. She went rarely and reluctantly, scurrying in and out as quickly as she could. This was the first time she'd sought it out, but today she had a purpose.

When she finally climbed off the bike, her legs were wobbly. The cobbles of the alley were thick with mud and paint flaked from the walls. There was a stench of rotting; some country farmers walked for days to get here, their produce packed in sacks and suitcases, so everything was dank and on the turn. She could taste a trace of mould and feathers, blood and faeces in the air.

Most vendors sold their wares from stools or little tables, while others squatted down beside a basket in the street. There were stalls selling sugar and flour, of course; soap and salt and half a dozen other products set to tempt her, but Maddalena passed them by. Today she wanted one thing only. Something hard to come by, even if you had the cash and goods to trade. She knew the man she was looking for; she'd seen him here before. She finally found him at an intersection with a narrow alley, which offered fast escape. He had his nose buried in a newspaper and his back against a wall, his feet propped on a sack of potatoes. Maddalena leaned Tito's bike against the nearest building and took a wax-paper package from the basket. The man didn't look up but he sneered as she came near.

'What are you looking for, girly?'

She pushed back her shoulders to show a confidence she didn't feel.

'Coffee.'

'You'll be lucky,' he snorted. 'Run along now.' But Maddalena knew the game – his dismissal was too glib. She had to show him she meant business, so she opened the waxed paper and handed him the pot. The contents were dark and dense, intensely red.

'What's that?'

'Plum jam.'

She felt his eyes crawl over her, lingering on the shape of her body beneath the floral print. Perspiration sprang up across the surface of her skin. She folded her arms, covering her chest.

'Try it. Free sample. I promise you it's good.'

He pried off the lid and dipped his finger in, holding her gaze as he tasted it, his eyes ringed with thick black lashes. She saw them narrow, his fingertip returning to the sticky vessel, tongue flickering, until in the end, he'd licked it clean. She knew it was good – Velare's gardens were well stocked with fruit of all kinds, but the plums were sweeter than any others she had eaten.

'How much you got there?'

'Four jars. But I've got money too.'

He grinned with a thin-lipped leer. 'Then think yourself lucky I've got a sweet tooth.'

Minutes later, she pushed her bike back down the alley with a small paper bag of coffee beans now nestled in the basket, a gift to show a gratitude she could not easily express. Her hands were still shaking when she climbed back on the bike – time for one more stop, before returning home.

It had been five months since Luca gave her his hand-drawn map of Rome. On Sunday after Sunday she'd left Velare to go and visit somewhere he suggested. She'd seen parks and ruins, galleries and churches. As she crossed each one off the list, she felt her world expanding. She'd set out to discover Rome and found herself along the way. Today she would complete the journey and meant to thank him the only way she could.

Maddalena rode the bike a few streets south and hopped off in front of the mottled marble wedding cake that was San Luigi dei Francesi. The exterior was grand enough, but it was nothing compared to the glory which lay within. The church was echoing and empty; held aloft by stone columns, the ceiling shone with burnished gold that seemed to glow, like the heaven she'd imagined as a child. Then, her singular experience of God had been a simple whitewashed chapel, but who could doubt in the Almighty when such a firmament was painted overhead? Still, she turned her gaze from it. She'd come here with one purpose: to see the Contarelli Chapel and its three depictions of the life of St Matthew by Caravaggio.

With no one else in sight, she went searching for the paintings, conscious of the noise her heels made, clacking on the polished floor. The shoes were new to her but second-hand,

and they gaped where someone else had worn them in. Like so much in her life, they didn't fit and so she bent to them instead. She found the little recessed chapel at the far end of the church, shrouded in darkness and the ghostly scent of incense. She strained to see the altar and the paintings – they covered three walls underneath a crescent window, which cast some daylight down.

In the first one, on the left-hand wall, a group of men sat at a table counting money. Christ stood nearby observing them, half hidden in the shadows. Too busy to notice the arrival of this holy stranger, all the men ignored him, except one: pinned in the light of holy transformation, Matthew gestured to himself, somehow knowing he'd been chosen. The beam which held him there was painted but seemed as if it emanated from the chapel's crescent window. It gave the tableau an uncanny realism – the image and the real world interacting, as if God's light had been burned onto the plaster, like the shadows of Pompeii.

The second painting was on the back wall, above the altar and directly underneath the glass. It showed an older Matthew turning to an angel hovering above him, its legs and body wrapped in white, receding back to black. Maddalena was surprised by Matthew's frailty, his rheumy eyes and gasping mouth, half covered by the curls of an unkempt beard. This Matthew seemed too fallible to be a saint – in other images she'd seen, he looked heroic, but he seemed frightened by the angelic apparition here. She saw Matthew's shock at witnessing the creature, understanding it was real; that its very existence meant God was real too and must therefore see his every action and hear his every word. She wondered how anyone could live with that and all that it implied.

The third and final painting sat on the right-hand wall. This was a crowd scene with a dozen or so subjects. She'd learned that Caravaggio often chose his models from the people who surrounded him. Not noblemen, but beggars, prostitutes and pimps – people who did daily battle with hunger and temptation. He often used them as stand-ins for the great religious figures, despite the fact it caused a scandal and the Church abhorred his choice. Caravaggio didn't care; how would sinners see themselves in these stories, if he did not reflect them?

In this painting, Matthew lay prone in the same light source as the first, a beam of light which seemed to issue from the window. A man stood over him, half naked and wielding his sword in a seeming frenzy. A crowd of people stood around, witnessing the murder. As Matthew shrank from his impending death, his terror seemed to radiate out into the mass of people which gathered round them. The entire scene was visceral, but Maddalena found herself most affected by the expressions of the bystanders, their horror and revulsion. In the top left corner, she spied a face she recognized – among these witnesses, Caravaggio had painted a portrait of himself, as powerless to intervene as any other. Standing in the quiet of the church, Maddalena felt herself included in their number.

She knew that Matthew had been killed in Ethiopia – Luca had mentioned it in passing, little knowing that it was a detail she wasn't able to forget. How could she, when her own brother, Dario, had met his fate on that same soil? He'd been eighteen when he left home to join the army, not yet twenty when he died. They were told he was killed in Addis Ababa, but she'd never really understood it. To a young girl in Sicily, it all seemed so unknowable. He'd left them, strong and handsome, never to return. She had no image of his passing, no real comprehension of that loss and yet here it was, in front of her – in Matthew, in the spectators, in the shock she felt reflected on their faces. Ordinary people, of the kind she saw each day, like the crowd in the *borsa nera*. This was a death in Ethiopia, as seen through Roman eyes.

When Dario died, she'd had little time to mourn. She'd grown up quickly, gone to work and moved to Rome. Now, with the distance of some four years, she felt the shock of recognition and with it, a recalibration. She stood for ten more minutes, staring up at all three paintings, then left the church on shaking legs. The day had frightened her, it made her feel . . . too much. She retrieved the bike and climbed back on, slipping past the chapel wall and its crescent window, knowing the light it cast had marked her too.

CHAPTER TWELVE

Standing under the red bulb, Luca watched the photographic image materialize in front of him. The white square swam as he sluiced it gently, washing it in waves. The whole top floor of Velare was stifling, but the little darkroom he'd built there was hotter still. He felt light-headed from the heat and all the chemicals, but even so, the process still enthralled him – chasing ghosts until the lines finally appeared, faint at first, then darkening, then deep. An alchemy of sorts, light and dark, contrasting and combining, bringing memory to life. One moment captured so it could last forever: developed, stopped and fixed.

The image coming into focus now had been taken at the start of the summer, before the family went north. It showed then four-year-old Sophia watching Maddalena, who had a bolster cushion on her knee. She was knotting lace, the neat rows of pins and bobbins barely visible. Sophia had been enthralled and their two heads bent close together. Luca had been compelled to take the picture because of the shadows cast by the olive tree above them. It dappled them both like a pointillist painting, and he was drawn to the simplicity.

He truly missed his daughters when they left for the summer. In their absence, he tried to keep himself occupied. Living in a city which had been reproduced in art for centuries, his challenge was to find a different way to see it, a new path on well-trodden ground. The war had, at least, redrawn the map.

After hanging the picture of Sophia and Maddalena up to dry, Luca turned his attention to a second print. This one showed a bakery in Testaccio. The shelves were empty, but the walls were plastered with posters, all showing the same image: a pair of hands breaking a loaf open, and above them the injunction 'Do not waste your daily bread'. The image encapsulated his feelings about such propaganda – edicts people didn't need and couldn't use.

In his third print, the dark silhouette of a bomber plane flew over Bernini's figures in the Fountain of Four Rivers. Their sculpted forms seemed to recoil in horror at the sight; like prey frozen at the sight of a raptor.

The fourth and final photograph he printed showed the shadows cast by a line of citizens queuing for their rations. They were observed by a row of wall-eyed pigeons, similarly stood in line. He titled it 'The Pecking Order' – everybody waiting for the crumbs. Like his hero Brassaï, he saw all these images as a form of journalism, commenting and reflecting without words. Violante would have told him to destroy them, that they could get him into trouble, but they were his only means of expression. Despite the risk, he felt compelled to document this time.

A tentative knock derailed his train of thought and he heard Maddalena's voice.

'Sorry to disturb you, but dinner's nearly ready.'

Luca checked his watch. Time passed differently in here. As her footsteps began retreating, he called out, 'Wait a moment. I have something to show you ... stay right there.'

He reached up and knocked the hanging bulb, which splashed the walls with red as it swung to and fro. He steadied the lightbulb and opened the door; Maddalena stood waiting. He held out the still damp image of her with Sophia.

'I thought you might like to see this. Here, hold your hands flat, it's still a little wet.' He placed it between her palms and watched as a smile lit up her face.

'When did you take this?'

'The week before they all left for the mountains. Do you like it?'

'I think it's lovely.'

'Keep it.'

Her eyes grew wide. 'Are you sure?'

'Only if you'd like it. I can always make another copy for myself.'

'Goodness. Thank you very much.'

She looked at the other images he'd taken, where they were hanging up to dry.

'When did you take all these?' She scrutinized the empty shop, the fountain and the pigeons.

'Oh, here and there over the summer.'

'I like that one of the bakery – no bread but plenty of commandments!'

'Exactly.'

'And that one ...' She looked at the round-eyed pigeons observing the queue. 'I feel sorry for them. The pigeons, I mean,' she added hastily. 'It's like the street cats; if we're all living off scraps, what hope is there for them?'

Luca raised an eyebrow. 'You think I ought to share my dinner with the cats?'

'They wouldn't thank you,' Maddalena snorted. 'It's only caponata, I'm afraid. Would you like to eat in the dining room, or will you join us in the kitchen?'

'I'll join the rest of you. Be down in a minute; I'll just finish up in here.'

Maddalena nodded and began to descend the attic stairs. Luca watched her go, delighted she'd seen the story he'd been trying to tell. He whistled to himself as he began to pack away, a tuneless ditty full of optimism. It had been a good day, so far.

In late summer the kitchen at Velare was chaotic. Maddalena made a simple supper for everyone still working in the house and it was consumed then and there, with less formality than normal. They took their plates out to a table in the courtyard, along with fruit and salads from the garden. For a city in the stranglehold of rationing, they ate modestly, but well.

Luca filled a bowl with ladles of caponata: a stew of olives, tomatoes and cubes of griddled, golden aubergine. He sat down next to Santino and his pregnant wife Maria, who was eating with enthusiasm. The mechanic started in on his favourite topic straight away.

'You seen the *Giornale d'Italia* is hammering the drums of war again? Against America, of course. Do you think they're likely to come in?'

Luca shrugged. 'It seems inevitable. The whole world is on fire – how long can they stay out?'

Santino glanced around the table. Although the household was somewhat reduced, there were still a dozen workers there, all with varying political sympathies.

'Been a lot of unrest in the north. Milan and Turin have had enough, and who can blame them? Seventy-five tons of bombs last week, can you believe it?'

Maria frowned at her husband and rubbed a hand across her expanding belly. 'Not while we're eating.'

'How are you getting on?' Luca asked her.

'A little tired,' replied Maria.

'It must be so hard in the heat. I remember the Contessa hating every minute.'

Santino put an arm around his young wife and said in a teasing tone, 'She's got nothing to complain of. She's fit and young, not like me!'

Maria rolled her eyes and then began to clear their empty plates. 'I'm going to help Maddalena.'

Luca took them from her. 'Let me do that. You relax with the old man.' He carried the plates back into the kitchen, where Maddalena was washing up.

'Thank you for supper. That was delicious.'

'You're very welcome. Are you heading back up to the attic?'

He shook his head. 'I'm done for the day. I think I'm going to go out to the loggia and listen to the radio, see if I can pick up any news.'

He often spent his evenings trawling for reports from different countries. The Italian stations were full of jingoistic rhetoric and stirring declarations of success. He knew the true picture was more nuanced, so tried to seek out different sources to help fill in the gaps.

Maddalena nodded. 'I've got something for you. I'll bring it out when I've finished clearing up.'

Luca went back through the quiet darkness of the salon. Despite the warmth of the September night, all the shutters and windows were kept tight shut – they were scrupulous about the blackout, even though it wasn't fully dark. So far, Rome had escaped the bombing raids which had pummelled other cities, but Luca believed it was only a matter of time.

He turned on the radio, which flickered into life, a scratch of static as he trawled the airwaves until he came across a British voice. He lit one of his rare cigarillos and let the words flow round him as he stepped out onto the loggia; the sky beyond was cobalt blue with wisps of pink. He was still contemplating it when he heard Maddalena's footsteps approaching.

'Here we go.' She was carrying a tray, which she set down on the table, quietly fussing over the contents. He noticed she'd set out the good china – white and apricot art-deco, delicate handles shaped like lightning bolts. She poured the contents of the pot into a cup, then handed it to him and stepped back, with an unexpected flourish of theatricality. 'Ta da!'

Steam curled off the gloss-black surface and he breathed in

the rich scent of coffee, so extraordinary and unexpected his tastebuds flooded in an instant. 'How on earth?'

She grinned in triumph. 'I have my ways.'

He closed his eyes and took in the aroma, then a sip, savouring the bitterness and heat with a sigh of deepest satisfaction.

'How is it?' Maddalena watched him with delight.

'Incredible! But you must have a cup yourself. Won't you join me?'

She hesitated. 'Are you sure?'

'Of course, it's better shared. God knows how long it will be till it comes again.'

'If you're absolutely certain?'

'Positive.'

'Well then, I'll go and fetch another cup.'

Luca was sitting on the terrace in the darkening twilight when she returned. She poured herself a cup and sat nearby. English voices on the radio captured her attention.

'What are they saying?'

Luca listened for a moment. 'It's the anniversary of the first German *blitzkrieg* bombing raids on London. They're discussing the effect it's had on the British psyche.'

Maddalena shook her head. 'I don't know how you do that; I couldn't ever understand.'

'I don't speak it fluently, I assure you, but I can get the gist. There's normally a music programme on at this time of night, if you'd prefer?'

She shook her head. 'This is fine. I didn't mean to interrupt.'

'Oh, it's not all that important, I just like to keep informed. We're spoon-fed so much propaganda here.'

'I imagine other countries must be too?'

'They are, you're absolutely right. Still, you get a clearer picture if you view it in the round.'

The voice on the radio continued to speak about the bombing. Luca couldn't help but lay the picture over Rome.

'More talk of the attacks – the British had it very bad, as has the north. I must say, I've feared the prospect of it since the first day of the war.'

Maddalena frowned. 'I can't imagine it ever coming here.'

'It's devouring the whole continent, so I'm afraid our turn will come.' He saw his words had frightened her and tried to lift the mood. 'Tell me: how did you come by this unexpected treasure? I hadn't heard there was any coffee in the shops again.'

'There isn't. Not as such . . . I hope you won't be angry, but I bought it from the *borsa nera*, in exchange for some plum jam. Which is yours, of course, by rights.'

'Why on earth would I be angry? You have nothing but my gratitude.'

'I wanted to thank you.'

'Whatever for?' Luca asked, bemused.

Maddalena put her cup down on the table. 'For everything you've done for me. The map you made, my guide to Rome. I went to see the last of them today, Caravaggio's paintings in San Luigi dei Francesi.'

'The Contarelli Chapel!' Luca beamed. 'What did you think?'

'I don't know.' She paused. 'It's hard to find the words.'

'Speak freely.' He reassured her. 'I won't judge.'

'No, you never do.'

She stopped and seemed to frame her thoughts. When she spoke again, her voice was thick with emotion.

'You mentioned once that St Matthew died in Ethiopia. I remembered because my brother died there, too. Mamma got a telegram, which she kept, of course. I read it many, many times. It said, "We deeply regret to advise that your son is believed to have lost his life as the result of ground operations in Addis Ababa."

'He was nineteen, nearly twenty. To me these places – Ethiopia and Addis Ababa – sounded like something from a story. Camels and sand and magic carpets . . . I've never lived anywhere but here and Sicily and so I think I couldn't picture it. Couldn't quite imagine where or how he died and somehow that made it all feel terribly unreal. I don't know why.' She looked at Luca. 'I expect that sounds silly.'

He shook his head. 'It doesn't. Not at all.'

'The third painting in the chapel, the one of Matthew dying? Probably looks nothing like Ethiopia today, but I never had a vision of it in my head and now I have. I can't explain it, I just know it helped somehow.' She shook her head in frustration. 'I'm sorry if that sounds like nonsense.'

'I think it's only natural to associate the loss of someone dear to us with the moment of their passing. A cruel irony perhaps, but crueller still if you can't picture it. I imagine it might make you feel . . . stuck somehow?'

It had grown so dark he could no longer read her expression clearly, but he saw that she was nodding.

'Stuck, yes. That's it exactly. You always know.' She leaned forward in her chair. 'I have so much to thank you for. That's why I went to find the coffee – to show my gratitude.'

'You didn't need to. I can't imagine how you managed it.' He realized he knew so little of her life. 'I wonder . . . do you like it here?'

Maddalena paused. 'I was homesick for the longest time. I missed my family, my little brothers and sisters growing up without me. But now I feel like this is where I belong.'

'Well, we are lucky to have you.' Luca sipped his coffee.

'I'm the one who's lucky.'

She said it with such force, he was surprised.

'This summer has changed me,' she said. 'I shall miss it dreadfully when everyone comes back from the mountains. Miss times like this, with you.'

The silence which followed seemed to pool between them, ominously heavy. The British voices on the radio had been replaced by music. It sounded so beguiling; he could imagine staying out here with her, talking, taking pleasure in the coffee and the warm night air. Far too late, Luca realized this was a danger more present than the threat of bombs falling from the sky. He stood up and said, rather stiffly, 'Will you excuse me? I think I might turn in.'

Maddalena sat upright. 'Of course.' And then, 'I'm so sorry . . . did I do something wrong?' She sounded anxious and confused.

'Not in the least, but I have work early in the morning. Do stay. Enjoy your coffee and the peace.'

She nodded but said nothing more. At the door, he turned back for a second.

'I'm very grateful, Maddalena – for the coffee and for

everything you said. You're right, it has been quite a summer, but all things end. Normality resumes: you understand.'

The only colour in the darkness was her hair, a deep mahogany, lit by the rising crescent moon. In another life he knew he could have stayed and lost himself entirely. Instead, he forced himself to turn and leave.

CHAPTER THIRTEEN

Rome, August 1997

When they finally got back to the pensione, Beatrice went directly to her room and shook the contents of the leather binder out onto her bed. She began to sort through every item, placing them on the bedspread like exhibits from a crime scene: tickets, identity cards, newspaper cuttings, receipts and photographs, all laid out in neat rows. She kept her Filofax to hand and made notes of dates, names and translations. Her hands were still a little shaky and the writing sprawled across the page.

Jude offered to go out and find them something to eat and she accepted gratefully, even though she wasn't hungry. She just needed space and quiet; time to think. In the bank she'd been so shocked, she felt almost catatonic. Thankfully Jude had the presence of mind to take charge.

'I think we'd better get you back to the hotel.'

She'd simply followed his instructions.

'Leave the painting here for now. I'll go and find someone, and they can put it in the vault. We'll come and get it later, or tomorrow, if you prefer. Safer than carting it round town, in any case.'

He helped her gather everything up – the passport, the photo of the painting and all the different documents, then led her outside and hailed a cab. Numb, she let herself be transported. Only once he'd left her room and she shut the door behind him, could she give vent to her true feelings. She sobbed until she felt thoroughly wrung out, then went into the bathroom to wash her face and gaze in disbelief at her reflection. Listless, she wandered back into the bedroom and retrieved the passport: her father's photograph above a name she didn't recognize.

She stared down at the pieces she'd laid out, trying to make sense of the bigger picture. What she now understood was that her father had another life she'd never known. The rows on the bed might be neat and orderly, but they threw her whole world into chaos.

Her parents' love, which had always seemed so solid, now felt tarnished in some way. She picked out a silvered photograph from the centre of the web. It showed a family portrait – four people standing on the steps of a house, in front of an arched doorway. Carved in the stone above it, that same double-headed eagle and heraldic shield from the cover of the binder.

Standing on the top step was her father, impeccably dressed in suit and tie, brilliantined hair and highly polished shoes.

One hand was in his pocket: the self-assured master of all that he surveyed. On the next step down, a woman with a handsome profile and tightly waved black hair – the kind you'd see in movies from the golden age. Her dress was severe, high collared with box shoulders and she wore a small pearl necklace. She was almost smiling. Almost, but not quite.

In front of them stood two small girls, their long dark hair in ringlets, which had been styled to perfection. Their outfits were neat and pressed and so old-fashioned – stiff sailor collars, buttoned shoes. Beatrice stared at both their faces in search of similarities. In her mind, there was no question: from the physical resemblance to the way the image had been staged, these adults and the children belonged together. She almost didn't need to read the proof printed neatly at the bottom of the page:

Conte & Contessa Montefalco with their daughters,
Costanza and Sophia. Villa Velare, Rome 1940

Her father's youthfulness was almost as shocking to Beatrice as anything, younger here than in any other portrait she had seen. He still had the same deep-set dimples in his handsome, smiling face and, unlike the mother, both girls in the photograph were smiling too, those same dimples on display. It made her wince internally; they were a trait she always wished she had inherited, instead of Maddalena's full mouth and straight, square jaw.

Beatrice stared at the four people in the photograph and digested every detail, then placed it back in the centre of the evidence now spread across the bed. Here was an identity card, granting Luciano Montefalco access to the Photographic Cabinet of the Vatican. There, a folded cutting from a newspaper, from much later on. She couldn't quite make out the date but thought perhaps it said 1953. It proclaimed one Sophia Montefalco had cultivated a rose which was entered into the international 'Premio Roma' competition and had won a commendation. The cutting included a picture of a young woman with those familiar dimples, now fully grown.

Beatrice wrote down a list of dates on which her father seemed to be known variously as Conte Luciano Montefalco, Luca Montefalco and Luca Fremont. Under other circumstances, such discoveries might have seemed clandestine and exciting, but at a stroke, she felt like he'd somehow become a stranger.

Still her daddy, but no longer hers alone.

Beatrice was in the shower when Jude returned. She'd turned her face into the stream of water, letting it needle at her skin. The knock on the adjoining door made her jump.

'Food's ready,' he called out.

'Be there in a minute,' she replied.

She let the shower beat down between her shoulder blades, easing the tension in her muscles. Her jaw ached and she realized she'd been clenching her teeth for hours, biting down on her anxiety. She stepped out of the shower and towel-dried her hair, then put on clean underwear, which stuck to her damp skin. She tiptoed barefoot across the wet tiled floor, pulled her jeans and T-shirt back on, then slid the bolt on the door to Jude's room.

'Knock knock.'

'Come in,' he said. 'How are you doing?'

'Much better for a shower.'

His room was a mirror of her own. A small double bed, with an ornate carved surround and a chest of drawers beside the open window. A warm breeze blew in, bringing with it all the sounds of the bustling square below. Jude handed her a plate, wrapped in tinfoil.

'Late lunch, or maybe early dinner. I went back to the same café we ate at yesterday. I tried to ask for takeaway but, as we have established, my Italian leaves a lot to be desired. Looking back on the interaction, I'm wondering whether they do in fact do takeaway at all, or if they just took pity on me ... Anyway, it's some variety of pasta. Not sure what exactly, but it smells good and I'm ravenous.'

Realizing she'd barely eaten since the day before, Beatrice lifted the foil. It released a cloud of steam and she felt her appetite returning. Jude picked up a bottle of Chianti.

'Glasses?'

'In the bathroom, by the sink. Mine's got a toothbrush in it, I'm afraid,' she called after his departing back. 'Would you mind if I perch on your bed? I've covered my own in paper-work and made it rather inaccessible.'

'Help yourself.'

Beatrice took the plate and a fork and sat down on the edge. Jude returned and handed her a tumbler of red wine, then took a seat on the window ledge, his back against the open shutters. 'While I was waiting for the food, I nipped back to that internet place by the station. Thought I'd try to do a search for Montefalco. I found nothing about a Luca or Luciano, but there was one site which mentioned Villa Velare and the Montefalco family in general. You might be pleased to know we now have an address.'

He pulled a piece of paper from his pocket and read his notes out loud. '"The House of Montefalco, a noble Roman family, with close ties to the Vatican since the Middle Ages. Villa Velare is a fine example of Renaissance architecture, with landscaped, terraced gardens, built on L'Aventino, one of the seven great hills of Rome."'

'Good sleuthing.'

'I thought so, but here's the thing. So far as I can tell, it's not a private home, at least it isn't anymore. I make no claims for my translating skills, but it looks like it's some sort of hospital these days.'

He handed her the sheet of paper, which she read.

'You're close. It's a hospice, not a hospital, belonging to the Church.' She looked up at him with a sudden realization. 'Oh my God, what do I do about burying their ashes?'

He thought about it for a moment, then shrugged. 'Might be easier if anything, I guess.'

She put her wine down on the nightstand. 'Well, that would be the first time any of this has gone my way.' She sighed, 'Honestly, it all feels so surreal. I hope you're not regretting coming all this way.'

Jude shrugged. 'I get that all this is complicated and deeply personal for you, but if I'm honest, it's pretty damned exciting.'

'Really?' She wasn't sure if she believed him.

'Are you kidding me? A trip to Rome to hunt down an

unknown Caravaggio which has been cut up into pieces. I'll take that over plodding round an auction any day. The photograph of those two pieces of the canvas blew my mind. It's clearly not a copy – it's something very different. We need to track it down.'

'Except we haven't got the first clue where the rest of it is, or how it came into my parents' possession in the first place,' Beatrice argued.

'Any more clues in the folder?'

'Possibly, though making sense of anything is quite another matter.' She hopped up. 'Come and take a look – a quick tour through the family scrapbook I never knew existed.'

Jude followed her into the other room.

'One thing which jumped out to me, for obvious reasons, is this photograph.' She handed him the silvered family portrait on the steps.

'My mum worked at Velare as a cook. She told me they met there in 1939, one year before this was taken.'

Jude looked at the photograph intently. 'I've been curious as to why there is no record of this painting anywhere, but if it was in a private collection and was taken by the owner, that would make sense.'

Beatrice thought back to Maddalena's letter. 'If it was his to take, why would mum feel guilty?'

'Do you think it's possible they ran away with it together?'

Beatrice looked sadly at the photograph.

'More than possible, I'd say.'

CHAPTER FOURTEEN

VATICAN CITY, NOVEMBER 1942

The thick autumn mist cast a milky silence over the Vatican, making it feel more remote than usual, a city within a city, cloaked in suffocating white. Luca shivered and shrank into his overcoat, walking quickly to the archive where he'd arranged to meet his brother.

Roberto had been busier than usual these last few months. They did not often get the chance to catch up outside work, so when the request came, Luca eagerly accepted. Besides, he'd been glad of the excuse. He and Violante had quarrelled the night before, something which seemed to be happening more frequently. Any respite gained by the summer months they spent apart diminished soon after her return. In fact, the entire household seemed on edge – a growing sense of claustrophobia, which built like static, warning of a coming storm.

The disagreement with Violante was born out of almost

nothing, a petty tit for tat which escalated far beyond the bounds of what was said. He'd been irked by the appearance of yet another painting in her little sitting room, a tormented Christ, mawkish and sentimental. Sophia had been having nightmares recently, visions of hell and eternal damnation, inspired in part by the paintings, the lurid sermons of Father Colonni, and her older sister's Bible stories, forcefully described.

Luca hadn't noticed the new painting at first; they had been discussing Signora Bianchi and her insistence on hanging up framed photographs of Mussolini around the house, having deemed the other members of the staff to be 'insufficiently patriotic'.

'It's our private home, not a railway station,' Luca had pushed back. Violante had defended her, saying she must be allowed to run the house as she saw fit. Since the start of the war, his wife had ceded almost all control to the housekeeper, though she took offence if this was ever pointed out.

'It's not her place to monitor the staff's beliefs,' said Luca. 'They're none of her damned business.'

Aggrieved by his blasphemy, Violante rolled her eyes and looked as piteous as one of her paintings. A dozen oils adorned the walls around her, each one more tortured than the last. The newest addition was Christ wearing an agonized expression, his forehead streaming with vivid rivulets of blood. Luca pointed to it.

'And while we're on the subject, I don't think it's helpful to have such graphic depictions where the girls will see.'

'They're sacred art.'

Luca snorted in reply, which raised her ire.

'I shan't apologize for raising our daughters to appreciate sacrifice and suffering. They need to be prepared – we are at war and any one of us could be taken any time.'

'They're children, Violante,' he'd sighed with exasperation. 'You can't possibly expect them to live in some state of perpetual grace.'

'Why not?'

'Because they're little girls, not angels.'

After months apart, he'd felt a gap between them grow. Now it seemed almost insurmountable. There were days when he could not remember what they'd ever had in common. At the start of their marriage, the nine-year age gap hadn't been a problem, but now it represented so much more. He'd just turned thirty-one while she was forty; he had a life outside their home, while she had little more than prayer.

Part of it was her nerves. She'd suffered for years, even before the threat of bombing. Now she openly resented living in the city. Luca argued that his work meant they must remain; that the castle and the summer house were inhospitable in winter and besides, the Aventine itself was unassailable. They ought to count their blessings. But Violante found the cloud of war unbearable, wherever they might be. She was more devout now than at any point since the loss of their infant son. She spent hours at prayer in case she should be called to meet her maker. Her fervour only served to highlight his ambivalence. Luca secretly rejected any notion of divinity and took no comfort that their son had gone before them to a better place, only certainty the boy was dead, as he himself would be one day. He wished he could talk about it with his brother; Roberto was wise but so caught up in all the complications of Vatican life, Luca didn't want to add more to his burdens. As they aged, their lives diverged; even after twenty years of fascist rule, Roberto did not seem unduly worried about the abstract threat of totalitarianism, which made Luca despair.

He found his brother waiting for him at the entrance to the *Galleria delle Carte Geografiche*. Luca kissed him on both cheeks.

'Roberto. Are you well?'

'A little tired.'

He did look weary, Luca thought. The city might be isolated, but it was subject to pressures few could imagine.

'Walk with me?' Roberto asked.

'Of course.'

The Gallery of Geographic Maps was quiet at this time of day. Their footsteps echoed on the geometric floor and a riot of images crowded Luca's vision. Detailed frescoes rolled out along the walls and ceiling, mapping every part of Italy. Almost inured to its charms, he couldn't help but marvel at the cost of human labour. He tried to match his older brother's step.

'So, what did you need to talk to me about?'

Roberto glanced toward him. 'You've been following the North Africa reports? They have entirely lost control.'

The Axis armies had suffered one humiliating defeat after another.

Luca nodded. 'I have. It hit us close to home. Dolorosa's son Matteo was lost in action a few weeks ago.'

Roberto looked stricken. 'I will pray for them both. Please

send her my deepest condolences. So much sorrow.' He shook his head in despair. 'I find myself asking what direction the wind might blow next with this war?'

Luca laughed. 'If I knew the answer, I might sleep better at night.'

'For many years, we thought Germany and Italy would prevail. Indeed, the Holy See has been preparing for that future, but now it seems less certain. The more the alliance deteriorates, the more precarious our position. We are reliant on the nation which surrounds us, are we not? Should the Germans choose to dispose of Mussolini or the King, well then, what next? There are rumours that the Wehrmacht forces plan to kidnap the Holy Father, intend to loot and pillage our collections. We remain neutral – as always – but we must consider our protection.'

Luca glanced at the map of Sicily as they passed, blue waters dotted with feluccas. Maddalena's home, he thought, the memory unbidden. He pushed it forcefully away, turning to his brother.

'Well then, how can I be of help?'

Roberto clasped his hands behind his back. 'My concerns are not those of the next year, or even the next decade, but the longer path of history. I am responsible for a collection which must be preserved, at any cost. Some items are too large to transport, but smaller pieces might be removed to safety. The question is, where might that be?' Roberto looked at him from the corner of his eye. 'The salt caves underneath our castle in the Dolomites . . . what state are they in?'

This question took Luca entirely by surprise. Though Castel

Gedächt had been in their family for centuries, Roberto never seemed that interested and hadn't visited in many years.

'Are you planning on going there? You do remember what it's like this time of year . . .'

'I don't wish to go myself, but I did wonder whether they might make a suitable place for storage.'

'For storing what, though?'

'Precious items, which ought not be exposed to the light of day. I can't say more than that, I'm afraid.'

Though desperately curious, Luca knew from long experience that Roberto was unlikely to be drawn.

'I haven't been down there myself in years, but I can ask for them to be inspected when the snow clears, if that would help?'

Roberto nodded gratefully. 'Thank you, brother.'

'When would you need access?' asked Luca.

'Springtime would be good. And discretion would be valued.'

'Always.'

Roberto put a hand on his shoulder as they walked. 'I rely on no one quite as much as you. Sorry for taking you away from the family.' They had reached the end of the corridor.

'That's quite all right.' Luca could not explain he'd been delighted to escape.

'How are my nieces?'

'Sophia has been having nightmares. Father Colonni's sermons have been focusing on fire and brimstone recently – he's frightened her somewhat.'

Roberto shook his head. 'Tell Sophia I will put up a prayer

on her behalf. I have better connections than Colonni, she need not fear. In fact, she should come to me for confession from now on. She will find I have a more sympathetic ear.'

After Luca parted from his brother, he wandered aimlessly for a while and found himself heading towards the *Pinacoteca*. Despite working close by, he hadn't visited the Vatican's art gallery in years. He thought about going inside to drink up the beauty, then realized he was just avoiding his return. He should apologize to Violante, make amends. The great paintings could wait for another day. Perhaps he could invite Maddalena to come with him? *The Entombment of Christ* by Caravaggio was something which she'd love to see in person, and he was certain she'd never visited the Vatican. He'd love to share it with her, see it through her eyes. But no – that would not be prudent. He still remembered their close encounter on the loggia the year before. There'd been no more signs of affection on her part, but better to be cautious.

He'd done his damnedest to suppress any thoughts of her. Perhaps he did look out for her sometimes, listen for her voice, but these were friendly feelings, surely? They were companions, nothing more. He thought about that word and its origins: companion – one with whom we break bread. Well, that was true and innocent enough. They lived under the same roof, and she cooked his food – it was simple. If he stayed vigilant then nothing bad could happen. He might then disregard these other feelings: the charge which shot through him when her fingers brushed his hand, or as she passed him on the stair.

Luca left the Holy City and crossed the great piazza, the stone saints watching from on high. They were not subject to such earthly concerns. They were dutiful and diligent, well-intentioned, pure. He was no saint and made no claims to be; he'd suppressed his basest instincts, with success. Why then did it feel like something had been lost?

When Luca returned home, he went straight to the nursery and was surprised to find his daughters there, unsupervised. Sophia was in a state of high anxiety; she ran to him and began tugging at his sleeve.

'Papa, Papa, Balia Carolina has been crying!'

Luca turned to Costanza, who was lying on a rug in front of the hearth, nonchalantly flicking through a book.

'What happened?'

Costanza shrugged her shoulders. 'Carolina had a fight with Signora Bianchi and now she's packing in her room.'

Sophia resumed crying. 'I don't want her to leave us, Papa. Tell her not to go!'

'What was the fight about?' Luca asked Costanza. She turned the page and refused to meet his eye. 'Costanza, I'm asking you a question.'

'It was Costanza's fault,' Sophia blurted. 'She told on her.'

'Be quiet, you baby!' Costanza shot her younger sister a chilling glance, then turned to him defiantly. 'If Balia Carolina is in trouble, it's because she brought it on herself.'

Luca tried to hide his frustration with her tone of righteous indignation. 'Where is Signora Bianchi now?'

'With Mama in her sitting room.'

He frowned at her. 'Comfort your sister, Costanza. Can't you see that she's upset?' He left the room and walked along the corridor, knocking lightly on the door.

'Come in.'

The sitting room was cold. Signora Bianchi stood at the window, looking out, her posture ramrod straight. Violante sat in a high-backed armchair, a mean little fire burning in the grate and a rosary and prayer book nestled in her lap. She seemed surprised to see him.

'I didn't know you were back.'

Luca had grown to hate this room with all its portraits of misery and torture. It had a beautiful frescoed ceiling, much prettier than those on the ground floor – soft colours, like a fabric which had faded over years. He remembered staring up at them during the long days of his wife's confinement, when their son was born. The time had left them both irrevocably changed. In the months after, Violante often declared she wished she had been taken in their son's place, despite Colonni's chastisement. He told her such thoughts were a mortal sin and she'd listened to him; began returning to the world, piece by piece, though Luca thought she never had returned to him. Not entirely. He looked at her now, stiff and seemingly unmoved by all the drama.

'Costanza tells me there has been a row.'

Violante shrugged with indifference. 'The girls were squabbling, so Signora Bianchi needed to step in.'

Luca frowned. 'They said it was about Balia Carolina.'

Signora Bianchi spoke for the first time. 'As I've explained to the Contessa, I'm afraid Carolina will be leaving us.'

'But why?'

'She said something inappropriate, that's all.'

Refusing to be so dismissed, Luca pressed her. 'I don't understand. What has she done wrong?'

Deep lines of disapproval scored the Signora's face.

'Carolina told Costanza she feared Sweden might be invaded. It isn't the first time I've had cause to doubt her loyalty to our cause.'

'But she isn't wrong. I agree, there's every chance.'

The Signora's mouth pinched tight. 'You may think that, but from a foreigner? I call those anti-fascist sentiments. She isn't one of us.'

Luca turned to his wife, who was staring into the pale flames of the fire. 'And you agree with this?'

Violante looked up, seemingly bewildered. 'Agree to what?'

'That Carolina ought to be dismissed.'

She waved her hand dismissively. 'I leave that to the Signora.'

Luca snapped. 'Surely she ought to be given the opportunity to explain herself? Not condemned outright on the word of an eight-year-old.'

Violante looked at him, affronted. 'Costanza never lies!'

'But what if she's mistaken?'

The housekeeper folded her arms. 'She'll get a chance to put her side of the story – I've telephoned the OVRA.' The acronym had a chilling effect on Luca. The Organization for Vigilance and Repression of Anti-Fascism were Mussolini's secret police, renowned thugs and feared by all.

The Signora continued, 'As I say, I've had my eye on her for several months. They were keen to take her in for questioning. I'm sure there's more to it, and they agree with me.' Her husband had been a squadrista of the first order, a true believer from the start, and she was every bit as devoted. 'As the contessa will vouch, I don't like to disturb the smooth running of the household. I try to give these people the benefit of the doubt, but some things should not be overlooked. Personally, I think young Costanza has been brave to speak up in defence of her country.'

Violante murmured her agreement. Signora Bianchi took a wristwatch from her pocket and checked on the time. 'I ought to make sure Carolina has packed everything she might need. If she is deported, as seems likely, we shan't want to be responsible for sending her things on to Sweden.'

At that, something in Violante seemed to stir. 'You think they will deport her? But then what shall we do? I can't look after the children single-handedly.'

'I'm afraid we are all called upon to make sacrifices. Italy's need is greater than our own and loyalty is required, now more than ever.' The housekeeper tucked the wristwatch back into the pocket of her apron. 'Will you excuse me? The officers will be here soon.'

Luca watched her go, irate but powerless to intervene. Would he stay so mute if it was Maddalena or Santino, he wondered? Violante sighed and opened her prayer book. He rounded on her in frustration.

'Carolina has been with us these past eight years. Are we going to let the Signora just dictate to us?'

Violante glared. 'I don't know why you're feeling so aggrieved. This will discomfort me, not you.'

'You truly doubt Carolina's loyalty?'

'As the Signora says, we can't turn a blind eye.'

He felt an urge to shake her. 'You seem to manage well enough.'

Luca heard wheels on gravel. He walked to the window and watched as two officers of OVRA climbed out of their car. Carolina descended the steps of the villa with Signora Bianchi carrying her suitcase. Behind her on the steps stood Dolorosa and Maddalena, clinging to each other. Luca felt a sinking sense of shame and dark foreboding; how had they let it come to this?

One officer opened the rear door and helped Carolina in, while the other stowed the suitcase in the boot. The housekeeper conferred with them both, then glanced up at the window; she saw him standing, watching. He thought she might look away, embarrassed, but then he realized – she felt no shame at all. He might still be the master of the house, but this was clearly her domain.

CHAPTER FIFTEEN

ROME, AUGUST 1997

Beatrice said nothing as they climbed into a taxi outside their pensione. Though every window of the run-down Fiat was cranked open, the day's heat was already on the rise and her handbag was heavy in her lap, weighed down by the metal canister which contained her parents' ashes. The driver scarcely acknowledged either her or Jude, chain-smoking one cigarette after another, even as he navigated gridlocked traffic. In any case, it would have been impossible to talk over the blaring radio, which played nothing but Annie Lennox for their entire journey west. The driver kept on the move, as much as possible, taking side streets and every rat run he could find. By the time they climbed out of the car, both passengers felt faintly nauseous, though the clean air of The Aventine soon revived them.

The broad avenues were a world away from the busy streets

of central Rome: stately and suburban, there were few signs of tourists. The driver dropped them between the cemetery and the gates of the Villa Magistrale of the Sovereign Order of Malta, whose keyhole had been polished by centuries of observers gazing at the far dome of St Peter's which it framed. The scent of fallen pine rose from the pavement as they followed signs for the Ospizio della Basilica Santa Sabina. It didn't take them long to find a pair of tall green gates shielding the building from the road. Beatrice looked around, uncertain.

'How can we be sure that this is the right place?'

Jude pointed to a tarnished plate, engraved with two faint words: Villa Velare.

She shot him a worried glance. 'Maybe we should have phoned ahead.'

'We've come all this way – we might as well just take a look.' He stepped across the threshold.

She followed cautiously, shouldering her heavy bag. The driveway snaked upwards, lined by tightly clipped topiary. As they came round the last bend, it widened to reveal a grand four-storey villa. Pretty and symmetrical, sage-green shutters punctuated the peach plaster walls. Formal gardens were laid out all around; a band of tall pines filled the horizon, their bony fingers reaching for the sky. To Beatrice, the place seemed preposterously grandiose for one small family.

There were signs of its new, more prosaic purpose everywhere: air-conditioning units hung at all the windows, while barbed wire and security cameras lined the perimeter. In front of the villa, white lines delineated several parking spaces, while cross-hatched yellow stripes marked out a loading bay for *zona di emergenza*. A broad flight of steps led to an arched doorway and above that, the carved crest of a two-headed eagle, which Beatrice recognized right away. This was where her father had stood in the portrait with his 'first' family. The photograph was sepia, while this was living colour, but there was no doubt in her mind. All that had changed was the door; what had been solid wood was filled with glass.

Fearing they might be called out at any moment, Beatrice approached the building with some caution.

'You think we should go inside and explain why we're here?' Beatrice asked Jude.

'I honestly don't think anyone will even notice us. Come on – let's have a look around.'

They found a cobbled terrace which ran beside the building, where thick vines of wisteria clung to plaster walls. Set among them was a stone plinth with the carved bust of a woman, her sculpted features black as coal. The long neck and elongated eyes were almost primitive, making her look striking, if not conventionally pretty.

Beatrice stated flatly, 'That's her. My father's wife.' She read the inscription, translating it for Jude.

'"Contessa Violante Montefalco 1902–1963. Commissioned by the trustees of the Hospice of the Basilica Santa Sabina. Contessa Montefalco graciously endowed her home to benefit the citizens of Rome, in gratitude for the sanctuary provided by the Church throughout her life. Her good actions will be rewarded in the kingdom of heaven."' Beatrice considered the choice of words. 'Actually, in this context, maybe it's more like "Her good deeds".'

'Makes her sound like a nun. Or a saint,' said Jude.

Beatrice stood face to face with the contessa.

'Interesting piece, though,' he continued. 'Modern, obviously, but made using ancient techniques, like the Etruscans.'

'I wonder what she'd think about me being here?' Beatrice shivered and repositioned the strap of her bag which dug into her shoulder. 'Not much, I suspect. Perhaps we should get on.'

They kept on past the house, where the pathway split: two branches meandering through formal flower beds. The garden sloped upwards, through a series of broad terraces; wide steppes filled with shrubs and herbs. As they climbed, they brushed through swathes of scented rosemary and thyme, picking out a path which avoided other visitors. Finally they came upon a little terrace with square beds full of roses, surrounded by orange trees and straight, tall pines.

'This must be the rose garden Mum mentioned in her letter,' said Beatrice.

They walked between the scrubby beds, the harsh sun bleaching out bare earth. The bushes were flourishing, but long past flowering. Beatrice opened her bag and stared down at the canister, which contained her parents' ashes.

'Now we're here, I can't think where or how to do it.'

Jude looked around them. 'This bit does seem quite exposed.'

They strolled towards the perimeter, where more rose beds were hidden by a long box hedge. It was still and quiet, shielded from the path below. Beatrice dropped her bag on the ground.

'I think this is the place.'

'You sure you're up to it?' asked Jude.

Lips pressed hard together, she nodded.

'Okay. I'll give you some space. I think I might just stick my head in at reception, let them know we're looking round the gardens. I'll come back in twenty minutes.'

'Thank you.' She gave him a tight smile and Jude walked back down the same way they'd come.

Beatrice retrieved the metal canister from her bag. It was warm, where it had pressed against her body. She knelt and tried to sweep away the topsoil, but it was bone dry and unforgiving; she suddenly wished she'd thought to bring some tools. Scraping at it with her fingers, she loosened the soil to make a hollow, wide but shallow. She thought it was enough.

Beatrice opened the lid of the metal urn and began to pour the contents out. A gritty grey powder spilled onto the ground, the larger grains bouncing as they fell. Beatrice pushed away the question of what they might consist of, or to which of her parents they belonged. Should she say something, she wondered? A blessing or a prayer, perhaps, though everything she thought of was a cliché: ashes to ashes, dust to dust, life returning to the soil . . .

She tried to picture them together: her parents, Luca and Maddalena, Mum and Dad, but no clear image came to mind. Just memories of memories, as Jude had said. She'd only been ten years old when Luca died; not enough time to lay down a store. She cupped her hand to slide the soil back over, covering the gritty powder, putting it to bed. Their words came back to her, from childhood:

'*Sogni d'oro, amore mio, ci vediamo nella luce del mattino.* Sweet dreams, my love, see you in the morning light.' A little prayer to guide you home from the lesser death of sleep.

She stayed there for a moment, crouching in the dust and heat, filled with a sudden sense of loss and liberation; as if the ropes which held her down had been untethered and she might fly up at any moment, hurled into the clear blue open sky.

Sometime later, she saw Jude from a distance as he walked back up the path towards her. His sandy hair was swept back by a warm breeze. *He suits this place*, she thought. Though he was barely tanned and resolutely blond, he seemed more comfortable than she was, even with her Italian blood and colouring.

'How are you getting on?' he called out.

Beatrice shrugged and forced a smile. 'I'm okay. All done.'

'Can I show you something?'

She nodded and he led the way along a path which followed the high perimeter wall. Beatrice put her hand in her pocket and found the carved wooden donkey she'd carried with her since her mother's funeral. She held onto it, the worn form oddly comforting to touch.

The beds against the high wall were full of vines and fruit and nut trees, all of which basked in the reflected heat. After a time, the planting ceased and the wall dipped down, running for a distance at chest height. Beatrice saw why as soon as they approached: the hill below it dropped away, a steep incline of pine and scrub which sloped down to the Tiber. Beyond that lay the entirety of Rome, spread before them.

'Wow.'

'Indeed.' Jude grinned. He pointed across the ranging rooftops. 'That's the Vatican, Saint Peter's Basilica, then close by you've got Trastevere. Over there is the Altare della Patria and beyond it, the Alban Hills.' The violet-blue horizon was softened by a haze. 'I thought you might like to see it.'

Beatrice looked around, trying to take it all in – the sprawling city, the heat, the scent of dry earth and the chatter of green parakeets in the canopy above. There was heavy traffic on the road below, though little sound of it appeared to carry. And there was light, glinting off the river; it was almost overwhelming. She shut her eyes and let the sun burn through the lids. A wash of bright blood orange filled her field of vision.

When she opened them again, Jude was standing close by, leaning on the wall beside her. He watched her intently, a small frown between his brows as if trying to puzzle something out. Faint freckles dusted the bridge of his nose. She hadn't noticed them before; they'd never been this close. She returned his look and held it. Something passed between them – a change, almost imperceptible – and she felt her own pulse beating in her throat. Unsure until that moment, she now imagined his hand coming up to touch her face and how she would lean into it, her lips parting, just a little.

Jude suddenly stepped back and cleared his throat. 'So we should probably get going.' He turned away and began heading down the path, pushing his hands deep into his pockets.

Flustered, she called after him, 'Go where?'

He didn't turn. 'To the Capitoline. To see St John.'

Beatrice watched him go, her cheeks aflame. She only hoped he hadn't noticed. Finally, she followed, wishing the ground would open up and take her.

CHAPTER SIXTEEN

Rome, July 1943

The swifts were leaving. After four months in the Eternal City, all but a handful had already flown away. A lone bird perched beneath a tile in the eaves of the Basilica di San Lorenzo. On the ground below, between the columns of the portico, twin boys were playing in the dust and droppings. Skinning ruddy knees, they moved their legions of lead soldiers into place.

'Let's play the siege of Carthage: you are Carthage, I am Rome,' the first declared, by dint of seniority. He'd lived on earth for fully one hour longer than his brother and, as such, he ruled the roost. The game proceeded, with repeated entreaties from both sides to 'pretend that . . .'. It was a fine game as the siege itself had lasted years, so they had no shortage of ideas. When they tired of it, they might walk the few streets to the railway yard, dodging the packed tram cars going to and from the market. They'd try to find their school friends, who were likely there already, pitching stones at passing freight trains and playing chicken on the tracks.

'Pretend this catapult wipes out all your infantry.'

Empty summer days stretched before them, if they kept out from underneath their mother's feet. Otherwise, they risked being forced to entertain their snot-nosed little sister. Freed from the constraints of education, they roamed across the city, clambering over ramparts and ruins, fighting skirmishes on ancient playgrounds. This was done as much for distraction as entertainment; their stomachs empty, thighs thin enough to circle with a hand, but who needed food when there were games to play? Especially a siege; and weren't the people of Carthage hungry too, before they burned it down?

'Pretend you're starving.'

Under the roof tile, the lone swift heard the call and yearned to stretch its wings. It fluttered upwards and crapped out a spattering of guano, which dropped down and down, onto the legionnaires below. The two boys shrieked with laughter, their hoots summoning the ancient priest who tried to shoo them both away.

The bird flew out, its body swooping like a missile, then soaring up. The day was perfect, bright and clear with all of Rome spread out below it, dissected by the roads and railway lines, converging and dividing. Seven hills, split by the ribbon of the Tiber. Layers of stone and sediment, sand and ash thrown up by long-extinct volcanoes. The city had been built this way forever: creation from destruction, the remains of one becoming a foundation for the next.

On this day there was little warning of their ruin, only the low and distant droning of the engines. The American Flying Fortress, 'Lucky Lady', was the first. She'd set off from North Africa that morning, cruising over Naples, then cleaving to the coast. A squadron flew behind her: B17s gliding on the currents, augurs of aluminium, their bellies full of bombs which dropped and seemed suspended for a moment, until gravity asserted. They fell to earth and sent up fire and flame and fury, which blotted out the sun. Great clouds of smoke obscured the ground, so on a second pass, the zone spread wider, like ripples in a pond: the airport and the shunting yards. Tiburtino, Prenestino, Casilino, Labicano, Tuscolano, Nomentano.

At San Lorenzo, the columns lay piled up like matchsticks in the rubble, fine painted frescoes already turned to dust. The two boys had tried to outrun the monster, although it had no form. They were together when it caught them, swallowing them whole.

Across the city, birds took flight: sparrows, pigeons, wrens and blackbirds, wheeling in the shock of conflagration. The swifts were all long gone.

Luca was heading to the basement storerooms when he heard the first wail of the siren and the patter of anti-aircraft guns. It was a familiar sound, not enough in itself to disturb him – likely just some Allied sortie. He began working, enjoying the meditative state which came over him as he sifted through large-scale prints of statues from the Hall of Muses, particularly the *Belvedere Torso*. The images were exquisite, the subject matter starkly beautiful.

He'd been relieved to return to work after a brief visit to the Dolomites the week before. The trip had a dual purpose: to ensure Violante and the girls were settled for the summer, and to transport several large crates on behalf of Roberto, which were now safely ensconced in the temperate salt caves underneath the castle. He wasn't sure exactly what the crates contained, but the size and shape suggested paintings. While he was at Gedächt, he arranged for extra stocks of firewood to be delivered, in case they stayed longer than expected. He already knew Violante would be reluctant to return to the city come September and saw no use in arguing with her anymore. Their private exchanges had become so barbed, they now communicated contentious subjects through intermediaries. In his presence, Violante and Signora Bianchi had discussed enrolling the girls at a boarding school in the mountains.

'Some would have us stay in Rome no matter what the danger,' Violante pronounced archly. 'Apparently, our placid Dolomites might be suddenly invaded, for goodness' sake. Can you imagine?'

Signora Bianchi had been quick to take her side. 'Never! I don't believe the government would let it happen. Or Herr Hitler, come to that.'

'No more would the Holy Father,' Violante vehemently agreed.

Deciding he no longer had the energy to fight her, Luca only insisted they would agree to an immediate return if the situation worsened in the north. He didn't point out Hitler might not be their ally for much longer – he had no desire to poke the hornet's nest.

'I just want to keep my family safe and I cannot do that if you're miles away.'

Violante had been bemused. 'God protects us, Luca. Where's your faith?'

On his return to Rome, he'd felt nothing but relief. The group which stayed back at Velare – Maddalena, Tito, Santino and Maria (now with Tommaso, their handsome little son), along with outside help from gardeners and cleaners and a maid – had all settled to their summertime routines. In the evenings, they'd often congregate to listen to the radio, openly delighting in Signora Bianchi's absence and the freedom it provided. It built a camaraderie such as they'd never known before.

Luca had been listening to the World Service in his study when the announcement came: troops landing at Castellazzo, Sicily. The Allied invasion had begun. He sprinted downstairs to find Maddalena and break the news to her. She'd been beside herself with worry, asking him for daily updates, charting their manoeuvres.

'What will happen to the locals?' she fretted. 'Will they be rounding people up?'

Luca went to the office of the British ambassador to the Vatican, who reassured him there was no need to fear – the Allies saw their role there as a liberating force. There would be casualties among the soldiers, but Maddalena's family were a good distance from Messina and so unlikely to get caught up.

When Luca told her this, she'd broken down, crying with relief. He'd put his arm round her and held her till the tears ran dry and then a little longer, reluctant to let go. They parted awkwardly, each acutely conscious of the other. In the days since, they'd circled one another warily, both uncommonly shy. When Luca left for work that morning, he'd watched her packing up a basket with the household ration books and offered her a lift.

'Thank you, but I can get the tram. I have a few more jobs to finish first.'

'Well, have a good day.'

'You too. I'll see you later.'

They both left smiling.

Luca's thoughts returned to this exchange as he was sorting through the prints. He spent a pleasant twenty minutes lost in idle daydreams. In the end, it was only the sheer volume of disturbance which drew him out. The sirens were still wailing, and two young priests were conducting an animated conversation right outside the door.

'What's going on?' demanded Luca.

Both men looked at him, aghast. 'You haven't heard? They've just bombed San Lorenzo. More planes are on their way – it's mayhem.'

Luca dashed straight upstairs to his office and tried to telephone Velare, but the outside lines were all engaged. He called his brother's rooms instead. Roberto answered right away. 'Seems they were targeting the freight yard, but they hit the basilica as well.'

Stunned, Luca asked, 'Was there no warning?'

'They dropped leaflets yesterday, although they seemed like empty threats.' The priest offered up a muttered prayer. 'The

Holy Father is talking about going to San Lorenzo, to see the damage for himself. Hundreds are reported dead. It's market day, so there were dozens of trams in the piazza.'

Luca felt a tilting roll of fear. 'I must get home and make sure everyone is safe.' He didn't mention Maddalena by name, though she consumed his thoughts.

'Surely you'd be safer staying here? They are unlikely to drop bombs on the Vatican, after all. Such a relief to know that Violante and the girls are far away.'

Luca was barely listening. What chance was there that Maddalena might have gone to the market at San Lorenzo? She didn't usually go that far, but with the lack of rations in the shops, it was entirely possible. 'I have to go now,' he said.

'Stay safe, little brother. I'll telephone you later.'

As Luca hung up, he realized he could smell the acrid scent of burning, faint at first, but growing stronger. He went to the window and saw columns of grey smoke rise across the city. Knowing the roads would be impassable, he left the Vatican on foot. Sirens and the stutter of the anti-aircraft guns kept up a constant conversation; Rome was reverberating but its citizens were oddly quiet. No one spoke as they hurried on their way, their drawn, grey faces turned up to scan the sky for danger.

Luca found himself envisaging the devastation; so many times he'd sat in the darkened cinema and seen the havoc wrought on Turin, Milan, Genoa and Naples, watched people stumble from their homes, searching for survivors. Seen footage of the fires which burned through buildings, leaving empty husks behind.

For more than an hour, he walked south as quickly as he

could, the sweat pouring off him, though he removed his
jacket and rolled up his sleeves. He stopped to gulp fresh
water from a *nasone* fountain, though he tasted smoke and
cinders. He sped his pace up as he got close to home, passing
the monastery of Sant Anselmo, where the monks incanted
prayers. The sound was haunting: a requiem which filled his
chest with dread.

When he finally got to the gates of Velare, the panic he'd
been trying to subdue flared up. His weary legs broke into a
trot and then a run, feet slipping on the gravel, heart hammering as he dashed past the front steps and round the corner
to the terrace by the fountain, to the open kitchen door. He
stopped there, breathing heavily. Maddalena stood beside the
table. Luca went to her directly, crossing the room to take her
in his arms. He sank his face into her hair and breathed the
scent: of flour and yeast and heat and fear. He buried himself
there until he became aware that she was crying, although he
couldn't hear a sound. He kissed her tears away and whispered,
'You're safe, my love, thank God you're safe. I came for you,
I'm here.'

And with that, he heard the roar of all the world returning.
The sound of sobbing, his ragged breath, the sirens and the
spitting guns. A chasm opened and everything rushed in –
wider than shame and deeper than denial. Words said could
not be unspoken; though each was but a single drop of water,
given time they'd carve a path through stone.

CHAPTER SEVENTEEN

ROME, AUGUST 1943

Throughout the day the birds refrained from singing, trying to preserve what little energy they had. Now, late in the evening, the warm air pooled beneath the rafters. The attic seemed to be swimming in a haze, even as it sank from blue to black. All Rome ached; no one could escape it. The city had been baking in the unrelenting sun for weeks now, ever since the bombs.

Luca looked down at Maddalena, her cheek resting on his chest, her tawny curls damp against his skin. She lay naked on the white sheet of the daybed, pearls of perspiration in the hollows of her collarbone. Their limbs tangled together, hands and fingers languorously entwined. He felt her breath on him and shivered, even in the tranquillizing heat.

Sleep was so elusive that Luca often woke with the sensation of a fever – that small, sharp flare of panic at the prospect of its onset, only then to realize the cause and shrug off the sheet. It was, he thought, no bad thing; they could not fall asleep together and risk discovery. He sometimes wondered if Maddalena really slept at all. On many nights her restless, twisting body had disturbed him. That, or the sound of gunfire, far away. When it woke both of them, they simply turned to one another and began where they'd left off, their skin a canvas waiting for the brush.

Weeks slipped by. It would soon be Assumption Day and *Ferragosto*: a time to honour the holy mother and more ancient fecund gods. Most years everyone escaped the city to head off to the beach for fresher air; now Rome was stuck together. After bombs fell for a second time, Maddalena said she wished they might just stay like this forever, shut up in a kind of twilight state. But even as the city burned, so life continued. Washing must be laundered, food must be grown, harvested and cooked. With half the household still off in the mountains, by sundown anyone who didn't sleep inside the villa was long gone. They'd close the gates at curfew and those few who remained – Luca, Maddalena, Tito, Santino, Maria and the baby – would all eat together, then retire to their rooms. The lovers would wait for total quiet, then climb the stairs up to the attic and creep onto the daybed, silent as could be. They feared any noise or voice above a whisper might be heard – a creak, a moan, a sigh might risk exposing them entirely. It made it more intense than anything Luca had ever known. Afterwards, the sweat would roll off their bodies and drip onto the floor. They licked their lips and tasted salt and knew it couldn't last.

The calls began the night after the bombs. Telephones, then telegrams and letters, back and forth. In that moment the mountains seemed so much safer than the city, but all knew the day of their return must surely come. Rumours of invasion grew, yet still they stalled. Violante said she wasn't ready; nor was he. Luca knew he ought to feel consumed by guilt, yet so far, he felt none. Perhaps because it seemed as if the gods were playing games. Within a week of the first raid, Mussolini was arrested. Finally, his faithful party turned against him, one by one. Luca heard it from the clipped tones of the BBC, translating it for Maddalena as they lay listening together. She'd been perturbed.

'I never thought the day would come. He's been our leader all my life.'

In the end, it took his own to bring him down – like all Caesars that surround themselves with loyal sycophants, who stay that way until they don't. He was placed under arrest at Villa Ada Savoia, after an audience with the King.

That night they opened several bottles of good wine and Santino raised a toast to the tyrant's end, though Luca cautioned them all to keep such sentiments within Velare's walls.

'They won't go quietly; you mark my words.'

Rumours spread of fascists being beaten by the enemies they'd made, their headquarters broken into and destroyed. Busts of Mussolini smashed, to shouts of *'Benito è finito!'*. Posters torn down and ripped to pieces, left to blow like blossom from a second spring.

Maddalena took great pleasure in removing Signora Bianchi's photographs of Il Duce. She threw them on the fire, saying, 'Damn the man and damn her too. I hope they go to hell.'

But though they relished this release, their country was not free. Caught between the Axis and the Allies, danger pinned them in on every side. German radio pledged to cover Italy with scars, while British leaflets dropped from the sky, warning of a rain of fire and steel. Everyone questioned what thoughts their neighbours harboured in their secret hearts. A country couldn't be crushed for twenty years then shrug it off within a day.

Nights in the attic turned into humid elegies, which swung from sorrowful to sweet. Their conversations took on a febrile tone, a yearning desperation as the hours and minutes slipped away. Maddalena went from reticent to eager, her passion shocking both of them with its intensity. Luca had been tentative at first – polite and gentle, so restrained – but now her whispered urging spurred him on.

Their daylight hours became consumed by news until finally, almost one month after the bombs, Rome was declared an open city. By abandoning their efforts to defend it, the government, such as it was, hoped to preserve both the people and the place. It was now safe for the party in the mountains to come home. They would arrive on *Ferragosto*, to celebrate together, best they could.

And so came their last night. Luca watched while Maddalena slept. Although the light in the attic was dim, he lifted down the Leica. Moving gently, so as not to disturb her, he held the camera to his eye and adjusted the focus, then pressed the shutter. As it clicked, her eyes flew open.

'I'm so sorry, I didn't mean to wake you.'

'It's all right. I shouldn't sleep.'

'There's no film in it,' he reassured her. 'I just wanted to remember ...' She pressed his hand against her cheek. They decided to slip out together, to the satin garden and the grove of orange trees, where the scented roses grew. It overlooked the city, a shielded place and, in the blackout, dark, dark, dark, except for the lantern bellies of the fireflies.

'This must be how Rome looked centuries ago.'

They returned to the attic and lay down. Luca dozed until a thin light came creeping in. Maddalena sat with the sheet wrapped around her; the rising sun had crowned her hair and made her look like Mnemosyne.

The time had come; the last dawn, the last hour, the last kiss. They moved from one place to another, without going anywhere at all.

CHAPTER EIGHTEEN

ROME, AUGUST 1997

The Capitoline Museum was heavily congested when they got there: a slow-moving legion, which trudged from gallery to gallery. Beatrice found herself pressed through the rooms, only glancing at the objects as she passed without ever slowing down.

She'd felt uncomfortable from the moment they arrived, propelled up the slope of the *Cordonata* with a squash of bodies on every side. Once they were in the building, not just the crowds, but the sheer volume of antiquity was overwhelming. Each room held so many layers that she didn't know where to focus her attention – a sculpted bust in front of a frescoed wall, intricate mosaics surrounded by a carved, gilt frame. At any other time, it might have energized her, but instead, she felt prickly and out of sorts.

As they trudged up the stairs together, Beatrice replayed

the events with Jude in the garden at Velare. Though neither of them had acknowledged any sort of attraction, she'd felt it growing since they'd got to Rome and presumed that he did too. Now she was left wondering if she'd imagined it all.

'Are you okay?'

Jude's question punctured her thoughts. She swallowed hard and nodded. 'Just got a bit of a headache. That's all.'

They'd reached a suite of rooms with white walls and polished parquet floors. After tramping further still, they entered the Hall of St Petronilla, which was occupied already by a large group with an enthusiastic guide.

'As you can see, *The Burial and Reception into Heaven of St Petronilla* by Guercino not only gives the room its name, it simply dominates the space.'

The guide continued at great length, so Jude and Beatrice skirted round the crowd and stopped in front of a smaller painting – Caravaggio's *Youth with a Ram*. For Beatrice, it felt bewildering to come face to face with it at last. The painting had consumed so much of her time and energy, it was shocking to be confronted with it as an object in the real world. The colour plates she'd seen in books had given no sense of the painting's vibrancy. With the overwhelming presence of Guercino so nearby, St John in its simple frame seemed almost modest by comparison. For Beatrice, the differences between this version and what she now thought of as 'hers' were surprising. This smiling boy seemed innocent and somehow guileless, while hers possessed a knowing grin.

It seemed the guide was done with Guercino as he now turned his attention to the Caravaggio, instead. 'St John, in

Youth with a Ram, was painted in 1602 when the artist was thirty years old. A mere eight years before he died, tragically early; who knows what more he might have been capable of, if he had lived?'

Jude had mentioned Caravaggio died young, but somehow, she'd forgotten. The fact of it in this moment made her sad.

The guide continued, 'Some of you might not be aware, but this is not the only version of this painting in the city. In fact, a copy of it, also painted by Caravaggio, can be found just a few miles away from here, at the Galleria Doria Pamphilj.'

Jude whispered to her conspiratorially. 'What do you reckon – should we tell him there's a third and blow his mind?'

The group leader moved on and began discussing Peter Paul Rubens and the Flemish Baroque, leaving Beatrice and Jude standing awkwardly together. Suddenly, seeing the painting in person seemed almost anti-climactic. She felt small and exhausted, too tired to wrap her mind around the meaning.

'I think I'd like to go now,' she said, without looking at Jude directly.

'Really?' He seemed surprised. 'You don't want to stay a little longer? The group will move on soon, then we can talk.'

But Beatrice realized that was the last thing she wanted. 'Why though?' She demanded. 'What's the point? We don't know who the painting belonged to, or where the rest of it is. I'm not sure what more there is to say. I'm feeling sick of the whole thing.'

Jude looked taken aback by her outburst.

'Sorry.' She pinched the bridge of her nose. 'I have a headache coming on.'

'It has been quite a day,' he frowned. 'Why don't you go back to the pensione, so you can take a rest?'

She nodded, eager to escape. 'What will you do?'

'Not sure. There have been one or two things I thought I ought to follow up on. Would you mind if I borrowed your notes?'

'Sure.' She dug the Filofax out of her bag and handed it over.

'Thanks. I'll look after it, I promise. How about I find us somewhere nice for dinner? Then we can make a plan before we head home. It is our last night here, after all.'

Beatrice had almost forgotten in all the drama of the day. She felt a wave of relief at knowing the whole thing would soon be over.

A few hours later, Jude sat at the table, nervously adjusting the cutlery on the crisp white cloth. He'd asked the young woman on reception to recommend a restaurant, somewhere with good food, but not too stiff or formal. She suggested Felice, a legendary trattoria in Testaccio, so Jude called to book a table and left a note for Beatrice, asking her to meet him there at eight o'clock.

Then he headed back to the little internet cafe by the station and paid for a two-hour session. Fuelled by multiple espressos, he started through the notes Beatrice had made. With numerous dates and names to play with, he was in his element, skimming web page after web page, building up the bigger picture as he went. The information he was looking for was hard to find. Some viewed the nascent internet as the

Wild West, but Jude saw it as an ocean; he cast his net far and wide, and slowly sifted through the catch.

When his two hours were up, he'd made some progress. Tentative findings, but still more than they had before. He went to find a telephone booth on the station concourse and made a call to corroborate the evidence he'd gathered. Now he had a real prize to present to Beatrice: a peace offering of sorts.

He wished he could rewind the day. The whole time he was trawling the web, he kept replaying the scene with Beatrice in the garden of Velare, and the choice he made to turn away. Looking back, he could not explain it; it was like watching himself on a loop, rewinding the tape, letting it go, and wincing as the moment was repeated, time and time again: pause, rewind, review. No matter how many times he did it, he couldn't fathom what went wrong.

Maybe he made the split-second decision because none of it was planned. He'd only wanted to distract her from her grief, but then she'd closed her eyes, and he found he almost couldn't breathe. When she opened them again, something in them both had changed, he knew she felt it too. This was the moment, but instead of leaning in, he'd turned and walked away. But why? The question came to plague him. Only hours later did the answer come to him: the red barn roof.

He called the woman the Parisienne, though her real name had been Céline. He preferred the playful monicker because she'd seemed unreal – more fantasy than flesh and blood. Céline Bertrand had commissioned him to find a trove of paintings stolen from her parents by the Vichy government of France, forcibly requisitioned from their gallery in Paris in 1942. If Jude could lay his hands on one and show a paper trail of ownership, then she would sue them for the millions they'd lost.

For months he'd thrown himself into the task, combing auction houses and gallery websites the world over, looking for any evidence of the missing works of art. Though he'd always maintained a professional distance from his clients in the past, he found their mutual attraction built like static before a storm. Calls went on much longer than was necessary, meetings extended into dinners. Despite his best intentions, he found himself falling hard.

He came across the suspected Paula Modersohn-Becker, with its red barn, on an auction website in the south of France. He'd presented it to the Parisienne in triumph and that night they slept together for the first time. She was everything he wanted and possessed all he lacked: she was worldly and sophisticated, free from all the doubt which plagued him. He was hooked.

As the auction day grew near, he came to convince himself that no one else could see the painting properly – only he possessed the seeker's instinct it required. Then, the Parisienne had called him late at night, to ask him for a favour: she didn't have the funds, but couldn't bear to let it slip away – would he bid and pay for it up front? Jude had been hesitant; he had no cash to hand or savings. He ought to look on it as an investment, she'd said – they'd make it all back ten times over. The next day, Jude persuaded his uncle to lend him the capital – an eye-watering sum – assuring him it was a short-term loan.

On the day of the auction, he'd woken early; St Jean de Luz was an hour ahead. He'd been calm enough in the beginning, until another, then another, bidder joined the fray. The numbers crept up, incrementally at first, then sharply, until all but one had dropped away. Still the price rose, and Jude realized his rival knew, they saw it too. He'd thought this would be a steal; instead he found himself at war. He went up to, then beyond, his limit, convinced it would be worth it in the end.

If he'd had the chance to stop, to breathe, to step away, to slow the flood of dopamine which tore around his body, he might have seen he was in trouble. That this was overreach, not merely speculation. But he did not. Instead, he clicked the mouse to bid, and bid, and bid again, until he won.

A few weeks later, after Kit Worseley informed him the painting was a forgery, Jude telephoned the Parisienne to break the news. His calls went unanswered, but she'd warned him she was heading into a busy period at work, so he didn't worry too much. He waited then reached out through her work email, but it bounced back straight away. Jude used his skills to dig into the details she'd given him – about her job, her identity, her friends. All were revealed to be a lie. In desperation, he flew to Paris to find her, but she was gone. She'd seemed too good to be true and so she was. Both Céline Bertrand and the man who sold the painting disappeared without a trace. Jude felt too ashamed to do much more than register the forgery and theft with the auction house and the French police. As well as the financial burden, he carried with him so much guilt and humiliation, he almost couldn't stand.

Now, as he sat in the restaurant in Rome waiting for Beatrice, he marvelled at his own naivety. Why had it taken him so long to connect those feelings to today? Shame had prevented him from seizing the moment. He'd ruined his one chance. He only hoped that what he'd found on the internet might help to broker peace.

When Beatrice arrived at the restaurant, she saw Jude straight away. As she crossed the tiled floor towards him, he seemed lost in thought.

After several hours of sleep, she'd woken to find her headache gone and a new perspective: grief was to blame. She'd let herself fall into a fantasy, soothed herself with its numbing balm.

On seeing her, Jude stood up and pulled out her chair.

'You found me.' He smiled.

'I did.' She glanced around the cosy room. 'This is nice.'

'It came highly recommended. Apparently it's something of a local institution.'

A waiter arrived with a bottle Jude had ordered. 'Join me?'

She nodded and picked up the menu. 'What are you having?

'The cacio e pepe, and then I think I'll have the steak.'

'I'm not all that keen on red meat. I think it's because my dad was always trying to force it on me, seemed to think it was a panacea, but all that blood just makes me squeamish.'

Aware that she was gabbling to cover up her nerves,

Beatrice trailed off and gave the waiter her order. When they were alone again, Jude asked, 'Did you get manage to get some rest?'

'I did. Much better now. Sorry if I seemed grumpy.'

'Not at all.'

'Was your afternoon successful?'

'Pretty good, all things considered.'

Jude began to explain how he'd used her notes as a springboard for his research.

'I went on the hunt for surviving members of the Montefalco clan. We know Contessa Violante is deceased. Next in line were her daughters, that is to say, your sisters . . .'

Beatrice interrupted him. 'Half-sisters.'

'Well, quite. Costanza and Sophia Montefalco – the two girls in the portrait on the steps of Villa Velare.'

'They could be dead for all we know. That photograph was taken more than sixty years ago.'

'But they're not. They're both very much alive and living here in Rome.'

'They are?' Beatrice was stunned and wondered why she'd been so quick to dismiss them.

'Remember when you read out the inscription on the bust of the contessa? It said it was commissioned by the trustees of the hospice and happily, those details are on public record. I did a bit of digging and spoke to a woman named Gloria Ferro – she works for the trustees. I told her I was in Rome investigating the provenance of a painting from their family's collection. The Montefalco Trust has quite a few significant pieces out on loan to the Doria Pamphilj Gallery, the Borgia

Collection and more besides. They're well-known philan-thropists in Rome.'

'And she bought it?'

'Thankfully I have some good contacts in the Italian art world who were prepared to vouch for me. Miss Ferro has agreed to meet us in the morning, at her office in the sisters' private home, though there's no guarantee they will assent to see us.'

'Did you tell her who I was?' asked Beatrice.

Jude shook his head. 'I didn't want to put her off. Besides, I thought there was a chance you might not want to meet them.'

Beatrice considered this. Though she felt a little blindsided by it all, surely she couldn't turn down such an opportunity?

Jude was watching her intently. 'Only you can decide if you're ready to pull on that thread. You know how much I want to solve this, but it's your family, your painting. This must be right for you. I can call and cancel – you only have to say the word.'

Beatrice voiced her reasoning out loud. 'If we don't go to this meeting that's it, we've reached the end. It was my mum's dying wish ... It scares me, but for her sake I think I ought to try.'

Jude looked relieved. 'I agree. You might regret it if you don't, but there's no need to tell them who you are until you're ready.'

Beatrice nodded. 'Maybe we just see what they have to say and take it from there.'

'Then after that, we can head to the bank and pick up the

painting on our way to the airport. The Montefalco sisters live in one of the streets above the Spanish Steps – prime real estate, I understand. They must be pretty loaded.'

Beatrice gave him a sardonic grin. 'Good for them!'

CHAPTER NINETEEN

ROME, AUGUST 1943

Late on the morning of Ferragosto, the party finally returned from the Dolomites. It had been, by all accounts, a trying journey. There were moments when they feared they'd get turned back and all were weary by the time of their arrival.

Maddalena hovered at the bottom of the kitchen stairs, ready to retreat to safety if anyone came near. She listened to the blend of voices which filtered down – excited chatter and Luca calling out to Santino as they helped unload the trunks and cases from the cars. She heard expressions of delight from Dolorosa on seeing Tito and the sound of running foot-steps as Luca's daughters dashed up to their bedroom. This was followed by a series of terse instructions from Signora Bianchi to the children's new nanny, Balia Paola, who called for calm. Maddalena strained to listen – the contessa's voice seemed entirely absent in the ebb and flow. She wondered for a moment if she might have stayed behind, then heard a quiet pronouncement: Violante had a headache and was retiring to her bed.

Hidden in the shadows, dread sank through Maddalena; the gravity of guilt returned and pinned her with its weight. Then Dolorosa shouted out that Tito had better help her take the bags down to the kitchen, unless he planned to send his mother to an early grave. Maddalena shook off her inertia and dashed back into the kitchen, preparing to look busy.

Dolorosa strode into the room. 'Maddalena!' The older woman wrapped her arms around her. 'Look at you. Have you lost weight? You're thin as a beanpole and pale as a ghost. We need to fatten you back up.'

'How was the journey?'

Dolorosa snorted. 'Don't ask.'

'Well, we're glad to have you back here, aren't we, Tito?'

The boy, who was laden down with boxes, made the same dismissive noise as his mother. Dolorosa reached out to pat him on the cheek then exclaimed at the soft whiskers growing there, which embarrassed him all the more. She handed him a box of cheese and charcuterie, wrapped in muslin. 'Take these down to the cellar.' When he'd gone, she turned to Maddalena.

'Did he behave himself?'

'For the most part.'

Dolorosa sighed contentedly. 'It's so good to be back.'

She walked into the pantry, which was full of jars of fruits and vegetables that Maddalena had preserved.

'How did you manage all this single-handedly? I thought the cupboards would be bare.'

'Tito helped, but it was honestly no trouble. We all ate together, most nights, so I had time at my disposal.'

Maddalena didn't say she'd thrown herself into these tasks to take her mind off their imminent return. Dolorosa nodded approvingly.

'Well, good for you. Would that I could say the same. Three separate meals: one for staff, one for the girls and one for the contessa and the Signora, who gives herself more airs and graces by the day. Wait till I tell you, she has the ear of the contessa now, for good and all. Dripping poison, if you ask me.'

Maddalena felt relieved to have her accomplice back.

'I'm just so thankful for the garden because there's less than nothing in the shops. So many things we're told we're supposed to have which simply aren't available. They're on the ration cards, but never show up on the shelves.'

The cook patted her on the arm.

'It's so much better in the country. Flour, meat, dairy, honey, you name it. I brought back everything I could.'

She took down her apron from the hook beside the back door. 'A good thing, too – did you forget it's Ferragosto? Come then, let's get to it. We have a feast to prepare.'

Maddalena was chopping fruit when she spied her little shadow from the corner of her eye. Sophia swung on the door frame, shyly.

'Do you still like figs?' Maddalena asked, holding one out. The girl nodded, dark eyes deadly serious. She popped half in her mouth and chewed.

Maddalena watched her. 'I bet it feels odd to be back home.'

Sophia nodded again and scraped her toe along the floor. She swallowed the fig and whispered shyly, 'Can I show you something?'

'Of course.' Maddalena set the bowl down and wiped her hands on her apron. 'Lead the way.'

As they climbed the stairs together, Sophia spoke about her new collection: precious little wooden carvings, brought back from the Dolomites. When they reached the bedroom, she opened her suitcase and showed the contents to Maddalena, who knelt down on the floor. Sophia could not contain her excitement.

'There's a town, not far from Castel Gedächt, where simply everyone can carve. There are so many shops and market stalls, you wouldn't quite believe!'

The girl handed her a carved Madonna and child, a donkey, a variety of cats and puppies and a little putti cherub with a rounded peach backside. Maddalena admired each one in turn.

'Aren't they lovely? Especially this donkey.'

'You can keep him, if you like. There are donkeys in the mountains, Maddalena, baby ones, as well as mamas. They come and nuzzle till you stroke them. They are the most beautiful and patient creatures that ever lived.'

Costanza, who was sitting by the window, watched her little sister with obvious disdain.

'Do you have your own collection?' asked Maddalena.

'Of course I don't,' scoffed Costanza. 'They're for babies.'

'I'm not a baby!' cried Sophia.

'Certainly not,' Maddalena said soothingly. 'I hardly recognized you – so grown up.'

'Did you miss us?' asked Sophia.

Maddalena nodded, then swallowed hard. Sitting here looking at the girls, her guilt was palpable, like a peach stone lodged in her throat, preventing her from speaking.

'Ugh! It's so hot here.' Costanza dumped her book down and slumped to the floor. 'Why did Papa force us to come home?'

'Did he?' Sophia looked to Maddalena in surprise. Her older sister stuck her chin out. 'Mama says so. *We* both wanted to stay.'

A new voice interjected and all three of them turned to see Luca standing at the door.

'You couldn't stay there, Costanza. It wasn't safe. Rome has been declared an open city now. There will be no more bombs.'

The young girl glowered, but didn't dare to contradict him.

'Well, I'm glad to be back home.' Sophia ran to hug her father's legs. 'Where is Mama?'

'Gone to bed. She's tired after the journey.'

Luca's face seemed pale, but Maddalena felt her colour rising.

'Perhaps I ought to get on.'

She moved to leave, trying not to meet his eye. As she passed him in the doorway, their hands brushed briefly and she felt the pull to him, deep in her core. Heart pounding in her chest, she walked along the landing quickly, then ran back down the stairs, eyes filling up with tears. When she got to her room next to the kitchen, she ducked inside and closed the door, chest heaving with every panicked breath. Maddalena sat on the floor beside the bed, knees tucked up against her chest. The small room was right above the cellar, so even in the heat of August, the boards were chilly to the touch. Gradually, her breathing slowed, she felt the racing dread diminish. Searching for a handkerchief, she put a hand into her pocket and found an unfamiliar object, small as a quail's egg and warm to the touch: Sophia's little donkey. She held it to her cheek and rubbed the softly sanded wood against her skin.

Like a child, she longed to run to Dolorosa for some comfort, or take to the confessional and beg forgiveness, be absolved. But then, she thought, some sins were too great to ever be forgiven; they just had to be borne. After the bombs fell, she became a woman. Now she only had herself to rely on. Only had herself to blame.

The rest of Maddalena's day was a blur of occupation, for which she was truly grateful. There were twice as many mouths to feed and a feast to prepare, albeit one in straitened circumstances.

While she and Dolorosa got to work in the kitchen, Signora Bianchi moved through the villa, inspecting all the changes wrought in her absence, eyes raking every surface.

'She's been sour as old milk since Mussolini's deposition,' Dolorosa observed. 'I recommend you keep out of her way.'

The family would eat first – Luca and the children in the dining room, the contessa in her sitting room upstairs, where she'd asked for her meal to be brought up on a tray. Chicken with peppers first, followed by poached pears stuffed with raisins, cinnamon and a dash of buttered rum.

The staff would eat more rustic fare: gourds simmered with eggs and a *palatella* sandwich of pickled aubergine and anchovy. The mountain flour was put to use to make the flatbreads. For those who'd stayed behind at the villa, this was the greatest treat as flour was scarce in Rome.

It was decided they would eat under the olive trees in the courtyard, so everyone turned out to help. Tito and Santino carried the kitchen table and Maria set the plates and cutlery, while young Tommaso tottered round between the chairs. Once the food had been laid out, Maddalena stepped back to inspect it. Despite the unexpected bounty from the mountain, the offering looked thin – far from the normal Ferragosto celebration of abundance. She tried to make it decorative instead, filling the spaces with bowls of fruit and jugs of herbs while Dolorosa poured a drink for everyone, a chilled red wine from the cellar, its rough taste disguised with peaches. They all took their places. Dolorosa sat between Tito and Maddalena, reaching out to take their hands.

'Before we begin, let us remember those who can't be here.'

Maddalena squeezed her fingers, thinking of Matteo and her own brother, Dario. El Alamein was as unknowable to her as Addis Ababa, so she placed Matteo in the Contarelli Chapel, beside her brother.

Dolorosa intoned, 'Happy Virgin, give your mildness to the world. Obtain by your blessed intercession grace for the guilty, recovery for the sick, strength for the faint-hearted, aid for those in peril.'

Maddalena glanced at the short, determined woman, who didn't cry. She was another mother to her now.

'Dispense to us thy servants, who on this day invoke your name: gentle Queen, the grace of Jesus Christ, your Son, our Lord and God, glory forever.'

As every voice joined with the amen, Signora Bianchi clapped her hands together.

'Some words for Mussolini now, I think.' Santino muttered something under his breath and the housekeeper whipped her head towards him. 'Do you want to start, Santino?'

He held up a hand, 'You go ahead. I couldn't do it justice.'

The Signora bowed her head as if in prayer and began. 'From the trench the hour of battle sounds . . .'

It was the 'Giovinezza' – the hymn of the National Fascist Party they'd had drilled into them for decades. Maddalena heard other voices round her joining in, though they seemed to be half-hearted.

'The Black Flame is always first. Lash out, a dagger in my hand and faith in my heart. It goes far, with glory and with valour.'

Though she knew every word by heart, Maddalena found her throat was thick and dry. Somehow, she couldn't speak.

Signora Bianchi finished her recital. 'Youth, youth, spring of beauty, in life's hardship your song rings for Benito Mussolini!'

When Maddalena lifted her head, she realized the Signora was staring at her.

'What's wrong – cat steal your tongue?'

She should have known her silence would be noted.

Maddalena began to stutter an apology, then stopped. Why walk on eggshells anymore?

'My tongue is not the problem.'

'I beg your pardon?' The Signora stared at her in shock. Though no one spoke or moved, Maddalena felt the bodies round her stiffen.

'I won't waste my breath on that man,' she said calmly. 'We all know he's a dictator and now he's been deposed.'

She thought of Carolina, sent away so brutally, and hoped she might approve. Then someone kicked her sharply underneath the table. Bianchi's thin lips pursed.

'That man has led our country since 1922!'

Maddalena knew she ought to stop, and yet found that she could not.

'That man led us into a pointless war and sent thousands to their deaths. My own brother was among them. Her son, too.'

She flashed a glance at Dolorosa who squeezed her hand so tight it hurt.

'How dare you speak about Il Duce in that way? If you want to work here, you'll show him due respect.'

Santino tried to intercede on her behalf. 'Maddalena's a grown woman. She can say what she thinks.'

Signora Bianchi turned sharply. 'Not if I say she can't.'

Santino began pushing back his chair, but his wife put a steadying hand out on his shoulder. 'Don't let's spoil the celebrations.' Maria's voice was calm. 'We mustn't let good food go to waste and there's a child here, don't forget.' She patted Tommaso's head as he nestled in her lap. Seeming to notice the boy for the first time, the Signora nodded stiffly.

'I only ask my staff to show their due respect, but I suppose we must be gracious and forgiving on a day like this.' She waved at them. 'Go on now – fill your plates.'

Dolorosa's grip loosened and they both stood up to serve the food. As she handed round the plate of *palatella*, Maddalena cast a surreptitious glance down the table. The Signora was quietly observing the proceedings, her sour lips pinched tight. As her sense of righteous indignation drained away, Maddalena felt her hands and arms begin to shake. Some part of her had sought release in their confrontation; it felt so good in the moment, but now she wondered – what might be the cost?

CHAPTER TWENTY

ROME, AUGUST 1997

Jude and Beatrice walked up the Spanish Steps together for the second time in just four days.

'Are you sure you're ready for this?' he asked.

'I suppose so. It's not like I've had much chance to prepare.'

Jude tried to reassure her. 'Maybe that's better. Try not to overthink it.'

'I still wonder if we ought to tell them who I am. It seems deceptive otherwise.'

'But that could put them on the defensive. It's your personal information – you get to choose how and when to share it.'

'What if it turns out my dad did take the painting from them – won't this give them grounds to simply take it back?'

Jude had thought about this already. 'Whatever happens, possession is the key. You might decide you want to let them have it in the future, but this is not about them. It's about establishing your claim.' He paused, seeing how nervous she was. 'I could go in without you, if you prefer? Get the lie of the land.'

She shook her head. 'You might need me to translate. Anyway, I think I need to look them in the eye.'

They turned onto a quiet street, near the Trinità dei Monti, and stopped outside a grand four-storey townhouse. Jude rang the bell.

'I'm not going to say anything about you or your parents, unless you give me the okay. Even then, I suggest we show our hand one card at a time.'

After a few moments, a uniformed maid opened the door and ushered them inside. She led them to an office on the ground floor where a matronly woman in her early forties was waiting to greet them.

Jude put out his hand and made the introductions.

'Jude Adler – we spoke on the telephone. And this is Beatrice Fremont, my colleague and translator.'

'I am Gloria Ferro, the Montefalco sisters' private secretary. Good to meet you, but I don't think you will need to translate. The sisters speak excellent English.'

Jude smiled warmly. 'Thank you for agreeing to see us at short notice. We've been trying to track the sisters down for quite some time and, as I mentioned, we're heading back to London later today.'

'Let me go and find out if they are ready and happy to proceed.'

Once the woman left the room, Beatrice raised an eyebrow.

'What?' said Jude, protesting innocence. 'It's all true, up to a point.'

'We've been trying to track the sisters down for quite some time, have we?'

He shrugged. 'Two days could be considered quite some time.'

Shortly after, Gloria Ferro returned.

'The sisters have agreed to hear what you have to say.'

She led the way up a sweeping marble staircase to the first floor, through a suite of rooms full of heavy furniture, the walls hung with decorative displays of crucifixes and hanging rosaries. The secretary stopped outside a pair of ornate wooden doors. She knocked lightly, then ushered them both in.

The sisters Montefalco sat side by side on a pair of high-backed chairs in the middle of the room. Jude guessed the elder of the two to be Costanza Montefalco: her silver hair was drawn back in a tight bun, a pair of half-moon glasses resting on her nose. The younger sister, presumably Sophia, seemed small and meek, although she greeted them both warmly.

'Please, take a seat.' She gestured to a little velvet sofa opposite their chairs.

Jude looked around the room. 'You have such a gracious home.' Both sisters seemed to accept this statement as demonstrable fact.

The wall behind them was filled with paintings: more than a dozen lurid images of saints and religious figures gazing down. In the centre, a huge portrait seemed to dominate. Its subject was obviously the contessa – she had the same long neck and tight, waved hair as the bust in the garden at Velare. In the painting she wore a high-collared dress, and her hands were clasped in prayer. The artist had obviously been intent on capturing a moment of devotion, but her expression was verging on delirium.

A maid arrived with a tray of tea and a little bowl of finely sliced fresh lemon. Gloria Ferro bustled round, helping everyone to settle and serving drinks before taking a seat in the far corner. Once a few sociable sips had been imbibed, Costanza indicated she was ready to begin.

'Gloria tells us you return to London tonight. A pity you must leave Rome so soon.'

'It is,' Jude agreed. 'Which is why I'm so grateful that you agreed to see us at short notice. And I'm delighted to see all these paintings. Am I right in thinking they were on display at Villa Velare, before your mother's kind donation of her home?'

The sisters nodded.

Jude continued, 'I ask because a client of mine has recently come into possession of a painting which we think might be of interest to the pair of you.'

Costanza eyed him dubiously, then turned to speak to Gloria Ferro in a rapid-fire exchange of Italian.

Beatrice whispered a hurried translation for Jude. 'Apparently Costanza thought we'd come here to buy something from their collection. They're puzzled by the change.'

Costanza shot a hard look at her secretary, then spoke to Jude directly. 'I think there's been some confusion, Signor. We are *not* art collectors and have no interest in buying art.'

Jude hurried to placate her. 'And our client doesn't wish to sell, let me assure you. They only want to establish the provenance of the painting. We believe it might have once been part of your collection.'

Costanza looked at him with frank suspicion.

'Impossible. We inherited our mother's collection in its entirety, and we know where every single item is – sold, on loan, or on display right here. We've never lost track of a single painting, I am certain.'

Jude glanced at Beatrice, who swallowed hard. Almost imperceptibly, she nodded acquiescence. He spoke directly to Costanza.

'We believe this painting did not belong to your mother, but to your late father, Conte Luciano Montefalco.'

The older woman stared at him with outright hostility. 'Why have you come here?'

'We're trying to recover an important work of art on behalf of his second wife. You were aware that he remarried?'

Pale with fury, Costanza stared at Jude. 'My father died during the war. And now I think you ought to leave.'

'Costanza, please . . .' implored Sophia. 'Let him speak.'

It was the first time she'd said a word since the terse exchange began.

Costanza glowered at her. 'I won't have his name – or that *puttana's* – spoken in this house. That man was dead to us the moment he abandoned his wife and family.' She turned back to Jude and Beatrice, her face stiff with loathing. 'He was a dissolute and a criminal and died in disgrace, bringing nothing but shame on his family. We don't know about any work of art which belonged to him and have no interest in his fate – his or that filthy whore's, may they both rot in hell.'

Beatrice put her teacup down with shaking hands.

'That's my mother you're denigrating. She had a name. It

was Maddalena and she and my father loved each other, more than anything.' She turned to Jude. 'I want to leave now, please. I can't stay here while they speak about my parents in this way. We need to go.' She stood up and strode out of the room.

Jude ran after Beatrice as she dashed through the front door and along the street until she reached the Spanish Steps, which teemed with tourists.

'Beatrice, wait!'

When he finally caught up with her, he saw she had tears running down her face.

'Are you okay?'

She shook her head and wiped her eyes. 'I'm sorry, I couldn't just sit there and take it anymore.'

'It must have been awful for you. I had no idea that she'd respond that way.'

'It isn't your fault. I put myself in that position.'

People streamed around them, the baking sun reflecting off the stone.

'Let's go somewhere, find some shade,' said Jude.

Beatrice shook her head. 'I just want to get my bag and go straight to the airport.'

He wondered if she'd forgotten about their plan. 'But what about the painting? We need to go and get it from the bank'.

She vehemently shook her head. 'What am I going to do with it – smuggle it back through customs?'

She set off down the steps again, pushing through the crowds.

'Beatrice, wait!'

'I wish I'd never come here in the first place; never seen the bloody thing!'

He finally caught up with her. 'Let's go and get a drink. Cool off. I can't imagine how hard all this has been, but we can't give up – we've come too far.'

'All we have is that stupid fragment,' Beatrice scoffed. 'What use is that without the rest?'

Jude wanted to put his arm round her, to find the right words to console her, but for a second time he waited far too long. Her jaw set with determination.

'Mum was right – she said the bloody thing was cursed. Well, it can rot in that bank vault as far as I'm concerned. I want nothing more to do with it. I just want to go home.'

CHAPTER TWENTY-ONE

ROME, SEPTEMBER 1943

The news came in the early evening, from Radio Algiers.

'All Italians who now act to help eject the German aggressor from Italian soil will have the assistance and support of the United Nations.'

The words they had been waiting for. An armistice with the Allied nations, at last.

'Marshal Badoglio offered to surrender, and Eisenhower accepts!'

'To Armistice – a toast, a toast!'

Luca brought up several bottles of Piedmontese wine from the cellar, while they trawled the dial of the transistor, stopping at Swiss, German and British broadcasts, which he made efforts to translate.

'Having recognized the impossibility of continuing an unequal struggle against overwhelming opposing forces, with the intention of saving the nation from further and graver misfortunes, the Italian government has requested General Eisenhower, Supreme Commander of the Anglo-American Allied forces, for an armistice.'

Signora Bianchi quietly slipped away, while Violante and Balia Paola took the girls up to bed. The rest stayed on drinking in the kitchen and charged their glasses, time and time again.

'*Finalmente, la pace!*'

Peace at last? Surely ending a war could never be so easy.

'What about the Germans?' asked Santino.

'What indeed,' Dolorosa sighed. 'It's all well and good the British telling us to rid ourselves of them, as if that was a choice! Don't they think that if we could, we'd be shot of them by now?'

Luca knew whatever happened, the fight must surely come to Rome. He watched Maddalena as she cleaned up behind the celebrants, her shoulders hunched protectively. He longed to speak to her alone, but both agreed that any form of assignation was too risky.

When all the wine was finished, those who didn't live inside the villa started making their way home. There were shouts and revelry in the streets but the curfew remained and by nine o'clock they were empty. Still, Luca loitered in the kitchen. Sensing Maddalena's mood, Dolorosa asked her what was wrong.

'Nothing really. It's only . . . I'm worried what comes next. Like Santino said, what about the Germans?'

'The Allies will invade and drive them out now, surely?' Dolorosa turned to Luca for support. He told both women there was every reason to be hopeful.

The next morning, he woke with a headache, to face a day

with little news and too much speculation. Radio Roma kept replaying Marshal Badoglio's proclamation from the night before, while rumours swirled that the Allies were storming the beaches at Salerno, the *Roma* battleship was sunk, and railway lines were cut. By nightfall, conjecture surfaced that Badoglio and the King had fled the city. They drank again, this time more out of dread than celebration. Sirens howled and lulled them into fractured dreams.

Luca climbed from his bed about an hour before dawn, wincing at the pressure in his skull. The quantities of alcohol consumed had left him with a restless, prickling anxiety. Looking out of the window, he saw a distant haze of smoke blanketing the city. He thought he ought to go and see his brother – find out what his contacts in the Vatican had heard. He dressed and crept through the silence of the sleeping house, down the driveway to the gates, hoping the newspaper might have been delivered early. When he got there, he found the postbox empty. From out of nowhere, two soldiers in uniform came rushing by.

Luca shouted after them, 'What's going on?'

One called back, 'They're almost here.'

'Allied forces, here already?' Luca frowned in disbelief.

'Not the Allies!' The soldier gave a hollow laugh and elbowed his companion. 'Tell him.'

'The German Wehrmacht's at the gate. Better arm yourself, my friend.'

Luca ran back inside the house, went directly to the dining room and took down the shotgun which always hung there on the wall. He laid it on the dining room table and started hunting through the drawers beneath, in search of shells. He found several boxes behind felted trays of cutlery and pulled them out. They looked as ancient as the gun; he prayed to God they weren't.

He ran upstairs to the desk in his study and pulled open the bottom drawer, taking out the sturdy little pistol which once belonged to his father. He felt the weight of it in his hands and realized he could barely remember how to load it. He'd only kept it out of some sentimental attachment; he'd never imagined he might have need of it in the quiet comfort of his home.

Luca thought of his children, sleeping on the floor below; he wished he'd never asked them to return. For a moment, panic almost overwhelmed him, but he pushed it down. No time – he needed to respond. He dashed back down the stairs and along the landing to the shadowed room where Violante slept. He put a hand to her shoulder and whispered her awake.

'Violante.'

He brushed back the hair which fell across her face. Still steeped in sleep, she knocked his hand away.

'Violante, wake up.'

She moaned. 'What time is it?'

'I'm not sure, but you must wake up – there's fighting south of here. It's the Germans. They're coming to invade the city.'

Guns sounded in the distance.

Violante levered herself up. 'They mean to occupy?'

'So it seems, unless they can be stopped.'

She was alert now and climbing out of bed. He went into the dressing room and took down a camera bag, dropping the pistol, bullets and boxes of shells into it. She watched, bewildered.

'What are you doing?'

'I'm going to see if I can help.'

'You can't, we need you here.'

'It's my duty, Violante.'

Her face drained of colour. 'I'll wake up the Signora, see what she thinks we ought to do.'

The sleeping house roused quickly. The Signora, Dolorosa, Tito and Maddalena gathered in the hallway in their robes and nightclothes. Only Balia Paola stayed upstairs, to look after the girls. Santino and Maria soon joined them with Tommaso. Luca handed the rifle to the mechanic, who hooked it over his shoulder and kissed his wife and son. The boy held tight to Maria, his fingers tangled in her hair. Luca exchanged a glance with Maddalena, who stood shivering alone.

'We'll lock the gates behind us when we leave. Go round and barricade the doors.'

'Can't I come too?' asked Tito.

Luca saw Dolorosa's fearful expression and shook his head. 'We need you here, to look after the women.'

Saying little to each other, the two men headed out. At the Clivo di Rocca Savella they caught up with a straggling band of men and a few women from the neighbourhood, all walking with purpose towards the distant sound of guns. In less than ten minutes they reached the outskirts of Testaccio. They went south, keeping to the side streets, toward Porto San Paolo and the old gates of the city. They could see the top of the Pyramid of Cestius, a white marble edifice at the centre of a web of roads. As they approached, the gunfire got louder, the acrid scent of smoke drifting to them on the breeze.

Finally, they reached a crossroads manned by soldiers building barricades. Each wore a different uniform: an infantryman, an artillery soldier, alongside obvious reservists and a dozen citizens all preparing to defend their city, come what may. Luca and Santino approached a ragtag group covering an intersection and making forays in to strengthen their barricade. The captain eyed them with suspicion.

'Got any guns and ammunition?'

Luca showed the man his Beretta. Santino patted the rifle, now slung across his chest.

'They'll do. We've seen far worse today.'

The scene at the crossroads was chaotic. Normally the road would be full of traffic at this time of day. Now it was littered with broken glass and hunks of rubble. Luca looked around him in astonishment.

'I can't believe they've got this far already.'

'We held them off at Garbatella, then got forced back up here.'

'Where's the rest of your battalion?' Santino asked.

'What rest?' The captain snorted. 'There are none – half of them disbanded after the armistice was announced. Can't say I blame them.'

Two young women, hardly older than Maddalena, came down the street, rolling a thick ring of barbed wire as if it were a child's hoop. The infantryman grabbed hold of it and began to stretch it from one corner to another. A couple of Carabinieri helped to hoist the lot over a pile of objects which lay across the street – sheets of metal, piles of brick and even kitchen tables.

The Carabinieri struggled to weigh the barbed wire down, their hands soon running with fresh blood. Occasional bullets struck the road ahead of them, sending up splinters of cobblestone. When the roll was finally in place, they crouched low and scuttled back to their respective corners. The infantryman sank down against the wall, his eyes dark and wild.

'Good men, those Carabinieri.'

One of the girls laughed. 'Good men? One of them tried to arrest me for carrying a gun. Seems like no one told them, we're not the bloody enemy!'

The infantryman shook his head. 'It's anarchy. The right hand has no idea what the left is doing.'

A machine gun started hammering from a rooftop at the far end of the street, beyond the barricade. The infantryman signalled everyone to take cover. 'Seen any reinforcements?'

'A few on the road behind us,' Luca replied. 'Some nuns as well, would you believe?'

The infantryman smiled. 'Good on them, though it doesn't sound like there's enough to make a difference. The Germans came prepared, with more equipment. They haven't had to ransack a museum for their arms.'

Santino stared in disbelief at all the turmoil. 'Why wasn't anyone expecting this? Anyone in charge, that is.'

'The hope was they'd spare the city, once they realized Marshal Badoglio and the King had gone.'

'That wasn't just a rumour?'

The infantryman shook his head. 'They left last night, I heard.'

'Doesn't seem their plan is working.'

Luca and Santino stared in disbelief at the neighbourhood they knew so well, now utterly disfigured. *'Chi siamo.'* Here we go.

Outside Velare, the howling sirens started up again, startling Tommaso, who'd only just dropped off to sleep. Maria bounced him on her knees while Maddalena fetched a rusk of twice-baked bread. She hoped sucking on it might help calm him down. Signora Bianchi had already barked at them both, saying the sound of his crying set her nerves on edge. Apart from the Signora, everyone was trying to treat Maria gently, understanding her terror for Santino; Maddalena's fears for Luca were known only to her.

Upstairs and downstairs, tempers frayed. Tito and Dolorosa bickered, even as they worked together making space in the cellar for everyone to hide. Signora Bianchi had decided they would all retreat down there, as a last resort. Maddalena knew she couldn't join them – the prospect of waiting in the dark for fate to find her seemed even more terrifying than meeting it face on.

Beyond these preparations, the adults did what they could to hide the truth from the children. Smiles and stoicism when they were all together, then out of earshot, the free exchange of fears. Maddalena stumbled over one such conversation between the contessa and the Signora. She'd been sent to fetch cushions and blankets for the cellar and was ascending the back stairs when she heard the women whispering in the hall. The contessa's voice was controlled but angry.

'You said it was madness, dragging us back here. How could he put us all in danger? If only I had known.'

The Signora made a soothing noise. 'It's not your fault. You must obey your husband, though I will admit I saw the writing on the wall. The north is so much safer – full of real Italians. If those damned Sicilian cowards had put up a fight, this might not have happened in the first place. Bunch of filthy inbreds.'

Maddalena slipped back down the steps before they saw her. She longed to confront the Signora, although she knew she'd come off worse. Still, it spurred her into action. She marched back into the kitchen, took down her raincoat, and pulled it on while Maria and Tito watched her.

'What are you doing?' asked the boy.

'I'm going out.'

She tightened her belt. Maria stared at her, aghast.

'Don't be mad! You've no idea what's happening out there.'

'That's the point – I can't stay here, imagining the worst.' She took down the set of house keys. 'I'll just go out and look around. Don't breathe a word, I'll be back soon.'

Without waiting for a response, she opened the back door and slipped through, shutting it behind her. Keeping out of sight, she ran round the side of the building, then headed down the drive. At the bottom, she peered through the gates. A column of smoke rose from the south and the warm September air had a pungent edge of sulphur, brick and burning. She opened the great brass latch, stepped through and locked the gate behind her, pocketing the keys.

Luca was somewhere out there. She would rather be near him in danger, than safely tucked away, alone.

CHAPTER TWENTY-TWO

Luca shrank down in the shadow of the fallen angel, his back against the cold, hard stone.

For several hours, he and Santino had camped out on the barricades. They'd seen their numbers swell, reinforcements joining them in ones and twos, compelled to help defend their home. They'd been optimistic then and held the Germans off, despite a high rate of attrition. The young women who'd brought in the wheel of barbed wire returned with a gelato cart and used it like a gurney, dragging bodies from the line of fire and leaving strokes of blood across the street.

Their makeshift battalion fought hard, but in the end, they were outmanned and outmanoeuvred. Forced back into the streets around Porto San Paolo, Luca and Santino made a run for the seeming safety of the Protestant cemetery. Protected by the Pyramid of Cestius and the towering city walls, this calm green space had been transformed. Men hid between the gravestones as stray bullets flew, splintering the marble. On the far side of the wall the battle raged on, unabated.

The two men became separated, but fear pushed Luca to keep going, running faster than he ever had before. He finally took shelter behind the stone wings of the angel, one hand pressed to his aching ribs, the other bracing the pistol tight against his chest. Luca fought to calm himself; how much time had passed since they had run in here? He had no sense, although the sun was higher overhead. Dust settled on the film of sweat across his chest and face. Conscious of his rapid shallow breathing, Luca looked around and tried to get his bearings. The cemetery was a short walk from the Aventine – he'd come here often to enjoy its peace and stillness, the stray cats curled up on the gravestones. Now, such familiarity only made it more surreal. On any normal day, he could be at his front gate in under fifteen minutes. He felt a stab of panic – had the battle got that far already? He thought not, though he doubted they could hold out much longer. An image of his family appeared to him, unbidden. He had very little faith remaining, but he prayed they were all safe and vowed to be a better man – a better father – if he survived the day.

A lull came in the fighting and the raging clamour briefly ebbed away, its absence somehow more shocking than the noise which had preceded it. Luca heard sharp orders being barked in German, urging their soldiers to press on and press up, then silence. Nothing but the sound of birds and his own breath. Had he ever been so frightened or alone? 'Santino, can you hear me?' he whispered in a rasping tone, but there was no reply. He could almost be convinced it was a normal day, sat in the dappled light of the cemetery, a stone's throw from the graves of Keats and Shelley, poets so beloved their words lived on long after death. Was it his fate to die with them, he wondered? If so, there was no time to repent.

'Touch has a memory. O say, love, say, what can I do to kill it and be free?'

As far as God and all the world would see it, Luca's greatest sin was loving Maddalena. He felt guilt, but no regret. Remembering her touch sustained him; he'd sooner die here than forget.

From the far side of the wall came a deep, rumbling vibration – the tanks were on the move again. The flamethrowers could be felt as much as heard, a rushing horror which rippled the air with a gyring haze, its white heat tearing through the barricade, lighting the pyre of rubble, planks and screaming metal.

All around him voices cried, 'Retrench, retreat, fall back. We cannot hold the line.'

One kilometre to the north, a band of students roamed the streets, pleading with people to come and help the resistance. 'We've suffered twenty years under Mussolini's heel. We can't exchange one tyrant for another.'

Maddalena stopped them to ask what she could do. A young woman took her hand. 'My name's Benedetta, come with me.' She led her to the Basilica of Santa Sabina, a few streets away. The church had been transformed into a makeshift medic station. The injured from the battle had limped up here, while others had been dragged or carried.

At first, she couldn't take it in. The church looked like a great baroque painting. The wounded lay between the pillars, their groans echoing off the walls. Maddalena walked up and down the rows, scouring faces in search of Luca and Santino. Finding no sign of either one, she went back to Benedetta, who was sorting through a pile of bedsheets which needed to be torn into strips for bandages. With no knife or scissors, Maddalena suggested they bite through the threads, then rip them with their hands. While they worked, Benedetta peppered her with questions: where had she come from, what did she do? Maddalena answered her, then asked the same things in return.

'I'm studying Latin at Sapienza,' Benedetta replied. 'At least, I was. My father lost his job when he refused to join the fascists. So now I'm working as a secretary at the Vatican. I hope to return to my studies one day, but who knows when?'

From the casualties, it was clear the fight was turning in the Wehrmacht's favour. Retreating soldiers tore off their telltale uniforms and picked up spare clothes thrown into the street by locals. When the first shell whistled overhead, they all cried out and ran for cover, but even that became familiar; they grew inured, only flinching at the sound. Maddalena attached herself to a bespectacled medical student named Vincenzo Sciori; together they tended to the wounds of a soldier brought down by a flamethrower, the skin of his hands and forearms blackened, sloughing off in strips. His screams were so loud they were almost grateful when he fainted from the pain.

Rumours passed among the volunteers: the battle had been all but lost. Those that survived now focused only on retreating. The afternoon sun broke through the selenite windows, a milky light which shone on the stars of the painted ceiling, and the sunken horror of the dead. Maddalena tried her best to avoid them and kept her eyes turned towards the doors instead. The casualties came in waves; at times they felt like they were drowning, then some respite would arrive. They'd go outside to wash the blood from hands and faces in the fountain, to share a cigarette and wait for the next onslaught.

Physically and mentally exhausted, Maddalena pushed up the sleeves of the raincoat she still thought of as Carolina's. She'd kept it on despite the heat, convinced she mustn't soil her uniform. It meant the coat was ruined, stamped all over with her bloody handprints. At one point she found herself vibrating, head to toe. She wondered if they were caught up in an earthquake, only to realize it was shock coursing through her body.

Maddalena was looking after an elderly woman when she finally saw them stagger in: Luca stumbled through the door, bearing all Santino's weight, the mechanic grey-faced and slumped against him. She called out Luca's name and saw the shock of recognition – he couldn't comprehend how she came to be in this hell. Together they carried Santino to an empty space between the columns and eased him down, fresh blood streaming from a deep gash on his thigh.

'What happened?'

'German sniper.'

Trying to staunch the flow, she pressed a clean dressing on the wound.

'It's pretty bad,' she said. 'I'll go and get some help.'

Vincenzo Sciori did his best to patch Santino up. The mechanic bore it stoically, until his wound was splashed with yellow sulfa. Vincenzo took Maddalena to one side.

'It ought to heal, although he's lost a fair amount of blood. For now, get him somewhere safe and try to keep it clean.' He placed an extra sachet of the sulfa powder in her pocket. 'I volunteer at a clinic on the Tiber Island. If he needs more treatment, don't take him to a doctor – he'll likely be arrested. Bring him to see me there instead.'

She grasped his hand. 'I don't know how to thank you.'

'No need, you've more than shown your mettle.' He looked at his watch. 'You'd better go – the Germans are threatening to bomb if the streets aren't clear by half past four. Rome might be an open city, but they're in charge now.'

Panting with exertion, Luca and Maddalena half dragged the injured mechanic from the church. Though Velare was close by – a brisk five-minute walk under normal circumstances – Santino was a dead weight now, passing in and out of consciousness. Luca tried to take as much of the burden as he could, but it was heavy going, nonetheless.

'What time is it?' asked Maddalena.

'I've no idea, but let's try to go a little faster. Not much further now.'

The street was empty and ominously quiet. The gunfire had diminished, although the distant sirens carried on, petulant and wailing. Maddalena leant in to the climb, until her heel slipped in a pool of blood congealing on the cobbles. She stumbled and felt her leg give way. Crying out, she dropped hard onto one knee. Luca twisted round to reach for her.

'Are you okay?'

She registered the shock and felt herself begin to crumble, but knew they couldn't stay there, so exposed. Clenching her jaw she levered herself up.

'I think so.'

Her knee throbbed: a clean and shining pain. She pushed through, forcing one step, then another. They climbed together slowly, at an angle to the street.

'Wait,' said Luca. A new sound, distinct and growing louder – the drone of an aeroplane. Maddalena craned her neck, trying to see out from underneath Santino's frame. She searched the skies but saw nothing.

'There.' Luca pointed to the east as a lone plane came into sight from behind a bank of cloud. It made a slow approach towards the city. Maddalena felt her stomach lurch and feared she might be sick. As the hornet whine of the engine grew louder, she braced herself. For what – a bomb? Perhaps the pepper chase of a machine gun? Panic overtook her, running like a wildfire. The prospect of death or madness almost came as a relief. What if she just stopped? What if she lay down and let the terror come? Desperate for air, she lifted her head and saw the gates ahead. Velare. Home and sanctuary. They'd made it back, at last.

Almost sobbing, she reached into her raincoat pocket and was relieved to find the ring of keys still there. Luca took hold of the mechanic's bulk as she fumbled with the lock then pushed, the metal scraping on the ground. They stumbled through together; dragging the man, they set him down. Santino mumbled something incoherent as they propped him up against the wall. Maddalena limped back to close the gate, locking it behind her. The plane droned on even louder, now almost overhead, as Luca sank down on the verge. Elbows on his knees, he rubbed his hands across his face.

'We must keep going,' she urged. 'We won't be safe till we're inside.'

'We're not safe, even then.' He beckoned her towards him. 'Let me see your leg.' He held out his hand for balance, then touched her swollen knee, feeling round it gently. 'It doesn't look too bad.'

She winced as she put it back down and murmured, 'Nothing broken.'

Except that wasn't true; she saw it very clearly now. He'd kept hold of her hand, though she had both feet on the ground.

'What is it?' he asked. 'What's the matter?'

She realized she must look such a fool. What had she thought would happen – that he might marry her one day? She felt the last hope die in her. She checked on Santino, who seemed to have passed out from the pain.

'I don't think I can stay here, Luca.' She forced the words out before she lost her nerve. 'I can't live here, with you but without you. It hurts too much, you see.'

Confusion clouded his brow. He opened his mouth, then closed it again, searching for the words to refute her claim. When he finally spoke, there was shock in his voice, but also resignation.

'Where would you go?'

'Back to Sicily, once things have settled down.'

Her hands were shaking so much she balled them into fists and forced them deep into her pockets. Luca stared up at her in shock.

'That's so unjust. You shouldn't have to leave.'

'You needn't worry. I'm sure I can find work.'

'It's not that.' A brief flash of frustration. 'I mean it is, of course, but more than that. I can't imagine life without you.' His voice dried and he cleared his throat. 'What if something happened to you? You might die and I wouldn't know.' His eyes had filled with tears. 'You think I'm being overly dramatic.'

She shook her head. 'I don't, I know exactly what you mean. I checked each body they brought into the church today. Every single one. It was terrible, but in the end I just felt glad that none of them were you.' She hung her head. 'I've no right to feel that way, Luca. I need you, but I know they need you more.'

She held his gaze and, when she spoke again, her own voice surprised her with its steadiness. 'You know I'm right. I can see from your expression.'

After a time, he looked away and nodded his agreement.

She turned her face up to stop the tears from falling. The sky above was bright and clear. The aeroplane had gone.

CHAPTER TWENTY-THREE

LONDON, AUGUST 1997

After landing back in London late on Friday afternoon, they went their separate ways. Beatrice told Jude she'd call when she was ready. On Saturday morning he took the photograph they'd found in the safe deposit box to a reprographic store on Tottenham Court Road. He had copies and enlargements made and, though the images were blurred and grainy, he marvelled at the contrast between them and the painting in the Capitoline. St John's expression was similar but subtly different, and then there was the swarthy hand which squeezed his thigh. It made Jude desperate to see the rest.

He felt unsettled, as he always did in the dog days of summer. London seemed dusty after the shimmering heat of Rome. He missed the excitement of their adventure, missed Beatrice as well. He yearned for change. It came sooner than expected, in an unpredicted way.

Jude woke up late on Sunday and flicked on the radio beside his bed to listen to the news. He dozed, half in, half out of sleep, paying no attention to the sombre music, which played largely uninterrupted, until a bulletin came through. Breaking news – Diana, Princess of Wales, dead after a car crash in Paris, in the early hours of Sunday morning. Startled into waking, Jude got up and went into the kitchen. He turned on the portable TV and watched the news unfold. He kept it on in the background as he went about his day, switching to the radio downstairs while he surfed websites of all the major auction houses, planning out the week ahead. Jude sorted through his cheque book and paid his bills while listening to a statement from the prime minister, Tony Blair. He knew the moment was historic, but he had no idea the whole country would convulse around it.

Monday came and he watched as the national outpouring of grief continued unabated. By midweek, London's landmarks were buried under a rising tide of wilting flowers and public sorrow. Jude felt affronted by it, though he couldn't fathom why. Several days passed before he finally made the connection: the similarities between this famous stranger's death and his own mother's. Both women taken in a car crash, their young sons left behind.

On Saturday morning Jude woke with a pounding headache and no intention of watching the funeral. He planned to spend the day working online instead, and yet he found himself flicking on the TV in the kitchen as he made a cup of tea. He ducked his head back in while he brushed his teeth, glancing at the images of familiar London streets, now eerily silent, lined with people standing dozens deep. The only sound was the tolling of a tenor bell and the horses, the cold clank of the livery rebounding under cloudless skies.

Jude went back into the bathroom, then heard an altogether different noise, one which made the hair on his arms stand up. It drew him back into the kitchen. A woman cried out in a keening voice, which rose and seemed to travel through the throng. The wave of sound crested then flattened and rolled on, passing between strangers in the body of the crowd. The long lens of the television cameras lingered on the royal family as they walked behind the coffin. The princes and their painful stiff-legged gait. He found he couldn't bear to watch them.

In the cold vault of his memory, Jude stood as a boy, watching his own mother's coffin going by, hoisted on the backs of strangers whose job it was to carry grief. They had to; at thirteen, his narrow frame could not have borne the weight. The darkness of the chapel seemed to muffle sound as much as feeling, until a voice cried out behind. He couldn't place it, then or now. It came from far back – one of the Welsh aunties on his father's side, perhaps?

'Oh Rose ...' Silence, then the punctuation. 'Oh Rosie, your poor boy.'

For years those elongated vowels had stayed with him. The grip of grief had taken hold that day and never once let go. He'd lived with it and even grown around it as it fossilized; a foreign body or a parasitic twin.

Jude realized he was crying. He turned off the television and went back downstairs to his desk. He flicked on the modem and listened to the whoops and whistles of the dial-up.

He tried his hardest not to think about his mother. He knew he'd have to face it one day. This year, next year, sometime, never. Maybe. Not today.

When the landline rang at 8 a.m. on Monday, it dragged Beatrice from her sleep. Her mother had long refused to replace the rotary phone, which still sat on the half-moon table in the hall. In her teenage years, Beatrice used to drag it into her bedroom, pulling the umbilical cord to its full extent and risking her mother's fury when she inevitably tripped over it. Now, bleary-eyed, wearing an outsized T-shirt, she picked up the handset and held it to her ear.

'Signora Fremont? It's Gloria Ferro. We met in Rome, at the Montefalco residence? I have Signora Sophia here and she wishes to speak with you. Do you have a moment?'

Beatrice leaned back against the wall and slowly slid down. 'Sure. I guess.'

She pulled the T-shirt over her knees.

'*Grazie.* One moment.'

Silence, then Sophia Montefalco spoke in her strongly accented English. 'Hello, are you there?'

'This is Beatrice.'

'I apologize for calling so early, but my sister Costanza is out attending Mass.' There was a pause. 'May I call you Beatrice?' She pronounced it Be-ah-tri-chay, like Maddalena.

'If you like.'

'I have been praying on this, Beatrice. I worry I am being disloyal to my sister, but I feel I owe you an explanation. And an apology.'

'Really, there's no need.'

'I want to speak about my father. He was not perfect, but he was not the man my sister has described. When he left . . . it was difficult for everyone, but no doubt he had his reasons. My mother was a devout woman, devout and very complicated. Costanza takes after her; perhaps you understand.'

Beatrice understood her all too well.

'My sister lied,' continued Sophia. 'We know my father did not die in the war. Oh, we thought it at the time, but found the truth out later. It was a fiction for my mother's sake. It made it easier for her, I think. The shame and humiliation . . .' There was another lengthy pause. 'In fact, my father tried to make contact with us many times, when we were children, then again as adults. Costanza would not allow it. She insisted we ignore him. He came to Rome in person, but she refused to meet, even when our uncle acted as intermediary and begged us both to reconsider. At that time, I didn't dare defy her. I thought there would be other opportunities, that I might gradually persuade her, but then he died. I missed my last chance to get to know him, because of her.'

Beatrice thought about their final trip to Rome. 'Was that the summer of 1973?'

'That's right. June or July, I think. I don't remember.'

'I was there,' Beatrice said, remembering the carousel. 'I went with him on that trip.'

There was another pause. 'If that is so, then I regret it even more.' Sophia's voice was shaky. 'Had I known who you were, I would have restrained Costanza. She prizes honesty over kindness, she always has.' Sophia sighed. 'The war was an ordeal for us, for the whole country. So many died, so many families torn apart. Ours was not the only one destroyed.'

'I can't imagine.'

'But you can, more than most. We both lost our father at an early age – we have that much in common. I want to get to know you and I don't have time to waste. I am sixty-one now. Both my parents died quite young. Time is a precious commodity.' Then tentatively, 'I wonder if you might consider coming back to Rome?'

Beatrice decided to speak frankly. 'I'm not sure if I can deal with any further confrontation and I'll be honest, I really can't afford it. Jude lent me the money for that last trip, and it was only because I was trying to fulfil my mother's dying wish.'

'Maddalena is dead?'

'She passed away in late July.'

'I'm so sorry. I was very fond of your mother, despite everything.'

Beatrice could hear her sincerity.

'Mum asked me to do two things after she died – first, to scatter their ashes in the garden of Villa Velare. Second, to return a painting to its rightful owner. That's why we sought you out – we thought it might belong to you.'

'Costanza wasn't lying about that. There was no missing painting, at least as far as I'm aware. I don't remember when your mother left, I was quite young, but I do remember Papa going. I will never forget, he took nothing but a suitcase and the clothes which he stood up in. I can picture him going, even now.' There was a catch in her voice. 'I don't know where this painting came from, but I'm sure it wasn't from my home.'

Beatrice sighed. 'Then it must have come into his possession between that day and when they both arrived in London, but I have no way of finding out what happened to them next.'

'Oh, but I know where Papa went!' Sophia sounded excited. 'We had a home in South Tyrol, Castel Gedächt. We stayed there many summers when I was a girl, but after the war we never once went back. That was where Papa was going when he left Rome. I'm absolutely certain.'

CHAPTER TWENTY-FOUR

ROME, OCTOBER 1943

Having gathered the entire household together, Luca tried to project calm. 'I don't want to be alarmist, but there are reports of the Germans targeting large houses like Velare. We might escape their scrutiny, but it makes sense to plan ahead.'

Dolorosa and Balia Paola exchanged a fearful glance. Within days of the occupation rumours of marauding soldiers, of theft and looting had begun. It was hardly a surprise – the wealthy suburbs were full of temptation. Many of their Aventine neighbours had chosen to escape the city early on, to ride out the war at their country estates. Now their empty Roman homes were being requisitioned by the German high command and they were powerless to object. Having often questioned his own decision to stay put, Luca found this vindicating.

'The contessa and I decided it might be best to place our valuables in storage and we think you're entitled to do the

same. Small items which hold sentimental or financial value –
watches, gold, jewellery, even firearms – will be hidden, until
such a time as peace can be restored. Santino has begun bricking up a portion of the cellar for this purpose.'

Luca hadn't been convinced the injured man was fit enough
to work, but Santino had insisted, and Maria seemed relieved.
By all accounts, her husband did not make a good or patient
invalid. Besides, building a false wall in the cellar kept him
gainfuly employed. The German authorities started confis-
cating vehicles in the first days of the occupation, so Luca had
taken the hard decision to lock the cars away.

'We all hope the Allied forces will come to our aid soon,
but until then, it's up to us to protect our possessions, our
home and, most importantly, each other.'

Even as he said the words, they sounded hollow. Every
anxious face was turned to him, except for one: Maddalena
kept her eyes averted, avoiding his gaze, though she could not
escape his company. They'd been forced to make a choice. The
life they longed for was impossible. All Luca could do now
was dedicate himself to the people in his care.

To that end, Santino had started working in the cellar,
covering the entire end wall with deep shelves, which would
house the items they planned to hide. Luca had heard of people
burying such treasures, only then to lose them. This false wall
would create a relatively clean, dry space and anybody going
into the main cellar would be none the wiser. They lost access
to the coal chute, but as the Nazis had requisitioned so much
of the fuel supply, it was redundant anyway.

Violante had embraced the plan with gusto, much to Luca's

surprise. She packed up her furs, couture dresses and most of her jewellery, embracing a more spartan existence. Since the occupation she'd turned her back on the world entirely, spending hours of time at prayer. Any interest in managing the house had long since been relinquished to the Signora. Now Violante saw her role as one of constant vigilance, looking out for their immortal souls. Signora Bianchi had complete control of the coin purse, the keys and the staff, who all lived by her rules, however capricious they might be. The Signora was determined to keep order.

'You heard the conte – you have until tomorrow morning to decide what you wish to put away.' The pinch-faced woman clapped her hands together. 'Now then, back to work!'

Luca had already put away the few items he really valued: some small works of art and all his wartime photography, his watches and the rifle, which Santino had used during the battle. He'd hidden his father's pistol in the wood store, not wishing to leave the house entirely without defence.

Two weeks after the battle, Luca had returned to the streets of Testaccio and the Protestant graveyard, planning to memorialize the places where they'd fought. He'd taken his camera and walked round in a daze, looking at the bullet-riddled marble, the fading bloodstains on the road now little more than shadows. Hundreds of men, women and children died in those days after armistice. In the end, Luca kept his camera hidden and left without taking any pictures. Furious with their former allies, the German occupying forces seemed intent on extracting some revenge. Luca encouraged everyone to exercise great caution.

'If anyone in authority comes knocking, let them in. Remember: people over property. Be courteous and helpful, give them anything they want, be they German soldiers, Carabinieri or the fascists.'

Any mention of the blackshirts made Santino swear and spit. 'I thought we'd kicked those *stronzi* bastards out for good.'

But as Luca had long predicted, they'd not gone quietly. In fact, they hadn't gone at all. Mussolini had been rescued from captivity by Hitler, remaining loyal to his old friend. Now the country was operating under three different systems of governance – one in exile in the south (General Badoglio and the King), one sharing power in Rome (the Germans and the fascists) and one in Salò, in the north (Mussolini's puppet cabinet, dancing madly to Hitler's tune).

None of it mattered. No one was going anywhere, not least out of Rome. Maddalena's vow to return to Sicily had been stymied. Despite the agony they both endured, they remained together, yet apart. Locked down, closed in, all waiting for the cavalry, which never seemed to come.

After Luca's speech, Maddalena and Dolorosa returned to the kitchen in a sombre mood. The older woman sighed as she lifted down a heavy saucepan. 'We'd better get a move on, they'll all be in here soon, trailing up and down to the cellar and whining for their food. What can we make?'

Maddalena shrugged. 'No milk for ten days, no flour, salt, sugar or butter; no oil. All we've got is cabbage, so you tell me. I can't think with all that banging. Santino woke me up this morning, hammering underneath my floorboards. I can't wait for this wall to be finished.'

'He's worried Bianchi will give her fascist friends the nod, before he has everything away.'

'She wouldn't do that to the conte and contessa, surely?'

'You think she doesn't steal from them already?' Dolorosa scoffed. 'She's got free rein. No one's had eyes on those accounts in years. She's on the take, you mark my words.'

'Never mind her, what are we making?'

'Cabbage ribollita, yet again.'

Maddalena went to the pantry to fetch some onions and the cannellini beans. 'I might go back into the city later, try Via Condotti this time, in case they've had a new delivery.' In truth, she just needed to escape. 'Maybe I can buy us a bunch of dahlias, to cheer things up.'

'There was nothing on Via Condotti last week,' Dolorosa grumbled. 'Only armoured cars and German soldiers. So depressing, they're bricking all the windows up and plastering them over. It made the whole street feel uncanny, as if the shops had been erased.'

Maddalena shivered at the description. 'Like the false wall in cellar, makes my skin crawl.'

'Well, I'm all for it if it stops the bastards looting. Will you put anything inside?'

Maddalena shook her head. 'Best not, in case they let me leave and go back home.'

Dolorosa scowled; ever since Maddalena declared her intention to return to Sicily, the cook had been trying to dissuade her. 'You'd be mad to go back there! Give it a year or two and you'll be head cook at some big house on the hill. You'll be set for life, believe me. They'd have to carry me out of here, kicking and screaming, to make me go!'

Maddalena smiled but wouldn't be dissuaded. She couldn't tell Dolorosa the truth: that were it not for the crater in her heart, she'd never choose to go.

The sound of sudden footsteps and a rattling of keys made both women stiffen.

'Look lively,' whispered Dolorosa.

Signora Bianchi came into the kitchen with a letter, which she proffered to the cook.

'This arrived, addressed to your son.'

'I thought the mail had been suspended?'

'Not for official documents.'

Dolorosa took it and turned it over in her hands.

'Well go on, open it,' snapped Bianchi. 'Don't just gawp at it, woman.'

Dolorosa tore the envelope with her thumbnail and extracted a single sheet of paper. She read it, then slipped it into her pocket without comment.

'All well, I hope?' enquired the Signora.

'No cause for your concern,' Dolorosa sniffed.

The housekeeper glanced around the kitchen, eyes alighting on the pan. She sneered, 'Soup again?'

'Ribollita.' Dolorosa bristled. 'Unless you have some way of conjuring up ingredients we haven't got.'

'Given there are two of you, I hoped your meal plans might be more inventive,' the Signora replied. 'The triumph of hope over experience.'

Knowing her friend was in no mood to spar, Maddalena interrupted with forced cheerfulness. 'I plan to head out this afternoon, in case any shops have been restocked.'

'See that you do.' Seeing no further chance for sport, the Signora turned and left the room.

Maddalena waited until she was out of earshot. 'Is everything all right? What did the letter say?'

Dolorosa reached a shaking hand into her pocket. 'Tito's been called to colours, Maddalena. Told to report for duty in a month.'

'That can't be right; he's not even eighteen!' She couldn't comprehend Tito being sent to fight. He was Dolorosa's younger son, her last surviving boy. Not knowing how to comfort her, Maddalena simply put her arms out and held her while she rocked. 'I wish there was something I could do.'

Dolorosa laughed bitterly. 'Get him out of Rome?'

She wasn't joking, though. Not really. Conscripted boys ran off all the time. Everyone had heard about them, absconding to the country, hiding in barns or abandoned buildings. Some fugitives found sanctuary in safe houses or convents, becoming known as the *sepolti vivi* – the buried alive – named after a sect of cloistered nuns who bricked themselves up and severed all communication with the outside world. Others chose to live rough in the hills around the city, but with winter on the way, that couldn't possibly be a solution. Dolorosa knew her son would not survive.

'Tito's full of bravado, but he's still a little boy inside, frightened of the dark.'

Maddalena kept thinking of a story she'd heard about a

group of boys, conscripted and stationed at Cremona, a camp outside Milan. The boys hatched a plan to escape through a storm drain, which ran beneath the local cemetery. The Germans got wind of it, but didn't bother trying to stop them; they simply waited till the boys were in the tunnel, then bricked up both ends and buried them alive. There had to be a way to save Tito from that fate, something which might make him exempt.

'What if there was a medical reason he couldn't fight?' asked Maddalena. 'Some sort of dispensation. I met someone, a medical student – I could see if he might help.'

Dolorosa's eyes filled with tears. 'You'd do that for him?'

Maddalena took hold of her. 'For both of you. You're family to me. This is the least thing I can do.'

Maddalena walked over the Ponte Fabricio quickly, heading to the Tiber Island. The river was swollen from the recent rain and rushed through the city with urgent force. As she crossed the bridge, she glanced up at the high walls of the Fatebenefratelli Hospital, which looked almost impenetrable. She'd come in search of Vincenzo Sciori, the student doctor she'd met in Santa Sabina, while tending to the wounded. He'd told her he volunteered at a clinic, and she hoped the bond they briefly formed might be enough to persuade him to help Tito; anything to save the boy from the desperate fate of conscription.

The sun was high, but her time was short. She had to find Vincenzo, convince him to help, then get to the shops on Via Condotti before they closed, or risk inviting Signora Bianchi's scrutiny. Maddalena felt upbeat about the mission when she set off, but seeing the hospital up close up, her confidence began to wane. The building was vast and imposing, a rabbit warren of corridors, clinics and departments. All she had was Vincenzo Sciori's name. She trudged from room to room, only to be hushed by harried nurses and sent away.

Finally, a young typist took pity on her and checked through the hospital directory, finding Vincenzo's name listed in a clinic which treated infectious diseases. Maddalena followed her instructions, searching out signs for *Il Morbo di K*. Fearful of time passing, she ran up several flights of stairs until she came upon the ward, at last. Signs on the doors warned of contamination. She peered through the glass and saw row after row of iron beds, all occupied by patients. Too scared to venture in, Maddalena loitered just outside. After some time, she managed to catch the attention of a passing nurse in a starched apron and a mask.

'I'm looking for Dr Vincenzo Sciori who works in this clinic. My name is Maddalena Viscuso.'

'Is he expecting you?'

She shook her head. The woman sighed. 'Wait here.' She disappeared inside the ward, returning a short while after. 'Dr Sciori is on his rounds, but he'll be back in twenty minutes – can you wait?' Maddalena nodded.

Light danced on the vaulted ceiling of the corridor as she stared out of the window. The high walls of the Jewish ghetto lay on the far side of the river. Its streets were empty, no children playing, few signs of life of any sort. Shortly after the start of German occupation, the new Chief of the Secret Police and Security Services, had told the city's community of Jews they had to pay to keep their freedom. The price, a million lire and fifty kilograms of gold; an impossible request, had Pope Pius not agreed to fund the shortfall from the Vatican's reserves. Weeks passed, enough to convince some that Rome's 'civilizing forces' could stay the Germans' hand. Some said the Jews of Rome might escape the cruelties the Nazis meted out elsewhere. They were wrong.

In mid-October, troops descended in the small hours of the morning, sealing off the entire Jewish quarter. More than a thousand men, women and children were rounded up and taken to Trastevere, then loaded onto trains at the Tiburtina Station two days later, bound for who knew where. Rumours circulated about the fate which waited at the end of such a journey.

Like everybody else, Maddalena had heard about the raid, but she hadn't been to this part of the city since, hadn't seen it so close up. The neighbourhood had once been vibrant, bustling, chaotic. Now it looked just like a ghost town; perhaps it was.

'Signorina Viscuso?'

She turned to see Vincenzo Sciori.

'Oh, it's you! Sorry to keep you waiting, I didn't recognize your surname.' Maddalena felt a wave of relief. 'Tell me, how has your friend been doing? Perhaps not well, given that you're here . . .'

'He's doing so much better, thank you,' she said gratefully. 'But I wonder, might we go somewhere private? I need to ask for your advice.'

He took her to an austere little office, with one desk, two hard chairs and a view of the deserted ghetto. He nodded over to it. 'You heard what that SS bastard Kappler did to the Jews? The whole community, snatched up in one night. It's beyond all comprehension.'

'I hadn't seen it for myself.'

Outside, the sun was dipping in the sky. Maddalena hardly knew where to begin.

'I came to ask for help, Vincenzo. We're desperate. My friend's son has been called up to fight, but he's not even eighteen yet, hardly more than a child. He couldn't possibly survive.'

'Him and thousands of others.'

'My friend, his mother, lost her eldest to the war already. She couldn't cope if he died too.'

Vincenzo didn't look convinced.

'Please, I beg of you. Name your price – I'll do anything you need.'

He frowned, obviously reluctant. 'You think you could deliver something?' She nodded fervently. He pulled open the desk drawer and took out a small square cardboard box.

'Can you to take this to an apartment in the ghetto? Not far from here: behind the synagogue, on Via della Reginella. You'll find a woman there who runs a laundry. Give her this and tell her to be ready. We'll come for them tomorrow night.' He scribbled the address out on a piece of paper. 'Do that, then come back here the day after tomorrow and I might have something which could help your friend. I can't guarantee it will work – he's not the only boy trying to escape conscription.'

Maddalena clasped his hand in gratitude and tucked the box and piece of paper in her basket.

'What should I do if someone tries to stop me?'

'You'll think of something; you managed to persuade me after all.'

Heart racing, Maddalena dashed back over the bridge and was about to cross the road when she saw an armoured car approaching. She froze, then realized it made her look even more suspicious. Straightening her shoulders, she took a breath and carried on, head held high. She passed the synagogue without incident, entering the tangle of streets beyond. The buildings here seemed to press in on one another, as if you might stretch from one window and reach the other side.

She held tight to the piece of paper with the address, her thoughts too scattered to retain the information from one moment to the next. Finally arriving on the Via della Reginella, she found the apartment in a block set around a central atrium. The windows were strung with washing lines which drooped from the weight of dripping sheets. Maddalena climbed a single flight of steps and knocked on the door, the sound echoing round the stairwell. After a moment a woman's voice called out, 'Who's there?'

The door had a tiny spy hole, which Maddalena stared directly into, trying to look braver than she felt. 'My name is Maddalena Viscuso. Dr Sciori sent me from the hospital.' She checked over her shoulder, almost certain she'd been followed. No one was there. The door opened a little and Maddalena found herself scrutinized by three pairs of eyes:

a harried woman in her fifties with a red-faced infant on her hip, and a little boy, half-hidden behind her skirts. The woman frowned.

'What do you want?'

Maddalena felt flustered, she didn't *want* anything, so she simply held out the basket with the box in it. She couldn't think what more there was to say.

The woman gestured for her to come into the cramped and crowded hallway. Every inch of floorspace was taken up by baskets of folded linen and buckets full of nappies soaking, half submerged and reeking. Strung above it all, a row of shirts. Maddalena couldn't fathom how to move forward, until the woman swept them back with her forearm and revealed an open doorway to the kitchen. A huge pan boiled on the stove and filled the room with steam, a pungent mix of chemical and animal. From the ceiling hung a drying rack, suspended by ropes and pulleys and swathed in socks and underwear. The woman passed the baby to the little boy, though it was more than half his size, then took the box from Maddalena's basket and pried it open, pulling out a paper sachet covered in tightly printed text. She stared in bafflement, then waved it at Maddalena.

'What does it say?'

Maddalena took the sachet and saw the directions were written in English.

'I don't know the words, but it's sulfa powder. I've seen it used to treat open wounds, to sterilize.' An image came back to her from that day in Santa Sabina, yellow powder on blackened flesh. At the time, her traumatized mind thought it looked like seasoning for human meat. 'You sprinkle the contents of the packet on the wound – it stops infection. Place a clean dressing on it, then wrap a bandage round.'

The woman counted through the packets in the box, while the little boy and the rash-cheeked baby stared at her listlessly. Maddalena smiled at them, though neither one smiled back. The woman put the sachets in her apron pocket.

'When you see that doctor, tell him there are twelve of us. I've got the children down here, because they ...' She jerked her head towards the ceiling, 'couldn't keep them quiet.' She looked Maddalena up and down. 'How long have you been a *staffetta*?'

'What's that?'

'A messenger. Aren't you working with the partisans?''

Maddalena shook her head. 'I'm just here to give you the package and deliver a message.'

The woman sighed. 'Well, go on then.'

'Dr Sciori said to say. "We'll come for them tomorrow night. Tell them to be ready". Does that make sense?'

'It does. And not before time.' The woman folded her thick arms across her chest. 'It's been a bloody nightmare. You tell him I need more food for the little ones.'

To Maddalena, the baby seemed as plump as any other, but the boy's cheeks were sunken and his bare legs looked like kindling. 'I'll let him know.'

'Next time bring us something useful, eh? Sulfa's all well and good, but better something we can eat.'

As far as Maddalena was concerned there would be no next time, but she nodded. The woman showed her to the door.

Relieved to escape the damp and squalor, she sucked in clean fresh air as she dashed back down the steps.

Her errand now dispatched, Maddalena found her anxiety turned into elation, a thrill which sped her through the winding ghetto streets. The sun was starting to sink over the rooftops, and she dreaded the thought of being out too close to curfew. On Via Condotti, the few windows which had yet to be boarded up displayed little but shoe polish and wooden plates. She joined a long queue at the bakery, though everything was stale. Afterwards she joined another queue for meat. The butcher slapped a block of coagulated black jelly onto the paper.

'Only blood today.'

She put it in her basket, then hurried back along the river and up the hill. She finally entered the kitchen through the back door and looked up at the clock: home with ten minutes left to spare. She was amazed to see Tito peeling vegetables in her place at the table. Dolorosa rushed across the room and threw her arms around her.

'You saw your friend?'

Extracting herself from the woman's grasp, Maddalena laughed. 'I did. He's going to try to help us. I'll go back the day after tomorrow and we shall see.'

The cook kissed her on both cheeks, then scowled at her son. 'Tito, you pig, tell Maddalena thank you.'

The boy mumbled his gratitude then sighed. 'You're going to hold this over me forever.'

Maddalena grinned. 'Oh, I can absolutely guarantee it. Now you have to show me some respect!'

As she tied the apron round her waist, she found she was still smiling. Little had changed, but doing something seemed like progress; felt like moving on.

Two days later, she returned to the island. It was late in the afternoon and a gathering of starlings circled overhead, their mass expanding and contracting, a thousand feathered forms with just one thought. She found Vincenzo working in his office.

'You went to the address I gave you?'

'I did. I gave her the sulfa packages, explaining how to use them and passed your message on. She said to tell you she had twelve and that she's taken the children in with her. They urgently need food – She was very clear I had to tell you.'

'I'm sure she was. It's difficult.'

'She meant twelve people in hiding, yes? Twelve Jews.'

Vincenzo paused, then nodded. 'The less you know, the less anyone can make you tell them. Remember that.'

'But you came for them? That was your message.' Maddalena felt an intense need to know the fugitives were safe.

'For the adults; for a few. We had some beds here, but not enough just now.'

Maddalena hesitated but felt compelled to ask. 'Aren't you worried they'll be discovered?'

Vincenzo smirked. 'Most of our German friends are very much afraid of infectious disease. We happen to have discovered a new one here – we call it Syndrome K, terribly contagious. So much so they don't dare come near or check too closely on the patients, which is very useful.'

He opened the desk drawer and took out an envelope. 'I hope this will help your friend – it's proof he's being treated for epilepsy, which ought to make him unfit for military service, although I make no guarantee. The authorities are not minded to be merciful.'

She took the envelope and shook his hand with gratitude.

'Thank you, Vincenzo. If there is ever anything I can do . . .'

He laughed. 'Be careful what you promise. I might just take you up on that.'

CHAPTER TWENTY-FIVE

Vatican City, November 1943

Early one morning in November, Roberto came to visit Luca at his office. The occupation meant there was intense pressure on the Photographic Cabinet to create a permanent record of the archives and Luca was working longer hours than ever before. Roberto rarely ventured outside the city walls and had come to rely on his younger brother to be his conduit to the outside world.

'I hope I'm not disturbing you?'

'Not at all,' said Luca, looking up from his desk.

Roberto hovered in the doorway. 'May I ask what you're working on?'

'Just going back through photographs of the Basilica di San Lorenzo Fuori le Mura, which was all but destroyed in that first bombing raid in August.'

Luca would bear the imprint of that day forever – the

falling bombs, the smoke, his mad dash through the city to find Maddalena.

'Plans are being made to start work on the restoration; I was looking at some of the details on the columns in the portico. I'm glad we have these records, or a great deal more might have been lost.'

'You're doing the Lord's work, brother,' said Roberto.

Luca considered denying it but thought better. 'Why don't you come in and warm up?'

They both sat down beside an electric heater. Roberto took time to settle his many layers of vestments, before enquiring, 'Has your work been much affected by last week's bombing raid?'

Though relatively little damage had been sustained, Vatican City had found itself the target of an aerial bombing for the first time.

'Not badly, but I was concerned for you. It was a great relief to learn that you were safe.'

Roberto brushed his concern away. 'It could have been much worse, though with all that glass blown in, the basilica has been absolutely freezing ever since. Shocking all the same. There are rumours it was the fascists, rather than the Allies or the Wehrmacht.'

Luca nodded. 'So I heard.'

'The suspicion is they were targeting the radio station. A desire to silence outside voices, although they singularly failed.' Roberto stopped at the sound of footsteps and a muffled conversation in the hall outside the door. He waited, readjusting the skirt of his robes, until the voices passed away. 'Where were we?'

'Talking about the bombing. Although I sense you might have more to share than idle gossip?'

The city was supposed to be a neutral state, but spies and double agents still existed in the precinct, factions within and between different countries and their diplomats. They sought many things: influence, control or simply information, a very powerful commodity. The bonds of brotherhood made such concerns unnecessary, but Luca and Roberto were never less than cautious. Lowering his voice, the priest leaned in to speak. 'You've heard the rumour, that the Germans plan to kidnap the Holy Father and ransack our museums?'

'They've been saying so for years, but surely even Hitler wouldn't dare risk it. That's tantamount to an attack on every Catholic in the world.'

Roberto pursed his lips. 'I thought so, until we intercepted a broadcast which seemed rather more specific. Coming in conjunction with the bombing, there is a feeling that we need to take this threat seriously.'

Luca was surprised by his brother's candour; he wasn't often privy to the internal workings of the Holy See. 'Capturing Pius would give them a powerful bargaining tool, I suppose.'

'It would indeed,' agreed Roberto. 'But I leave the Holy Father's safety to the experts. My main concern is how I preserve my own collection.'

'I thought we'd seen to that in the summer?'

At Roberto's behest, Luca had transported a number of wooden crates to their family retreat in the Dolomite Mountains, long before the occupation. They remained there still, secured in the salt caves underneath the castle. Luca knew he wasn't the only Roman charged with hiding treasures on behalf of the Vatican; the crates he'd transported were likely matched a dozen times over, in cellars and attics across the country. It was an open secret, though only a handful of senior clerics knew of the precise locations.

'We made a decent start,' agreed Roberto. 'Although some items were simply too large or heavy to be moved. Or too sensitive, quite frankly.' He leaned down to warm his hands by the thin bars of the fire. 'There are some items which, both literally and figuratively, have never seen the light of day.'

Luca knew the Vatican's Biblioteca held artefacts which required delicate handling and preservation, but he hadn't realized any of them fell under his brother's jurisdiction.

'I wonder . . . what do you know about the concept of *damnatio memoriae*?' Roberto asked, steepling his fingers.

Luca frowned; the 'condemnation of memory' was a term he was familiar with from ancient history. He had a vague recollection of certain leaders from the Imperial and Republican periods, who fell from grace and found themselves erased from history.

'I've come across a few classical busts which were violently defaced: Caligula, Nero and the like. Problematic emperors and controversial figures, all thousands of years old.'

Roberto observed him thoughtfully. 'You weren't aware then, that the practice still continues? The expression of it has changed a great deal over time, though the principle remains the same: someone or something fallen so far from favour it must be expunged. For instance, during the Renaissance and Baroque, it was not uncommon for transgressive work to have the artist's signature removed. Some were destroyed altogether.'

'Seems rather draconian,' said Luca flatly.

Roberto nodded. 'Censorship so often is. There are cases where it might be justified, but some think even immoral work can be blessed with some divinity. I count myself among them. We touched on this a year ago, in the Gallery of Maps, do you remember? I was obtuse back then, by necessity, although you helped me without question. Now I feel I owe you a more detailed explanation.' He squared his shoulders and sat up in the chair. 'I have the stewardship of an especially sensitive collection, artefacts the Vatican decided to conceal some few centuries ago, deemed so dangerously subversive, they needed to be kept hidden. I call them the *Damnatio Memoriae*, for want of a better title. As to the form they take, I cannot be too specific. I hope you understand.'

Luca was intrigued to learn such a collection existed, but not surprised. He'd observed the secret inner workings of the Vatican for many years.

'Forgive me for asking, Roberto, but why are you telling me all this now?'

'Because if the larcenous Nazis were to get hold of them, it would be a disaster. It's my duty to ensure that doesn't happen. You were kind enough to store some of the smaller items for me, but other works cannot easily be moved – their size or scale prohibits it. There is one such piece – rare and very precious. I discounted it at first – too cumbersome and too conspicuous, but now I wonder if there might not be a way . . .' Roberto reached out and placed his hand over his brother's. 'My dear Luca, would you be willing to undertake another journey on my behalf?'

'Where to?

'Castel Gedächt, of course. Where else?'

Luca frowned. 'But everything north of Salò is in the German Operational Zone now, under the rule of Mussolini's puppet government. I understand you might want to conceal whatever this is from the Nazis, but there must be better places than in the lion's den itself!'

'But Gedächt belongs to us, brother, and you are the only person I can trust.'

'What about roadblocks and checkpoints? What about fuel?'

Roberto cut off his protestations. 'Anybody travelling under the flag of the Vatican is guaranteed safe passage. Our vehicles journey through the Brenner Pass most days!'

Luca couldn't help but laugh at his brother's misplaced confidence. 'The Vatican's supposed neutrality didn't stop it being bombed, Roberto. You want me to undertake a reckless journey into enemy territory, while the country fights a war on several fronts, all for the sake of an inanimate object?'

'I wouldn't ask if it wasn't so important. I cannot go myself, but you can travel with impunity,' Roberto entreated him. 'This is my privilege and my burden, Luca, my life's work. I vowed to preserve it, come what may. You once asked me if the life you were leading was all there was. You wanted greater purpose? Here it is.'

Luca felt the pull of who he'd been back then. But that was before Maddalena. Before the battle and the occupation. He'd changed, had glimpsed another life, before the door slammed shut. He didn't have the strength to open it again.

'I'm honoured you would ask me, but it isn't possible, I'm

afraid. I have a duty, as a husband and a father. My life is not my own.'

Roberto sighed. 'I understand.' He looked saddened but resigned. 'You'll let me know if you change your mind?'

'I will, of course,' Luca promised, though he knew it wouldn't happen.

Roberto gave him a thin smile then gathered himself up. 'I'll leave you to your work.' He turned back at the door. 'I sometimes think by answering my calling, I sealed your fate as well as mine. That was never my intention. It weighs on me, more than you can know. You sacrificed so much for me, little brother. Perhaps one day I can return the favour.'

Mid-November brought the cold, but very little fuel. The Germans liked their requisitioned villas to be luxuriantly warm and so kept the bulk of the supplies which made it through the Brenner Pass. In Velare, the fires in the children's nursery and the Signora's sitting room got most of what they had. The rest of the villa made do with seasoned wood, but it was often cold enough to see your breath. Even the kitchen was chilly, although the need to cook necessitated some little warmth, at least.

Coal was not the only scarcity in Rome. They hadn't had a soap ration since the start of October, which made Maria's work in the washroom all but impossible. She persuaded Maddalena and Dolorosa they should try to make their own. They somehow scraped together the ingredients: fat, caustic soda, resin, alum, talcum powder, even perfumed oils. Eventually they made something which at least approximated soap and shared it out among the other members of the household, with some left over.

'We could sell this and buy so much,' said Dolorosa. 'Salt, sugar, matches – just imagine!' But Maddalena had a different plan in mind.

'Could we give it to the laundry woman in the ghetto?' She'd told Dolorosa about her mission in service of Tito's letter of exemption. Not all parts of it – she'd kept the existence of the people hidden in the attic and Syndrome K to herself. 'A little soap would make a difference; she's washing everything in ash.'

'Of course,' Dolorosa readily agreed. 'I owe her, for helping you to help my boy!'

The following Sunday, both women made a large batch of ribollita and found such clothes and blankets as they could spare. Tito and Maria helped them carry it all downhill and past the synagogue. They knocked and this time were gratefully received. In helping the woman, each felt their own fortune more acutely.

Tito's eighteenth birthday came, with somewhat muted celebrations; the time arrived for him to present himself for service. Though they were nervous, Vincenzo's letter gave them hope. Dolorosa and Tito rose early the next day and Maddalena waved them off. For the rest of the morning she was easily distracted, imagining mother and son's progress across the city to the barracks. She hoped they wouldn't be kept waiting long; with any luck they'd make it home again by dark. She was astonished when she heard the back door open shortly after three o'clock. Dolorosa's face was a mask of anguish.

'They refused the letter.'

She looked as if she'd aged a decade in a day: hair dishevelled, her jowls drooping and a web of veins beneath her panicked eyes.

'The sergeant just handed him a ticket and put him on a truck to the station with a load of other boys. I tried pleading, but they wouldn't listen. Before I knew it, he was gone.' She gulped for air. 'They didn't even let me say goodbye.'

Maddalena took her hand. 'Which camp did they send him to?'

Dolorosa threw her hands up in despair. 'I've no idea, they wouldn't tell me.' Her lower lip began to tremble. 'He doesn't even have a change of clothes – I didn't think he'd need them. What kind of mother am I?' She grabbed a clump of her own hair and wrenched at it. 'They've taken him! My boy, Maddalena,' she sobbed. 'My only living boy!'

CHAPTER TWENTY-SIX

It was just before 5 a.m. when a noise woke Maddalena. She lurched up onto her elbow and whispered 'Luca?' But there was no one there, just the empty silence of pre-dawn. She shivered and her empty stomach rumbled – perhaps that was what woke her? It wouldn't be the first time. She'd been dreaming of focaccia, the texture of it pressed between teeth and tongue. Though she longed to turn over and nestle back down under the eiderdowns and blankets, it was almost time to rise. The oblivion of sleep was lost; no point languishing when there was so much to get done. Oh, but it was hard to leave her bed. It was so cold in her little room above the cellar, going to bed sometimes felt more like hibernation.

Maddalena swung her bare feet to the floor and lit a stub of candle in a jar. In the dim glow, she pulled on a pair of thick socks and her gown, then threw a heavy woollen blanket round her shoulders. She went into the kitchen and turned on the light. Her first job was to get the stove going. The firebox worked best with coal, but there was almost none of that, so they used seasoned wood instead, making each part of the process more laborious – the foraging and fetching, sweeping and disposing of the ash. The wood basket in the kitchen had just enough to get her started, but she'd have to go down to the cellar soon, to refill it for the day. When the bright flames flickered into life, she snuffed the candle out. The clock above the back door said it was just after five o'clock. Almost time to rouse Dolorosa, though that seemed cruel, given her current state. Three days had passed since Tito was sent off to camp and his mother had barely slept. Maddalena decided to let her rest a little longer.

She opened the back door and went out into the courtyard to fill the *concha* from the fountain. It was dark and the villa was veiled in a heavy mist. The cold had a bitter edge so early in the morning, but she thought the fog might burn off later. Maddalena carried the full jug back into the kitchen, shooing the cats which prowled around her feet. The room was warming up; she shrugged the blanket off her shoulders and hung it on a chair, before checking on the fire. It was burning well, but faster than expected, so she scooped up the empty log basket and headed to the cellar. She opened the door, switched on the bare electric bulb and discovered Tito sitting on the stairs, looking up at her. Maddalena gasped and crossed herself, offering a hurried prayer. Tito hushed her with a frightened whisper.

'Be quiet, you might wake someone!

Maddalena hissed back, 'Holy mother, Tito! You scared the life out of me! What in God's name are you doing here?'

'I couldn't stay there; I had to run away.' His cheeks were dirty and streaked with tears. 'They were going to send me off to Germany to fight! Please help me, Maddalena.'

Maddalena sat down on the cold step next to him.

'What on earth were you thinking, coming back here?'

'I had to come home, I had nowhere else to go.' He looked mournful. 'I won't die fighting for those bastards.'

'What's your plan then, to just sit here? Because it only took me a minute to discover you and your mother's in and out of here all day!' Maddalena felt an urge to shake the boy. 'You know they'll kill you if they find you?' Tito didn't answer, but looked like he might cry. She hadn't the heart to stay angry. 'Are you sure you can't go back?' He shook his head. Maddalena sighed. 'Then we'll have to find you somewhere better to hide while we work out what to do.'

It sounded simple enough, but the prospect terrified her. The risk involved seemed unimaginable, and yet there were *sepolti vivi* everywhere, their numbers growing day by day. There were people in hiding throughout the city – across the entire country, for pity's sake. Instead of surrendering to their fate, many of the men and boys being forced to work in German labour camps or conscripted to their army chose to conceal themselves instead. Maddalena thought about Vincenzo Sciori and his fake contagion, Syndrome K – an entire ward of fugitives, hidden in plain sight. Perhaps he might he be persuaded to take Tito in as well? It had to be worth a try.

From far above them came the sound of a creaking floorboard and a flushing toilet, which made Maddalena jump to her feet.

'Dear God, what time is it?'

She opened the cellar door and looked out: almost 5.30 a.m., which meant Balia Paola would rise soon to start getting the girls ready for school. In an hour they would be down here, wanting breakfast. Time was running out.

'Perhaps we ought to wake your mother up and tell her.'

Tito's response was emphatic. 'Don't be daft. She'd fall to pieces the moment she was questioned. She couldn't hide something like this if her life depended on it, which it might.'

He was right: Dolorosa was bullish but a bad liar and a worse actress. She'd soon be exposed if the Carabinieri came knocking, as they most surely would.

'You can't stay here, though. Somebody will find you.' She looked around the cellar in despair – there seemed like nowhere to conceal him, until an idea came to mind.

'Come with me.' She took his hand and led him out into the kitchen. The house was pin-drop quiet, but it wouldn't stay that way for long. Maddalena thought they had half an hour at most.

'Where are you taking me?' asked Tito.

'To the coal chute.'

When Santino bricked up part of the cellar, he'd enclosed the chute as well. There'd been no other way to configure the space, and it was basically redundant. The access hatch was outside in the courtyard, against the kitchen wall. The coal-chute dropped into the walled off section of the cellar at a steep diagonal. She knew it would be tight and dark and dirty, but it was dry and entirely hidden. Tito went very quiet and pale.

'I don't think I can do that.'

'Well, we haven't got much choice.'

She grabbed the heavy blanket from the kitchen chair, along with the candle stub and a box of precious matches from the stove.

'Come on.'

She opened the back door and peered out. Nothing moved, not even the slinking feral cats. Maddalena checked the clock: it was already 5.40 a.m..

'Come on, it's now or never. I'm not joking.'

Rigid, he began to move.

'Stay completely quiet,' she whispered. 'We can't risk someone coming to the window.'

They stepped out into the dark courtyard together and she shut the door behind them. The sun would rise soon enough, but for now, the only light came from the setting moon. It cast a blue sheen on the cobbles and the cover of the coal chute: rectangular pressed metal, with a handle on its outside edge. In the days when quantities of coal were still delivered, the men would bring the fuel round in a barrow, lift the hatch and simply tip it down. Maddalena passed Tito the blanket, then grabbed the handle; although it hadn't been used in months, it opened easily enough. They crouched down together and peered in. The shaft disappeared into the dark cellar below: she only hoped it would be wide enough for Tito to fit through.

'Drop the blanket down first, so you have something soft to land on.' She tried to sound encouraging, even as Tito stared into the darkness of the void.

'I can't go down there,' he muttered, turning to face her: 'What if I get stuck?'

'No one made you run away, you idiot. That was your decision.' His panic was beginning to infect her. 'You ask for help? Well, here we are.'

From somewhere high above them came a noise. They both sprang up and pressed their backs against the wall. The shutter on the window next to the nursery creaked open – Balia Paola was awake. Maddalena put a finger to her lips, and they waited. After what seemed like an eternity, the shutter closed again. Maddalena peered upwards. The house was dark and quiet. At least the blackout and the mists were working in their favour.

'She was probably checking on the weather.'

Even in the chill morning air, Tito was sweating. He stared down at the gaping maw of the coal chute, seemingly paralyzed by fear. Maddalena wanted to comfort him, but there was no time – he needed to be galvanized and if he hated her, then so be it.

'Come on now, pull yourself together. You're eighteen. Time to be a man.'

His derisive snort turned into a sob of fear. She pressed him harder.

'You realize they'll shoot you for desertion if they find you? Me too – for aiding and abetting.' She snatched the blanket from him and started shoving it into the open shaft. 'Now get on your knees, or I swear I'll push you in myself.'

Obedient at last, Tito sank onto the ground.

'That's better. Slide your legs in then turn over on your belly, so you can wriggle down and then let go.'

She guessed the drop was a couple of metres but kept that thought to herself. Tito put one leg in, then the other, before turning over and wincing as he forced his broad hips and buttocks through the gap. More than half his body was now inside the shaft. He wriggled further, bracing himself with his elbows on the cobbles. He seemed to be making good progress, until it came time to tuck his arms in. The girth of his shoulders, and the awkward angle of his limbs made him stiffen up.

'I can't move.'

There was rising panic in his voice. His whole body suddenly convulsed, once, twice. As long as he stayed locked in that position, he wouldn't budge. He needed to relax and let his own weight pull him through. Tito started crying, trying to lever himself out, though he didn't have the strength. His lungs filled with rapid, hitching breaths, which only served to wedge him further still.

'I can't move.' Fear made his voice unconscionably loud. 'Help me, Maddalena!'

She slapped her palm across his mouth and pressed it tight, looking up in terror at the windows, expecting them to open, one by one. Now she was crying too; she whispered, 'I'm so sorry.' The windows all stayed shut. Eventually, Maddalena took her hand away and stroked his hair until the hitching spasms passed. Tito slowly came back to his senses, the tension dropping from his shoulders, allowing his reach to lengthen.

'Keep going, you're nearly there.'

The tips of his fingers turned white as they gripped the edge, his legs dangling in the void until he suddenly let go. There was a heavy thump as he landed.

'Are you okay?'

Empty air and blackness until he finally replied. 'I think I might have hurt my ankle.'

Maddalena slumped to the ground, exhausted.

'There's hardly any space down here,' Tito whined. 'Just shelves of people's stupid things.'

Santino had built sturdy ledges, which ran the full length of the wall. 'Wait . . . I think I can climb them, like a ladder.'

'Are you sure they'll bear your weight?'

'We'll soon find out.'

She heard him grunting with exertion, then saw a hand extending towards her from the dark.

'Wait a moment . . .' With shaking fingers, she lit the stubby candle in the jar and leaned deep into the chute, stretching her arm out as far as she could reach. Tito finally caught hold of it, then began to climb back down. Maddalena looked up; though the house was still dark, the sky had begun to lighten.

'I have to go now,' she whispered.

'I'm hungry, Maddalena.' His voice was wretched.

'I'll bring you something when I can, but that might not be till later.'

'The candle won't last long.'

'Then only use it when you need to.'

She threw the box of matches down.

'Make some space under the shelves and try to sleep. I'll come and see you when it's safe.'

She looked away then. She couldn't bear to watch as she shut the hatch and closed him in.

When she walked back into the warm, dry kitchen it was almost six o'clock. She washed her hands, relit the stove, then stood in total silence. There were no noises from the cellar, only her own frightened, racing heart. She took a deep breath in and started along the corridor. The time had come to wake his mother and feed her friend a pack of lies.

That afternoon an officer from the Carabinieri pulled up to the villa in an armoured car. Luca met him at the door, to be informed that Tito, along with several other boys, had failed to report for duty and were now wanted for desertion.

'Seen any sign of him?' the officer asked.

'Not a hair. His mother's downstairs now and she's utterly distraught.'

The officer sniffed. 'You sure?'

'I'm absolutely certain. The poor woman is beside herself with worry.' Luca frowned, 'I can't believe he'd run away – he's always been a diligent young man. I'm sure he'll turn up soon.'

'Better hope so. If he doesn't, they'll stop the ration cards for your whole house and take his mother in his place.'

Luca bit back the retort he longed to give, knowing it would only make the situation worse. 'Well, if he turns up here, I'll be sure to let you know.'

When the officer had gone, Luca went down into the kitchen. Dolorosa was at the kitchen table, red-eyed, a hand-kerchief twisted tightly round her fingers. Maddalena stood behind.

'Did you hear all that?'

The younger woman nodded. He looked at Dolorosa. 'And you've had no word from him at all?' She shook her head decidedly. 'If he comes here or gets in touch, you must tell me right away. I'll take him back myself and try to persuade them to be lenient.'

'You think they would be?' Maddalena asked. It was the first time she'd spoken to him directly in many days.

Luca shrugged. 'He can't possibly hope to outrun them. If he has absconded, I only hope he has the sense to stay away.'

CHAPTER TWENTY-SEVEN

LONDON, SEPTEMBER 1997

Looking for clues, Beatrice sat on the floor surrounded by boxes and bin bags. She was upstairs in what used to be her father's office, though it had become a dumping ground for anything unwanted – a product of her mother's fear of throwing things away. The scale of the task was daunting; Beatrice had spent the morning sifting through reams of paperwork and had barely scratched the surface.

Outside it was raining heavily. Water poured off the skylight in sheets as an endless stream of traffic swept by on the road below. There was an ominous, rust-coloured stain on the wall which expanded every time it rained. Beatrice did her best to ignore it; another threat to the house she loved and feared she would soon be forced to sell.

In their younger days, her parents had each had their own domain: the basement belonging to her mother, while her father had this bright and airy space. She used to call it the sky room when she was little; built in an optimistic moment at the turn of the nineteenth century, these houses were designed for artists. She supposed the light was what had drawn her parents to it in the first place. It was certainly why she loved it and was so desperate to stay.

As a teenager, Beatrice often felt embarrassed when her school friends came over. She wished she could wipe out all traces of Italian and have a 'normal' English home. Proper mothers made chips and beans and Findus crispy pancakes; put Frazzles in their children's lunch box, not zucchini fritti, and treated Viennetta as a luxury, instead of an object of scorn. But oh, what she wouldn't give for a plate of her mother's cooking in this moment.

After Luca died, Maddalena found it difficult to let go. Everything got filed away, though none of it was needed. So much flotsam, weighing mother and now daughter down. None of it offered Beatrice any insight into her parents' life in Rome, or beyond it. She only knew they'd arrived in Britain after Rome's occupation and before victory in Europe was declared – somewhere between 1943 and 1945. Beyond that, she had nothing and the deepest strata she had found only went as far back as 1949, the year they bought the house on Talgarth Road.

In less than twenty-four hours, Beatrice was due to return to Rome, to meet with Sophia. They'd agreed to spend some time together over a long weekend, to 'get to know' one another. Although Costanza wanted no part of the arrangement, Sophia had generously offered to pay for her flight and board. Beatrice booked a room at the same pensione where she and Jude had stayed, relieved to have somewhere familiar to escape to.

She'd phoned Jude to share the news, and he seemed excited for her. He was hard at work, preparing a preview of her father's collection at the gallery to raise interest before the auction. Despite her outburst on the Spanish Steps, they both felt the pull of the painting, but with no new leads, there seemed nowhere left to go.

'I've started going through my parents' papers, but there's nothing so far,' Beatrice complained

'Maybe something will come up in Rome, a new direction.'

'Maybe, though as far as I can see, they left Rome with nothing and started here the same. God only knows how they acquired a Caravaggio along the way. I'll just keep looking.'

For now, though, she'd had enough. She stood and stretched and looked up at the London sky. Beatrice loved the bones of this building, and knew already it would break her heart to leave. She walked slowly down the two flights of stairs to the kitchen, then put the kettle on to boil. Perhaps she ought to make herself some lunch, something complex enough to occupy her hands and quiet her overactive brain. She browsed the recipe books on the shelf, many of which she'd bought herself as gifts, before realizing that although her mother loved to cook, she had little interest in other people's methods. Maddalena was a work in progress, always competing against herself. She kept kitchen diaries like a scientist might keep notes on their observations – refining and improving day by day. If these ledgers amounted to a cooking bible, Beatrice's favourite was the equivalent of the Old Testament: stuffed with pamphlets from the 1950s and 60s and instructions for kitchen aides her mother bought and then discarded. Beatrice turned to it when a memory of food from childhood floated up. With instructions involving innards, eels and catfish, it had long been an object of ghoulish fascination.

Now Beatrice took it down from the shelf and flipped it open at a recipe for a chocolate bombe, which her mother had made for her thirteenth birthday. Long before that, there were notes on the purees Maddalena made when Beatrice was weaning: carefully recording the results: apparently, baby Bea adored pea and even sweet potato but could not abide the *carciofi*. That made her smile – only her mother would feed a baby pureed artichoke.

Standing at the kitchen table, Beatrice found herself reading the book in reverse: past 1960s dinner parties made with too much gelatine and pâté and detailed notes about what Luca did or didn't like. It was touching to see the efforts she went to for him – corrections to her methodology and personal observations which gave a window into their early married life. She skimmed through the 1950s, the frugal meals for two and cuttings encouraging a housewife to 'make her pennies stretch'. Then came the late 1940s, conversion sheets from metric to imperial and shopping lists, along with scribbled protests at the lack of good ingredients. These were familiar to Beatrice already. Maddalena often complained that, for years, the only place to buy olive oil was from Boots the Chemist.

The book went back further still. Suddenly impatient,

Beatrice flipped it open to the front. These early recipes were all in Italian, her mother's writing scratchy; less assured. Very few were dated, but they seemed to be from the early 1940s. Maddalena had made shopping lists for different markets, the names of which made Beatrice realize they were in Rome. Excited now, she sat down and worked through the recipes, one by one. They seemed standard, just a list of ingredients and Maddalena's method, but a few gave hints of her interior – a note about missing home, or a list of things to send back to her mother. Beatrice was touched to find these as her Sicilian nonna died long before she was born.

One or two of them were given titles – A Recipe from a Roman Kitchen for Sugarless Gelato, A Recipe from a Roman Kitchen for Snails. Beatrice realized she'd reached the war years when she came across a ration card from 1941. Elsewhere, a long list of items which were no longer available, and possible alternatives. Pressed between the pages, there was a little hand-drawn map of Rome and a diagram of what was growing in the garden, and when it might be harvested. Instructions on how to make soap, how to press walnut oil, how to grind oats into flour and milk. She even came across a dried red rose, the petals so dark they were nearly black, delicately wrapped in tissue paper. Beatrice reached a section where a dozen pages had been torn out, before a recipe for bread which could be shaped into loaves or little rolls. It looked incredibly complex – hours of proving to get just the right consistency. It was entitled: A Recipe for Rosette di Pane from a Dolomite Kitchen, January 1944.

*

A dial tone, then a beep. 'You have reached the Adler Gallery, I'm sorry I can't take your call. Please leave a message.'

'Jude? It's Beatrice. I think I might have found something ... You know how Sophia said my father had gone somewhere, after he left Rome? Well, I think my mother went there too. There's a recipe she wrote which certainly seems to fit the time frame. You're so good on the internet, would you mind looking into it while I'm away and see what you can find? It's called Castle Gedacht G, E, D, A, C, H, T, and it's in foothills of the Dolomite Mountains, close to the Austrian border. I'll be back in London early next week, but if you need me, I'll be staying at our pensione in Rome. Speak soon.'

Jude turned his hire car off the *autostrada* and began the long climb into the hills. His eyes were scratchy from lack of sleep – an early flight into Verona meant he was up long before dawn. He hadn't slept well the night before, questioning his decision to set off on this journey alone, without Beatrice's knowledge.

He'd picked up her answerphone message and gone straight to his computer, struggling with the search terms until he realized the language was misleading; he needed to be looking for Castel Gedächt, not the English spelling of castle. That helped, though there was still precious little to be found online. Finally, he came across a photograph which took ten minutes to download, the lines of pixels appearing slowly, like thread pulled across a loom. It revealed a fortified building, perched in the South Tyrolean mountains: an oval keep with three towers at the top of steep stone walls. Beyond that, the internet wasn't useful – just one tourist website which mentioned the castle was open to visitors, though it had no webpage of its own. He'd almost given up entirely when he came across mention of it on an auction site, a notable sale of early twentieth-century paintings from the castle's private collection, which had raised tens of thousands, five years before. It was not proof, but it was a connection; he felt the familiar, slightly sickening rush of his seeker's instincts kicking in. By then, Beatrice was already on her way to Rome. He rolled the dice and booked an early flight for Verona the following day. Though he still felt some trepidation, he'd learned his lesson – this time he was going in with eyes wide open.

After a wearying two-hour drive from the airport, Jude checked himself into an anonymous hotel on the outskirts of the nearest town. It was gearing down from summer and felt empty and abandoned, so he decided to head to the castle right away. He wound the hire car up the narrow mountain road; steep, serpentine bends, which turned and doubled back. The hillside dropped away to rolling slopes of vivid green, flat and dense as velvet. The castle came into sight from a considerable distance; the steep walls of the keep appearing between switches in the road, surrounded by a canopy of trees in all their autumn grandeur.

Jude pulled into the car park and turned off the engine. All was quiet, half a dozen cars parked up but few signs of other tourists. Jude locked the doors and wandered through a birch-lined avenue, which led to the gated entrance. Hens pecked in the gravel and the sun was warm on his back. It all looked so bucolic, though he guessed it would feel different in the winter, under sheets of ice and snow.

A sign on the gate indicated the castle was due to close within the hour and the last guided tour of the day had already started, so Jude broke into a run. The steep stone path led up towards the keep, whose towering walls appeared to loom away. By the time he reached the central open courtyard, he was almost out of breath. A woman in her late fifties stood in front of a small group of visitors, all dressed in walking gear. Jude suddenly felt conscious of his cords and long twill overcoat, a city dweller's uniform which made him stand out from the crowd. The guide was wired like a spring and filled with energy, speaking volumes with her hands. She was in the middle of an introduction, cycling through languages – first German, then Italian and finally in English.

'Welcome to Castel Gedächt, or Schloss Gedächt, if you prefer. The castle which you see today was first constructed in the thirteenth century. Built on salt caves, it has remained in constant occupation till this day. For those latecomers . . .' she looked pointedly at Jude, 'I reiterate: no photography and please do not enter any area marked private – the family are in residence today. We are grateful to them for sharing their home with us and they deserve their peace. Now, if you would like to follow me, we begin our tour with the armoury.'

They trailed after her, ambling around the first few rooms filled with an array of weapons, including bayonets, pikes and staffs. Jude hung back by the door, taken by a painted wooden shield: it was ivory and crimson, with a double-headed eagle stencilled in the centre – an exact replica of the emblem above the door at Villa Velare and stamped on the leather binder which once belonged to Beatrice's father. Jude felt a huge surge of relief. His impulsivity seemed to be paying off.

The guide ushered them on impatiently, sending them back out into the courtyard. It was cold in the shadow of the surrounding walls, a place which rarely saw the sun.

'You might not realize, but beneath your feet lies one of the many mining tunnels which can be found throughout the site.'

Jude looked down and saw he was stood on a metal grid above a pitch-black shaft. He stepped back abruptly as the guide continued.

'It's said that convicted criminals were dropped into the caves below, saving the authorities the trouble of dispensing with their bodies.' Uncomfortable laughter rippled through the group. 'This entire building was extended and converted in the sixteenth century, becoming the Renaissance marvel which you see today. Notice please the frescoes and the repeated motif of the double-headed eagle – the crest of the Montefalco family who owned this castle for two centuries, until Heinrich von Niedermeyer took over in the 1940s, and whose descendants are still in residence today.' Jude found himself shivering, chilled by the shadows and the all-pervasive damp.

'Now we will go up to the ramparts, to see the private chapel. Everybody, follow me.' The guide led the group up a flight of narrow steps cut into the wall of the keep. Their sturdy walking boots were suited to the climb. Jude followed behind them but turned and ducked into an open-fronted balcony which ringed the inner courtyard. He'd seen and heard enough to know that he was in the right place; his next challenge was to make contact with the owner.

The signs marked *Privato* seemed especially numerous on one door; Jude took it as a good indicator of the fastest route to an inner sanctum. He turned the handle and nipped inside, heart thumping in his chest. He'd always loved the buzz he got from sniping a painting at auction, but that felt like nothing compared to this. He found himself in a corridor, which led to a grand dining hall, full of dark wood furniture. The walls were decorated with mounted antlers and boars' heads, round wooden shields and the same esoteric weapons he'd seen down in the armoury. A huge wagon wheel, dripping with candle wax, hung over a long table. Jude found it all so incongruous and gothic, he could hardly believe he was still in Italy.

'Guess you got lost, huh?'

The woman's voice came out of nowhere, her American accent immediately evident. Jude span round and saw a trim blonde woman in her early forties standing by the door, dressed head to toe in Lycra. He smiled in what he hoped might be an appealing, self-effacing way.

'I think I might have taken a wrong turn. I do apologize.'

The woman's face lit up. 'Oh, you're a Brit!' Then, in an exaggerated British accent, '"Don't get many of those to the pound".'

'Guilty as charged,' grinned Jude, thrusting out a hand, determined to press home his advantage. She laughed as she shook it.

'Brits are always so funny. I'm Cindy von Niedermeyer.'

'Julian Adler. But call me Jude.'

'Well, Jude, I just passed your group on the way to the

map room. If you head down there a-ways, you ought to find them.'

Stalling for time, Jude mumbled in an embarrassed way. 'The thing is, I was actually looking for a loo and I got a bit confused.'

'Oh! I got you – come this way.'

She took him down a different corridor, far shabbier than any of the public spaces, and opened a door into a bathroom which looked like a sanatorium from the First World War. The walls were arsenic green, with peeling paint and covered in a tangle of water pipes.

'All mod cons!' Cindy said brightly. 'I'm afraid you take us as you find us, as they say. I'll wait outside and show you the way back, in case you get lost again.'

Deciding he ought to relieve himself, in case Cindy was listening, Jude stood at the toilet, then washed his hands and came back out.

'Quite the museum piece.'

'Right?' Cindy agreed sardonically. 'One of the many joys of living in a Schloss.'

'Yes, I've been meaning to ask about that. Schloss or Castel, which is it? So Germanic, considering we're in Italy.'

'You sound like my husband! He's German, but he went to school in England. In answer to your question, we're, like eighty kilometres from the Austrian border here, so it's pretty much its own thing, you know what I mean?'

Jude didn't, but he smiled and nodded. Cindy led him back into the dining room and they were almost at the exit to the courtyard when he spoke up again in desperation. 'Might I ask where he went to school? Your husband, I mean.'

'*So* British.' Cindy laughed. 'You are *so* British! He went to Winchester College – do you know it?'

'I should say so, went there myself.'

Cindy's mouth dropped open. 'You did not!'

Indeed, Jude had not, but he rather relished saying he did with such conviction. He found this kind of high-wire act both terrifying and enthralling.

'Emil will be blown away when I tell him. What a small world!'

'I'd love to meet him,' said Jude.

'Really? He'd get such a kick out of the Winchester thing. He's always going on about that place.'

'Ah, don't we all?' asked Jude, beginning to wonder if he could really pull this off.

'Listen, he's out in the vineyards right now, playing on his tractor, but he'll be here tomorrow morning, looking after the kiddo. I host a yoga class on the roof – sun salutations mean so much when you get up this high.' She smiled again, showing two rows of perfectly straight white teeth. 'Why don't you drop by then, come for coffee, keep him company. Say 9 a.m.?'

Jude nodded, wondering how he might pull off a deep dive into Winchester College between now and then.

'I'd like that so much, Cindy, thank you. I can't wait to pick his brains.'

The following morning was misty. Jude drove the ten miles back to Castel Gedächt with some caution, the hairpin bends and drop-offs far less appealing when they appeared without any warning. He feared that Cindy von Niedermeyer's sun salutations might be cancelled, but the American was made of sterner stuff than he gave her credit for. At 8.50 a.m. the car park had five cars in it and a trail of middle-aged women carrying yoga mats towards the building. He followed them through the avenue of birch and back up the sloping path towards the keep. Wreathed in fog, the castle felt even more ominous and imposing.

Jude retraced his steps to the private door, but this time rang the bell. A short while later it was opened by a great bear of a man in jogging bottoms and trainers, a faded Led Zeppelin T-shirt and a long towelling dressing gown, all of which had seen much better days. The man had wild, curly hair, with streaks of silver, and an equally dishevelled beard. He carried a boy toddler on his hip and seemed bemused to find a rogue Englishman at his door so early in the morning.

'You must be Emil!' Jude beamed.

The man frowned. 'And you are . . . ?'

'Jude Adler. Met your wife yesterday – she told me to drop by. Winchester College?'

'Oh. Right!'

The pained expression which flashed across Emil von Niedermeyer's face suggested his visit hadn't been a source of great anticipation. Jude tried to look sheepish.

'You probably need me turning up about as much as an infestation of rats right now.'

'Oh, we have plenty of those already, I can promise you!' Emil laughed.

'Ha ha, very good.' Jude smiled determinedly, wanting to give Emil little choice but to invite him in. After a brief but awkward pause, the bear stepped back. 'Well then, come on in.'

Jude patted down the pockets of his coat. 'Might be like bringing coals to Newcastle, but I picked up some rather good coffee at the airport . . .'

As he held out the bag of Kenyan ground, Emil's face broke into a broad grin. 'Now, that is a welcome sight. We're in the back of beyond out here – I'd have to go to Innsbruck to pick up something so exotic.'

He led Jude into a large kitchen, a chaotic space with a mix of fittings, traditional and professional: an inglenook fireplace with a cast-iron stove, alongside a catering-sized hob. Stainless steel shelves filled with copper pans and racks of knives, an old ceramic butler's sink and an industrial dishwasher. In the middle of the room was a large wooden table, scrubbed raw by many years of service. It was covered in toy cars and trucks, brightly coloured plastic bowls and a scattering of cereal. Emil dumped the little boy into a highchair and watched for a moment as he set about driving his vehicles through the landscape of his breakfast, then he turned and rubbed his hands.

'Right then, let's see about that coffee.' He took the bag from Jude. 'So you're a Wykehamist, I understand.'

This was the moment Jude had been dreading. His attempts to educate himself on the history of the college had fallen short, due to poor dial-up connectivity in the hotel's business suite.

'How old are you?' asked Emil.

'Twenty-eight,' Jude replied.

'Ah. You won't know any of my lot, then. Perhaps their younger brothers. Was Sanders there, or Alabaster?'

Jude considered trying to bluff his way through, but feared he couldn't pull it off. Besides, the lie had already served its purpose.

'Afraid not,' he said. 'I wasn't there for very long.'

'Oh.' Emil sounded disappointed.

Wanting to keep him on side, Jude sought to cast the blame elsewhere. 'Cindy seemed keen for us to meet, though, all the same.'

Emil scowled. 'My wife does this to me every now and then – hands out invitations based on spurious connections. I only hope this morning hasn't been a pain.' Subtext: it was a pain for him.

'Not in the least,' said Jude. 'Difficult to find like-minded people up here, one imagines.'

'Well, quite.' There was silence as Emil screwed the coffee pot together and lit a flame beneath. Jude cast around for conversation; he might not have been to the right school, but he'd spent years valuing collections for impoverished gentility and could mimic the language they spoke.

'How do you find it, big place like this?' he asked. 'Must be hard to get it to wash its face.'

'Very hard,' sighed Emil. 'We've done everything we can to diversify. Weddings, B & B, you name it. Yoga retreats are the latest thing, according to Cindy. I'm not convinced, myself.'

Jude nodded sagely. 'It's about stewardship though, isn't it? You have a responsibility to keep it up; to hand it on in better shape for the next generation, so it isn't such an albatross around their bloody necks.' He'd heard some version of this at every estate sale he'd ever attended.

Emil warmed up appreciably. 'Land-rich, cash-poor and sitting on a money pit. If someone offered to buy this place, I'd bite their arm off in a minute.' He looked at Jude with naked speculation. 'I don't suppose . . .'

'Does it need a lot of work?'

That clearly piqued Emil's interest.

'Might I ask what do you do for a living, if you don't mind?'

Jude didn't mind. In fact, this had been his sole intention.

'Art dealer.'

The coffee pot burbled into life.

'Interesting,' said von Niedermeyer as he lifted the pot from the heat. 'My father was a gallerist. Quite a collector in his day.'

'Oh really – whereabouts?'

'Munich and Berlin.'

Jude tried to tamp down his excitement.

Emil sighed discontentedly. 'All the good stuff's gone now, I'm afraid. Sold to keep this sinking ship afloat.'

Jude felt the familiar fluttering of panic; what if he was too late?

'All of it?' he asked, as casually as he could muster.

Emil looked at him shrewdly. 'Well, maybe not quite all . . .'

Once his son had been deposited back into the Lycra-clad arms of his mother, Emil von Niedermeyer took Jude on a whistle-stop tour of Castel Gedächt.

The layout was eccentric – one wing of airy rooms at the

top and a cluster of subterranean cells at the bottom. The only unifying element was that it all looked tired, almost to the point of exhaustion. At each stop, Emil presented Jude with another item which 'might be made available, for the right price'.

Jude tried to feign enthusiasm, though none of it had much value so far as he could see. There were a few wooden shields which had a certain charm; the odd watercolour and a trunk inlaid with malachite, but none of them were Beatrice's St John.

Jude kept pushing Emil, trying to entice him. 'I specialize in the Old Masters. That's what brought me out to Italy – the reappraisal of Gentileschi means there's such a strong market for all that sort of thing. Baroque, Renaissance, anything like that.'

He watched Emil's face carefully and thought he saw him register the words, but if he did, no more than a flicker.

'Those were my father's favourites, too. You'd have liked each other, I dare say.'

They were in a warm and sunny sitting room, at the top of one of the towers. Stained glass in leaded windows gave a view across the valley, to rolling lawns of verdant green. Flies buzzed around and a dozen little desiccated corpses lay baking on the sill. They seemed to have come to the end of the tour and Jude still had no idea if the Caravaggio was now, or had ever been, in Emil's possession, though his intuition told him something was off. The time had come to take a more direct approach.

'Tell me about your father.'

'You want to know about the old man, eh?'

Emil strode over to a glass-fronted dresser and pulled out
an aged photograph album. He sank back down next to Jude
and cracked open the first page. There was a photograph of
an oil painting – a stocky man with a small moustache, curly
hair and a severe side parting. It was quite apparent the man
shared his DNA with Emil.

'Portrait of my father as a young man.' The bear smiled.

Jude looked at it closely. For its time it was a highly nat-
uralistic interpretation – overly sentimental and romantic, a
style of art which was particularly favoured by certain parts of
German society, during the rise of the Third Reich.

'When was this then, '33, '34?' Jude enquired.

'You do know your stuff,' said Emil admiringly.

'Quite different to a lot of Germanic art around this
time ...' He left the statement open.

'Father had no truck with the expressionists. He was in
favour of the classics. Italian masters, like I said.'

'Earlier on, you implied he acquired a few pieces of his
own,' Jude said, affecting innocence.

'Rather. He had an eye; you couldn't question that.'

'I'd imagine a grand old place like this must have had a sizeable collection at one time. How did your father come to own
it? Did he buy the castle or was it requisitioned in the war?'

A frown crossed Emil's brow. Jude pressed on.

'Your tour guide mentioned the Montefalco family, but
they have no record of it being sold, so I imagine something
like that might have happened. Quite a lot of Germans ended
up round here in the later stages of the war.'

Emil shifted uncomfortably. Jude waited, leaving space to

let him speak. He watched as a fly got caught up in a lace-draped lampshade which hung above them: grey, with a heavy coat of dust.

'Did someone send you? Are you with Interpol?'

'Nothing like that. I'm just here looking for some answers.'

'On whose behalf?'

'The daughter of Conte Luciano Montefalco. We believe you might know the whereabouts of some property which belonged to him.'

Emil slumped back and put his great paws over his eyes. 'I always knew this day would come.'

Concerned he'd pushed the man too far, Jude asked hesitantly, 'Are you okay?'

Emil looked up, his eyes glittering with tears of evident relief.

'You have no idea how long I've been waiting; how much it weighed me down.'

CHAPTER TWENTY-EIGHT

ROME, DECEMBER 1943

Santino took out his hammer and a paper bag of tin tacks. Signora Bianchi had given him instructions to replace all the photographs of Mussolini which had been removed over the tumultuous summer. At the same time, he was to display the new curfew hours – 7 p.m. to 6 a.m. – and a list of crimes and punishments, by order of Herbert Kappler, the chief of the SS and Gestapo, overseeing occupied Rome:

A comprehensive programme of punishments to be meted out to Roman civilians, published here today in brief:

- For harbouring or helping escaped prisoners of war: death.
- For making contact with them: hard labour for life.
- For printing or publishing or circulating news

derogatory to the prestige of the Axis Forces: penal servitude for life.

- For owning a wireless transmitter: death.
- For instructing wireless operators: hard labour for life.
- For looting in evacuated areas: death.
- For desertion of work, or sabotage: death.
- For not fulfilling labour obligations: death.
- For not acquainting the authorities of change of address: twenty years prison.
- For taking photographs out of doors: hard labour for life.

Santino nailed the order to the kitchen door. While he worked, he cursed the bloody woman and her friends, the *stronzi* fascists, and the godforsaken Nazis. He cursed them all to hell and back, but quietly, and only after making sure nobody could hear.

Maddalena never did get to eat any of the oranges she picked that early winter's morning. They were the first citrus fruits to ripen, and she was excited to twist the stems free and feel their scented oil buttering her fingers. She filled her pockets and could not wait to show them to Sophia and Costanza, who yearned for sweetness when so little was available. And to Tito, who'd had nothing to enjoy these last seven days.

She looked back towards the house and thought of him lying behind the false wall in the cellar. Dawn's light would soon come creeping round the edges of the coal hatch, though the courtyard would remain in shadow for several hours. Tito complained bitterly of the cold, so she'd gone in search of every spare blanket and warm item of clothing she could find. He told her how much he hated waking up down there, hardly knowing if it was day or night, listening for noises from the house above to give him any clue. He would climb the ladder of the shelves and peer through the gap, see just enough to know if it was wet or dry, day or night. Perhaps an orange might lift his spirits; something to distract him from this desperate situation.

Maddalena walked back down through the garden. Steam was drifting from the upper terrace, where the sun hit first. This had become her new routine: she would head out at first light, gather a few vegetables or herbs, fill the water jug, then kick the cover on her way back in, to signal to Tito that the house was soon to rise. The two of them might exchange a few words, if he was awake already, though this was rare. Their hushed and hurried conversations always ended the same way,

'Stay strong.'

'You mean stay quiet.'

He tried to make a joke of it, pretend it was ironic, but there was bitterness in his tone. They had much longer conversations when the household went to sleep. Tito would climb out and walk up to the top part of the garden to stretch his legs and breathe the fresh night air. He'd bend and even run a little, his limbs cramping from the hours squashed in the narrow space between the walls. Maddalena would stay nearby to keep a watch.

'You know you can't stay down there forever,' she whispered. 'They're looking for you.'

'I know.'

'It's dangerous to stay. What if someone hears you? Signora Bianchi would hand you over to the secret police without a second thought.'

'I know, but where else can I go?'

She didn't have an answer. She'd gone to the clinic to plead their case and Vincenzo had been sympathetic, but regretful: the ward was at capacity and besides, they couldn't take in every boy who wanted to avoid conscription – there were far too many. He promised to reach out to his friends in the partisans to see what they could do. Until then, Tito ought to just stay put.

'He should be thankful you found him somewhere safe. There's many far worse off than him.'

But Tito didn't seem particularly grateful when she broke the news.

'I can't live like this, Maddalena. I wish I could just disappear,' he groaned.

'You have! At least as far as the army's concerned.'

'Then maybe they'll stop looking for me.' He needed to believe it, his eyes pleading with her to agree.

'Maybe.'

He paced the ground, agitated, wired. 'If they catch me, I'll kill myself. Rather that than die fighting for the Germans.'

'And I'd rather neither option, if it's all the same to you.'

She tried her hardest to divert him, but still he persevered.

'This cellar is my tomb. *Selpolti vivi* – you might as well brick me up and leave me here forever.'

'Don't be so morbid, Tito. You're not dead yet, although you will be if you carry on like this. I'll kill you myself!' She punched him in the arm until he laughed.

'I don't know how I can ever thank you,' he said, gazing at the clear December sky.

'What for, keeping you locked up like a gaoler?'

'For helping me and bringing food.'

She grinned. 'Now that's more like it.'

'When all this is over, I'll take you out for dinner and dancing and dessert.'

The wistful look he gave made her feel uncomfortable. She knew that he'd begun to fall in love with her a little. Wanting to discourage it, she changed the subject.

'When all this is over, you'll go off and find some great adventure.'

'Will you come with me?'

'I'll be too busy recovering,' she yawned. 'All you do is sleep all day. I work, then stay up all night long with you. Bianchi will probably fire me for nodding off in the soup and you'll be left there all alone.'

'Then you might as well go right ahead and kill me. You'd be doing me a favour.'

'Would I now?'

'And in return, I'll haunt you for the rest of time.'

'Promise?'

'Cross my heart.'

She thought they were too young for all this talk of death, but not too young to die.

*

At the breakfast table, Maddalena surprised Costanza and Sophia with two ripe oranges to take with them in their bags to school. The sight of the delicious spheres led to such squeals of excitement, their father put his head around the door.

'Now that is a rare treat,' Luca smiled. 'What do you say, girls?'

They chorused, 'Thank you, Maddalena.'

She dipped into a playful curtsy. 'You're very welcome. These are the first ones to ripen, so make the most of them. More will come in the next few days; we just need to be patient and then we'll have fresh juice and *insalata di arance Siracusana.*'

They shrieked again, only to be shushed by Balia Paola.

'Come along now, time for school. Don't cling on so. Let your father leave for work.'

Maddalena returned to the kitchen, where she and Dolorosa finished clearing up. They'd just sat down at the table for a rare moment of respite, when Maria came rushing in looking stricken.

'Soldiers. A truckload of them, pulled up on the front drive.'

'What do they want?' asked Dolorosa fearfully.

'The sergeant's asking after you.'

Maddalena saw the blood drain from her face and exchanged an anxious glance with Maria.

'What do we do?'

The cook wiped her trembling fingers on her apron. 'I suppose I'd better go and find out what they want.' She untied it and hung it on the hook. She didn't hurry, she wasn't able. It seemed as if it took every ounce of her effort just to walk towards the door. Maddalena reached for Maria's hand, and they followed on behind.

The sergeant was waiting on the front steps: a young man, bored and haughty, with a thin moustache and hooded eyes. He watched them approach with an expression of distaste.

'Which of you is the mother of Tito Senese?'

Dolorosa stepped forward.

'Well then,' said the sergeant. 'You need to come with me. You're under arrest.'

Her shoulders slumped. Instantly defeated, she started moving towards him. Maddalena put out a hand to hold her back.

'Stay where you are.' Blood was pounding in her ears as she rounded on the sergeant. 'Why are you arresting her? What has she done?'

The sergeant wasn't much older than her, but he spoke slowly and deliberately, as if she were a child.

'Her son is a deserter, absent without leave – you understand? He failed to report for duty, so we're taking her instead.' He grasped Dolorosa by the forearm and began to drag her across the threshold. 'Come on, I haven't got all day.'

Maddalena followed them both out onto the steps. 'You're "taking her"? What do you intend to do with her, send her off to Germany to fight?'

The sergeant waved her away. 'It's no concern of yours.'

A flat-back truck was parked on the driveway at the bottom of the steps. A dozen soldiers sat on benches, six either side. The sergeant called to Maddalena, 'Go back inside, unless you want to come with us for the ride. What do you say, boys?'

The soldiers shouted their agreement. Burning with anger, Maddalena hissed, 'You're utterly pathetic.'

Maria gasped. 'Don't, Maddalena!'

The sergeant was no longer laughing. 'Speak to me like that again and I'll arrest you, too.'

Maddalena whispered to Maria, 'Don't worry about me. Quickly, go and get Santino!'

The young woman dashed down the steps, heading for the garage. Then suddenly another, sharper voice chimed in. 'What's going on here? Why wasn't I informed?'

Signora Bianchi was marching down the steps towards them, a look of furious indignation on her face. Seemingly disinclined to discuss the situation, the sergeant carried on, 'This woman's been arrested and will stay in prison until such a time as her son makes an appearance.'

As they reached the bottom of the steps he shoved Dolorosa towards the truck. Signora Bianchi called after him, outraged.

'And pray, what happens if her son turns up?'

The sergeant didn't answer. Whatever the outcome might be, it clearly wasn't good, but Signora Bianchi kept on insisting, 'I asked you a question, sergeant, don't ignore me!'

The sergeant paused, narrowing his eyes as Signora continued her tirade, 'It is my understanding that the young man in question was sent away and told to report for duty. He hasn't been seen since. Therefore, the army lost him, not his mother. I ask again – what happens if he turns up?'

'Nothing good, for either one of them.'

'You cannot possibly hold this woman accountable!'

'We can,' he said. 'We do.'

They'd reached the truck now. Two soldiers stood, ready to help pull Dolorosa up. Unused to having her authority denied, Signora Bianchi shouted at them both to stop.

'I am head housekeeper here, and I answer to our employers, the conte and contessa Montefalco. What am I to say when they ask me where their cook has gone?'

The sergeant snarled, 'Tell them I'll come back and take their ration cards if any of you say another word.'

The waiting soldiers took hold of Dolorosa's arms and yanked her up. She staggered then sank onto the wooden bench, visibly shaking, tears streaming down her face. The sergeant climbed up after her and slammed his palm down on the cab roof, signalling to leave. As Maddalena watched, she felt every ounce of strength and bravado draining from her body. The driver started the engine and began to pull away.

'Wait!' A strangled cry echoed off the walls, then came the sound of someone running. The voice called out again, 'Please stop, Mamma, wait for me!'

Tito flew round the corner, skidding on the drive. His clothes and face were filthy and dishevelled, brown hair almost black with soot. He tore after the truck, as it began to pick up speed. Maddalena cried out, 'Tito, no!' But he ignored her and kept going, his bare feet pounding on the gravel. Once more he shouted, his voice so loud and panicked, it could be heard above the engine's growl. 'For God's sake stop, you have to wait!'

Seeing him at last, the sergeant hammered on the cab roof, shouting at the driver. Tito kept after them, his arms and stocky legs like pistons, until the truck came to a sliding halt.

Exhausted, Tito dropped to his knees, his chest and shoulders heaving. The sergeant jumped down from the truck and began to walk towards him.

'Are you Tito Senese?'

It was clear he couldn't speak, but Tito nodded, then dropped his chin onto his chest to signal his surrender.

The sergeant reached for his sidearm, aimed at Tito and shot him in the head. The crack of the bullet echoed off the villa walls, the boy lurched backwards; in an instant a third eye, black and ragged, spread across his brow. He fell arms out, palms up, in supplication, even as a second bullet punched his chest.

Maddalena felt the first scream from Dolorosa, as though it had been torn from her own breast. Although the truck was far away, she reached toward her. Like a siren, the woman stood and expelled a howl with every breath.

The sergeant dug a polished boot under Tito's shoulder, making certain he was dead. The body lay immobile, sightless eyes turned towards the sky. The sergeant gestured to a couple of the soldiers, who tried to drag Dolorosa from the truck. Now she was actively refusing, scratching and screaming, desperate to hold on. It was a futile struggle; the men were strong and quickly overcame her. They jumped down and pulled her after them so carelessly she landed in the dirt.

The soldiers were on Tito's body in a second. Lifting under his armpits, they dragged him, bare feet scraping on the ground. They flung him on the truck bed like a sack of coal and ashes. The engine roared to life, the soldiers and the sergeant climbed back up and then were gone, leaving Dolorosa weeping on the ground.

CHAPTER TWENTY-NINE

VATICAN CITY, DECEMBER 1943

Luca was returning to his desk from the darkroom when one of the young secretaries chased him down.

'You're needed on the telephone, sir. Some sort of emergency at home.'

He dashed to his office and snatched up the handset. 'What is it? What's going on?'

Signora Bianchi's replied, 'So sorry to disturb you, but an incident has taken place at the villa. After you left this morning, a group of soldiers came looking for Dolorosa – they had a warrant for her arrest, due to her son's apparent desertion. They'd begun to execute those orders when the boy suddenly appeared. It seems he'd been in hiding hereabouts and the commotion flushed him out.'

'What then – did they arrest him?'

There was a pause and Luca wondered if the line had been cut.

She finally continued. 'No, sir, they shot him dead. Mercifully they have removed the body, but the household is in disarray. The contessa asked if I might call you on the telephone – she would greatly appreciate your presence here, at your earliest convenience.'

Thirty minutes later, Luca knocked on the door to Violante's sitting room.

'Come in.'

She was sitting by the window, with a rosary held loosely in her hands. Signora Bianchi stood close behind her. Violante turned to him, her face and fingers waxy in the winter light.

'You got back quickly.'

He nodded. 'Roberto arranged for a driver with Vatican plates to bring me home.'

She rifled through the beads. 'We have been harbouring a fugitive, Luca. Though I find it impossible to believe.'

Thinking she might still be in shock, Luca asked gently, 'Did you see it happen?'

'No. I became aware of a disturbance, but I was praying. When I heard the shots, I got up and looked out of the window and saw him lying there, quite dead. The soldiers took his body, drove away.' She shook her head, as though trying to cast off the image. She reached up to pat Signora Bianchi's hand where it rested on her shoulder. 'I'm so thankful for my dear Signora. She brought calm and order to the chaos.'

Except for the low crackle of the fire, the rest of the house seemed cloaked in silence.

'Where is everyone?' he asked.

'The boy's mother had to be taken to the doctor.'

Luca frowned at her choice of words. *The boy's mother* – why not simply Dolorosa?

Violante carried on, 'She was quite inconsolable, hysterical in fact. Maddalena and Maria had to carry her between them.'

Desperate to make sense of the day's events, Luca turned to the Signora.

'On the telephone, you said Tito was hiding. Do you know where?'

The woman sniffed. 'By the state of him, I'd say the garden or the cellar – he was filthy. I've asked Santino to look about, though I already have some suspicions . . .' She patted Violante's shoulder. 'With your permission, I think I ought to go and speak to the Carabinieri. The captain was a friend of my late husband, as you know.'

Violante agreed. 'He's always been so kind.'

'But why?' asked Luca.

'To try to get ahead of any trouble.' She looked surprised, as if this ought to be self-evident. 'A dreadful thing has happened here and I want to be assured it won't have any impact on the rest of us. Our ration cards, for instance – they threatened to revoke them.'

Luca was amazed by her callous self-regard. Violante seemed oblivious.

She looked up at Luca. 'I believe – and the Signora agrees with me – the girls ought to be shielded from this whole debacle. Thankfully they are still at school for several hours, but when they return, nobody must tell them. It would be too traumatic.'

Luca frowned. 'I don't know if that's possible . . .' What did she imagine, that everything would carry on as normal?

The Signora looked at her watch. 'I must go; will you excuse me?' Violante watched her leave and let out a deep sigh.

'I can't help feeling something in our country has gone awry. Young people used to feel a sense of duty. We've lost our dignity somehow.'

'What are you talking about?' asked Luca, baffled. 'There isn't any dignity in war. There never was.'

She shuddered. 'It was an act of violation. I can't believe he was here, in hiding all along.'

'It's terrible; that poor, poor boy.'

Luca had known Tito since early childhood. He could picture him as a toddler, running through the garden on his sturdy little legs. He couldn't begin to imagine what he'd endured in his last few days on earth.

'Poor boy?' Violante's agitated voice broke through his thoughts. 'If the soldiers hadn't come here looking for him, we'd be none the wiser and he'd be out there still. The thought of it . . . night after night, and we had no idea!'

She turned to stare out of the window, stone-faced. Luca suddenly understood. The act of violation she was talking of was not Tito's murder in cold blood, but him hiding in the first place. They'd been talking at cross purposes all along.

Her lips pursed in disappointment. 'I suppose it's to be expected, without a father to show the way. His mother was always far too lenient.' She shot him a look of disapproval.

'You were too fond of the boy, I might say. Blind to all his faults.'

He turned his back so she couldn't see his furious expression, his throat contracting like a fist.

'I think the shock of this has affected your composure. Tito did nothing to deserve such callous disregard.'

'Please don't speak to me in that tone, Luca. I haven't got the strength.'

He realized he barely recognized Violante as the woman he once married; the mother who'd had to forfeit her own son.

'I've got such a dreadful headache.' Violante pinched the bridge of her nose. 'Santino has been instructed to wash down the drive and clear everything away before the girls return from school. Could you go and check in on his progress? Make sure every last trace of this dreadful business has been removed. If not for my sake, then for our daughters. Or are we less worthy of your pity than that boy?'

Without another word, he left, relieved to escape her.

Feeling deeply unsettled, Luca walked down the stairs towards the kitchen. It was rare to find the room so cold and uninviting: no smell of baking, no industry, no chatter. He ducked his head into the cellar, but it was dark and there was no sign of Santino there. Wondering if he'd gone back to the garage, Luca headed out into the courtyard and found the mechanic lying on his belly, his head and upper body deep inside the coal chute.

'What are you doing?'

Santino jumped at his voice and began to back out of the hole.

'You gave me a fright,' he muttered gruffly. 'I thought that bastard sergeant had come back.' As he stood up, Luca saw he was holding a high-powered bicycle lamp.

'What's going on?'

Santino scowled. 'That bloody stupid boy, that's what.'

Despite his curt tone, Luca knew Santino had been very fond of Tito. He was the closest thing the boy had to a father, since his own had passed away. Santino gestured to the chute.

'That's where he was hiding, if you can believe it.'

'But how?'

'See for yourself.'

Luca took the proffered lamp from Santino and knelt on the cobblestones. He leaned into the shaft, holding the light before him, the beam swinging wildly across the shelves and walls. He steadied the bulb, so it cast its light down on the floor. The tight space was stuffed with a surprising amount of detritus – a nest made out of pillows, eiderdowns and what looked like Violante's best fur coats, all piled up on the floor. The shelves were full of plates and cups and remnants of half-eaten food. The scent of urine and tallow candles wafted up, almost making him recoil. A flash of colour in the corner caught his eye; he swung the lamp back to reveal an orange peel, discarded on a blanket. After a few moments, Luca lifted his head out of the shaft and looked at Santino in abject horror.

'How long was he down there?'

'He absconded ten days ago. By the looks of it I'd say he's

been here for most of that.' He shook his head despairingly.
'The bloody fool.'

'Does the Signora know?' Luca fervently hoped she'd left
before Santino made his discovery.

'The hatch was wide open when we came back here and
there's not much gets past her, as you know.'

Even now, she might be telling the authorities.

'You think she'd share her suspicions with the Carabinieri?'

Santino furrowed his brow. 'I don't know. I don't think so.
It doesn't look good for anyone to admit this room is here. She
knows as well as we do that the Carabinieri would just come
round and help themselves. She has things of her own down
there; I saw a good bit of cash and quite a lot of jewellery when
I was closing up.'

Luca slumped against the wall, trying to assess the situation.

'Did you see how it happened?'

'I missed most of it; I was in the workshop. Maria saw the
soldiers arriving – some bolshy young sergeant who decided to
cart poor Dolorosa off in Tito's place. I suppose the boy must
have heard all the shouting and realized what was happening.
He climbed out and went after her. I was too late to stop him.
If I'd have been there a minute earlier, I'd have tackled him
to the ground.' Santino sat down beside the coal hole. 'That
poor, deluded boy. I've known him since he was a baby. I was
friends with his father, Gio.'

'I didn't know that,' Luca said.

'It was before you took over. This place was still in your
parents' hands back then.' He scratched the greying stubble
on his chin. 'When Gio died, I promised Dolorosa I would

keep an eye on him. Before Tommaso, he was like my son. He had a good heart, you know? But even as a kid, he didn't have the wit to stay out of trouble. Makes me wonder how he managed this at all.'

Santino wasn't looking at him, but Luca sensed an undercurrent moving through the conversation.

He thought about the discarded orange peel lying on the blankets. Santino started to lever himself up, wincing with the effort.

'Can I help?' asked Luca. Santino waved him off.

'I just need to keep it moving.' He massaged his thigh where the bullet had clipped him on that dark September day. Luca pictured him bleeding, slumped unconscious against the outer walls of the villa, while he and Maddalena talked. He wondered how much he remembered of that day.

'People can surprise you,' said Santino. 'What they will risk for those they love, what they'll surrender. I keep my eyes and ears open, and my mouth shut, but I would be ready, if my help was ever needed.'

The men were sluicing the gravel with diluted lye when Maddalena and Maria returned. They walked with their arms linked together – like sisters, Luca thought – though in truth, they were holding each other up. Remnants of bloody water ran in rivulets, which the women gingerly stepped over.

'What did the doctor say?' asked Luca.

'She needs to be sedated, so they're admitting her overnight.' Maddalena sighed. 'They've no idea when she will be well enough to come back home.'

Maria began crying quietly. Maddalena stroked her hand in sympathy. 'You need something hot and sweet. Why don't you come back to the kitchen? I have a tiny bit of honey left, maybe with some lemon and hot water?'

Maria shook her head. 'Thank you, but the only thing I want now is to hold my son.' She turned to Santino. 'Where is he – where's Tommaso?'

'Upstairs in the nursery. Balia Paola's been looking after him.'

'I need to go and get him. Will you come?'

Santino nodded and put a steadying arm around his wife. Luca watched as they walked towards the house together and Maddalena followed. He called after her.

'Maddalena, wait. Can we talk?'

She seemed reluctant. 'I ought to get back to the kitchen. No one has eaten any lunch, and I need to start on supper. It seems I may be on my own for quite a while.' She was trying to sound brave, although the tremor in her voice betrayed her.

'Perhaps I can help, if you would let me,' Luca insisted.

'Very well.'

When they reached the courtyard, Maddalena stared down at the closed hatch of the coal chute, the colour draining from her cheeks.

'Are you all right?' he asked. 'Perhaps you ought to go in and sit down for a moment.'

'Thank you,' she nodded. 'I think that might be a good idea.'

She sat at the kitchen table and sank her head into her hands. Luca found himself filling the kettle and setting it to boil on the stovetop.

'You said you had some honey?'

She moved to stand, but he put a hand gently on her shoulder and pressed her back into her seat.

'Let me get it. You do everything for everyone – I should like to take care of you, just for a moment.'

She nodded gratefully and he saw her eyes had filled with tears. She pointed to the pantry cupboard.

'The honey's in there, on the top shelf, and there's a bowl of lemons lower down.'

He cut the lemon into slices and poured over boiling water, placing the cup in front of her, along with the honey and a little spoon. He pulled out a chair and sat down opposite, as she stirred in the sweet brown paste. The scent released was deeply comforting.

'I really ought to be getting on,' she said, glancing at the clock.

He nodded. 'But I think we need to talk about Tito first, don't you?'

Maddalena swallowed hard as Luca started speaking.

'He was hiding in the secret room, in the cellar. By the looks of it, he'd been down there quite some time. We cleared it out, Santino and I. Threw everything away, but I fear that won't be an end to it.'

Maddalena sipped at the lemon water, her hands cradling its warmth.

'The difficulty we have is that the Signora is probably aware of Tito's hiding place. She told me earlier that she has some suspicions . . .'

Her eyes widened, the pupils dilating. Luca continued, 'I

think we both know that she is likely to be dogged in her pursuit of answers. How Tito came to that idea, how he got down there in the first place. How he stayed there undetected for so long.' He watched her clasp her hands together, thumb and fingers rubbing one over the other. 'All of that is hard to fathom, knowing Tito as we do.' He rapped his knuckles on the wooden table, making Maddalena jump. 'Sound travels and your room is right above the cellar. It's a wonder that you never heard him.'

Maddalena stared down into her cup, blinking rapidly.

'I can't prevent her coming back here and turning this place upside down. I can only help you if you tell the truth. Did you do it, Maddalena? Did you help Tito hide?'

A single tear dropped onto the table; she nodded once. Of course, he'd known the truth already. Had known it from the moment he saw the orange peel discarded on the blanket. Seen whose hand had plucked it from the tree and given Tito his final meal, though neither could have known it. Some part of him had simply hoped she might deny it. That she could do so with such conviction, she'd persuade him she might stay. Now he knew that couldn't happen; her fate had been decided. He looked at the clock above the door. It was an hour since he'd got home. He expected the Signora's footsteps on the stairs at any moment, the warning jangle of her keys.

'We have so little time. Is there somewhere you can go?'

She took in a shuddering breath. 'There is one place . . . a woman who might take me in and hide me.'

He reached across to take her hand; both of them were trembling.

'Then go now and go quickly. Pack a bag and leave here right away. I'll stay and try to hold her off, as best I can. I only wish I could do more.' His voice cracked and it took all his strength to hold himself together. 'You have to know; I'd give my life to keep you safe.'

CHAPTER THIRTY

DOLOMITE MOUNTAINS, OCTOBER 1997

In the tower of Castel Gedächt, Jude watched as Emil von Niedermeyer blinked back tears.

'Excuse me. I knew this moment had to come, but I wasn't quite prepared ... My father was a Nazi, Mr Adler. I rather think you might have guessed that much already. I long suspected it, especially since the other fellows in my house at Winchester accused me of the same, by dint of my German ancestry. Such are schoolboys.' Emil sniffed. 'I returned here when I finished school. My father was already ill by then, although he hadn't warned me – didn't want it to bugger up my A levels, apparently. It was an awful shock; he was emaciated and erratic, taking a cabinet full of painkillers each day, not all of them prescribed by a doctor. I stayed with him, those last weeks before the end, hoping I might finally get to know him. In retrospect that was a decision I regret. He told me how he came to own this place – a kind of deathbed confessional, if you will, high on ketamine and morphine and the promised liberation of his imminent release.'

Emil ran a hand through his hair, making it stick out at all angles.

'He wanted to pass on his '*Geheime Kunstsammlung*' to me – his private collection. He truly thought it was a gift, though I came to see it as a malediction. It ruined me. I'm not ashamed to admit that now, although I was for many years.'

The bluff and bluster of the great bear was gone. This version of Emil seemed infinitely frail.

'As my father told it, the story started in Hamburg in 1938 when he first met Hildebrand Gurlitt, the infamous Nazi art dealer. Gurlitt took him under his wing and together they stormed through Western Europe, looting art on behalf of the upper echelons of the Party. They ransacked museums and galleries across the continent, appropriating items for the Führer: paintings, sculptures, books, coins, furniture and weapons – you name it. It was like a bloody Viking siege. They took city after city.'

Emil gave a hollow laugh. 'I say this in the most dispassionate of ways, but it was really quite remarkable what they were able to achieve. They laid waste to European culture, took what they liked and destroyed what they hated, though even then they were pragmatic – they still kept what they thought had monetary value, even if they disliked it. My father amassed a huge amount of expressionist art, which he and the Nazis deemed "degenerate". He kept it hidden so he could sell it later and we lived off the proceeds until he died in 1966.'

Jude was familiar with the subject already. He'd had to hunt down many missing works on behalf of disenfranchised clients – Jewish families whose entire fortunes had been stolen by the likes of Heinrich von Niedermeyer.

Emil continued, 'Gurlitt was an egomaniac and encouraged that trait in others, or perhaps it was a question of like seeking out like,' but by the summer of 1943 they'd plundered most of northern Europe, and meant to do the same with the Vatican and Rome. They needed somewhere safe to store the spoils of war; Allied bombings were frequent and unpredictable, leaving anywhere above ground at risk, so they hit upon the idea of storing their stolen artefacts in salt mines. Underground systems so deep and vast and complex, they stood no risk of being discovered or being hit by falling bombs.'

Jude frowned. 'I would have thought keeping anything as delicate as art in that environment would cause huge damage.'

Emil shook his head. 'The conditions in a salt mine are constant and the climate is good for preservation – between 40 and 47 degrees and a steady 65 per cent humidity – ideal in many ways. There's a little spa town in Austria, named Altaussee, where they created a vast underground storage facility for the Linz *Führermuseum*. It was intended to showcase the art Gurlitt "acquired" for Hitler – his legacy – but although these men worked on behalf of the Führer, they stole almost as much for themselves, in part to satisfy their own desire for money and, in my father's case, an insatiable thirst for possession.

'He came here in the autumn of 1943, already planning his retirement. He'd seen the writing on the wall by then, wanted to get out of Germany before it all went to hell. As you said, a great many powerful and wealthy individuals sought sanctuary in the Dolomites around that time. Himmler envisaged this so-called "Alpine Fortress", a sort of haven for party officials and pro-fascist governments in exile. It covered an area from southern Bavaria, across western Austria and all the way down here, into northern Italy.

'My father was on the hunt for a suitable place to buy when he came across Castel Gedächt. It was unoccupied – the owner lived in Rome – but it was the salt caves which really interested him. He paid some people off with a Chagall and had the castle "requisitioned", so he could move in. Then he arranged for the work he'd amassed over years – most of it forbidden "degenerate" art, remember – to be smuggled out of Hamburg and hidden in the caves here, underneath the castle. Imagine his surprise when he discovered a secret cache of paintings concealed there already. Buried treasure – baroque masterpieces. Beautiful, priceless and, seemingly, unknown.'

Jude muttered, 'The Caravaggio . . .' almost to himself.

'Oh no, Mr Adler. You run ahead of me. The Caravaggio didn't make an appearance until later.'

Emil looked at him sadly. 'Perhaps it's easier if I just show you. I can lend you a jumper if you like. It's rather cold down there.'

Emil led Jude out of the family quarters and down to the armoury, in the lowest part of the keep. The mist had not yet cleared and gave the place an atmosphere of damp suppression. Jude could only imagine how isolated and unforgiving it might be once the snow came and the occupants were locked inside together, for months on end.

Emil walked over the metal grate, whose sheer drop had seemed so terrifying to Jude the day before. He gazed forlornly into the dark below.

'This was where they dropped criminals who'd been sentenced to death.'

'So I heard,' said Jude, skirting round the grate this time.

'I don't suppose the fall would kill you, but you'd never get back out.'

The stocky man led Jude to a low wooden door, covered in stencilled images of the dual-headed eagle, oxblood on ivory. He took a set of keys from the pocket of his dressing gown and unlocked it. Beyond the doorway, a flight of wooden stairs descended steeply. The walls were clad in planks of ancient pine, which narrowed to form a tight arched ceiling overhead. Emil's frame filled the space entirely and Jude felt the first whiff of claustrophobia – not only at the confinement of the space, but at its shape, so reminiscent of a coffin. To his relief, the stairs soon levelled out into a tunnel. There were rough boards of whitewashed wood on the walls and a long swag of cables, providing electricity to bare bulbs which lit the way. Although the gradient was gentle, Jude could tell they were heading further underground. Emil glanced back over his shoulder.

'Mind your head, and your footing while you're about it. I take no responsibility for your safety.'

It grew colder as they descended, a smell of damp must and something else. Something acrid, which burned in the back of his throat. The whitewashed boards ended abruptly, revealing rough-hewn walls, which gave off a dull gleam.

'Looks like marble, doesn't it?' said Emil.

Jude ran a hand across the surface. It felt like cold hard stone.

'Rock salt,' Emil continued. 'Lick your finger if you don't believe me.'

Jude did and felt his mouth pucker.

Emil laughed without much humour. 'It carves like marble, too. This tunnel and those steps ahead? They hacked them out with picks and axes. Amazing really, when you see it all up close.'

The passage came to an end ahead. A metal handrail and a flight of steps led down, disappearing into shadow.

'Go slow from here, it's very slippery,' cautioned Emil. 'I'll go ahead and get the light.'

Jude focused all his attention on where he was going, placing one foot after another in the gloom. When he reached the handrail, the space around him opened up and the darkness sucked him in.

'Mind your eyes.'

Jude heard the clunk and stutter of a fluorescent lightbulb and winced at the sudden brightness. The space was bathed in a sickly blue-white glow. It revealed a rough chamber, no bigger than the dining hall upstairs. Emil gestured all around him, 'This is what the castle was built on, in every way. Salt used to be called white gold. The Habsburgs built their fortune from it, though this is very modest in comparison. When larger deposits were discovered, this place fell into decline. The workers turned to carving wood instead. Our nearest town is known for it, though I don't suppose many tourists understand that when they buy a souvenir.'

Jude shivered as he felt the cold seep in. Emil seemed oblivious.

'They used to call this place the Chapel. It's an antechamber, really – the caves go down for more than ninety metres. It always gave me horrors as a child, thinking of those workers down here in the dark, wriggling around like maggots, trying to squeeze through tiny gaps. I think it's about being so far from the surface. No quick escape route if you need it and a thousand tons of minerals above you, pressing down . . .'

'Dear God,' said Jude.

'One can imagine why they'd want to offer up a prayer.'

Standing there in his dressing gown, trainers and jogging bottoms, Emil seemed curiously detached.

'Why did you bring me here, Emil?'

'Because I needed to atone.'

Jude realized with a sudden dull certainty that no one knew he was down here. Not even Cindy von Niedermeyer. Only Emil, with all his secrets.

'Some enterprising soul decided to carve a small baptismal font down here, because of the name, I suppose. In case you need a dousing before descending to the underworld. Would you care to see it? It's quite peculiar.' Emil crossed the chamber to the far wall, where a deep recess had been cut. 'My father was responsible for bringing electricity down here in the 1950s. They only had candles and oil lamps before that.'

Above the baptismal, an ornate brass chandelier hung from the cavern ceiling.

'One of Father's little affectations.'

Emil reached over and pulled a cord to switch it on. The light of the chandelier wasn't the ugly violet of fluorescence, but a rich, warm gold, though Jude didn't notice at the time. He only saw what it illuminated: a gallery of paintings, dozens of them hung in gilded splendour across the jagged wall. He gazed at them, entirely lost for words.

Emil sighed, his barrel chest expanding then contracting with a great release of air. He gave a pathetic sort of flourish. 'Behold, my father's damned collection. I've kept this secret far too long.'

CHAPTER THIRTY-ONE

ROME, JANUARY 1944

The new year began with shots fired shortly after midnight. At the Hotel Excelsior, the occupying forces picked over what remained in Rome. They might be down to the dregs, but that didn't stop them celebrating. They vowed to murder the old year and went out into the night to fire off rifles, pistols, shotguns and machine guns – any weapon they could lay their hands on.

The next day the first snow fell, casting a cold mantle on the hills outside the city. No one had believed this bloody occupation would last so long. Rumours of an Allied invasion persisted, but never seemed to come. Life, such as it was, ground on and on and on.

For Luca, the weeks following Tito's death were some of the hardest he had known. Tortured by his fears for Maddalena, he did no more than exist. Though she had managed to escape before the Carabinieri came to arrest her, he'd no idea where she had gone. Now she was a fugitive, though he attested to her innocence. He followed every rumour about the vicious torture of prisoners, of young women raped and murdered by their captors. At times he tried to comfort himself, believing he would have an instinct if she'd died or been arrested. It seemed likely she was still in hiding somewhere, though the prospect of her succumbing to slow starvation was hardly any better. He drove himself half mad with his imaginings and found he couldn't eat, or sleep, or concentrate on work.

Ordinarily this depression might have drawn attention, but Velare was a house in mourning. All the adults lived together, yet alone. Luca felt so full of fury, he couldn't speak to Violante or to the Signora. He loved his daughters, but their presence brought no respite, only guilt. He felt as if he'd brought a blight into their lives and couldn't shake the feeling they'd be better off without him. After weeks in hospital, Dolorosa returned home and finally to work, filling her days with labour. With both sons and a husband gone before her, Luca knew he couldn't offer any comfort. Like him, she existed as a shadow – cast from other people's light, but giving off none of her own.

Weeks passed, the new year came and went and still no word. The only thing which kept him going was faith in her and hope – sometimes enough to fuel him, at other points no more than a fume. The man he'd been was gone. If he was going to live, he had to be reborn.

*

Luca was in his office in the Vatican when a knock came at the door. It was his first day back after the new year. He'd been trying to commit himself to work, desperate for distraction, but could do little more than stare at a stack of images before him. The knock was hesitant. He thought about ignoring it, then reasoned that it might well be his brother. He shouted out, 'Come in'.

The young woman who opened the door wore a neat brown jacket and had an agitated air. She was in her early twenties; Maddalena's age, he thought. He'd seen her round the building, though he didn't know her name.

'Sorry to disturb you.' She hovered half in, half out of the room. 'I've come about a friend.'

'A friend?' asked Luca, utterly perplexed.

She stepped further forward. 'A friend I met in Santa Sabina, last September. I think you might remember – she said you were there, too.' Her intense expression was obviously trying to convey some meaning. Luca cast his mind back; though the basilica of Santa Sabina was close to home, he hardly ever went there. Couldn't think of a recent time, except of course when he had staggered in there carrying the burden of Santino, after he'd been shot . . . Luca sat bolt upright in his chair. 'Yes! I know your friend!' He fought the urge to rush across the room. 'Have you seen her? Is she well?'

The young woman's eyes widened. She shook her head and whispered, 'Not here.' Then raised her voice again. 'I'll be in the *Sala degli Animali* in half an hour – perhaps I might see you there?'

'Of course.'

She nodded then ducked back out into the hall.

Luca walked slowly round the Room of the Animals, a low winter light on the inlaid marble walls. He had to force himself to stop in front of every sculpture, even though a torrent of adrenaline was burning through his veins. He pretended to admire a carving of a human-looking monkey, a nutshell cradled in its paw. The room was open to the elements and bitterly cold. Outside, the frozen water in the fountain looked like it had been rendered out of glass. This winter was one of the harshest anyone could remember. He blew on his hands and stamped his feet, all his attention focused on the door.

At last, the girl came running in, her cheeks pink from exertion. 'Sorry. It was hard to get away.'

Luca was too anxious to waste any time on niceties. 'When did you last see Maddalena?'

The young woman glanced around, making sure they couldn't be overheard. 'I haven't seen her myself, but I've been told that she's quite well. My boyfriend knows her. He's a doctor and he's in contact with the place where she's been hiding.'

'Please, tell me everything you know. How is she?'

'Desperately cold and hungry, I suppose. They've almost nothing and there are quite a few of them in hiding there together. Rations don't go far. The partisans help where they can, but I shan't lie to you, it's a dire situation.'

Despite the terror flooding Luca's mind, he tried to focus. 'Is she safe?'

'For now, although it only takes one wrong move and the secret police will be all over them. Vincenzo fears they may be compromised already. They need to move them, but there's nowhere they can go.'

'How long?'

'Who can say? I'm sorry. That's all I know. I really need to go now, but I'll come again if I have news.'

'And if I need to reach you?'

'My name is Benedetta Camilo. I'm a secretary in the Latin Letters Office. Leave a note in my pigeonhole with a time and, if I'm able to, I'll meet you here.'

Luca nodded, then gripped her arm and whispered, 'Tell her to hang on. Tell her I'm going to find a way to get us out of here. I mean to leave Rome and take her with me. Tell her *both* of us, that's terribly important. Make sure she knows.'

With this news and Benedetta as an ally, Luca felt the cloud of his depression lift. He finally saw a path ahead and money paved the way. With help from Santino, Luca went back down through the coal chute and brought up gold coins and cash, which he'd stored away the year before.

He gave a large amount to Benedetta, who bought food from the *borsa nera* and delivered it to the people hiding Maddalena. She also secured the services of a partisan forger who specialized in passports. Luca's request was specific and therefore expensive: two service passports, like those issued by the Holy See, in the names of Mr and Mrs Luca Fremont. Benedetta gave the forger stamps and seals from her own department, while Luca worked for hours in his dark room, isolating portraits of them both from negatives in his collection. In the end, he produced two neat, square passport photographs in black and white.

Within a fortnight, Benedetta brought the finished passports to him. Luca hid them in his desk in a leather binder. The time had come to tell his brother about his change of heart.

'Oh, thank you, Luca. I can't tell you what this means to me, that you would risk so much for the *Damnatio Memoriae*.'

Luca felt a pang of guilt. Roberto's relief was almost palpable.

'You know we're taking in art and artefacts they got out of Naples just before the Allies went in? Six hundred cases. Nowhere is safe! Tell me, when would you plan to go?'

'As soon as you can have my cargo ready,' Luca replied.

'So fast?'

He'd guessed Roberto might question his change of heart and the need for so much haste. 'I've been thinking about what you said, and I realized how important this was to you. Right now, travel north is still possible, but who knows how long that will last? There are rumours of a full Allied invasion any day and increasing partisan battles on the border. I think it's now or never.'

Roberto stared earnestly at his younger brother. 'But are you certain? You seemed so reluctant last time we spoke.'

Luca couldn't lie to him outright, so instead he raised an eyebrow. 'You assured me I'd be perfectly safe travelling with Vatican plates and papers – has any of that changed?'

'Not in the least. There would be a major diplomatic incident if anyone, even the Germans, interfered with an official
operating on the Vatican's behalf. Our trucks go up and down
through the Brenner Pass quite frequently. The infrastructure
works, and we are neutral. No-one wants to incur the wrath
of the Catholics, I can promise you.'

'Then I am glad to do my part.'

Luca was determined to keep moving. If he stopped, even
for a moment, he might stall, and that was not an option.
Maddalena's life depended on it.

Roberto showed him the painting just once before the conservator cut it into quarters.

'Behold the greatest treasure of my *Damnatio Memoriae*.'

Luca was stunned. 'It's a Caravaggio. Based on *Youth with
a Ram?*'

Roberto nodded solemnly. 'It is. Brought here the year
after the artist's death, it's been concealed ever since. I trust
only you and one other to have sight of it. It will be your task
to preserve it twice over – first, by making a record for the
archives, and second by transporting it to its hiding place at
Gedächt. The conservator's job is to cut it with such precision
that it can be transported from here and put back together in
the future, when it's safe for it to return.'

Luca and the conservator worked together late into the
night. Luca took a photograph of the intact painting with
a large-form camera. He then went into the dark room to
develop this single print, while the conservator surgically
incised the canvas.

When cut, each piece was the length of Luca's arm. They encased the four large rectangles in a flat box, made with a thin veneer of pine. It fitted comfortably inside the lid of a good-sized suitcase. Sturdy brown leather, reinforced, and lined with silk, it was heavy, but fully half of it was free for him to store his clothes, as well as a dozen gold coins for emergencies, and anything else he might take with him from Velare. The time had come. He left a message for Benedetta, telling her to stand by.

The night before he was due to leave, Luca embraced his older brother and took the suitcase from him. Roberto had arranged for the loan of a Lancia Astura from the diplomatic fleet. Luca had been somewhat surprised to see its sleek green two-toned polished curves.

'Isn't it rather conspicuous?'

'Diplomatic cars are meant to be. You don't want to go unnoticed; you want people to see you coming and let you through. The plates and the papers are proof you are an agent of the Pope, acting in the world on his behalf. You have fuel cans and touring maps and I've arranged for you to spend the night at a monastery which helps maintain our vehicles. You'll be well looked after, but I beg you, go straight there and come right back. This painting is the most precious part of my collection, but you are more important.'

Luca hugged his brother tightly, reluctant to let go. He had no idea when he might see him next; knew Roberto wouldn't countenance his choice. He only prayed that, given time, he might forgive him.

When he got home, Luca parked the car at the bottom of

the driveway, fearing an unfamiliar engine might wake the entire street. Rome's curfew lasted until 6 a.m. and he meant to get started at first light. Given the unpredictability of the weather and the journey, he had a long, long road ahead.

Violante had been appalled at his proposal to leave the city on an errand for Roberto, but as this was a service to the Catholic Church, she could hardly object. In the days prior to the journey, Luca spent as much time as he could with his children, though Balia Paola became increasingly frustrated.

'Am I not trusted?' she asked.

'It isn't that. I'm going away for a while, and simply wish to spend time with my girls before I go.'

He'd played card games with them, read to them and crept from the room when they finally slept. Then he'd gone upstairs and wept, stifling the sound. He had no doubt this decision would alter all their lives. His daughters would never look at him with the same innocence again, and yet he had no choice. Ahead of him lay a narrow path, full of hazards. Taking it seemed like the only way for everyone to live.

*

Luca woke in the dark before dawn and pulled his clothes on. He passed the doors of his sleeping family, knowing that to wake them would risk breaking his conviction. Better to act as if his journey had already begun.

Carrying the suitcase, he left his house and closed the door quietly behind him. He walked down the steps and across the gravel driveway, where Tito's lifeless body had once lain. So many paths had crossed here, departures and arrivals.

At the corner, he looked back over his shoulder. Two little silhouettes stood at their bedroom window – too small and distant to make out their expressions, though he thought he saw them waving. He put down the case and lifted his hand to wave back, but they had gone. Fearing he might stay there, frozen like a pillar, Luca forced himself to turn away and carry on.

The bells of Santa Sabina started ringing. The sound sent up a mass of starlings, which had been roosting in the stone pines. Luca flinched, in that moment mistaking them for a cloud of flak from anti-aircraft gunners stationed on the hill. He scanned the skyline for a bomber's silhouette, but there was none; only this convulsion, flocking together and flying apart. Fleeting and ephemeral; mortal but divine.

The ancient Romans thought if the gods cared for humans, they would send a sign of their will in the movement of the birds. Luca wondered what the starlings might have told them, then decided he'd had enough of superstition. He defied augury; the readiness was all.

CHAPTER THIRTY-TWO

Luca stood beside the car, nervously waiting in the cold shadow of the building. He'd no idea where Maddalena had been hiding; Benedetta only told him where and when to rendezvous with them. He was pacing to and fro when he heard footsteps and a murmured conversation. Suddenly the two young women appeared in the half-light, Maddalena leaning heavily on Benedetta. Even from across the street, he could see the bones of her face were razor-sharp. There was a sallow tone to her complexion. Her clothes hung off her, the coat belted so tightly at the waist, he thought he could wrap it in the span of both his hands. Her wrists so frail and slender he feared they might break, though she carried very little – just a small cardboard suitcase in one hand and the ledger which held her recipes tucked underneath her arm.

The two women started across the Via della Reginella. Luca's eyes sought Maddalena's out, but she kept her gaze averted. When they reached the car, the women hugged each other tightly. Benedetta opened the passenger door to help Maddalena in, all the while checking up and down the street to ensure they went unnoticed. She bent down, kissed her friend on the cheek, then closed the door. Luca walked around the car to meet Benedetta. 'This is for you.' He pressed a thick envelope of money into her palm. 'It doesn't begin to express my gratitude.' Benedetta's eyes filled with tears, which she quickly brushed away. 'There's no need. Just promise me you'll get her somewhere safe.' Luca hesitated till she laughed, 'Well, go on then!' Finally spurred into action, he jumped into the driver's seat, started up the engine and pulled away, the blood in his temples pounding so hard he could barely see.

Even as he navigated the narrow alleyways and cross streets of the ghetto, Luca tried to keep one eye on the road and one on Maddalena. She sat beside him, bolt upright, her slim legs pinned together, holding the suitcase and the ledger in her lap. Her knuckles were white, her jaw clenched – all raw nerves and spiky sinews. Neither of them said a word, but he reached out to take her hand, letting go only to change the gears, then reaching back to hold it once again. He drove that way across the entire city.

Roberto had been right. The two-toned green car was so conspicuous, it seemed to exert its own gravity. At checkpoints the soldiers would be polite to the point of deference, simply glancing at the paperwork, then waving them both on. The service passport Roberto had provided languished in his suitcase. Instead, he presented the two partisan forgeries which Benedetta had obtained. Maddalena Viscuso and Conte Luciano Montefalco no longer existed – they'd been replaced by Mr and Mrs Luca Fremont. After a long period of silence, it occurred to him to show these passports to Maddalena. More than a little perplexed, she took them from him, opening the first to see her picture there, along with her new name. When she opened the second one and saw what it suggested, she started weeping silent tears, which nearly broke him. Luca had to pull the car over, unable to continue. He put his arms around her, the feeling so familiar and yet half forgotten. He held her till her sobs subsided, stroking her hair as little by little, the tension ebbed away. He kissed her on the top of her head, feeling oddly chaste and shy. When she spoke at last, her voice was feather-light and fractured.

'I'm so sorry, Luca. I've taken you from them and that was never my intention. I made you break your vows . . .'

He shook his head fiercely. 'The war did that. It frayed them till they tore; our own sharp edges did the rest.'

She turned her face away. He put a gentle hand on her cheek, to turn it back.

'You are not to blame, surely you must see that? You've suffered quite enough. I can't imagine what you've been through, but I can see that it was hell. You don't have to say a word if you don't want to. I shan't make you.' Searching for distraction, he leaned over and pulled four maps from the leather pocket inside the upholstered door. 'I have a task for you instead. Be my navigator? I would be truly grateful. Stop us driving round in circles, getting lost.' He handed her the stack of *Carta D'Italia* touring maps.

'Where are we going?'

'To Castel Gedächt in South Tyrol, where I can finally protect you.'

The act of travelling proved a balm for their discomfort, giving them shared purpose. This was the longest journey Maddalena had embarked on since leaving home. Even the touring maps were unfamiliar, though she applied herself gladly to the task. The hours passed and so did the kilometres, despite the frequent checkpoints. Each time they stopped, a hush descended on the car and they both held their breath until they pulled away again. After a time, Luca remembered that Dolorosa had packed a wicker basket for his journey. Knowing how much she mourned for Maddalena, he'd longed to say she was alive. The cook would have been thrilled to see her open the basket, to find fresh ciriola bread and a leather-wrapped thermos of hot soup.

'Don't eat too much too quickly,' Luca cautioned. 'You'll need to build your stamina up slowly.' He need not have worried; she felt full after a few mouthfuls, having little more appetite than a bird. Somehow, this shared act helped ease the way. Luca told her about the days after Tito's execution; how he had attempted to defend her and keep the Carabinieri off her trail, realizing it was safer for Maddalena's sake to keep the Signora in his debt and close at hand.

In turn, Maddalena began to say a little about her time in the tiny attic on Via della Reginella. She'd shared it with two Jewish women, Naomi and Ruth, and their four children. The adults had taken it in turns to sleep alongside the children on two dirty mattresses laid out on the floor. Maddalena had happily shared the childcare and the cooking, though there was barely any food: steamed cabbage in a weak stock made up most of their diet, plus one small morsel of precious bread, which each of them consumed throughout the day. They would chew on a tiny piece at the start and finish of each meal, drinking cup after cup of water to try to fool their empty bellies.

Hardly knowing how she'd endured these weeks of torment, Luca tried to help her look ahead. 'When we get to Castel Gedächt, I'll go and pay a visit to the neighbours. They're farmers; with any luck they'll have some food to sell. A little meat, a few vegetables, maybe even flour. It's not like it is in the city. It's always been a hard life up there in the winter, but they usually have good stores of food.'

'Won't they question what we're doing there together?'

'The locals know me and the family, of course, but I doubt we'll see that many people. If we do, we only have to say you're there to cook and clean for me, but that is ever so unlikely. Try not to worry.'

Luca didn't voice his real concern, that Maddalena was still a wanted criminal, and he a married man.

'Let's take this one day at a time. Once we get to the Dolomites, with any luck we can relax.'

'What happens after that though, Luca? What next?'

'I don't know. The hard truth is, there are no easy answers, but we have time to make a plan.'

The road ran north, through flat frozen fields and sudden craters, where stray bombs had gone to ground. There were German tanks ploughing in the opposite direction, driving south towards some future conflict, buildings pockmarked by machine guns and donkeys lying dead, their rough carts abandoned by the roadside. After several hours, a grey mass of clouds gathered on the horizon and began to turn a sickly yellow. Soon the sky was full of slanting snowflakes.

They stopped overnight at a Benedictine monastery a few miles off the road, for food, fuel and snow chains. The monks had been expecting a single man and were surprised to receive a married couple. They apologized − they had no double rooms − and put them both up in separate, austere cells. Each was quietly grateful for their solitary space, and slept deeply. Luca wondered what Roberto might think if word got back, though there was nothing he could do to prevent it.

They took to the road again early the next morning and watched the landscape change − rice fields, vineyards, orchards, farms and factories. Maddalena slept and a dozen kilometres slipped under the wheels, and then a dozen more. Hours passed as Luca drove through nondescript countryside, and the outskirts of much bigger towns. Then slowly, the vistas in the distance grew. Hills turned to white-capped ridges, turned to mountains, their peaks lost in the clouds as the light began to fade. The chains on the tyres bit in; though these high roads could be perilous at times, they were not impassable. His Roman friends were amazed whenever he chose to visit in the winter, but as he explained, snow and ice were part of the fabric of life up here for almost half the year.

The sky over the Dolomites was dark as steel when he finally turned the steering wheel onto the track, below the castle. Maddalena slept beside him, curled up in a woollen travel blanket which he'd found on the back seat. Looking at her, he felt the same lurch of love and anxious pity as he had when she'd walked towards him at dawn on the previous day. He brushed her cheek, the skin soft and luminously pale.

'We're here.'

She stirred and murmured in her sleep.

'I'm sorry, I wish I didn't have to wake you.'

Maddalena opened her eyes and stretched, taking a moment to adjust – to him, the snow, the jagged mountains now close by, and the towering keep which loomed above them.

'Welcome to Castel Gedächt.'

She stared up at the steep walls. 'It's like something from a fairy tale. I had no idea ...'

'This is the gateway to the Alps. This castle has been standing guard for seven hundred years. It's also absolutely freezing and will take an awful time to get warmed up. Now, bring that blanket and we can camp out in one room until we get the fires going.'

He lifted their two cases out: hers small and light and almost empty, his weighed down with contents more precious than he dared contemplate right now. Maddalena leaned against him as they climbed the snowy path up to the gatehouse. He took the keys from his coat pocket and wrestled with the heavy wooden doors, pushing them apart to reveal a steep courtyard inside the castle walls: a clock tower, a high chapel in the ramparts, a covered well. Archways and balconies and pale plaster facades with fading frescoes.

Suddenly a terrifying volley of barks assailed them. Two huge dogs leapt out of the shadows: great, vulpine beasts – black and tan, and bristling with muscle – they were tied to lengths of chain, which only just restrained them. Maddalena clung to Luca's arm as the dogs snapped and snarled at the very limit of their stays.

'*Halt die Klappe!*'

A thickset man appeared on the balcony which overlooked the courtyard. He came running down a flight of steps towards them, brandishing a shotgun.

'*Dummkopf!*' he growled at the dogs. He raised the barrel of the shotgun and trained it on Luca and Maddalena. 'Who the hell are you and what are you doing on my land?'

Luca moved himself between the snarling dogs and Maddalena.

'I'm Conte Luciano Montefalco and this is my ancestral home.'

'Show me proof.'

Luca put his suitcase on the ground and opened it, handing over the Vatican service passport which Roberto had provided.

'You work for the Vatican?'

'I do.'

The man seemed a little mollified, at least enough to lower the barrel and point the shotgun toward the ground. He gave the passport back to Luca and held out his hand.

'Heinrich von Niedermeyer.'

Somewhat reluctantly, Luca took it. Von Niedermeyer's hulking frame was reminiscent of his dogs'.

'I apologize for any confusion – the castle was requisitioned for use by the Gauleiter's office three months ago. You should have been informed.'

Luca narrowed his eyes. 'I received no notice.'

'Well, I can hardly be blamed for that.' Von Niedermeyer shrugged. 'I am a good soldier, and I go where I am sent.'

'You're an officer?'

'I was speaking rhetorically. I deal in art, on behalf of the *Einsatzstab Reichsleiter Rosenberg*; cultural appropriation for *der Führer.*'

'And you think that gives you the right to occupy my home,' Luca stated flatly. Von Niedermeyer gave him a humourless smile in reply.

'It was deemed to be suitable for my purposes. Since the entire South Tyrol now falls under the *Operationszone Alpenvorland,* I suppose my needs outweigh yours.' He de-cocked the shotgun, laying it open across his arm. 'Whether you received a telegram or not is irrelevant. This castle was legally requisitioned, and the law is on my side. No need take it personally, *Signore.*'

'This castle has been in my family for centuries, so forgive me if it does seem somewhat personal to me. And it is *Conte* Luciano Montefalco,' Luca said deliberately.

Von Niedermeyer turned to Maddalena. 'And how should I address you – as *contessa*?'

She hadn't been expecting the question and cast a nervous glance at Luca, who abruptly intervened.

'No. No, this is Maddalena. She's here to look after me. To cook and clean. I'd burn water if I was left to my own devices in a kitchen.'

Von Niedermeyer smiled at Maddalena as he replied. 'I am the same. Someone comes up from the village once a week and brings a few supplies. She's an old crone and not very capable, but we manage.' He paused briefly and then said, 'Have you eaten? Signora Carpetti made me some sort of mutton stew. Perhaps instead of standing in the snow like savages, we could all go inside and continue our conversation in the warm?'

When Heinrich von Niedermeyer led them into the large kitchen, Maddalena couldn't help but draw a breath. It was not dissimilar to Velare, except that all the wood was dark and varnished with carved edges, but she was amazed by the sheer quantity of provisions. On the table were two large pies, wrapped in waxed paper, and an apple strudel on a cake stand. A row of enamel bins sat in descending size: flour, sugar, tea and coffee, and a wire basket with a dozen deep brown eggs. Cavolo nero, two little cabbages and a fat head of broccoli sat in a box on the marble counter, while a fresh loaf of bread lay sliced up on a chopping board, the crust a nutty brown. Maddalena felt her mouth water even as she looked at it.

On the stove, a huge pot of stew was bubbling away – far more than one man could hope to eat, even if he were exceptionally greedy. She went over to stir it and inhaled the rich odour, thinking for a moment she might pass out.

Von Niedermeyer didn't seem to notice. 'I know you Italians like to eat later, but you'd be very welcome to dine with me, if you haven't made other plans.'

'Our plans were to eat here,' Luca said, his tone still a little sour. 'But thank you, that's extremely generous. We've been on the road all day and we are hungry.'

'Especially this one, eh?' Heinrich grinned at Maddalena

while elbowing Luca in the ribs. 'We need to put a little meat on your bones, young lady!'

Von Niedermeyer clapped his hands together. 'I have an idea! Why don't you both stay here for the night. I can hardly turn you out into the snow. Then we can all go to Bolzano tomorrow, to the Gauleiter's office, and see what they say. Straighten out this business with the telegram. They may not realize you're working for the Vatican. I have no wish to tangle with the Pope.'

'Thank you,' said Luca. 'That's very generous. I accept.'

His smile was gracious, but Maddalena could tell he was reluctant. Von Niedermeyer turned to her.

'Well then, why don't you take the little bedroom at the end of this corridor and the conte can take the larger room next door? There are clean linens in the blanket box, and you could light the fires in there. Shouldn't take a moment.'

Luca interjected. 'I don't mind bunking down in the study. Save Maddalena from going to all that effort.'

'No, I think not,' the German replied curtly. 'That room is being used for storage and besides, Maddalena doesn't mind, do you my dear? After all, that's what you're here for.'

'Of course.' She glanced at Luca, his face a mask of placidity, though she knew he was on edge.

'While you are about that, we gentlemen can relax. I am keen to hear all about your dealings with the Holy Father. I think this calls for a bottle of something, don't you?'

After making the beds and laying the fires, Maddalena retreated to the kitchen to serve out supper. Von Niedermeyer insisted they eat in the formal dining room next door, a grand space with weapons, shields and taxidermy hung on every wall. All three of them sat together at one end of a dark-wood dining table, with candles lit and a roaring open fire. The food was simple but it felt like a sumptuous affair. Maddalena still couldn't stomach much; knowing her appetite needed to be grown, she ate a little of everything and let her taste buds simply savour the variety. She allowed the conversation to flow around her, still utterly overwhelmed by such a dramatic change in her circumstances. Only two nights before, her dinner had consisted of half a cup of watery soup with a morsel of bread. More than anything, she wished she could send the full plate in front of her to the children in the attic.

After dinner, the men moved through to a little library, while she made them coffee and then cleared up. She tidied everything back and made a plan for the breakfast she would prepare in the morning. Von Niedermeyer's cook had left a bowlful of *biga*, an excellent starter dough for bread and she whipped up a little batter for *crespelle*, Luca's favourite pancake, which she hadn't made in years. She could not get over the quantities of butter, flour, oil, salt – even a tiny amount would have been enough to transform the meals she made while in hiding.

Balancing a tray of coffee, cups and cream, Maddalena knocked on the door to the library. Both Luca and Heinrich simultaneously called out, 'Come in.'

Heinrich, whose face was red and shining from the wine, found this hilarious. He slapped a hand down on one knee. 'Did you hear that? Both of us at once. Come in!' His shoulders shook with mirth. 'What can we do for you, Maddalena?

Your wish is our command. A glass of wine, perhaps?' He picked up the bottle, which was almost empty.

'Thank you, no.'

'No more for me either,' said Luca, sliding his own glass out of reach.

'Oh, please don't make me drink alone! Indulge me.' Von Niedermeyer leaned forward and sloshed the remains between both men's glasses.

'I hope you don't mind, Herr von Niedermeyer, but I made a batter for some *crespelle* for breakfast. There was a little milk left out, which I didn't want to go to waste.'

'My kitchen is yours – help yourself to anything you need. I have a very good grocer who supplies everyone important in the Alpine Zone.'

'I can't think how long it's been since I had *crespelle*,' sighed Luca. He turned to von Niedermeyer proudly. 'Maddalena is the best cook in Italy, bar none.'

'Is that so?' He raised his eyebrows. 'Then I look forward to sampling your breakfast. Now, will you come and join us?'

Though it was only eight o'clock, she felt utterly exhausted. 'If you don't mind, I should just like to turn in.'

Von Niedermeyer nodded. 'No doubt you're tired from the journey. I've had a little tankless water heater fitted in the bathroom; if you like, you could run yourself a bath.'

'Thank you, Herr von Niedermeyer.'

She exchanged a look with Luca, saw that he felt forced to stay. Maddalena left the room and closed the door behind her, pausing for a time to catch her breath. She heard von Niedermeyer's slurring voice.

'I know you haven't brought that girl up here in the midst of winter purely for her cooking skills, am I right? Tell me if I'm wrong and I'll have a crack at her myself!'

Half an hour later, Maddalena stepped into a deep bath of steaming water. She sank her head to rinse away the musty odour of the attic and felt it softening her tight-wired shoulders. She lay there until her fingers pruned and the water started to go cold. Afterwards, sitting on the horse-hair mattress, she felt transported: the fire in the grate sent flights of orange dancing round the walls; she was utterly clean and warm at last. In her ledger she jotted down a list of all the food she'd make for breakfast. But for the abrasive company of Heinrich von Niedermeyer, this place was as close to heaven as anywhere she'd ever known. Outside, the deadening snow made the world unnaturally quiet. After spending a month at such close quarters with six others, the silence was almost overwhelming. She thought perhaps she wouldn't sleep, and yet she must have, because when she stirred again the fire had all but burned out in the grate. There was just a smouldering of embers. A figure sat in the little armchair in the corner, lost in thought.

'Luca?'

He turned his face towards her. 'I didn't know if I should wake you.'

'What is it – what's happened?'

'I'm so sorry that I brought you here.' He glanced towards the door. 'That man is very, very dangerous. I think he may have stolen some things belonging to my brother. I fear we're in grave danger. We have to leave here first thing in the morning.'

'But where will we go?' Maddalena asked.

'I've no idea. I only know we cannot stay.'

At 6 a.m., Maddalena dressed in the dark and walked along the corridor, into the kitchen. She'd planned a menu like no other, for a very special purpose.

First came the bread.

She would bake two types. A dozen *filone* loaves, long, thick sticks with a light crumb. The fermentation and the first and second rise meant she needed to get started straight away. Then two dozen *rosette di pane*, the traditional rose bread of the region, which puffed up into delicate little rolls. The cook's starter, the *biga,* would be put to good use. Maddalena had made both breads with Dolorosa on dozens of occasions, though not for quite some time. They still might prove a challenge; without the right ingredients or proving, they would not rise correctly. She only hoped she hadn't lost her touch.

She opened her recipe book, the product of nearly five years in the kitchen of Velare, where she'd honed her craft. All those skills would be called upon today. The room soon filled with the rich scent of yeast from the dough, rising gently under cloth. Maddalena moved on to the *crespelle* while she waited, then to grinding up two sweetened pastes of hazelnuts and almonds, to fill the bread rolls when they came out of the oven. Added to the table were slices of wafer-thin mortadella and a hard alpine cheese, as white as snow. Outside, the sun began to rise over the mountains; crisp and bitterly cold, but promising. There were no clouds, only a bright ice blue beyond the pale peaks of the Dolomites.

The bread needed her attention, a second prove, knocked back and left to rise again. She sank her hands into its flesh, rolling the heels in deeply, time and time again. The oven made the kitchen warm and fragrant. Having barely slept, it lulled her into a soporific state, although she knew she had to stay awake and stay alert. She and Luca had sat up for hours the night before, discussing their predicament and trying to reason a way out. Luca shared his fear that von Niedermeyer had them trapped and knew more than he was letting on. A meeting with the *Gauleiter*, the Nazi prefect of the region, could be their undoing – it would only take a telephone call to expose them. The punishment for Maddalena's crimes would be death by execution. Of that, he had no doubt.

Luca told her about the paintings, his brother's secret works of art, how they'd been hidden here to protect them from Nazi looters and the bitter irony of von Niedermeyer's presence. Maddalena had thought this place a fairy tale. It was, but so much darker than imagined – a seductive palace and the wolf within it, waiting to devour them.

'Something smells delicious.'

She spun round at the sound of von Niedermeyer's voice. 'Good morning, Maddalena. I didn't mean to startle you.'

Luca stood beside him, tired and pale, though von Niedermeyer seemed oblivious. He looked around the kitchen at the signs of her endeavours – the bread roses and *filoni* waiting for the oven, the plates of cheese and ham.

'You've made a feast!'

'It's almost ready. Why don't you gentlemen go and sit down at the table? I'll bring it to you shortly.'

'You were right, Conte, she is a real treasure. She'll make a wonderful wife one day.'

Maddalena felt her skin crawl even as she smiled. She exchanged a look with Luca. He nodded, almost imperceptibly, the signal that things were as bad as he suspected. Not mere concern, but now proof they were in mortal danger. Maddalena's hands shook as she put the bread into the oven. She only prayed that it would rise.

*

Luca fixed a broad smile on his face and kept it there throughout breakfast. Although the food was delicious, he could barely swallow; a knot of anxiety tying his throat. Von Niedermeyer went back for one bread rosebud after another, filling them with sweet and savoury concoctions.

As he watched the big man gorge himself, Luca kept replaying the events of the night before. His evening with von Niedermeyer had started awkwardly enough – he found Heinrich pompous and boorish and resented having to defer to him in his own home. It was only when the wine loosened his tongue that his true nature was revealed.

Von Niedermeyer's questions about his work with the Vatican showed he knew a good deal more about the family than he'd professed. The more intoxicated he became, the more he let things slip. He knew Roberto's name and his position in the church. Luca pretended to match him glass for glass, filling the German's each time he ran low. He volunteered to go and fetch more bottles from the kitchen; on his way back he stopped to try the study door. It was locked, but Luca was not without resources. He returned to the library and waited until the large man drank himself unconscious, lying slumped and utterly inebriated in his chair. Luca carefully lifted the ring of keys from Heinrich's pocket and went back to the study with a lighted candle. Slipping the key into the lock, he crept inside and saw two dozen paintings lined up against the walls, some still in the pine-wood crates he'd personally transported from the Vatican so many months before. He was certain this was his brother's secret collection: the *Damnatio Memoriae*.

Luca returned to the library and gingerly replaced the keys in von Niedermeyer's pocket then tiptoed away. He went to Maddalena's room and sat in the dimming light of the fire, trying to calm the panicked inner voice which screamed they were in danger. He shared his fears with her when she woke and they spent the next few hours devising a plan for their escape.

Now Luca watched warily as von Niedermeyer tucked into yet another plate of food and spoke around each mouthful.

'I telephoned the Gauleiter's office – they're expecting us this afternoon. I'll put in a good word for you. Who knows, they might decide your claim is greater, in which case I'll be happy to vacate.' His slow smile suggested he thought nothing of the sort. 'In the meantime, it looks like it's going to be a clear day. We ought to make the most of it.'

'I promised Maddalena I would show her a decent view of the Dolomites. It's her first time in the mountains. We might take a little picnic.'

'That sounds wonderful. What time shall we leave?'

It was Luca's turn to smile, though his was hesitant, embarrassed.

'I wonder if I might be candid. Man to man, as it were.'

Von Niedermeyer looked intrigued. 'Please go ahead. I am the very soul of discretion.'

'It's just . . . I hoped to have a little time with her alone, you understand. So grateful to enjoy your hospitality, but this was the whole point of the trip. Obviously, with you in residence, it didn't quite turn out the way I'd planned.'

Von Niedermeyer leered. 'You sly dog. I knew it! Of course. Enjoy your picnic and make sure to take a blanket.'

Luca watched Maddalena as she crossed the courtyard, carrying a wicker basket to the car. She walked with stiff, straight shoulders. If you looked closely, you might see her hands were trembling, although that could just be the cold. Only Luca knew the basket contained a dozen *pane di rosette* rolls. Puffed and hollow, the base of each had been cut open, and now concealed twelve gold coins. Sticking out of the basket were four *filone* – straight, stick-like loaves, each as long as Maddalena's arm. She looked for all the world as if she might be going to the market, though were she to sell these wares at the *borsa nera*, she'd never have to work another day. He'd watched as Maddalena rolled each of the four quarters of the Caravaggio as tightly as she dared, working them into the hollow core of the loaves and stuffing the ends with bread. Underneath them all, she'd placed her ledger, a constant through these last chaotic years. He knew it meant much more to her than simple recipes.

Von Niedermeyer and Luca were standing in the courtyard, the two dogs lying at their feet. Heinrich slapped him on the shoulder.

'Enjoy the view. I'll drive us all to Bolzano as soon as you return.'

'Right then,' said Luca, his smile feeling like a rictus grin. 'I suppose we'd best get on.'

'By the way, I loaded your cases into the boot of my car, in preparation. You don't need anything, do you?'

Luca shook his head, thankful that the service passports for Mr and Mrs Fremont were hidden safely in the glove compartment.

Surprisingly nimble on his feet, Heinrich ran to open the door of the Lancia for Maddalena. She settled into the passenger seat with the basket on her lap. Luca got in beside her and started up the engine. He was about to pull away, when von Niedermeyer called out 'Wait!' He gestured to Maddalena to wind down her window. She did as she was told, and the stocky German leaned his shoulders in.

'Now then, Maddalena. Don't be greedy.'

He grinned as he plucked two of the four long *filone* loaves from her basket and tucked them underneath his arm.

'Have fun you two. Don't do anything I wouldn't do.'

CHAPTER THIRTY-THREE

SOUTH TYROL, OCTOBER 1997

Jude and Emil stood before the gallery on the wall of the salt cave. There were two dozen paintings in total, some by artists Jude recognized – Titian, Vermeer and Guido Reni – as well as many others he did not.

Emil gestured to the paintings glumly. 'My father made all this for his own perverse pleasure. I think his chief delight was their possession; something even Hitler couldn't claim. When he first came upon the paintings hidden here, he believed they belonged to some private collector with a taste for the erotic.'

Jude scanned the images and saw that a few were sexual, the subject matter of some quite shocking, even to his modern eyes. There was a small but highly charged depiction of Adam and Eve and the serpent, their limbs and coils entwined in a knot of writhing flesh. Another image showed a papal figure blessing dozens of naked women, who had fallen to the floor in paroxysms of ecstasy.

Emil continued in his flat tone. 'Quite a few of them are salacious, but by no means all.'

There were several plain portraits of people Jude didn't recognize, a sable-skinned Madonna and several bucolic landscapes which could not possibly cause offence. Emil gazed at them all sadly.

'One painting changed his whole perspective.'

'The Caravaggio,' said Jude.

Emil von Niedermeyer looked at him with curiosity and some suspicion. 'You knew it was here.'

'I thought it very possible, although I had no idea what to expect, until now.'

The Caravaggio took up the most space on the wall. Hung in the centre, in a gilt frame, it was meant to be the focal point. It was no surprise to Jude that the entire left half of the canvas was missing. What was shocking was what was there. The right half of the canvas showed a male figure, kneeling. Had St John been present, they would have been intimately close, one wrapped around the other.

The face of the kneeling figure was one Jude recognized right away – a self-portrait of Michelangelo Merisi, otherwise known as Caravaggio. He was familiar with those dark curls, raven-black eyes and arching brows. The artist had painted himself many times: as a youth and before his death. His face was even on the 100,000 lire note which Jude had folded in his wallet, for goodness' sake. The difference here was in Caravaggio's expression – not fraternal love, but carnal longing. If the rest of the canvas had been in place, he would be gazing at St John with lust, intent on feasting on his flesh, Eros fallen on Narcissus.

Jude walked closer to examine it. The glow from the chandelier was dim, which made it hard to make out all the details, but he saw the painted shadows right away. A telltale circle, like a halo, on the oak leaves in the background. On the ground, a pattern suggestive of a fish. This was not just a painting of two men filled with erotic tension, but Jude was certain Caravaggio had also chosen to depict himself as a Christ-like figure, embracing young St John. Were it complete, it would not only be a masterpiece, but a scandal which would shock the art world to its core. An unknown Caravaggio was one thing, but one which suggested homoerotic blasphemy was more than Jude could ever have imagined.

'Quite something, isn't it?' said Emil mildly.

'That's an understatement.'

'My father came across the Caravaggio more by luck than judgement. The owner of the castle – your client's father, I presume – turned up here in early 1944 with a young woman. He was travelling as an emissary of the Pope and his brother was a senior prelate. My father realized the Vatican had to be the source of all the hidden paintings, which made them even more valuable in his eyes. He planned to have both the conte and his companion arrested, but they must have caught on, because they absconded. They'd concealed the Caravaggio in loaves of bread which they were attempting to smuggle out. This half of the painting was inadvertently left behind. My father never knew what happened to the rest. He believed the couple escaped to Switzerland – to live in exile or die in the attempt.'

Emil scuffed the toe of his trainers on the cavern floor. 'Like so many, after the war my father went back to being an ordinary citizen. It was chaos. Europe was a battlefield and it was relatively easy to cover one's tracks. Few asked questions, and if they did, he paid them off. He married my mother, they had me, my mother died and then he shipped me off to boarding school in England.'

Emil looked at Jude forlornly. 'My father relayed all this to me right before he died. I was eighteen years old. He told me how fortunate I was to inherit his secret treasures, that these were the rarest works of art the world had ever known. He never understood – it wasn't a gift to me; it was a curse. I took no joy from it, only horror, understanding who my father really was. My whole life built on these poisonous foundations. I drank my way through my twenties and most of the money he left. I tried to get sober quite a few times, but could never stay that way, until Cindy. We met in recovery, in Innsbruck. Both of us were addicts, but she saved me, then gave me my son. Through their existence I finally found a reason to keep on waking up each day.'

Jude had feared Emil when he'd first brought him down here; now he saw he was a tragic figure. 'Does Cindy know about the paintings?'

Emil nodded mournfully. 'Until you, she was the only person I'd ever told. She's always begged me to get rid of them. I couldn't, though. I gave Father my word, though I was tempted to destroy them.'

'What stopped you?'

'Father thought great art ought to be immortal – that its beauty transcends the bounds of history and morality. Not sure I agree with that entirely, but I couldn't do it, nonetheless. Couldn't have it on my conscience; sins of the father, and all that.'

Jude felt like dropping to the ground when they emerged from the dark and found daylight. He delighted in the warmth of the sun, which had finally burned through the mist. Emil was rather more circumspect.

'I thought I'd feel lighter once unburdened. Now I'm not sure if I do.'

'How long have you been keeping this a secret?' asked Jude.

'Thirty-one years,' Emil replied.

'Well then, give it time.'

They walked back up through the courtyard.

'I ought to let Cindy know where we've been. Do you mind if I just pop my head in?'

'Of course. Take your time.'

Jude wandered up to the flat, sedum-covered rooftop of the castle and leaned against the ramparts. He looked out across the hills, to the steel-grey mountains on the horizon. The air seemed preposterously clean and every shade of green and russet filled his vision: fields and cliffs and forests. Out of time and utterly romantic.

In the valley below stood a red barn with a mansard roof, reminiscent of the forged Modersohn-Becker painting which had come so close to destroying him. The sight of it brought back that sinking dread, somehow now diminished, less vivid than before. It felt like the end of everything when it happened, but now he wondered if it might just have been the closing of a chapter. If Emil could face his demons, so could he. Make a choice, decide if it defined him. The ever-present sense of dread, while not replaced with optimism, was at least tempered with relief. He thought about his mother: would she be proud of him, he wondered? Perhaps she might be, after all.

Some time later a subdued Emil rejoined him on the rooftop.

'I'm afraid you're in Cindy's bad books.'

'Oh dear,' said Jude.

'She isn't pleased you lied to her.'

'I might have a way to get back in her good graces.'

'How so?'

'Your father thought the conte ran off to Switzerland or died in the attempt. Except he didn't. He escaped to England with the other half of the painting. No one knows where the bottom left-hand section is, but the conte's daughter, Beatrice, has the top part and that's what led me to you.'

Jude couldn't imagine what Beatrice's parents must have endured in order to escape, with the awful knowledge of what they'd had to leave behind.

'Like your father, I'm convinced these paintings came from some secret archive of the Vatican. There have long been rumours of erotic art collections hidden by the Church, but what you've shown me seems more complicated – not merely a chapel of sin. In the case of the Caravaggio, it's blasphemy and homoeroticism combined, and that's potentially explosive. Let me talk to Beatrice, but I think if we play this right, we can rid you both of this burden, ease your financial worries and protect your reputations.'

After a moment, Emil shrugged. 'I would say what do I have I to lose, but I think that's already been established. Talk to your friend, come back with a plan and I'll get Cindy to take a look. She's the one you'll need to convince.'

Jude took his hand and shook it. 'It's a risk, I won't deny it, but the Vatican kept those paintings hidden for centuries, then your father did the same. You don't have to; it's time they saw the light of day.'

Beatrice got the call from Jude when she was sitting on the loggia of the pensione, drinking coffee with Sophia. The receptionist offered to transfer it to her room, so Beatrice dashed up the stairs and grabbed the handset.

'Hello?'

'Beatrice, is that you?'

'You found me!'

'I've been calling you for hours – they said you were out.'

'Sophia has been showing me around.' Beatrice felt shyly happy. 'She took me to this gorgeous villa – the Doria Pamphilj. We wanted to go and look at Caravaggio's St John, but we couldn't get tickets to the Capitoline, then I remembered you said they had another copy there.'

'And how was it?'

'Beautiful, but Sophia's absolutely certain – she has no memory of seeing it before.'

Jude couldn't contain his excitement any longer. 'It doesn't matter. The search is over.'

'What do you mean?'

'I mean, I'm calling you from a weird little hotel in the Dolomite Mountains, about an eight-hour drive from Rome. I went off-piste.'

'Miles off, by the sound of it.'

'I got your message about Castel Gedächt and decided I'd be able to find more out on the ground, so I hopped on a flight to Verona. I wanted to establish a connection, some concrete link between the castle and the painting.'

'And did you?' She felt infuriated and delighted.

'You could say that.'

'Then tell me!'

'I found it, Beatrice. I found the missing half, saw it with my own eyes! It's ... incredible, you won't believe it. A self-portrait of Caravaggio as Christ, embracing St John. I mean, it's very clearly meant to be erotic. It's going to blow everybody's minds ...'

'But how?'

'A long and very complicated story, but for now you'll be relieved to know I don't think either your mum or dad were actually to blame for this in any way. They didn't steal the painting. They escaped to England while trying to save it from a Nazi who was going to have them both arrested.'

Beatrice sat down on her bed, hardly able to take in what he was telling her.

'His son owns the castle now. I actually feel really sorry for the guy – he was burdened with all these painful secrets and a collection of stolen paintings which he's kept hidden all these years. There's dozens of them. He thinks they all came from the Vatican.'

'So what now?'

He paused. 'Here's how I see it: if we hand them over to the Vatican, there's a good chance they won't be seen again. You need money, so does Emil, and I think the world deserves to see these paintings. What if we go to the media with the story, find one of the big museums or a private benefactor who will buy the whole collection and put them on display?'

Beatrice couldn't answer; she needed time to think. Jude ploughed on, caught up in enthusiasm at the scheme.

'Let's face it, the Vatican doesn't need the money – they have literally billions. But you deserve to get something out of this. If you give me your permission, I'd like to draw up a plan which both parties can sign on to – say a 40/60 split on the Caravaggio between you and the von Niedermeyers, if we can find a buyer?'

'Would they buy it even though it's not intact?'

'I hope all the publicity might unearth the final piece. Whoever has it might not know what they're sitting on.'

'My God, Jude. Do you really think it's possible?

'I think that's entirely up to you.'

After hanging up, Beatrice walked back down to the loggia in a daze. The sounds of the piazza floated up and Sophia turned at the sound of her approaching footsteps.

'Is there something wrong, Beatrice? You look pale.'

'I'm not sure, to be honest.' She sat back down beside her, still in shock. 'That was Jude Adler on the telephone – the man who was with me when we first met. He called to say he's found two more pieces of the Caravaggio.'

'But this is very good news, no?'

'I mean ... I think so. And in part it's thanks to you. He went to visit the castle you told me about and found it there.'

'Castel Gedächt?' Sophia looked stunned.

'I don't know all the details, but Jude says it's been there since the war. Some Nazi had a secret collection of stolen art hidden in caves beneath the castle. My mum and dad got caught up in it – that's why they fled to London, in order to escape him.'

'The salt caves ...' Sophia placed her palm on her chest. '*Oh cielo!* That's incredible. What will you do now?'

'I've no idea. The Nazi's son owns the castle now. Jude thinks we should band together, find a buyer. We could make a substantial amount of money that way, which would help me save my home and honestly, that's all I want, except ...' Even as she was speaking, Beatrice realized there was something else she wanted, too.

'Except what?' asked Sophia.

'Mum wrote to me, right before she died. In her letter, she spoke a lot about guilt and sin and forgiveness. Her dying wish was to return the painting to its rightful owner, but if I try to honour that, I stand to lose everything. I really don't know what to do.'

The older woman sighed. 'I understand this, more than you might think. When my mother died, we discovered she'd left Velare to the Church. Costanza and I lost our home, where we'd lived all our lives.'

'That must have been awful – were you angry?'

Sophia shook her head. 'Not for a moment. We gladly gave it up. It was our duty; we were honouring her memory.'

She reached out to squeeze Beatrice's hand.

'And now I must leave you. As a good Catholic, I still take confession once a month. Not that I have much to repent these days! Shall we meet again tomorrow?'

'I'd like that very much.'

'Then I shall leave you to your conscience; I'm sure the right choice will present itself in time.'

The next day, Jude made his way back to Castel Gedächt. The weather was on the turn; heavy cloud meant the mountains were no longer visible. In the gloom, it looked less like a storybook, more like a vampire's lair.

When he pulled into the car park, the yoga ladies were all leaving for the day. They stood in groups of twos and threes; rolled-up mats tucked underneath their arms. Jude raised a hand to them and walked through the avenue of birches, along the steep path to the sloping courtyard. The sign by the gate now said 'Closed for the season'. He went directly to the von Niedermeyer's private apartment and knocked on the door. There was no answer. He thought perhaps he ought to have telephoned ahead. Emil might be anywhere on the estate, or even in the mountains – he'd talked about bringing the donkeys down from their high pasture.

Suddenly a voice came from behind him. It was Cindy, shining with perspiration, a purple towel around her neck. 'If you're looking for my husband, you'll be waiting quite a time. He's not here.' Her once-friendly demeanour was now chilly and remote.

'When will he be back?' asked Jude.

'A day or two, I think.'

He was puzzled. 'But he knew I was coming – we were going to make a deal.'

'Yeah, so I heard. Only I'm afraid we got a better offer.'

'I beg your pardon?'

She smiled. 'I think you overplayed your hand. You lied to me and put my husband in a vulnerable position. It's taken years of therapy to get him to a good place, then you had to go and bring it all back up again. At least it helped him finally see sense. I guess I owe you some thanks for that. He wasn't going to get there on his own.'

'Get where?' asked Jude, feeling utterly bewildered. 'No one else knows about the paintings, or so your husband led me to believe.'

'Well, someone clearly does.'

'I don't understand.'

'My husband told me about your proposal, and we considered it, but we received a counter-offer yesterday and decided, on balance, it was a better fit. Complete anonymity and a six-figure finder's fee. In light of that, it won't surprise you hear the paintings are gone, Mr Adler. He boxed them up and drove them down to Rome himself last night. He asked me to apologize on his behalf, but you ought to know, my husband is far more generous and forgiving than I am. I'm not in the least bit sorry – I'm glad to see them go, and you with them. Now, if you wouldn't mind, I've got to go and relieve the babysitter. You're resourceful; I guess you can find your own way out.'

CHAPTER THIRTY-FOUR

In a daze, Jude drove the hire car back down the mountain and rejoined the autostrada, heading towards Verona Airport. After spending so long in the winding hills of the Tyrol, he felt utterly bewildered by what he saw as Emil's betrayal. About an hour into the journey, the rain came. It lashed the road, and low cloud obscured the wider view entirely. His world narrowed down to a tunnel of cars and metal barriers.

The sinking dread he felt was only too familiar; the same as when he found out the Modersohn-Becker was fake, only this time so much worse. Who could have known about the paintings? No one knew where he was, only Beatrice. He reasoned she might have shared the news with Sophia Montefalco, but who would she tell? She had no reason to pull such a bait and switch. He considered driving down to Rome directly, to break the news to Beatrice face to face, but found he couldn't stomach the idea. All he wanted was to give up and go home.

He pulled onto the slip road to the airport, yearning to return to London and all its bland familiarity. After checking in his suitcase, he wandered through departures. Anonymous among the tourists, he found himself staring at a large display of Scotch and cigarettes, wondering if this calamity might justify their purchase, when a hand descended on his shoulder.

'Signor Adler?'

It belonged to a man in a navy suit, with a walkie-talkie and an airport security lanyard round his neck.

'Your boarding pass and passport, please.'

Jude handed them over before it hit him: the man had addressed him by name and in English. How could he possibly have known?

'What's this about?'

The man flicked through the documents and spoke without looking up. 'There is an issue with your luggage. Come with me.' He nodded to a nearby Carabinieri with a holstered gun and they started walking through Departures, Jude's paperwork in hand. With little option but to follow, he saw heads turn to watch him go.

'I think there must be some mistake . . .' Jude flushed, trying to catch them up. They led him down an empty corridor.

'No mistake.' The man stopped in front of an unmarked door and swiped a keycard through the lock. 'In here, please.' The room was bare – a table, a single plastic chair and a large, mirrored window on one wall, which gave no illusions to its purpose. Jude felt certain he was being observed.

'Wait here.' The man stepped back into the hallway and closed the door, leaving the armed Carabinieri standing guard outside. Jude sat down in the chair. What could be the issue with his suitcase? Was it connected to the painting? Had his passport somehow been flagged? When he and Beatrice had arrived in Rome, they'd been smuggling a stolen Caravaggio, albeit unbeknownst to them. This time he had absolutely nothing to declare.

The minutes ticked by, and Jude had started to wonder if he should demand to call the British Consulate, when the door opened. An attractive woman in her early thirties came into the room. She was small and svelte with glossy dark brown hair, high heels and a tailored suit.

'Signor Adler, sorry for the inconvenience.'

'Why am I being held?'

'You're not – I see no restraints. But this is airside, and we are conscious of security. If you want to return to Departures, I can ask someone to escort you there.'

Jude's curiosity got the deciding vote; he said nothing.

'Alternatively, I have a helicopter here, on standby. If you agree to go with me, I can have someone extricate your luggage from the plane.'

'I don't understand – go where?'

'To Rome. My client has asked me to make this transport available to you. It takes a little over an hour, although the rain may slow things down.'

'And you are . . . ?'

'Ines Manori.'

'May I ask who you work for, Ms Manori?'

'For the Vatican, Mr Adler. The Holy See.' She wagged a finger at him. 'You left the Dolomites a little faster than we were expecting, otherwise we could have done this in a more relaxed way, but we were anxious to prevent you flying home.' She looked at her watch. 'Your baggage is about to depart for London. Whether you return there with it is entirely up to you.'

Jude climbed out of the helicopter at Roma Fiumicino Airport and saw two white Mercedes S-Class saloons waiting on the tarmac. Ms Manori, who'd barely spoken during the noisy flight, climbed into the first car, which slid away and merged into the traffic. Jude got into the car behind and found himself experiencing the kind of travel he had only heard of – a world without queues, where all static was removed. It had taken less time for him to get here from Verona than it had to wind down the one-track mountain road. Jude settled back into the leather seat and found the novelty of the entire situation dulled the sting of Emil's duplicity. The worst had happened, and so he felt peculiarly rudderless, content to lie back and let the current take him.

The Mercedes slid through the inner-city traffic and finally turned at Piazza san Pietro. Jude spied Ines Manori's limousine ahead and they entered in convoy at Via Sant'Anna, their tyres a pattering whisper over cobbled ground. After the great press of humanity outside, Vatican City itself seemed almost empty. The car slowed to a halt in front of a large white marble building and the driver got out to hold open the door. Ms Manori stepped from her car at the same moment, mobile phone still pressed against her ear. She smiled and raised a hand in greeting. Something about the way she maintained eye contact made him certain she was speaking about him. Then a voice called out from behind.

'Jude? What on earth are you doing here?'

He turned to see a third Mercedes with Beatrice Fremont standing beside it. They stared at each other, utterly confounded.

'Don't ask me – they sent a helicopter to pick me up from Verona.'

Beatrice frowned. 'I'm supposed to be meeting Sophia. She left a message saying she'd send a car. I thought we were going to look around Velare together.'

'And so you shall.' Ines Manori came towards them, smiling coolly. She introduced herself to Beatrice. 'I took the liberty of adding in a little detour to your journey, in order to reunite you with Mr Adler. There is something I think you might both like to see – please, come this way.' She walked ahead, towards the entrance of the building.

Beatrice hissed at Jude, 'Are we on *Candid Camera*? This feels like an elaborate joke. What's going on?'

'I've no idea. I went back to Castel Gedächt this morning to talk to the von Niedermeyers, and it turns out they've sold the lot, including their half of the Caravaggio. Emil's wife told me someone made them an offer they couldn't refuse. He'd already packed up the paintings and driven them to Rome. Surely it must all be connected?'

Beatrice reached round to her handbag and pulled out the cardboard tube protruding from it. 'The chauffeur took me to the Banca Roma on the way here. Sophia asked to see the painting, so I arranged to retrieve it.' She looked horrified. 'My

God, Jude – do you think she's working with them? But I never mentioned the Vatican to her, so how did we end up here?'

They followed Ines Manori into the lobby of the marble building. She walked over to a security desk and picked up two steel clipboards, handing one to each of them

'Before we can proceed any further, I must ask you both to sign these. Standard non-disclosure agreements, but by all means look them over.' She gave them each a ballpoint pen. 'Of course, you're under no obligation, but if you don't sign then I'm afraid I cannot take you any further.'

Jude looked at Beatrice and shrugged – what did either of them have to lose?

'Very well then, come with me.' Ines clipped down the hall ahead of them in her high heels.

'Where are you taking us?' asked Jude.

'The *Archivio Segreto Vaticano* – the so-called Secret Archive.' She glanced back. 'That makes it sound more mysterious than it really is. It just means private, but *segreto* has such intriguing connotations, don't you think? They name things well round here.'

Ines led them down a shallow flight of steps to a set of doors which opened into a sparsely furnished room. Beatrice had never seen anything like it; built under a rib-vault ceiling of carved stone, the walls and floors were pristine white. In the centre stood a large worktable and next to it, a surgical lamp, its face a metre wide. The light from it was so blinding, it made her wince. Ines Manori strode over and tilted the face down, so it pointed at the table.

'It seems the conservator has stepped away for a moment, but I'm sure he won't mind if you take a closer look.' She beckoned them both forward. 'I wanted to show it to you before the work got fully underway. Such strong illumination would not normally be tolerated, but under the circumstances, it can be allowed until the reconstitution has taken place.'

Beatrice exchanged a fearful glance with Jude as they crossed the room together. On the table lay three separate rectangles of canvas: the reimagining of St John in *Youth with a Ram* by Caravaggio, almost complete, except for the missing top left quadrant. Beatrice gasped and looked to Jude for his reaction; she was surprised to find him smiling.

'Well, well. What do you know ... You wait a lifetime for one piece of a missing Caravaggio then three come along at once.'

With the pieces side by side, the image coalesced. Ines Manori pointed to the spaces in between.

'As you can see, the conservator has already removed the rather crude method used to stick these two parts together. Thankfully it caused very little damage, and I'm told it won't be apparent when the repair work is complete. Synthetic material will be placed behind the cuts, a bond made with conservation grade adhesive. In some places the canvas may need surgical intervention – to be sewn back together – before the entire painting can be lined. That will help to keep all the quadrants in place. Then comes the colour, once the structural repairs are complete. Any gaps will be in-painted before a varnish is applied to unify the surface. Thankfully the separation was done with great skill in the first place. And we are fortunate to have an excellent record of what the painting looked like before the separation.'

She picked up a large black and white photograph of the painting, which lay on the desk and handed it to Beatrice. 'It is my understanding your late father, Luca Montefalco, actually took this photograph himself.'

'My dad?' gasped Beatrice, astonished.

'According to our records, he took this image on 14 January 1944, the same day it was cut into four quarters, by order of your uncle, Father Roberto Montefalco.'

Beatrice frowned. 'I had no idea.'

'This was the centrepiece of his collection. Everything that happened during the war was done to facilitate the painting's removal to a place of safety. At that time there was a reasonable fear that Vatican City was under threat, from bombing or invasion. Many items in Father Roberto's collection were of a ... sensitive nature, shall we say? Their theft or exposure would have been extremely problematic, so he sought to remove as many of them to safety as he could.'

Jude interjected, 'A lot of other European galleries and museums did the same during the war.'

'The only difference being this collection was a tightly guarded secret for several hundred years. This wasn't just about their monetary value, but also their importance to the Vatican.' Ines Manori smiled. 'I'm told Father Roberto called his collection the *Damnatio Memoriae,* after the ancient Roman practice where tyrants or traitors would be erased from history. The practice continued into the Renaissance and extended into art – sometimes a single piece of work might be condemned, sometimes an artist.'

'For what reason?' asked Jude.

'They might have been seen as blasphemous or sinful, perhaps an unflattering depiction of someone powerful. There are more ways to offend than please.'

'And what about the Caravaggio? Who did that provoke?'

Ines Minori shrugged. 'No extant records exist, but we believe this painting was one of Caravaggio's last works. He was a rather complex character. In 1606 he was exiled from Rome for murder. Four years later, he made it known he wanted to return. He negotiated a deal with the Pope's nephew: clemency in return for the gift of several paintings.

'He set sail from Naples on a felucca in 1610, but he was mistakenly arrested en route. When he was finally able to escape, he went looking for the ship and his paintings. He died in the attempt, aged just thirty-eight years old. Whether it was from sunstroke, syphilis, malaria or from wounds sustained in a street fight, no one can say for sure. Neither can we be definitive about those final paintings – what the subjects were, or where they ended up . . .'

She trailed a fingertip along the edges of the canvas.

'Certainly, we can imagine this image would have been deeply offensive to the Pope – it suggests carnal desire. The figure on the right, a self-portrait of Caravaggio himself. On the left, his friend and sometime student, Francesco 'Cecco' Boneri. There is some evidence of a relationship between the two men – a letter written by an English traveller referred to Caravaggio and Cecco, his apprentice, who 'lay with him'.

Idle gossip, perhaps, but it may have been enough to condemn the work.

Jude raised an eyebrow. 'I think it might be more than that.'

He indicated the crescent painted on the undergrowth. 'What looks like a halo over Caravaggio, here. And on the ground, a shadow shaped like a fish. Both symbols of Christ.'

Ines peered closely at the areas he pointed to. 'Perhaps you're right. All the more reason why the Church would have wanted to suppress such an image.'

Jude laughed, without much humour. 'Suppression is a polite term for censorship, which has been going on in here for centuries.'

Ines Manori put her hands up in surrender. 'What can I say, Mr Adler? I don't deny it, but times change and progress can be made. No doubt this painting would still cause huge controversy in some quarters today, but as a society we're more inclined to have a conversation than lock these things away.'

Jude couldn't hide his disbelief. 'Does that mean you intend to share the *Damnatio Memoriae* with the public?'

'That decision has yet to be made, but I will say, a generous private benefactor has offered to fund any resulting exhibition in the future. Of course, it would be better if the painting was intact.'

She looked meaningfully at Beatrice, whose hand dropped to the cardboard tube protruding from her handbag.

'I'm told both your father and your uncle longed for its return. I wonder, Miss Fremont, in light of everything you've heard today, what do you wish to do with your portion of the canvas?'

Beatrice glanced at Jude. A simple choice, and yet it would have momentous repercussions on her life. With shaking hands, she pulled the rolled-up canvas from her bag.

'It was my mother's dying wish that I return this to its rightful owners. I'd like to do so in her memory.' She passed it over.

'We are indebted to you, Miss Fremont. And to both your parents.' The dark-haired woman smiled. 'As you no doubt realized, this half of the canvas was given to us by Emil and Cindy von Niedermeyer, along with a significant number of other paintings from the same collection. The Vatican does not expect such largesse without reward. We agreed a very generous finder's fee with the von Niedermeyers. I wonder, might the same terms be agreeable to you?'

Jude interjected. 'Cindy said six figures. Would that be enough to save your house?'

Beatrice nodded, her mind reeling with relief. 'But wait, what about Jude?'

'Indeed,' smiled Ms Manori. 'None of this could have been achieved without your efforts, Mr Adler. We would like to offer you a reward and discuss further work, if you will consider it. We could make good use of your expertise. The pay is very generous, let me assure you.' Stunned by the proposal, Jude could do no more than nod. Ines Manori looked distinctly pleased by their reaction. 'As far as the world is concerned, the paintings were missing and have now been recovered in the very place they were left for safety more than half a century ago. A satisfactory conclusion, I would say.' She looked at her watch. 'And now you need to go. Sophia Montefalco is waiting for you in the limousine, so you can all travel together.'

'Go where?' asked Beatrice, confused.

'To the Santa Sabina Hospice on the Aventine Hill, so you can meet your uncle and give him the good news – his entire collection has been returned, at last.'

CHAPTER THIRTY-FIVE

Father Roberto sat in a vinyl-covered chair, gazing up at the frescoed ceiling. He needed to distract himself while the dialysis machine performed its thrice-weekly miracle. It was disagreeably warm for October and the seat was unforgiving, but he took solace in the process. He'd come to see the cleansing of his kidneys as an act of communion. The wound in his chest was from a needle, not a spear, but he thought of that as a covenant of flesh.

Trying to find a more comfortable position, he shifted in his chair. His robes stuck to the damp skin in the small of his back; he shuffled forward and looked up at the painted flowers, the shells and ribbon sashes, which had survived for centuries. Their colours might dim, but their curves were drawn with sculptural precision, as close to perfect as anything on this side of the veil.

He found it a strange irony that he'd ended up back here, after all these many years. As a younger man, he'd turned his world upside down trying to escape it; had the hubris to think God had a different plan for him. Yet here he was, in his ninety-second year ... Villa Velare had been his destiny, after all. Like so many lessons, this one had taken him a lifetime to absorb.

He was tired, an aching exhaustion which sapped his spirit. He might sleep a little later, though he couldn't do so now – too many clanging bells and pipes and whistles, too much static in his blood. Soon the nurse would bring him a glass of water and a *pasticcino*, make sure all the lines were functioning and clean. He would ask her when his niece was coming. He knew he'd asked her once already, but the answer seemed to fade. His memory was mercury these days – the more recent, the greater its tendency to escape him, slippery as a fish. Only a trace of it remained.

Older recollections stayed more or less intact: his boyhood with his brother, playing outside in the winter snow. Or in the summer, daring one another down and down, into the underworld below.

The last time he saw his brother they'd stood together, side by side, watching his little daughter on the carousel, whirling round and round. Luca had come to Rome to give him one quarter of the Caravaggio – a promissory note. The other quarter stayed in London, a guarantee of Maddalena's safety. He showed him photographic proof. As to the rest, Luca thought it might be anywhere, but he had an idea of where to start. He wouldn't say more in that moment, just swore he would move heaven and earth to recover and return what had been lost. But Luca died before he could make good his undertaking. Roberto wept and then began to wait; he'd promised his brother he would do nothing more while Maddalena lived; he would not break his word.

Lately he had begun to accept he'd likely leave the earth before his task could be completed. It pained him: a loose thread in a tightly woven life. But then his niece, Sophia, came for her confession, as she did every month. She told him about Luca's daughter, her joy at their connection, and how sad it was her mother passed away.

With Maddalena's death, the seal was broken. The priest could speak at last.

Beatrice hung back as Sophia entered the room before her. She didn't want to crowd an elderly man. On the journey over Sophia had warned that her uncle was not always lucid. He often seemed to forget important details – the names of his nurses, or which of his contemporaries had died.

'He might not know what day it is, but he can tell you everyone in attendance at the Papal conclave in 1958.'

Beatrice loitered in the corridor, trying to keep out of the way. There was a tremendous amount of traffic between the rooms, nurses and orderlies passing from place to place. The underlying beauty of the building was evident in the tiled floors and moulded plaster ceilings, but it was overwhelmed by all the medical equipment and the strong scent of disinfectant.

Sophia opened the door and beckoned her inside. The room

was bright, with large windows which overlooked the driveway. A neatly made hospital bed took up a good deal of space, though it was unoccupied. Father Roberto Montefalco sat in an upholstered chair beside a large piece of medical machinery, which appeared to be plumbed into him in several places. Beatrice was surprised to see him dressed in layers of vestments. Liver spots speckled his skin and he was small and sallow, as washed out as a watercolour left too long in the sun. Sophia took his hand and bent over, so her mouth was level with his ear.

'This is Beatrice, Uncle. Remember, I told you she might visit?'

He turned his head, and his eyes seemed to brighten as he focused on her. His hands and arms floated up, becoming tangled in the cords which bound him to the machine.

'È diventata una bellezza!'

Beatrice smiled, a little embarrassed as she translated his words in her head – She had become a beauty . . . She fought an overwhelming urge to cry.

Sophia bent down again. 'Perhaps we should speak English, Uncle?'

'Don't worry for my sake,' said Beatrice hurriedly.

'It is only polite.'

'Honestly, I was a translator. I speak fluent Italian, though Mum always used to tease me about my accent.' Beatrice felt a pang as she realized she was talking about Maddalena in the past tense.

Roberto's shoulders dropped. 'I was very sorry to hear about your mother. I said a rosary for her this morning.'

Surprised, Beatrice turned to Sophia. 'Uncle Roberto has

been my confessor since I was a little girl. I came here to see
him after we spoke on the loggia.'

'So that's how how the Vatican learned about the paintings
at the castle?'

Roberto interjected, 'I promised my brother I would keep
my silence until your mother passed away, but when I heard,
I had to act. I cannot rest until my collection is restored.'

Sophia knelt beside her uncle's chair.

'That is why we came to see you – to tell you the good
news. All the paintings have been returned at last. Beatrice
brought back Maddalena's canvas, the collection is complete.
There is no more need for worry.'

The old man's eyes filled with tears. He patted Sophia's
hand, his jaw working silently, the only sound the whisper of
the machine. Finally, Roberto found his voice.

'Thank you.'

'It's my mum who deserves it. She asked me to do this. It
haunted her for years.'

Roberto nodded. 'Your mother was always good and kind
and true.'

'You remember her?'

'I knew her a little, of course, but I learned more about
her from your father. When we met in Rome, when you
were still a little girl, I almost did not recognize him. We
had both aged, of course – it had been thirty years – but it
was more than that. When he was young, Luca was always
restless, unfulfilled. There was an *agita* . . . I can't explain.
But when he came to Rome with you, I saw he was a different man. He was contented. He knew himself. What

greater blessing can there be? I have no doubt your mother gave that gift to him.'

Beatrice felt her lip trembling. Sophia came and put her arms around her while Roberto continued, his own voice thickened by emotion.

'Luca told me what she did, the sacrifice she made. Maddalena risked her life trying to save a young boy named Tito Senese. Tragically he died and she was forced to go into hiding. He told me she had courage beyond her years. She didn't seek danger out, but when bravery was required, she never turned away.

'Even decades later, your father still wanted to protect her – she was concerned that the Vatican would seek retribution, or that there might be reprisals for her part in poor young Tito's death. Of course, I don't believe anyone in authority would have sought to punish her, but I can understand why she would have such little faith. So, I promised to say nothing. How could I deny my brother, when he gave up so much for me and asked for so little in return?'

A stillness settled in the room, all three of them preoccupied by thoughts of those who'd lived here, now long gone. Sophia broke the silence.

'You look tired, Uncle.'

'I am, but it is necessary. The nurse will be here soon, to release me.'

'I should give you some privacy,' said Beatrice. 'Besides, I ought to go and find Jude. See where he's wandered off to.'

She went over to the chair and took Roberto's hand. 'Thank you so much for telling me all that. I hope we can meet again?'

The elderly man put his shaking hand on hers.

'My dear Beatrice, of course. We are family.'

Jude walked up through the soft green landscape, along the rising path, looking for the rose garden where Beatrice had buried her parents' ashes. It was much cooler than the last time they came here. It looked as if it might rain later, but for now there was a gentle breeze and soft, flat light. He strode through swathes of fragrant herbs, now dry and leggy. When he finally came upon the little terrace, he was surprised to see its transformation. Roses in every shade of red rambled across the wall which overlooked the city, an unexpected second flush.

Jude sat down to wait on a stone bench with far-reaching views. When Beatrice was ready, she'd come to look for him and would undoubtedly be drawn up here. It was tranquil and isolated, as good a resting place as he could imagine. He realized there wasn't any one singular location he associated with his mother – her ashes had been scattered in the manicured grounds of some municipal cemetery outside London. He'd never felt the need to find out where or visit; she wasn't there and so it hadn't seemed to matter. Now he wished he had a place like this, somewhere to rest and to remember. He gazed across the domes and terracotta rooftops, then closed his eyes for a moment. He could no longer recall her voice, or the feel of her arms surrounding him. There were flashes of her, but they were memories of memories, the presence of her absence. He was ready to let go.

When he opened his eyes sometime later, he saw Beatrice heading up the path towards him. She raised a hand to wave, but didn't break the silence. The only sound, the chattering of starlings flying out and then returning. They would soon mass and take wing, filling up the sky. He thought he might wait to see it – that would be something to remember.

Beatrice came and sat down beside him; their fingers almost touching. He met her gaze and something passed between them. This time he didn't turn away.

AUTHOR'S NOTE

I started writing *The Seeker of Lost Paintings* in 2023, on the heels of finishing my debut, *The Porcelain Maker*. I felt absurdly pleased to have completed one novel but daunted by the prospect of starting another. I knew my story would be set in fascist Italy, but I wanted to tell the story of ordinary citizens – so much of history is written about great figures, far less about the common man. It was only through discovering the published diaries of four extraordinary women that I found my way in. Were it not for them, I don't think the story would exist in this form.

Iris Origo was an Anglo-American living in the Italian countryside, between Rome and Florence, in the run up to the second world war. She had friends in high places, but that wasn't what made her diaries so vital; it was the way she described the minutiae of her life and how the conflict closed in on her family and community over time. Her journals offer the clear-eyed view of an outsider who loves her adopted country, watching as it gets crushed beneath the heel of an authoritarian regime.

Whether she's describing the splendours of the Italian countryside or the realities of rationing and propaganda, Origo's writing is precise and beautiful but unsentimental. Iris led me to the *selpolti vivi* – the boys and men who went into hiding out of desperation. Both her pre-war diary *A Chill in the Air* and *War in Val d'Orcia*, written during occupation, revealed the bravery of ordinary Italians in the face of exceptional cruelty. These stories inspired Tito's incarceration and death, both all-too-common tragedies those days.

I kept Victor Failmezger's thorough history, Rome – *City in Terror: The Nazi occupation 1943–1944*, by my side throughout. He explored these events in forensic detail, including many stories of ordinary people who were witnesses to history. He led me to the diary of 'Jane Scrivener', the pseudonym of Sister Luke, an American nun who lived in Rome and worked in the Vatican throughout the occupation. Her journal, published as *Inside Rome with the Germans* (Macmillan, 1945), included meticulous notes which helped me understand the regime of rationing and restrictions which ordinary Romans endured.

Both these books showed how the people of Rome fought back against the occupying forces. On 10 September 1943, Porta San Paolo was a scene of devastation as the Italian army took a desperate last stand against the German occupation of Rome. Dozens of ordinary citizens turned out to fight alongside them. Though the Wehrmacht forces eventually prevailed, they held back 49,000 troops for a full day. Almost six hundred Italian men and women died in defence of their beloved city and their homes.

Researching the Italian resistance led to some extraordinary stories, including that of K Syndrome and the Fatebenefratelli Hospital. Within weeks of the occupation, Heinrich Himmler gave orders for the Jewish citizens of Rome to be rounded up and sent to Auschwitz. Herbert Kappler, the head of the German police and security forces in Rome, demanded that community leaders hand over 50 kilos of gold to secure their safety. Though the ransom was finally secured (with help from the Vatican), it was all a ruse. Early on the morning of October 16, German forces sealed off the Ghetto and 1,022 people, including 274 children, were loaded onto trucks, then train cars at Tiburtina Station and sent to their final destination: Auschwitz-Berkenau. Of their number, only sixteen survived.

Those that managed to escape the round up went into hiding. For every person sent to the death camps, eleven remained behind, desperate for sanctuary. It's estimated there were 200,000 to 300,000 people hiding from the Germans in Rome at this time and more than 10,000 of them were Jews. The Catholic Fatebenefratelli Hospital on Tiber Island, opposite the Ghetto, was already known as a haven, but with large numbers of refugees suddenly requiring help, they needed to be bold. So was born *'Il Morbo di K'* or K Syndrome, purporting to be a highly contagious and deadly disease. Incredibly, the scheme worked: Nazi soldiers did not dare to enter the ward, allowing doctors to protect the courageous refugees. Maddalena's friend Vincenzo Sciori is a fictional stand-in for the brave staff of the Fatebenefratelli who risked so much.

The part that women played in these efforts is often over-looked. Caroline Moorhead has written extensively about Italian women in the war, from *A House in the Mountains: The Women Who Liberated Italy from Fascism* (Vintage, 2020) to *Edda Mussolini: The Most Dangerous Woman in* Europe (Penguin, 2023). Caroline's incredibly crafted histories brought the time into focus, and it was through her, I learned about the incredible courage of the 'staffette': the women and girls who faced unim-aginable danger to resist. Ada Gobetti was one such fighter and her *Partisan Diary* (Oxford University Press, 2010) informed Benadetta and Maddalena's fictional forays into fighting back.

James Holland's books and podcasts helped my understand-ing of the events of 1943, particularly *The Savage Storm: The Battle for Italy 1943* (Penguin Books, 2024) He even inspired the name Dolorosa, which proved to be so fitting for Velare's tragic cook. The villa's kitchen is at the heart of the story, from high days and holidays through to their response to rationing, Maddalena's passion for cooking even helped her conceal the Caravaggio.

I've always loved Anna del Conte's writing about food. Her choice of words feeds the imagination, even as they make you ravenously hungry. *Risotto with Nettles* (Vintage, 2010) is a wonderful memoir which combines vivid recollections of her early life in Italy, alongside the recipes they inspired. Her descriptions of a wartime kitchen, the food and flavours she remembers, all proved to be a stimulus for me and therefore Maddalena.

Like so many, I was captivated by Andrew Graham-Dixon's seminal work, *Caravaggio: A Life Sacred and Profane* (Penguin,

2010). Of course, he is not responsible for the liberties I took with the life of Caravaggio and his final, fateful journey, or the paintings I imagine were lost along the way. Although the lascivious re-working of *St John Youth with a Ram* is entirely my invention, it is known that Caravaggio died enroute to Rome, trying to buy his way back after being exiled for murder. Those paintings have never been definitively identified, so perhaps we have license to imagine. As for the concept of *Damnatio Memoriae*, it's real enough and existed in different forms for centuries. I will leave it to the more conspiratorial among us to decide whether the Vatican might have one or two such treasures tucked away.

With thanks . . .

So many people have helped to bring this book to life. I am especially grateful to Jevon Thistlewood ACR, Conservator of Paintings at the Ashmolean Museum of Art and Archaeology, who was so generous in teaching the art of conservation and suggesting ways in which my imaginary Caravaggio might be made to seem authentic.

I am indebted to friends and family for the personal stories they shared. Special mention must go to Marilyn Marchetti, whose beloved husband Wally was the inspiration for Santino, Velare's stoic mechanic. I know Wally is much missed by all who loved him.

Also, to my dear Walter Iuzzolino, without whom this book would simply not exist. I have him to thank for Maddalena's method of escape. During the Second World War, his grandmother, Nella Superina, fled to Italy from Croatia, having smuggled coins concealed inside a basket of bread rolls.

Writing is, by necessity, a rather solitary existence, so I feel very lucky to have the company of some fantastic women. Huge thanks to Leila Alabaster, Rebecca Fletcher, Claire Fuller, Judith Heneghan, Amanda Oosthuizen and Louise Taylor. Thanks also to Barbara Serra whose story of discovering a fascist in her own family was a catalyst for me.

And to my own coven – my mother Denise Mallender and sister Andrea Marchetti, who read every draft, corrected my appalling grammar and supported me through thick and thin. 143, now and forever.

Finally, to Phil and Esme, who are everything. Thank you for cheering me on, despite the long hours and all the piles of research on the kitchen table. Love you (and the dogs).

March 2025

Also by Sarah Freethy . . .

The Porcelain Maker

**Two lovers caught at the crossroads of history
A daughter's search for the truth**

When Max, a Jewish architect, is sent to the Dachau concentration
camp, it's only his talent for making exquisite porcelain
figurines so admired by the Nazis that stands between him and
certain death. Avant-garde artist and Max's partner, Bettina,
has no idea where he's been taken but, when she learns of his
fate, she's determined to rescue him whatever the cost.

A lifetime later, Bettina's daughter, Clara, sets out to unravel the
mystery of her identity. As she weaves together the fabric of her past,
she discovers the terrible answers her mother wanted hidden forever.

'A page-turning journey to uncover a past of
heroism, betrayal, love, and loss'
Heather Morris, bestselling author of
The Tattooist of Auschwitz

'A gorgeous debut'
Heat

'A standout novel of heartbreak, survival and
hope in time of war' **Rachel Hore**

AVAILABLE NOW IN PAPERBACK, EBOOK AND AUDIO